ACCIDENTAL PARENTS
Two Gay Dads and Two Teens

Also by Peter Melillo

Improbable: Male Love Stories

Fairy Swatter: Stories

ACCIDENTAL PARENTS
Two Gay Dads and Two Teens

a novel

PETER MELILLO

For Bernard Cowan

who bravely risked taking a bullet for me

CHAPTER 1. Country House

For over a year, Bob and I had spent weekends searching to buy a rural getaway. We wanted to experience all four seasons of the year, at least on weekends. We craved more than the two puny city seasons. Urban trees are green all year, or never, tall buildings blot-out what the sky is up to, and below ground mechanical systems kept the sidewalks warm no matter the outside air temperature. We were eager to re-experience earth's dramatic, big sky magnificence and night's soft moon-shadows or total-black.

Searching during a buyer's market, we found flawed almost but not quite lovable leftovers. After sixteen months, second house hunting became tedious, then we saw Dan and Bill's place. Their country home seemed to say yes even before we fully checked it out and said a resounding yes back.

It was remote but not isolated, a century old but well maintained, all our boxes were checked. The purchase price was less than we budgeted, and most importantly it exuded a welcoming vibe. A fishing stream ran through the five acres that surround the residence. Much of the land was covered in old growth hardwoods or newer fruit baring trees and berry bushes. Near the house on one side was a small barn containing antique farm equipment and on the other a detached four car garage with small workshop tucked in back.

Entering the three-story Victorian house's front vestibule, to the left was a good size den. Dead center was a grand high ceiling formal parlor and behind it an elegant dining room separated from the parlor by wide pocket doors. In back, the width of the house was a massive old-fashioned eat-in kitchen with generous pantry, connected to the den and dining room by smaller pocket doors. A small maid's room with bathtub was behind the kitchen, and a half bath was tucked in next to the side-entrance mudroom. There were four huge bedrooms and two large full bathrooms on the second floor. The third floor and basement were for the most part used as storage by the previous owners. Attached to the house a wraparound covered porch connected to an elevated, open to the sky, massive back deck. The raised deck was complete with high-end, stainless-steel barbecue grill, fire pit, running water fountain, outdoor furniture, and fabulous views.

We bought the place for a little more than its assessed tax valuation, plus the cost of oil in the tank and cords of seasoned firewood stacked under the deck and porch.

We were told the price we paid was less than half its value in a seller's market. But our sellers were motivated to have a fast sale go finalize their divorce.

After the house-closing's legal-formalities handing checks out around the table, Bill slipped me a note, *"Good luck with the property, we were happy there once upon a time. I hope you men will find the joy we knew. Just be aware owning an old house means lots of constant little headaches. Mike Morgan and his tag-along helper can fix most problems and keep your grass mowed on the cheap. He is the area's best handyman and lives close by. Be nice to him, he's thin skinned so needs kid glove handling. His helper may be developmentally delayed or crazy or both. But they have been good to the house, and consequently us."*

While moving clutter from our city condominium apartment to the country house, we broke the tread on a mudroom stairstep. On close inspection, other well-weathered side entrance stairs were ready to snap. As the previous owners recommended, we called Mike Morgan the handyman.

He came right over with his teenage assistant who he introduced as Joey Hall. Mike looked about sixty, 5-foot, 6-inches, 140 pounds, craggy face, gray hair mostly bald in the middle, and deep-set honey-brown eyes. He was dressed in a threadbare flannel shirt, faded-thin bib overalls, and high-top scuffed work shoes. Mike was not chatty other than about the job at hand. We learned later by association Mike always wore a serious angry face, and at that moment our damaged side entrance steps seemed a particularly weighty matter.

His assistant Joey was mid-teens, maybe 5-foot, 4-inches, at around 125-pounds. He had pale blue eyes that stared out with a blank expression. Joey was either dull normal or his brain was idling under his straight platinum blonde hair cut around a soup bowel, leaving eyebrow length bangs in front. He wore a light blue holey-T-shirt, threadbare patched cheap-jeans, and worn-down off brand high-top sneakers. At first, I thought the teen was mute, he answered my questions with head nods, yes or no. Then later he answered Mike with complete, well-constructed sentences. I'm guessing he didn't know he came off as rude toward us. On the other hand, Bob and I can be off-putting. We are big, still military hard, and never would win a beauty contest. But we love each other, which goes deeper than mere skin-deep beauty.

Mike and Joey replaced our mudroom steps for the cost of materials and a miniscule charge for labor. We were pleased with the quality of their workmanship and work ethic completing the job quickly without drama. So, walking them back to their truck, I tried to hand Mike a tip in acknowledgement of a job well done. After all, tips were expected of us in the city.

Mike waved the tip money away with a scowl. "My motto is safety first. Those steps were a safety hazard, someone could have been injured. We done the job up to county code, so no tip required."

Without thinking, I put the bills in his blue bib-overall's top-pocket and said, "It's not much, let us buy you and the boy lunch." I turned and headed back to the house, suspecting I had just offended Mike unintentionally. Later Bob suggested I had a lot to learn about rural people and their pride around city folks.

Despite my steps repair tip faux pas, twice a month, Mike and or Joey showed up early on Saturday and quickly cared for the lawn and shrub around the house. One spring morning after breakfast I was reading in the glider-lounger on the back deck when Joey showed-up alone on a motorcycle, it was not a lawn care day. Without a word he went to what had once been Dan and Bill's vegetable garden. He pulled up weeds by hand without gloves, went to the barn, collected tools to turn the soil over. Then he added Dan and Bill's compost and planted seeds from folded used envelopes in his pocket. At the end of the month, Mike and Joey had not charge us for preparing and maintaining an unasked-for eatable garden. It seemed counter intuitive to give a speech about doing work without being asked first and then not asking to be paid. So, we would handle it like we did in the city when our doorman went above and beyond without being asked. We would be extra generous at Christmas time, rather than risk offending Mike again.

Then quite by accident we discovered Mike was doing, little odd jobs around the house and not charging us beyond our agreed upon, low, monthly lawnmowing, shrub pruning fee. For example, a roof-gutter came loose during a windstorm while we were there and was dangling half-way off the house. When the roofer we called came later that week, Mike had already fixed the gutter, unasked. When I mentioned the gutter, he would not accept payment for the unasked-for labor. Mike even offered to talk to the roofer for giving me a tongue lashing for wasting his time.

When Bob and I sat Mike down to raise his fee to cover the extras he did, he said, "Small tasks to keep your place presentable are included in what you already pay me. It's a fair amount, I don't expect, nor will I accept more."

The last Saturday of every month, after the lawn and grounds work were completed, Mike knocked on the mudroom door to be paid. He preferred cash, so cash he got. If we were not planning to be home, I put his money in an envelope under the door mat, on top of the spare house key.

For the first year of owning the country house, Bob and I settled into a routine. We would leave work early on Friday afternoon, get up to the country with time enough to throw food on the outdoor grill and relax with a beer on the deck to watch the sunset. Long holiday weekends were the best for enjoying our part-time rural life. When it was too cold for relaxing outside, we moved inside to watch the snow fall while sitting by a crackling fire in one of the several fireplaces.

Late Sunday night or early Monday morning it was back to the city and the drudgery that paid expenses for two-homes. Bob taught high school and I bought and sold businesses. At the country house we slept better and longer breathing the vegetations' oxygen-rich air. Consequently, our moods were brighter waking to wild bird songs and squabbling squirrels.

Rural life was a pleasant improvement over the cities' noisy neighbors stomping-around-upstairs, pigeons fucking loudly on the window air conditioners, and honking traffic down at street level twenty-four-seven in all seasons. Over busy, tightly time structured urban dwellers during the week, we thoroughly relished our freeform rural peace and quiet weekends and holidays. At only age thirty-two we had achieved what we had been looking for, the best of both worlds, Bob and I were happy with each other and living our dream.

Then Mike made an uncharacteristic visit late, on a Saturday night, though he wasn't due to be paid again for a week. He said, "Would it be possible for you men to do me a big favor. It's important or I wouldn't ask."

Bob and I said, "Shoot," in unison.

"My wife, Eleanor, and I have to rush down south. We can't take Joey, there is no room for him. Could you keep him temporarily? He will work hard for his keep and be no trouble. I guarantee it."

Bob asked my question, "What happened Mike?"

Looking at the ground, he rocked back and forth in his scuffed work shoes. "If you must know, Eleanor's sister Yolanda has been taking care of their mother, who's gone senile. Just now the hospital called, Yolanda's had a stroke, and they cannot keep her in the hospital without insurance. If we don't do something, tomorrow they will put her out on the street in a wheelchair. The hospital says both Yolanda and her mother require feeding, washing, toileting, *the whole bloody shooting match.* There are no relatives left, and we don't have money to pay strangers for that, so we are going. They live in a small house trailer, there is no room for Joey."

Surprised he'd asked us, we didn't know them beyond yard work. So, I asked, "What does Joey say?"

"He'll do as told."

"Does he have any other options ... I only ask because Joey never seemed to warm to us. I don't think he even likes us."

"He's that way with everyone. But Joey is the son I never had, and you men are his best option for the moment."

"We never intended to be parents."

"The boy needs to finish high school up here. He didn't do well down south. He'll behave for you, or I'll fix the reason why not."

Bob looking how he does when we have a big problem asked, "What's your best guess how long you'll be gone?"

"Don't know, but if we're not back in time. After Joey graduates' high school and turns eighteen, he'll join the Army. Same as I did, and he'll be out of your hair."

"You caught us off guard, we weren't expecting to raise a kid."

"Honest, he won't be trouble, and like I said he'll earn his keep and then some. At worst you're looking at two years of keeping him fed and housed. He doesn't eat much more than he shoots or catches fishing. Of course, that is if you are willing to keep him." Mike was acting out of character begging a favor. His angry face was replaced by a beseeching one. Clearly, he was out of his usual comfort zone and uneasy asking us something important to him.

I sensed Mike never approved of us, from his condescending scowls. I looked over at Bob and could tell he was thinking the same thing I was. The unacknowledged homophobic nine-hundred-pound gorilla in the room wanted attention. "Mike, you do know Bob and I are gay, right?"

"I sort of figured that."

Bob chimed in, "Is Joey gay?"

"To tell you the truth, I don't think he knows. The boy had a hard life before he came to us. He hasn't completely gotten beyond that yet. If you are asking my opinion, I expect that's the way he will go sooner or later. Then again, some folks never do find themselves, he could be one of them you never know."

"Mike, is that why you picked us?"

"No, not only that, but we'll be also living to North Carolina. It's one of those hate states. A few years back the governor and state legislature passed a mess of discriminate against homosexuals' laws. Joey has had it hard since he was born. I don't want him to have to put up with that crap, no matter how he turns out. *I do care about the boy.*"

"Does Joey have any friends or family who will take him in? We don't know him or have experience with kids. Bob and I weren't planning on parenthood."

"No. He was born in South Carolina and got passed around a lot until he was finally sent to us as a last resort."

"Mike, you hear me, right? Bob and I never even talked about raising a child."

"Okay, I understand I'm asking a lot, and we don't know each other all that much, so no hard feelings." Getting ready to leave a lost cause, Mike replaced his meek beseeching face with his usual angry one. The one with all its deep creases.

Bob used his command voice to stop Mike walking away and said, "What happens if you can't find a place for Joey?"

"The county welfare office has a group home for boys his age. I've heard it's not too good, and Joey didn't do well in group homes down South. But up here has to be better than a hate state."

"When are you leaving, Mike?"

"This came on quick, we're going right now. I'll drive all night."

Bob and I exchanged a couple's look and I said, "What was your plan if we *can't* help?"

"Eleanor and I will drop Joey off at the state police barracks near the highway. They'll keep him until Monday morning when the welfare office opens. I telephoned already it is setup ready to go if need be."

Searching each other's eyes while speaking in unison we said, "You caught us by surprise, Mike."

"Look, I'm sorry how this all happened. But believe me it will be hard on us too when we get to where we're going. What I mean to say is I understand if you can't take him in. Like I said, no hard feelings."

Bob gave me a look that was easy to read. I nodded okay, and said, "Mike, we'll take him if you sign a paper from when to when you housed Joey, a statement why you can't continue, your new address and phone number, and give us permission to keep him until something else can be arranged. That's on condition, Joey is on board, will cooperate, and not give us grief."

"Where's the paper?"

Bob led Mike to our den. "Gus will write it all down using the computer in the den ... this way."

To keep my mind off problems we didn't need, want, or were trained to handle, I asked, "Where is Joey right now?"

"Out front, in my truck with Eleanor, he's got a knapsack with his clothes. He doesn't have much beside a deer rifle, shotgun, and fishing gear. I taught him to be self-reliant and to live off the land."

"Mike, we'll try giving Joey a home until you return. But you tell him if it doesn't work out, we'll take him to the state police or welfare office, like you set up. I want him to hear that from you."

With the paper fresh from the computer printer and signed by us three, Bob and I walked on either side of Mike out to his old pickup truck. Joey sat by the passenger's door Eleanor sat in the middle. Mike stuck his head in the driver's door window, said something and Joey climbed down, slung on a large backpack, and took two long-guns and fishing case from the truck bed. Mike and Joey talked at the truck's tailgate. Meanwhile, we shook hands with and told Eleanor how sorry we were for her family's troubles.

When Mike and Joey walked over to where we were talking with Eleanor, Joey head down moved to stand a short distance behind Bob and me. Mike got in his truck, started it up and he and Eleanor waved as they drove off. The look on their faces was funereal sorrowful. Joey stood stony faced resigned.

We walked back to the house in silence. Back inside I said, "Joey, we three need to talk and get to know each other, but not tonight, it has gotten late. I don't know about you, but I always feel sad saying goodbye."

Bob said, "Would you like something to eat or drink before bed?"

"No! *We need to talk right now.* I have to know if this is going to work out or find another place."

What the kid said made sense to him. But letting him overrule us and call the shots right from the start didn't work for me. I'd been a full bird colonel in the military, as had Bob. "Any decision for tomorrow, need to be slept on tonight. That's our house our rule, follow me to your room."

Joey didn't look pleased but said nothing as we went up to the second-floor guestroom. At night it was an airy room with lots of moonlight and moon shadows.

By day, the room was full of sunshine. Our plan was to eventually paint it, get some lamps, buy window-shades or blinds and lined-drapes for winter. The room had a queen size-bed, two dressers, two bedside straight-back chairs, and two comfy-upholstered reading chairs in the wide bay-window. All the furnishings were left by Dan and Bill.

"What are your other house rules?"

Bob and I exchanged a look mouthing, "Rules?"

"Showers at night or the morning, who goes first and last?"

With a smile I said, "Your choice, you share a bathroom with the unoccupied room next door. Breakfast is at seven-thirty we won't wait for you. In the morning we can get to know each other over coffee. Good-night, welcome to our home, sleep well."

****

As usual, Bob and I working in tandem swiftly assembled our weekend breakfast plus one. It was coffee, juice, fresh fruit, waffles, bacon, and scrambled eggs. We liked big breakfasts, we're big guys.

Freshly showered Joey came downstairs at exactly seven-thirty. He looked less stony-angry-sad and more stoic than the night before. "Morning, what you're making smells good."

"*Good morning.* Grab a seat, we're just about ready to eat. The coffee and such are there, fix a mug the way you like it."

Bob followed my comment with, "Hi, Joey, if you don't see something you'd like, ask, if we don't have it, we'll get it."

I tag-teamed Bob and said, "What's your favorite breakfast, Joey?"

"Oatmeal, that's been my old reliable. But I have nothing against the spread you have here."

With that said we three tucked-in and made short work of snarfing-down the fragrant morning meal. After the dishes were taken to the sink, I suggested, "Let's take our coffee out to the deck."

We took places at the old rustic picnic table, me, and Bob on one side Joey on the other. Bob said, "Last night you had questions, how about we take turns, one question per person?"

"There are two of you."

"Then you can ask two questions to each of ours. Is that better?"

"It's still two against one. But okay, it's your home, your rules."

"Why don't we see how it goes? Worse case you and Bob talk and I'll listen and take notes."

"Whatever, like I said, it's your house. You probably want to know more about me than I have questions for you. No matter what or how you slice it, you have me at a disadvantage."

I didn't hold back Joey was a taught negotiator. "How do we equalize that?"

"No, like you said Gus, let's see how it goes."

I looked over at Bob and saw he was thinking what I was; *We'd hardly begun, and Joey took charge, and scored points.*

Nevertheless, Bob responded like someone in command. "For our edification, Joey, tell Gus and me the first thing you remember remembering?"

"Bob what I remember remembering seems too personal and irrelevant for this moment. I think what you really want to know is whether I'll steal your stuff, die of a drug overdose, burn down your house, or murder you in your sleep. Well, just for the record, I won't, never did, and don't intend to in the future. The reason is, I've seen how drugs and alcohol ruin lives, and know better than to bite the hands that offers me a place to stay."

"That's encouraging to hear, since Mike and Eleanor gave you quite an endorsement, addict and psychopath weren't listed. So, who are you, Mr. Hall?"

"I don't know, I haven't figured me out yet. Just so you *do* know, I've been a disappointment to everyone I have ever known except Mike and Eleanor. So, you shouldn't expect much of anything good from me. But I won't disappoint you on purpose."

Diminishing my expectations, I asked, "Why is that do you suppose?"

"I'll tell you what I know, that's what you really want, right? My mother died giving birth to my sister who then died just after being born. I've heard said my father was young and disappeared when my mother died. My mother's mother raised me until age six and then she died. Apparently, I have that effect on people who care for me, they die or kick me out. Be sure to pay up your life insurance, I'm a jinx."

"Who knows maybe we can change your luck?"

"You're funny ha, ha, change my luck, that's a good one. My bad luck is permanent."

"Then tell me all about it. What has it been like being bad luck you, Joey?"

"I got handed around until I ran out of relatives. Then I was regularly beaten for no reason in two different group homes. Mike an Eleanor rescued me from an extra bad group home when I was thirteen and tried to hang myself. The beam I tied the rope around broke."

"Are you still suicidal?"

Joey's posture shifted in his seat to support his words. "No. Mike taught me to be self-reliant and live off the land. I have life skills now I didn't then."

Bob's schoolteacher persona showed when he said, "I want a promise you will talk to one of us before harming yourself."

"Promise."

I suspected Bob was doing what I was, mentally shifting through what we'd got ourselves into. Then Bob aid, "Finish your thought before I interrupted."

"I really thought my luck had finally changed with Mike and Eleanor, until last evening when they got a phone call and had to run to change adult diapers. So, now I'm homeless *again*, and been dumped on you two, and that's my story up to now. I accept I'm a loser who spreads bad luck everywhere I go. Don't do it on purpose, it's just my role in the grander scheme of things."

"Thank you for sharing. Do you have questions for us?"

"Sure, Gus, now that you know my history, do you really want to risk life and limb or whatever to give me a home. That I'm here proves all before you failed."

"The way I see it, if you're willing to work with us, we're willing to work with you."

"So, is this where you want me to strip so you can inspect my body and take photos to prove I've no marks or bruises?" With that said Joey stood and lifted his shirt about to pull it over his head.

"Stop! Why do you think we want, to photograph you naked?"

"Gus, don't you need proof I'm unblemished?"

"For what? If you have blemishes, just tell us."

"But now that you know my screwed-up history, you should have proof there is no damage on the outside too. You wouldn't buy a horse without checking his teeth, right. I don't mind stripping, most of the others wanted it."

"You're not a horse and we're not buying you. How about we let the dentist examine your teeth when you're due for a dental checkup." I could not figure out how my tête-à-tête made a wrong turn and got off-track, or did it? Why was I blushing, embarrassed at underage Joey offering to strip down for our inspection? The idea seemed grossly embarrassing, slightly titillating, and totally inappropriate, for us all.

Bob saw my dismay and joined the conversation with the determination of a well-trained teacher. "Joey, have you had sex with adults in exchange for housing or food?"

"Yup, I was violated at age eight, by a cousin twice my age. We were supposed to be sharing a bedroom in his family's home. He made me bleed, a lot. So, his family kicked *me* out and I became a homeless ward of the state."

Bob, stood, refreshed our coffee mugs, saying, "Mutual consent and self-respect are essentials for sex, otherwise it's a serious crime called rape."

"Oh, so that's what you want ..." After a brief silence, Joey, shrugged his shoulders and said, "Okay, I hereby give you both my consent to use my body for sex in exchange for a place to stay and three-square meals."

"We didn't ask for or want that from you. Is that what you want from us?"

"No. I thought that was what you want."

"It's not."

Bob, my hero, asserted control of a discussion that had gotten well beyond my comfort level. "Joey don't take what I'm about to say as rejection. Gus and I are married and sexually exclusive. We love each other and are not interested in exploiting you. But we *will* defend you against anyone trying to take advantage of you. Do you understand?"

"*Then what do you want from me*? Why would you take me in for no reason? You don't even know Mike, Elanor, or me. What do you want? I don't think you even like me."

"Mike asked us for a favor, to feed and house you. What gave *you* the idea we'd want to sexually take advantage?"

"I was in two different group homes down south, the boys got by giving sexual favors to staff and bigger boys. I know what works to make the world go around, sex, with whoever."

Having caught my breath after Bob intervened, I got up and walked over to the deck railing and leaned out looking at the view, and said, "Joey, look around, this is no group home, and we don't want sex with you. But just imagine if we'd not had this talk today and all three had a misunderstanding about what was necessary to get along."

"Maybe you'll change your minds. I was told if you got nothing to sell you sell your self-respect. I never had or have anything."

Bob looked as uncomfortable as I felt. Hitting the kid's concern from a different direction he said, "In this part of the country you are called jailbait. You dispensing sexual favors is not an option while you live with us. If you need something, just ask us for it." Bob said this sounding irritated at Joey's view of the world.

"Oh, I didn't understand. I've been called stupid my whole life. I keep forgetting that I am."

"You are not coming across as stupid. I can't figure out what we did to make you think you could come into our home and boss us around. If you don't want to stay with us, just say so. We know where the State Police Barracks are."

"I know nobody does anything for nothing. All I have to offer you is my body or manual labor. I'm just trying to understand what exactly is expected."

"How did Mike and Eleanor learn to be your foster parents?"

"I don't know, they made rules."

"How about we three make rules you can follow?"

"Okay, I can see I'm pissing you both off royally, sorry about that. How about, just give me a list of work you want done?"

I can give as good as I get. "Joey, from here on out if you want something, preface it with please. Mike told us he talked tasks with you. The only labor we expect is what Mike told you workwise. We have no ulterior motive in offering you shelter. If you are convinced this won't work out, then so be it. Grab your stuff and I'll drive you to the state police. Otherwise, give us a chance, your choice."

Joey dropped his tough guy in charge act. His face took on a lost puppy air and he said, "What Mike told me was mostly what I do for you already. I take care of the grounds, fix what breaks, and keep an eye out for future work. How am I supposed to earn my keep that way? What am I supposed to do to make you happy enough to feed me three meals with a warm place to sleep? See my worry?"

"We are pleased with the work you do, that's enough. While we are on this topic, do you want to transfer to a school in the city and live with us during the week?"

"No thank you, big cities make me anxious. I should do more here because I like to eat every day and be warm in winter. How about, if you want, I wash your cars, and paint inside and out, I can build things, and do all kinds of other work. Just tell me what you want, I'll do it. I don't mind being alone during the week, honest."

Bob and I exchanged a look at Joey's change in tone and I said, "When we all three live in this house, we all three pitch in with housework, food preparation, and clean up. It should be a collective effort on the inside of the house, share and share alike. When we are not here, pickup after yourself. We don't like a mess."

"What about the outside?"

"Joey, the outside of this property was your domain before we bought it, make us all proud to live here. But no wild parties, no drugs or booze whether we are here or not. As we said before, you are underage."

"Is that it?"

"We expect you to brush your teeth, eat three *nutritionally* balanced meals a day, get eight hours sleep, shower every day, make your bed, and cleanup after yourself. Keeping up with your schoolwork will make Bob happy. Any questions?"

"Why are you acting like parents?"

"Maybe we only look tough and are really nice guys."

"Then I have a question. No. Actually, it better wait till you know me better."

Picking up another shift in tone, I said, "Some questions won't survive to see another day. What's on your mind? It might be important?"

"Every time I have trusted people I got screwed, one way or another."

"Even Mike and Eleanor?"

"No. They made me feel safe and secure, until yesterday ended that. What you wanted to know is if you can trust me. Can *I* trust you? You have all the power and I'm one mistake away from being thrown out with the garbage."

Bob has said I don't know when to keep my mouth shut. "You said the word we have been heading toward so far today, trust. For me it is not static, it must be constantly renewed. If we three are talking, there shouldn't be any big mistakes or surprises about trust."

"Surprises!"

Bob came to the boy's rescue. "How about all big decisions decided unanimously, if possible. For example, we all agree, no one here wants *you* living in a group home. Agreed!"

"Agreed!"

"Agree."

Bob the schoolteacher was showing his vocation. "Let's set building trust as our primary reason to communicate, and use it to work out small problems before they grow big?"

I added an addendum. "Joey, that's if the sheriff or other authorities aren't involved with you."

"Phew, I feel relief ... Maybe my next question is too personal."

Like Bob says, I do not always think before speaking. "Take a shot."

"How did you guys know you were gay?"

I was not expecting the question. But maybe the kid was trying to get to know us, *I think, I'd suggested that.* "Bob says he knew at birth, and since then won't let anyone forget."

"What about you Gus?"

"For a long time, I attempted to be who I thought was wanted. Then I discovered it wasn't possible for me to be someone else. Once I got that figured out the rest fell in place easily."

"Did your family still love you?"

"They did, and showed it more often than before I came out, and I even got support from places I wasn't expecting, like in the Marine Corps. But not everybody has it that easy."

"At my school, calling something or someone gay, is an insult. The boys use gay or fag nonstop as putdowns or to mean stupid bad."

"That kind of thoughtless intolerance hurts many LGBTQ kids trying to accept themselves."

"You mean it's the same as for blacks, Jews and other minorities?"

"Not exactly, most LGBTQ people don't have family members, or even any LGBTQ role models. Without support it is crazymaking to try and understand hate from strangers just for existing. But hey, Bob and I survived. So will your LGBTQ classmates. Did I answer your question?"

Before Joey could answer, Bob spoke up. "Joey don't confuse your classmates' political incorrectness with the disease of homophobia. Underlying a lot of current societal disruption is Caucasians going from majority to minority status and looking for scape goats to blame. But hey, that's only my point of view."

"Bob, what should I do at school about the blaming?"

"Be generous, your classmates may be getting a double whammy, adolescent sexual insecurity, and their parent's resistance to social change."

"Wow, that's more answer than I expected ... ugh. You know, after all this yapping I think I might like you two guys after all."

"Because we give good breakfast?

"No. People don't usually talk to me like I have a brain."

"If you give us a chance, your feeling could be mutual."

"I'm impressed you didn't ask me if I'm gay. After I told you, you were. I expected you to ask."

"Since you brought it up, what would your answer have been?"

"Maybe. The truth is I don't know, and that's another big worry of mine."

Half to himself, Bob said, "Identity confusion might explain why we got off on the wrong foot."

Then he perked up, smiled, and the real Bob showed up as he said, "I'm going for a short run. Anyone care to join me?"

"I'm in."

"Me too."

It was interesting Joey could ask us about being gay and not ask about Bob's race-ethnicity, he is Vietnamese American. Could it be country folks are less interested in mixed race gay relationships than about LGBTQ identity. I doubt that. Or maybe, Joey, just wasn't ready to talk about race.

****

Bob and I fell into our regular exercise run to the highway and back. Joey just barely kept up, so we did not let loose for a final sprint to the house as usual. Back at the house catching our breath on the porch, Bob said, "Joey, how about I wash, and you dry the breakfast dishes?"

Gasping for air, leaning on the railing with both hands Joey cawed. "Sure, sir. But I don't mind doing both."

"Sir is not necessary, I resigned my commission five years ago, now I'm just plain Bob. Around here we like to do chores together. They go faster."

"While you do that, I'll dust and straighten up the den for our first official family meeting to discuss our schedules and expectations. That is if there are no objections?" No objections tendered, I grabbed my hot pink-feathered-duster and got busy.

CHAPTER 2. Family Meeting Formality

I know most people view meetings as hum drum bummers. But since we got off on the wrong foot with Joey, setting down ground rules to avoid future misunderstandings made sense to me. We gathered in the den, and I said, "Gentlemen please take a chair with a white-foolscap pad and pen on it. Take notes, write down ideas, or doodle. Since this meeting was my idea, I'll chair our first family meeting, and without objection Joey will chair the next, in one week. All in favor say aye … the ayes have it. The first item on my list, Joey, how do you get to school?"

Joey, sitting on the love seat, told us the big yellow school bus picked him up and brought him back to Mike's place. When asked how to change pickup and delivery points. He said the assistant principal's secretary, in the school office managed buses. With no objection, I put a visit to school office to change address on my to-do list. Joey had an objection to Bob or me meeting with the school principal on the visit.

"My counselor is pretty okay if you want to say hello to her?"

"Will our being gay cause *you* problems?"

"Don't think so, that's how it is right now. I have two gay dads. If someone has a problem, I'll tell them it's better than being homeless."

"Bob, do you have a contribution to this first family meeting?"

"Joey, do you have a bank account?"

"No. Never needed one."

I said, "Open a bank account goes on my list. My guess is savings accounts are still free and checking requires a three-or four-digit balance or pay a monthly fee."

Bob cut me off asking, "Joey, do you have a cell phone?"

"No. Don't need one. Who would I call?"

"We might want to call you about a last-minute change of plans, or if you were alone up here and had an emergency."

Joey shook his head no and said, "I can handle emergencies by myself."

Bob addressed me saying, he'd call in sick the next week and take care of three errands and whatever else came up. Then he asked, "Joey, can you leave school grounds during your lunch break?"

"Sure, with a counselor's note or a parent present to sign me out."

"I'll sign that you'll be returned in the same condition I found you."

"Ha, ha … promises, promises."

I was surprised Bob was willing to give up a week's work and lesson plans for the sake of our new adventure in unofficial foster parenting. Bob taught high school English in Brooklyn and developed thoughtful effective lesson plans as a matter of pride. He must have grown fond of Joey fast. The jury was still out with me, nevertheless I suggested a compromise. He called out sick Monday and Tuesday. I had meetings I couldn't miss Monday through Wednesday morning. If he drove Joey to school Wednesday early, he'd still get to work on time. Then I'd drive up and pick Joey up after school. That way we each only lose two days' work.

A new thought arrived and showed on Bob's face, so he said, "Gus, keeping on the same page, how much should we put in his bank account to open it?" Bob was a bit of a worry-wort about money.

"How about one hundred dollars, it's a good round number, then each month we'll add fifty. Fifty was what we paid Mike for lawn service, right?"

Looking disturbed, Joey threw his hands in the air and jumped to his feet. "You just-wait-one-goddamn-minute! I don't need a babysitter, and you aren't supposed to pay me for taking care of me."

Officiating as chair, I said, "Who says Joey?"

"We all agreed, including Mike, I'm honor bound to earn my keep, *and I will!* I'm not a welfare bum or charity case, never was, never will be!" Joey's face was flushed and showed determination.

Right on cue, Bob used his schoolteacher voice and said, "Nobody suggested you are a bum. The cell phone and bank account are for our convenience. I only used fifty dollars as a reference point. That's what we paid Mike for mowing the lawns. Having the bank account may be required to get the phone."

"But you paid Mike cash."

It felt like my turn, so I said, "I'd rather write a check. And a guy your age needs a bank account with a monthly allowance to establish credit and prove he can manage his money. Consider it part of your educational experience ... don't make a face over it. This is not a punishment, it's as much for our convenience as a learning experience for you. Indulge us, Joey."

"I'm not convinced, but you're bigger and bossier. Before I met you two my biggest problem was being short."

"And now?"

"The kids at school walk around like zombies staring at telephone screens in their hands. They look hypnotized, *I don't want to be a zombie in some trance like them.*"

"Then don't be. Like I said before, the phone is for our convenience, we split our time between two homes. If something comes up at the last minute, we can talk and not leave yon hanging hungry waiting for dinner."

"*Just so you Understand!* I'm not okay with you buying me things. My job is to work for my keep!" Quieting down a notch lowering his voice, Joey said, "Look, I need a place to stay, don't make this harder than it has to be ..."

I saw Bob's face register a new topic, his posture went on alert, and he cut Joey off. "Can you ride a bike?"

"Sure, of course, but I never owned a bicycle. Wait what does that have to do with what we were just talking about? Please, please don't buy me a bike!"

"Hey Bob, he said no bicycle. What do you think about a motor scooter, like a Vespa?"

"Joey, can you ride a motor scooter?"

"I don't know what a Vespa is. But you've seen me ride a motorcycle when I came here to work your garden."

"You know, Gus, a small Japanese motorcycle would probably cost a lot less than a quality European motor scooter."

"True, Bob, but which one is safer for a rider talking on a cellphone?"

"Neither Gus!"

Joey was visibly uncomfortable with how we kept changing the subject. So, he tried to best us by changing the topic too. "What are we going to do with the food in Mike's freezer? It would be terrible to waste it with so many hungry people in the world. Oh, and since you care, they left their motorcycles behind."

"Whoops, now what are we talking about, Joey?"

"When the electric gets turned off all that meat will rot, and the smell will permanently ruin the freezer."

"What's in Mike's freezer?"

"Mike and I bagged our limit of gobblers this past turkey season. Also, there are fish leftover from trout season, oh, and a quarter of my last year's venison is still there cut in steaks."

"When do you expect the power to be cut?"

"When Mike stops paying the bill. I overheard the kids at school say you can only get one month behind before electricity is shutoff."

"Gus, you ever cooked a turkey?"

"Never did, how about you?

"Nope, I don't like the taste."

Joey ignored Bob's comment about turkey flavor, and said, "Don't you guys worry, I can roast, or fry, or grill turkey and fish. Venison is a little tricky, there is no fat in the meat. Eleanor uses a really hot pan with lard, it improves the flavor."

Bob moved the conversation away from eating wild animals and said, "Hold on, if no one is living at Mike's place, the cost of running the freezer can't be much. Gus, we could cover it until they get back, and not worry about all that game meat turning bad."

"Capital idea. While we're at it, does Mike get his mail delivered, or picked up at the post office?"

"Delivered."

"Bob you probably want to add a trip to the post office for a change of address for Joey and the Morgens to our post office box. Joey when you write Mike, ask if he wants his mail forwarded or held, and if he minds, if we pay his utilities."

"While you're at it, Joey, ask if you can buy or borrow one of their motorcycles to ride to school."

"Wait a second, Bob, won't Joey need a license to ride a motorcycle on the street. It's eighteen to drive a car in this state, isn't it the same for motorized two wheels?"

"Several kids my age ride motorcycles to school and the auto-shop teacher helps them with repairs after last period. He only charges for the cost of parts. The shop teachers at my school are the best."

"We got a lot accomplished for a first family meeting. Next week, with Joey chairing, we should go over the results of this week's plans before new business. Now, shall we lunch or brunch and then you two looks to need a nap. I can't wait to begin reading the last novel by that famous author who just died."

CHAPTER 3. Hans

An unexpected consequence of Bob, then me spending alone time with Joey during his first week with us was a perceptible relaxation of nonverbal anxiety. It was surprising how quickly Joey's running ability improved up to our level. He showed pride when we acknowledged him our equal running, and that cut resistance we had tried not to speak about but couldn't ignore.

At the start of the second week, after a nutritious breakfast, Joey chaired our family meeting with reluctance, then fell into the job and kept Bob and me to the agenda. Within the boundaries we set, he grew into controlling the meeting like a budding leader learning his job.

Bob recounted his visit to Joey's school. He told us at first the office staff was disinclined to accept a photocopy of the paper signed by Mike and us unofficially acknowledging Joey's change of living arrangements and new address. They wanted judges, lawyers, bureaucracies, signatures, and all notarized in triplicate.

Since Bob taught high school, he knew the work-shirking ways of bothersome low-level administrative office workers. He successfully accomplished his task moving up the pecking order to a person who would facilitate the straightforward process without need of lawyers and such, the school principal.

As bob told it, meeting with Ms. Limane, Joey's guidance counselor, also met with inflexible opposition by administration staff. It seemed at Joey's school prearranged appointments were mandatory due to Limane's over-booked schedule and individual students' emergencies. Miraculously, after direct persuasive persistence, she became available for a quick meet and greet, between her other work. Initially, she only offered the barest of demographic information about Joey and then tried a bum's rush us out the door.

Misinterpreting Ms. Limane's blandly stated confidentiality restriction as personal, Joey, jumped to his feet and said, "Go ahead, talk about me without me. You adults are all the same. I'll wait outside until your done trashing me." Then he stormed out of her office, loudly banging the door shut.

Expecting to soon follow Joey out the door, without the information he came for. Bob said he made direct combat Colonel in charge, stare down eye contact, and then loudly demanded, "Are you even able to say if the boy is in a vocational track or dropout prevention protocol?"

Bob says Ms. Limane cringed back in her chair, then heaved a big sigh and made a show of another look at the photocopy we signed with Mike. Then sat up straight in her chair, dropped her officious facade, and started talking. It appeared to Bob, she was breaking rules for our boy's sake and wanted us to know it.

She told Bob, when Joey arrived to live with his other unofficial foster parents, he was already in eighth grade and tested well below average for New York children his age. So, the school district assigned him a tutor two days a week for four months. Upon retesting after tutoring, his scored went from the lowest to the highest percentile. So, he became eligible to take advanced placement (AP) curriculum when he arrived in high school. She said Joey has been taking and passing AP classes ever since then. He continues to be an unexplained conundrum for our inhouse testers. Now, in eleventh grade, Joey has a 4.0 grade point average, and taking our most difficult college level courses. He is in the top five percent of the school's college prep tract."

Bob spoke up to cover his surprise. "Mike told us Joey was in special education class."

"What I told his other foster father was the boy lacks social skills and we don't have special education for that. Most students handle socialization on their own. The man must have misunderstood."

"Joey told us he has no friends because he's called names for being short. Are you aware of that?"

"He's got thin skin. You just saw how sensitive he is. I know somethings bothering him, but he isn't ready to tell me what."

"Do you have any suggestions for us new foster parents?"

"Joey's only extracurricular activity is the woodcrafter's club. They meet once a week after school and do woodworking. Their projects are individually chosen by the student with the teacher, and done in the school's vocational wood shop, it's hardly social. If Joey wants to get into a decent college or university and have lucrative future employment, he needs extracurriculars showing he's a team player. Here I'll print you out a list of what else the recruiters look for."

"Thank you … this is quite a long list. Is there an abridged version?"

"Sports teams, student government, or helping the less fortunate, anyone could give his future prospects a boost."

After telling us about his encounter with Ms. Limane, Bob turned to Joey and asked, "Are you interested in sports or student government or helping the needy?"

"Give me a break, sports, I'm the shortest, lightest weight guy in eleventh grade. The humongous football goofballs would crush me into the ground. Mike said all politicians are lying thieves, and with two gay dads I need a social worker, not be one."

As Bob often says, sometimes I speak just to hear my own voice disconnected from my brain. "Really, there are no sports that interest you. I thought you purported to be an all-American boy with indeterminate sexuality and altitude was your only problems. Or did I get that wrong?"

"Look, football, soccer, and basketball all reminded me of being beat-up in group homes. Baseball is too slow and boring, what else is there?"

Still wagging my tongue, I said, "How about individual team sports?"

"Like what?"

"Hmm, there's tennis, badminton, ping-pong, swimming, track, or wrestling." Bob said he saw a light flick on, then fade when I mentioned wrestling. He shot me a look did I see it? *I had not.*

Then ever at the ready, Bob followed-up perceived interest with a question. "Joey have you ever tried wrestling? I could show you a couple of holds, if I can remember back hundreds of years, to my high school wrestling foray."

"What do wrestlers do? I mean besides feel each other up?"

"We lifted weights and had to run with the cross-country squad."

"There must be more to it?"

"There is, to win you pin your opponent's shoulders to the mat for a count of three. It's a thinking man's game, you are both of equal heft. The first round is thee-minutes, then two, two-minute rounds, you get two points for a take down and one for an escape, pin your opponent and win. I don't recall any points for ass grabbing."

"I can't do it … don't have weights to lift."

"You'll need a better excuse than that. Every wrestling room I've seen had plenty of free weights and floor mats to wrestle on."

I offered without being asked, "We have weights in the basement of this house. Dan and Bill left a complete set, and we brought our own up from the apartment, along with a much better weight bench."

Joey didn't say yes or no but looked interested. "I'll check to see if my school has a wrestling program. If they do, I'll get back to you on weightlifting. Bob, are you going to tell Gus about my phone call with Mike?"

"Why don't you? I only heard one side of the conversation."

"What'd he say?"

"Mike said if you don't like turkey meat, I should donate the four gobblers in the freezer to the senior citizen center lunch program. He thinks we should eat the fish and venison and empty his refrigerator, unplug both the freezer and refrigerator, and leave the doors open. I'll clean them first."

"How are Mike and Eleanor doing in North Carolina?"

"I'm guessing it's pretty bad, but he'd never tell me that. They are both looking for part-time work and have their hands full caring for a helpless mother and daughter. He said we should either bring his chickens and duck here or turn them loose."

"Gus, do you see poultry farming on your resume?"

"Sorry Bob, nothing personal, I'm not entertaining such a fine feathered idea."

"I do miss having a dog for company."

"Hold on a minute Joey, how can you manage AP classes, wrestling, your outside chores, and give a dog the attention it needs."

"I have good time management skills. Ask Mike?"

"Then what happens in two years when you go marching off to war. That's what Mike said you want to do."

"That's what Mike expects, it wasn't my choice."

I looked at Bob, he was thinking the same thing I was, *Maybe we bit off more than we could chew taking in a homeless waif with frontier survival skills. He wasn't only disturbing our peace and tranquility he came with issues.*

Oblivious to Bob and my silent communication, Joey kept talking and hardly stopped for a breath. He said, "Mike says he doesn't want to sell his motorcycles, but we can use them on loan for however long need be, until he's back. He said it would be better for the bikes to run rather than fall into disrepair standing idle."

Mindful of the two-year commitment we made and wish to make it work despite new information. I said, "At our next family meeting we should talk about boundaries."

Bob to the rescue said, "Another way to resolve the bird problem would be to let it be known we will give them away free to good homes. What do you guys think?"

"But Bob and Gus, what will the senior citizens eat?"

"Let them eat turkey and venison steak."

Joey looked disappointed and slouched in his seat, so I changed the subject. "Do you want to ride Mike or Elenore's motorcycle to school, weather permitting?"

"That way I could try out for wrestling and not have to beg for rides after practice."

"You never mentioned begging for rides."

"I have to do it on Mondays after woodworking. I hate feeling beholden by asking favors."

"Why is that?"

"The school bus schedule is strict, it won't wait. There is no school transportation for afterschool activities."

"Are you sure beholden is the word you want to use?"

"Why not?"

"Your guidance counselors said you need to develop social skills. Asking for a ride is social."

"I accept I come from nothing and will always have nothing except my pride, which doesn't beg favors. Why would I want to advertise I'm without wheels?"

"If you get nothing else from Bob and me, we are not losers and you by association are not either. Just believe it, you'll find it's true."

Bob was looking antsy and finally said, this meeting is running long, preachy, and we three have reservations for brunch with friends two villages over. He proposed buying Joey a new motorcycle helmet, getting him a license and insurance before our next meeting. Then said, "Don't worry Gus, I'll take care of it. With no objection, Mr. Chairmen I move we end this funfest and go Sunday brunching with gay compatriots."

"Hold on Bob, our friends can wait a minute. I'd like to talk about getting a dog. In the past you felt we were too busy to give a dog a well-balanced life."

"Got it, now going from a duo to a trio there is more people time for a dog. When Joey joins the Army will the dog travel back and forth with us to the city to see a professional dog walker?"

"Why not? I'm game if the dog is."

"Sure, Gus why not get a dog to keep Joey company during the week? I'm adaptable."

"And our apartment cat could use an occasional four leg fury visitor for stimulation. It might cut some of that holier-than-thou-aloofness."

"Then it's okay by me. Joey what do you think, a puppy or an older dog with a history?"

"Rescued dogs are a lot of work, but usually worth it. Wow, really, we'll get a dog. Then I won't miss Mike and Eleanor when you are in the city."

"Let's go to the dog-pound next Saturday.

"That's a plan, and with it I move to end this meeting and go brunching."

"Okay, all those in favor … the ayes have it."

****

The county sheriff rescued a young German Sheppard when she raided a mobile home meth-lab out in the boondock. The dog was big, handsome, tan with a black snout and saddle. He was starved, beaten, and made into a crazy-mean guard dog. He had been attached to the house trailer entrance with a heavy chain when the sheriff and her deputies raided the place. They used a tranquilizer gun to get past the guard dog.

Joey named the rescued K-9 Hans. We three humans worked to gain his trust and bring him back to doggy sanity with gentle firm instructions, rewards, measured affection, and when milestones were achieved bountiful love. Once Hans learned to be a domestic housedog and behaved accordingly, our close-knit trio became a quartet adding a four-legged fury member.

As matters came up affecting the family, they were swiftly decided by consensuses at Sunday meetings. Our family of four settled into a peaceful routine as fewer and fewer issues needed resolution as newness wore off. After six months, the need for weekly family meetings became superfluous, and replaced by a notepad magnetically affixed to the refrigerator.

CHAPTER 4. Wrestling, New Suit

As it turned out, Joey's high school wrestling team did not have a 133 pounder, and so he was welcomed by the coaches and teammates as potential to fill a hole in their roster. Adding three pounds to his weight meant second helpings of pasta, rice, or potatoes. He resisted overeating at first, then discovered extra endurance running with us. Once he reached 133 it became about maintaining the weight after each morning on the scale.

Without another 133 pounders on the team Joey practiced with heftier trained wrestlers, or with wirier fast 125 pounders. With the coaches' encouragement and teammates support, Joey looked like he found his sport. His apprehension about joining the team dissolved once he got into a regular training routine. At home, his beaming smile showed up more regularly to replace his usual anxious on guard Mike Morgan like face. He wasn't ready to admit it but was blossoming learning to wrestle through hard physical workouts and supportive comradery.

Then transfer student Austin Bennington, another 133 pounders joined the team. He was a twelfth-grade late transfer from a city high school, where he regularly won his wrestling matches. Initially Joey learned much having Austin as a practice partner. Then he saw many of his anticipated matches given to Austin. Joey found it hard to accept a diminished role on the team. Against other rural schools Austin was unstoppable, he won every match barely breaking a sweat. Meanwhile, Joey slid into self-identified bench warmer role even though, when possible, he was matched against less experienced opponents, and often won.

Bob, I, and Hans noticed Joey's slow-slide down a dark psychological hole. Bob called a family meeting ostensibly about the county's transfer stations change in days for accepting recycle materials and other new rules.

With a scowl plastered on his bright young face the first thing Joey said after the recycling rubrics change was, I'm quitting the wrestling team on Monday.

Foster parenting was new to Bob and me, and it wasn't something we went looking for, so I said, "Why?"

"I'm just quitting, that's all. I don't need a reason!"

Unlike me, Bob was used to working with adolescent turmoil and said, "Hold on, buckaroo, we know the reason you joined. We deserve to know why you're quitting."

"Because I don't like how I look in a singlet. Is that a good enough reason?"

I did not have all day to waste playing word games with a teenager. I said, "What narcissistic bullshit is that. When did you suddenly grow so vain?"

"I joined the team I can quit it."

"Huh, you never cared about your appearance before. In fact, if I didn't threaten to cut your hair myself, you'd never see the barber, and he even likes you. Don't say it, Joey, I know, there's just no accounting for your taste. I'm sorry I mentioned that to you."

Bob jumped in for stability. "There is accounting for taste, science just hasn't found it yet. Joey, it'll be faster to tell us the real reason. Otherwise, we won't leave you alone ... come on we have a busy day planned and wresting fashions haven't changed since the ancient Greeks were forced to compete in their Olympics clothed."

I couldn't help imagining fit ancient Greek wrestlers doing combat naked. "Bob, that was a sad day indeed."

"You know you guys can be so thickheaded sometimes."

"Enlighten us."

"Okay, so my singlet makes my crotch look small. Satisfied? Monday, I quit."

Bob the peace maker gave Joey a mollifying look. "That reason won't work, Joey. The ancient Greeks, founders of wrestling as sport, considered small genitals attractive representation of Platonic love. Compare Greek male nude statues to the big-dick ancient Roman's lustful sculptures and you'll see what I mean."

Joey quickly realized he had started something expecting little resistance, and we were not about to give him an easy out. "I'm not small for my height, compared to the other boys I see in the showers after Phys-ed class or wrestling practice."

"Does your school have rulers in the showers?"

"No. But I'm bigger than average, soft, and you know what else? It is not good for my skin to take two showers a day Monday through Friday. So, how about that for the reason I'm quitting wrestling tomorrow."

I could see Bob was not buying what Joey was selling any more than me. He was about to bring his often-harsh schoolteacher reality into focus. I jumped in with a softer approach. "How would it be if I buy you a dry skin lotion and a falsey to stuff in your jockstrap to make it a more comfortable size?"

"You want me to wear a falsey? In case you haven't noticed, I'm not a girl, and if I were, I'd need two falsies."

"The problem I see is when you guys wear your white singlets too much information is visual. Your black uniforms are a better choice for discretion."

"You're bullying me to keep wrestling when I want to quit. I should have known this day was coming."

"Hans." His ears shot straight up, and his body went to alert. "Come." He stood, shook himself, marched over with German Sheppard authority, and then stood expectantly in front of me. "Good boy," I stroked the top of his head then his snout. "Hans, sit. Should Joey stay on the wrestling team?" Sitting, he wagged his tail and smiled his tongue out, so I stroked his chest. "We have one vote for quitting and Hans votes for staying on the team."

"What do you think you're doing?"

"Our house rule is all important decisions must be unanimous. No need for me or Bob to vote since it's already a split decision. May I recommend the topic of quitting wrestling be tabled till next meeting?"

Body language ridged, strength of character showing on his face, Joey said, "I think not, we settle this here and now."

"Joey, you're breaking protocol."

"See, I knew you'd try some trick. We talked about my joining the team at a family meeting. Now we are talking about my quitting at this meeting. There is no need to wait until next week."

"I don't recall me or Gus ever saying no to you about anything."

"Good, then tomorrow I quit."

"No, Hans voted for you to stay on the team. Make a case, convinced us three to agree with you, and I'll talk to Hans on your behalf if he gets stubborn." Bob could be judicious when he wanted.

"Okay, then I'll make my case. *Which I shouldn't have to*. The chickens and duck had to get adopted because they weren't wanted here. The team doesn't need or want me any longer either, I'm just the same as the poultry."

"Is someone harassing you?"

"Just the opposite, they hardly know I'm alive. Austin is winning all the challenging 133-pound matches. I only wrestle the pushovers!"

"So that's it, the real reason to quit is not enough action at matches? Want me to talk to the coach for you? I can be persuasive?"

"Definitely not Gus. They are busy planning the after-season awards celebration and might even be anti-gay."

"What makes you think they're anti-gay?"

"The boys trash talk gay people a lot and the coaches never scold them. Anyway, I've not earned any award, why should I go to sit on my hands. Plus, I don't have a date for that party. So, what's the point of going."

"Bob, you want to take the oppositional view or should I … okay then, it's mine. The thing about athletics is the human-apparatus can be fragile, it gets strains, pulls, tears, breaks, or even illness that interfere with competition. And you my young friend, are there, ready, to save the day at 133 pounds in case of such a catastrophe."

"Yeah, yeah, into the breech or something."

"No team wants a loss by default. In your long view, Austin graduates this year. Using what you learned from him, next year you should be the number one 133 competitor. But only if you can maintain that weight *and don't quit.*"

"What about the other thing?"

"Adolescent boys who struggle the hardest recognizing they're gay often express gross homophobia until they can acknowledge being queer as acceptable. Neither Bob nor I doubt your sexual indeterminacy or would be intimidated by your teammates or coaches. Would we Bob?"

"Let me at the bastards!"

"Joey, for my dense sake, is antigay also about you living with two gay dads."

"No. I'll still be the only one at the party with no award, and no date. I never liked parties it's all bullshit boring chit chat."

"Joey, if I recall correctly, you didn't join the team to win awards, show-off your dating skills, or prove yourself a party animal. If you complete the season, you achieved your goal of getting on the team to gain applications' extra points for extracurricular activities. In the adult world points are given for showing up."

Bob chimed in with his two cents, "See it through, finish what you started. It's about your future job prospects."

"How's it going to look? I live with two gay men and don't have a steady girlfriend. You know what they'll say."

"You didn't choose to live with us or us you. Let people talk it's no skin off your nose, and you won't be the only wrestler at the party without a date."

Joey's stiff body language showed his frustration at not getting his way. "You can't know I won't be the only single."

I leaned in toward Joey, attempting to turn the heat down. "When I was your age, I often went places without a date and had more fun than the guys whose dates were obnoxious and no fun at all."

"Gus, are you preaching at me?"

"Right now, this year's party may look like no fun, but next years will be a triumph to measure it against."

"Who says?"

"Rudyard Kipling said, 'Triumph and disaster should be treated the same.'"

"That's from his poem 'If.'"

"Did you read Kipling in school?

"No. Mike and Eleanor gave me a birthday card with "If" printed on the front. It was my first birthday living with them. They said I should memorize the poem and live by the words. I forgot a lot already."

"If I gave you a collection of Kipling's coming of age in India stories, would you read them?"

"I guess, sure. I liked "If." Was he gay too?"

"Not that I know. But he did write about boys growing up in difficult circumstances. Looking at the change on your face, has this conversation drifted into another uncomfortable place for you?"

"That's okay, it's my fault I started it." Dropping his hands into his lap Joey said, "Can we talk about something else?"

Bob's expression looked thoughtful. Sometimes, he couldn't resist showing off his academic chops. "You know Gus, Herman Hesse would be a better choice for Joey's coming of age reading."

"Except Hesse didn't write "If.""

"Oh, right you are. But he still might find Hesse helpful. Let's get him both authors."

"Please don't buy me gifts. I need to earn my keep."

"Joey, is the end of season party a dress up event?"

"How'd you know? Wrestlers like to wear suits and ties when not in singlets. I guess it's one extreme or the other with them."

"It also fits a certain macho jock image."

"If I wanted to attend, you'd have to drive me to the Goodwill store to buy a suit and tie. But wait, see, that's another reason not to go."

"Goodwill?"

Joey explained Eleanor bought all their clothes there and fixed them to fit nice, using her old foot-powered sewing machine. Except of course, Goodwill doesn't sell underwear and socks. She got those from the factory seconds closeout bins. "What's wrong with Goodwill?"

"There is nothing wrong with Goodwill. But now that we are living together, why not get a suit where we buy ours? Then we'd look like a family. If they need to talk, let's give them something to talk about like how fashionable we are. What do you think, Hans?"

Hans eagerly approved, stood, and wagged his tail hard in assent. He liked to be included and had me figured out and used the knowledge for extra doggy treats. It was a symbiotic relationship.

After looking approvingly on Hans and my interaction, Joey's face shifted to disapproval and said, "Gus, I'm supposed to be earning my keep around here. I can't with you two spending money on me. Money, I'll never be able to repay."

"Repayment will be seeing you dressed up to celebrate achieving your goal, joining, and completing the wrestling season. Does that about cover this meeting?"

"Ugh, not quite, just now when I got upset, I admitted to checking-out guys in the showers at school. I know that sounds perverted. But I'm not really a deviant. It could be I'm simply curious about who has what. You know the haves and have nots hiding under pubic bushes in underpants. Curiosity is a good thing for a student, right?"

"Everyone should have a hobby."

"Don't blame yourselves if I'm gay, it's not your fault. I was interested in cock watching long before I met you two. The group homes I was in had us all shower together while staff watched and commented. That's where I learned to watched, monkey see monkey do."

Physically adjusting his body, Bob brought his teacher's training into a sensitive topic for Joey, but not urologists. "Many children who were sexually abused share your interest. Research suggests it's from disturbed development, then trying to fix it, not voyeurism."

"I don't understand?"

"Sexually abused kids either become hyper-sexual or sexually shut-down when most children their age are discovering sex play naturally."

"I don't like the word voyeurism it sounds … like a horror movie. Since I started this, do you think there is a test to find out if I'm gay? Knowing would prove I'm not as crazy as I feel most of the time."

"Where's this coming from?"

"Right this minute I am ashamed I told you my deepest dark secret, cock watching. I didn't mean to it came out unintentionally. But if I were gay, wouldn't my interest go beyond just looking?"

"Maybe there is a way for you to find out?"

"Okay, but before you tell me that, *know*, I want to be straight. Just like Mike and Eleanor. That's my wish … nothing personal."

"We aren't looking for converts. But why wouldn't it be okay to be gay?"

"When I came here from the south, Mike already had Dan and Bill, the guys you bought this place from, as customers. Everybody knew they were queers, but they never caused any trouble and paid in cash, on time."

Physically hunching up to show he wanted to speed the conversation along, Bob said, "And?" Most likely he needed to pee.

"Well, in truth, I felt creepy uncomfortable around them."

"Why was that?"

"They were soft, and sometimes they acted like silly girls. Even called each other Miss Thing or Queen Mother when they thought no one was watching."

"I'd find that offensive too. Was that it?"

"Dan leered at me, and it reminded me of the look just before I was raped. Once or twice, I saw Mike or Eleanor look at me hard, like to see if I was as girly as Dan and Bill. But maybe, it was just my imagination."

"It's possible to misunderstand other's looks."

"No. I felt judged, like I do when bullies at school call me faggot."

"Do you want me to show you some moves to put them on their ass?"

Joey's body language stiffened to show his male macho attitude on guard. "No, I can take care of myself. But for all I know my destiny may be to end up a shorter version of Dan or Bill."

"Do Gus and I give you a creepy feeling because we *are* gay?"

"No. If there was a bad fight, I'd want you guys on my side. I don't fight the bullies because my grades matter to me. Don't worry I could knock them on their ass if they went too far."

"Joey, Bob and I, decided we are going to love you no matter what team you play for in bed."

Bob pitched in to help and said, "Exactly. There are many ways to be gay or straight, but only one way to be Joey Hall. Chill out, time provides the answers we seek, if we're patient."

"I hear you, but don't you think it would be unusual for me not to be in a hurry to know? I'm a teenager, we want everything yesterday."

"Keep talking, I sense there's more on your mind."

"Gus you're a mind reader?"

"Spill the beans bucko."

Joey went on to tell us part of him thought he should feel ashamed for comparing boys' cocks in the school showers or peeing at the long trough urinals. And half of him liked looking, comparing, and remembering who had what clothed. He said it felt naughty, like being in on their secrets without them aware. But not in a gay way, because in his heart of hearts he wanted to be heterosexual."

"Joey, take all the time you need for self-discovery; we'll support you whoever you are."

"You two treat me right. I guess if I turn gay it could be worse."

"Are we done with this?"

"Since it seems so important to most people do you think I'm a twisted fuck for not knowing what team I play on at age sixteen?"

"Let's put it to a vote, Hans and Bob, 'Is Joey a normal cock-curious teenager?' … look, there is your proof, three wagging tails vote for normal."

Not always the quickest to get the discussion was over, Bob capped it. "Back full circle to where this started, research shows all human males would prefer bigger penises, even those with ridiculously huge impractical tools. That's why you want a singlet showing a bigger bulge. So, there!"

"Gosh, now I feel better."

Wary, I anticipated upset, after just calming Joey down. But we were gaining insights. "What do you think about when jerking off, girls or boys, or both?"

Joey's fair skin bloomed a bright red blush, and his face went stone like ridged, to show I had broached an unspeakable taboo. Bob and I assumed Joey did what most sixteen-year-olds do for stress relive. We never had a reason to mentioned it before he mentioned cock watching.

"Joey don't misunderstand me. I don't want to know the content of your fantasies, only their gender."

Bristling, back ramrod straight Joey aid, "How could you ask that, ever heard of personal space, Gus?"

"The test isn't foolproof, and fantasies change over time. Don't be such a prude Joey."

Hans stirred, went to a clearly bothered Joey and lifted the boy's hand with his head. Joey automatically petted the dog. Blushing deeply, Joey seemed to be chewing on something he wasn't sure he wanted to spit out after revealing so much of his inner life already.

Good old Bob tried to repair the mood I had disrupted. "These days the consensus indicates many girls and boys your age don't have masturbatory fantasies, like previous generations. My advice is, don't let Gus's good intentions disturb you. He means well, and I'm throwing you a lifeline, take it."

"His question was out of line. I should have said fuck off! It's none of your business."

Hans looked confused but nevertheless barked to answer Joey's raised voice.

"Having been raped may have disturbed your public private boundaries. Maybe we should end this conversation? I think, I just step in something off limits."

"I was told touching myself down there is an unspeakable act. Now you sound like it's normal. Every day I work so hard to be good, and then fail and jack off. That's why what you asked, hit so hard. I'm a failure who can't even *keep a promise to myself.*"

"Huh, a generation gap, in my day we just let nature take its course with a little friendly friction and then didn't think about it afterward."

"Gus, I know I'm fighting a losing battle, but you're not helping saying cock watching is my hobby. That isn't who I want to be. I only halfway enjoy watching and then imagine those cocks doing what I'm doing. I told you I'm a loser."

Not always one to know when he's being appropriate, Bob pressed on academically. "Joey, statistics show the majority of human's first, last, and most frequent orgasms come from whacking off, alone. Whether you want to think of it as yielding to temptation or celebrating your body the outcome is the same. I call it basic biological function, with or without helpful imaginary."

"Here we go we're finally getting down to it. Did Mike leave me with you two because he thought I'd turn out queer? He did, didn't he?"

Without realizing it, I'd been zoning out, no doubt as a remedy to Bob and Joey, yammering back and forth about hand jobs. "Your question is for Mike, ask him. You have his phone number."

"Why can't you or Bob tell me?"

"It's Mike's question."

"Damn it, now I have a headache. May I go take a nap?"

"Sure, take Hans with you. He loves napping."

As far as we know Joey, never asked Mike why he had chosen two gay men as foster dads. It also seemed wrong to mention Mike's judgement about North Carolina being a hate state best avoided by young people of any persuasion.

****

After thoughtful consideration of style and fabric, our tailor set to work constructing a suit that fit Joey perfectly. Initially, he resisted going into the city with us to meet Mr. Wong, our tailor. Dense urban areas made Joey anxious. By then we had learned ways short of putting a black bag over his head to overcome opposition for his benefit. Joey said the final fitting caused a lump in his throat looking at his well-tailored stunning reflection in the full-length mirrors.

Driving back to the country house, caressing the fine English worsted dark-wool fabric, Joey said, "This suit smells new. I've only worn secondhand outer clothes. I feel like a different person when I put it on! Thank you, dads."

"Bob and I thought you'd like the look of a new suit. Mr. Wong dresses us to our best advantage."

"May it serve you well, Joey."

The suit became his most prized possession and yet the post wrestling season party remained a dread for him. He had convinced himself he'd be all alone sitting in a corner shunned by his teammates. To counter his self-deprecation, I volunteered to attend the party as transportation provider and adult sidekick. Joey begrudgingly acquiesced to attend, but only not to disappoint his adult wingman foster father. He expected to have a terrible time, even with my promise to crack cringe worthy bad jokes.

CHAPTER 5. Austin

Driving up to the country house after work, traffic was abysmal due to roadwork, two accidents, and the gods' disfavor of internal combustion engines all traffic jammed together. When at last I arrived, I did not have time to change suits, let alone shower. Joey had ridden his motorcycle home from school, changed into his new spiffy outfit and was about to change into afterschool clothes because I was so late.

Joey looked sharp, projecting a new self-assurance into which he was growing. It allowed him to be angry at me for being late and happy not to have to attend the much-dreaded party because *I was irresponsibly late*. Bob had afterschool parent teacher meetings he could not skip. By necessity he would forgo the party but have time to shower and change before joining us at the restaurant. So, it was fated I would be the scruffy one in our little family group. To counter Joey's contrary mood, I decided to have a good time despite everything going off the rails thus far.

Even with my tales of woe, having left work extra early to be a good supportive-parent-substitute, and explaining the highway gods' ire, Joey made excuses not to go, right up to walking out the door. My repeatedly declaring how good he looked got him in my car. In my travels, when all else fails, flattery works.

The post-season wrestling awards presentation and party happened in the high school cafeteria from four PM till cleanup, on Friday. The decorations were minimal-masculine-conservative, emitting a strong hint of patriotic testosterone. Out of habit, I looked over the crowd when we arrived. Most student attendees did not have dates or dress better than work-rumpled me. Consequently, Joey stood out dressed like a well-tailored adolescent fashion model. He got looks, even stares. Here and there party rules were put up, hand-scrawled on white-poster paper, "No shop talk allowed during the party."

Pointing to a poster Joey said, "This is a first, wrestlers and coaches talking about something other than wrestling. They don't know anything else."

The ceremony started with unnecessarily long rambling speeches from middle-aged, muscle-bound men elaborating on; rah-rah team, excellent job men, go Lions. The speakers were wearing ill-fitting, bulging muscles straining seams of off the rack cheap suits. I felt right at home wearing my almost worn-out, rainy-day office-wrinkled-suit.

We were both pleasantly surprised when Joey's name was called first for an award. He was given the most improved wrestler of the year little plaque and coaches handshakes all around. His face showed a radical mood shift from dread to pride. When he relaxed Joey was a good-looking teen. It was fantastic to watch and worth the price of his suit, Joey began to radiate delight.

Then about three-quarters through the droning presentations, Joey was called to the microphone area with a small group of other wrestlers. They were each given a winner's medium-size trophy-cup. Joey had won more matches than he lost.

Finally, at the end of giving out awards, his team-mate Austin received the only undefeated wrestler's big trophy, and then the school's overall best wrestler of the year, the biggest trophy. Even though Austin started the wrestling season late, he scored the most wins by pinning opponents, and scored the highest number of team points. Austin broke school records. But by the look of it, Austin's self-aggrandizing speech did not win him any points from his teammates or coaches.

After the award presentations and thank you speeches, we were told to socialize. The head coach said, "Remember to be excellent citizens on and off the wrestling mat, so no shop talks tonight."

Then high school girls circulated among the mostly male audience with trays of healthy canapés and cups of nutritious fresh-fruit-juice-punch. Just after the refreshments arrived, Joey got nervous and wanted to leave. I was ready to go as well, we had accomplished our mission. Just then Austin slid into the empty chair next to Joey and the two began a casual chit-chat review of the event. Joey admired Austin's trophies, which Austin relished beyond good manners. After my perfunctory introduction and brief handshake, I left them chatting and wondering, *Was that shoptalk or socializing tête-à-tête about grappling holds.* I went in search of coaches to praise for encouraging my foster teen to win trophies and self-esteem almost against his will.

Rather than get into the weeds with coaches explaining why Joey had two foster fathers, my gaydar indicated I was, for the most part, singing to the choir with these men who grabbed and held other men. Even though, most student wrestlers appeared straight, I had to wonder how that was working out, until remembering the school's wrestling program ranked highest in its class statewide. Joey shared that fact with Bob and me when he first joined the team and needed our parental signatures to participate and absolve the school from future lawsuits.

Thanking the coaching staff was more rewarding than humbling or off-putting, depending on point of view. In fact, if I had been single, I could have scored telephone numbers for dates with older than me muscle-bound ex-jocks on the make. But hey, I was never into rough sex, and I love my man, Bob, and he loves me back. So, to keep my virtue intact, I gravitated back to my seat and safety of teenagers.

When I left, the two teens' conversation appeared superficial wrestler talk. Returning I noticed they had gotten into serious subjects. I thought, *That's interesting, these two must know each other's physical strengths from daily wrestling workouts.* But a light was shimmering behind their eyes, an almost palpable energy pulsated back and forth as doors opened, and they shared who they were. The more I watched them it became clearer they knew each other's bodies in detail from grappling practice and showering, and now after they had been publicly acknowledged winning awards, they were sharing their backgrounds in personal detail.

Normally my rational self would require I discreetly leave again and give the boys privacy. But my inner bitch demanded to know if self-centered Austin was trouble for my ward. Soon it became clear to me Austin had a personality disorder. The way he flaunted his accomplishments without acknowledging Joey's gave Austin away. I based my opinion on his inability to read his audience and going from indifferent to Joey's instant best friend at warp speed. My foster-parenting skills were nascent but stirred protectively the longer I eavesdropped. So, I stuck to my seat not sure the teens had noticed I'd returned.

Joey told Austin an un-upholstered, safely abridged version of his story, as I knew it. He ended with he only attended the event because his two gay dads insisted. But was glad he came after all.

Then smirking Austin said, "Do your gay dads hit on you and give free blow jobs to your friends?"

In a sharp ominous mood shift, Joey scowled hard. "No. And if you say anything like that at school, *you'll regret it.*"

"Chill, bro, I'm not a tattle tale. I've told you all about how my life hasn't been so wonderful, right?"

I overheard Austin brag his parents were successful agronomists, in fierce competition with each other for fame. They were so busy out doing each other's research, they often forgot they had hungry children at home. Because his parents were away much of the time, his older brother Nyles parented him as best he could when they weren't dumped, uninvited on unwilling relatives to feed. I imagined the experience of being shuffled about didn't leave room for character development.

When unplanned baby brother Bix was born, Austin was old enough to begrudge losing what little attention he received. So, he ran away from home. After eight days on the streets with other homeless waifs, the police found Austin using the tracking chip imbedded in his ear lobe by a veterinarian. His parents were working in Africa at the time. Nevertheless, they were charged in their absence, with using unapproved veterinary devices on children, a felony. Austin found this out from his older brother who had regular run ins with law enforcement.

A family court judge had Austin's chip removed and sent him to live with his widowed paternal grandfather. Granddad had tried out for the U.S. Olympic wrestling team when he was young. To keep Austin's rambunctious energy controlled, gramps taught the boy wrestling exercises with repetitive training to the point of exhaustion. At the beginning of Austin's third year of high school, grandpa died at home after a long illness.

Nyles, four years older than Austin, was arrested that year. He got an expedited trial, and convicted of computer hacking, and treason against the United States of America for releasing classified government documents onto the internet. Nyles was sent to a federal prison called super-max to serve three life sentences without the possibility of parole. He was twenty-one years old at the time.

It could not be proved that Bix, the youngest brother was the genius brains behind Nyles' crimes. So, he became a ward of the state's child-welfare system and sent to a group home for chronic-delinquents until his eightieth birthday. Bix was elven years old at that time.

Based on the seriousness of Nyles' crimes, and absent parents the police took Austin into custody. He was living with his Malaysian girlfriend, Mung. They had cohabitated in his deceased grandfather's apartment and were the old man's only care givers. Gramps was of the Christian Science faith and held an antipathy toward the medical profession.

When the authorities could not connect Austin to his brothers selling national secrets on the dark web to hostel powers, he was sent to live with his mother's retired aunt in the country. At her advanced age she didn't have the strength or resources needed to fight the court system dumping her grandnephew on her.

Austin said, "Living with my aunt is hard, it's like I'm constantly walking on eggshells. I'm a city kid, I know nothing about all this rural shit. But if I screw this up its jail for me on a trumped-up charge. It would be ironic; my aunt loves living in quiet solitude like prison solitary-confinement. Except when she goes crazy becoming a screaming ninny over stupid stuff, like I changed the radio station she was listening to. Then she says she'd rather see me locked up in prison like my brother than in her house."

Not a skilled conversationalist Joey said, "All I've known is country life. It works for me. The secret is enjoy it. Know what I mean?"

"Yeah, right. I was supposed to go to a fancy college after high school. No more … now my mom says I'm on triple-secret-probation to live with my aunt or be locked up for life like Nyles."

"Does your aunt pay you to do chores?"

"Joe, she doesn't want anything to do with me. Most people treat dogs better than she does me. She's so crazy she still chops her own wood for heat and cooking. I know she can afford gas and oil, I've seen her social security check."

"I never met my parents. I would have liked to."

I noticed two things at once; custodians congregating with push-brooms at the rear of the cafeteria, and the number of attendees had dwindled to a few. Glancing at my watch, I nudged Joey with an elbow. He looked over showing surprise I was there. I tapped my timepiece. Joey's face then Austin's registered my silent indication the party was over. Without a word we stood and exited the school.

As we approached the parking lot, I whispered to Joey. "If *you* want, you may invite Austin to dinner with us."

Joey paused, most likely considering what he wanted. Then settled on a conclusion and said, "Austin, would you like to eat with me and my dads tonight?"

Austin's face lit up. "Sure!" Then his enthusiasm flickered and dimmed, "Oh sorry, my aunt will expect me to eat dinner on her back porch tonight. I'm being punished, I called her a bad name, *the fucking bitch.*"

Never one to know my place, I said, "Can you give her a call for permission and offer to take your punishment another time?"

"I was stripped of my cell phone when banished out here to the sticks."

"You may use my cellphone." I reached into a pocket and handed it over. After a brief, whiny one-sided begging call, we three were off to meet Bob at the restaurant. I was running late again, the story of my day and not my usual style.

****

There was no sign, or any identifier for the nondescript building behind a large full parking lot sitting well back off a heavily traveled road. To its left was a huge barn and other farm outbuildings. I turned my big Mercedes into the restaurant's car park and stopped next to Bob's Volvo. He had held a parking space for me. We were eight minutes late for our reservation, not good. Standing alongside his car, Bob was wearing a peeved look. His punctuality is one of his things I live with. When three of us disembarked from my vehicle, Bob's expression changed from how I imagine him chastising a student in his classroom to curious. When my guy Bob, is caught off guard the corners of his mouth turn-down and his eyes narrow. Once he had made sense of a surprise diner, his face relaxed to welcome an unexpected guest. Nevertheless, I still got a scorching look for being late.

"Bob this is Austin, Austin this is Bob." They exchanged a brief butch handshake as I hurried us into the eatery entrance.

Inside the ultra-elegant, exclusive farm to table restaurant, I went directly to the maitre'd's podium, and said, "Good evening, Brent, sorry to be a few minutes late."

"I was just about to give your table, to *two* walk-in couples. See over there, they are at the head of that longline waiting for cancellations."

"Please don't. Is there any chance you can accommodate an additional person in our party?"

Brent motioned over a busboy and spoke softly in his ear. As the busboy left to create a fourth-place setting, Brent did an approving visual inspection of my companions' dress, and then said, "Will the young gentlemen be having wine?"

"No. Too young, they'll have soft drinks?"

"No problem, your table is ready, right this way please."

Looking around Bob's and my favorite eatery for special occasions, Joey noticeably went agog. He studiously examined the ambiance from original pastoral fine art hanging on the walls, large sculptures mounted on pedestals amid arrangements of beautiful cut flowers. Opulence enveloped, us from delicious smells wafting to plush pile Persian carpets underfoot. Tranquil live classical music played by violin, viola, and cello, in a soft lit alcove. It all enhanced the dining experience for the well-dressed patrons enjoying themselves. Joey was unsophisticated but acclimating fast.

With false bravado, Austin informed no one in particular, "My parents like these kinds of places. No menus, right? You eat what the grouchy old chef feels like cooking that day and happily pay six months' wages to eat it, isn't that so?"

"The chef here is a black woman. She owns the farm next door where the food is produced. You'll have choices, she's not a tyrant." My Austin patience was running thin.

Bob reads me like a book and firmly said, "Austin, reserve judgment till you taste her food."

Busboys brought glasses of ice, filled with slightly effervescent spring-water, and hand-woven cloth-covered wicker-baskets of hot bread and rolls accompanied by tubs of herb-butter.

Then our server, Marc, spoke main course choices for the day. If we choose the fish it would have to be caught in the pond out back, so it would take longer to prepare than the other menu items. No one at our table ordered fish, and the salad of the day was served with the scrumptious house dressing.

Austin looked from Bob to me, measured the intensity of dislike for him and said, "Actually, this place is nicer than I expected for the boondocks. There must be a bunch of you rich guys hanging out incognito."

Bob muttered, "Are you working undercover?"

With his right arm extended like a roman emperor, Austin gesture at the opulence and said, "Actually, I could write up this joint for the high school newspaper."

Once again to keep Bob civil, I said, "For the record, we are not rich. We don't come here too often."

Bob cooled off a modicum, reading my intentions he joined the conversation. "Tonight, is a celebration of Joey's success during the wrestling season. It is how our family celebrates special occasions. Tonight, Austin, you are Joey's guest, remember to thank him."

"Oh okay, I'm sure Joe will improve his wrestling just to get more celebration dinners like this. And he will be sure to invite me."

Bob looked ready to attack so I said, "That string-trio piece being played is by Vivaldi, it's a favorite of mine. How about we all relax and enjoy tonight. Let's soak up the ambiance and enjoy the food."

What I said was followed by a lull in conversation, then the wine and drinks were served, and we began grazing in earnest. Finally, Joey broke the silence with, "Austin, did you love your girlfriend?"

"This may sound funny but being with her I didn't make my usual blunders turning people off. I never offended her, that was a first for me. And she loved having sex with me after granddad got too sick to do it with her."

Looking over at me and Bob, Joey asked, "Is being in love wonderful for you guys?"

"Yes, because Bob is a tiger in bed. Oh sorry, you probably didn't want to hear that."

"I don't mind what you horny old men do, as long as you take me to places like this to eat. Do you think they'd give me the recipes?"

"Doubt it. Gosh, Bob, Joey just indirectly gave us permission to get randy. *Are you busy later tonight*? We should try doing it with his permission for a change."

"I don't know, Gus, it could be Joey's trying to impress his wrestling buddy with his benevolent spirit by releasing my tiger." Then after a pause, hand on chin, pretending profound contemplation, Bob said, "Un huh, no, most likely Joey intuitively knew we were cooling intimacy at the country house. And now he gives us license to appease his guilt for denying us. You see what a nice dinner can buy?"

Joey blushed red during Bob's remarks. His face showed little wheels turning in his head thinking, *Could it be Gus and Bob stopped having weekend sex when I moved in with them? Why? How crazy is that? Should I care? Is it important for me to know?*

"What's on your mind, Joey?"

"Nothing, oh nothing really." But his face showed continued deep contemplation. He was thinking, *I know Mike and Eleanor always had personal-time Saturday nights. Unasked, I would take their dog for long late-night walks until they finished their huffing and puffing. Why would Gus and Bob stop weekend sex because of me? Or could they be worried about being a bad influence?* Then Joey stopped ruminating, took a long look around the restaurant, and realized he had a lot to learn about people, life, love, sex, fine dining and how to fit all the pieces together to make a complete picture.

Austin insecure with the conversation not being about him tried to steer it back. "Is dessert good here? I love chocolate desserts."

Bob joined me on the same page, *Keep the evening pleasant.* "The dessert cart is indulgence carried to infinity."

"For me it's temptation itself." My comment produced another lull in conversation. I'm guessing sugary visions of confections danced around the table in our musings.

After an awkward pause Austin broke the silence. "Joe, you pull off this country bumkin lifestyle like a natural. Any chance you could do this urban boy a big country favor?"

"What favor?"

"My aunt once had an herb garden, now it's mostly weeds and a few ratty pots inside her kitchen window. She said she couldn't keep up with the weeds and do all her other chores."

"Everyone hates weeds."

"My aunt might cut me some slack if I gave her herb garden a new life. The thing is, I don't know a weed from an herb or where to start. Would you help me?"

"Sure, I don't mind."

"You don't have to do a good job, any old slap dash will do for her."

Austin's place at dinner was irking me. "What's in it for Joey? And just so you know, Joey doesn't do slap dash. We all take pride in our work."

Caught off guard, Austin stuttered, then said, "Gosh Gus, I didn't think he needed a reward with you two adult men looking after him."

"You want something. So, what does he get?"

"Okay, maybe doing a good deed for me will improve his karma?"

"Austin, Joey's karma is certified pristine. It's yours we are talking about."

"Oh, so, you are going to be like that. How about I offer to help Joe with his chores around your place? I mean, you know, occasionally, not too often, maybe once would be enough."

"We share routine chores. Our schedule is set, try something else."

Speaking in a rush, Joey tried to intervene. "I don't mind putting in an herb garden, payment is not necessary. I know where to get plants and seeds for free."

After watching a while, Bob pushed in. "If you put out, you're supposed to get back, right Austin?"

"That sounds like prostitution." Austin looked unsure, clearly, he was on shaky grownup territory dealing with my man who had been giving him a fisheye much of the evening.

I for one was curious to know what Austin knew about prostitution at his age. But held my question for another time and place.

Bob asked Joey, "What's involved creating an herb garden?"

"Let's see … maybe three days tops."

Feeling left out, I jumped back in and said, "Austin, we never got Joey's room painted, and we have two other bedrooms in need of paint. Are you up for bartering interior painting for exterior gardening?"

"If one of you shows me how. I don't mind learning new things, when I don't make a big mess as I usually do."

"I'm sure Joey is capable of closely supervising your painting and showing you how to clean up after yourself. We have a house rule; you make a mess you clean it up."

"You drive a hard bargain. I didn't expect street haggling over a nice dinner. When do I start painting?"

"After the school year finishes, you, Joey, and Bob will have free time to supervise you."

Bob tuned back into the banter, "Austin, have you gotten approval beyond hints from your aunt for creating a renewed garden?"

"She won't mind, she likes to cook with all sorts of wild things in her food."

Supporting what Bob said by offering a united front, I said, "Most people are territorial about their homes. Asking permission prevents misunderstandings and that can avoid unpleasantness. While we are on the subject, the work at her place must be on her schedule. A little thoughtfulness goes a long way." That was follow by a heavy silence.

Joey tried to fill the void that followed by feeling his way around social discourse, in unfamiliar surroundings. "So, you lost your grandfather, girlfriend, and brothers all at the same time. That had to be tough. Is it too personal to talk about?"

"Joe, I'm surviving despite being victimized, I did nothing wrong. You saw the size of my trophies tonight they make up only a little for being exiled to live with a Bible-thumping witch bitch."

"Austin, you mentioned personal losses tonight, but only showed sadness at losing your girlfriend's touch. Pardon me for being nosey, but that seems odd."

"Then Joe, don't be nosy."

I couldn't hold back. "In whose honor is this dinner?"

"My granddad didn't want me around and kept me busy doing stupid exercises until he got too sick to push me around. Mung was his lover-caretaker before she came to my bed because he couldn't get it up. I don't know how I'm supposed to feel, other than I miss Mung and I'm horny all the time."

"Didn't your grandfather take you in when you had no place to live?"

"The court made him give me a home. It was against his will. My brothers got what they deserved, my grandfather too. Why are you picking on me?"

"You sound cold."

"It wasn't okay when my brother Nyles started using drugs to get high and then blamed my parents for it."

"Where were your parents?"

"My parents are divorced, thanks to my criminal brothers. After Bix was born, they forgot I existed. I know everyone is supposed to love their mother, I don't. People are only out for themselves in this world."

"Do you have any contact with your brother Bix?"

"No, we hardly know each other. What I do know is something is seriously wrong with that child, and just between us I think my folks were afraid of Bix."

"That's quite a family history you should write a book."

"I keep being told I've had it better than most by people. So say people who are jealous of me. But I won the biggest, best trophies tonight, that proves I'm special."

Joey seemed to get antsy listening to Austin talk in an off way. So, he said, "Austin what subject would you like to talk about?" Joey was hoping the conversation would get back to normal, whatever that was."

"Only because you asked, I'll tell you. I like talking about myself best."

"Ugh, okay."

Bob the schoolteacher showed his training. "Austin, do *you* sometimes think the world is crazy?"

"Definitely! I'll tell you why, I make friends easily, and then they always disappoint me. There must be an epidemic of bad friends."

"My guidance counselor says I need to have more friends. I'm not sure I do."

"You need to be my friend and let me sleep over your house when my aunt is on a tear."

"You two don't know each other that well."

"Come on, I'm a displaced urban dweller exiled to rural backward America for punishment. I'm entitled to a little relief occasionally."

Bob and I exchanged a knowing look, and I said, "Step by step, let's see what kind of job you do with painting Joey's room in exchange for an herb garden. Then we'll see if he wants to know you better."

"You two men are too tough. Let Joe make his own mind up he's not a child."

Without giving it a thought, Joey came to our defense. "They are always fair with me. I have to use the restroom be right back." With that said, Joey headed to the head.

Addressing Austin, Bob said, "Tough works for us. Gus, Joey, and I transformed a rescue dog, Hans, from a snarling, snapping K9 psychopath, into a cuddly oversize lap dog. And yet he maintains the ability to tell good intentions from bad and acts accordingly. Austin, watch yourself around him."

Before Austin could put voice to defensiveness showing on his face, I said, "And with that family lore, I think we are done here. Check, please."

"Gus, wait a second. Austin, it was nice you could join us for Joey's celebration dinner. But understand this, you are older and have had more advantages. If you hurt him, even unintentionally, we will bring our wrath down on you without mercy, and that is not a threat it's a promise. Do you hear me boy?" I could tell Bob had been wanting to say that all evening. If my man hadn't spoken those words, I would have.

"Yes sirs, understood, that is the second threat I received this evening and I always take threats seriously, I'm a wrestler ... Thank you for a lovely dinner, it was threat worthy."

Then Joey returned looking relived.

"CHECK, PLEASE."

****

I drove Austin and his trophies to his aunt's house. I didn't attempt small talk I was sated after a lavish meal. Austin babbled on relentlessly how unfair the universe was to him. When I suggested the universe might have cause, I was treated to silence. Silence fit my mood perfectly. But I played traveling music to discourage further talking. His face showed dislike for my taste in music. My initial estimation of Austin had been poor and went south over the evening.

Meanwhile, Joey rode with Bob going back home. With an ever so small tinge of envy, I imagined them chatting away replaying the evening. Joey rehashing the wrestling awards party's high points and then his impression of the restaurant and meal. I know them, they would-be laughing, having fun, and not trashing Austin as I was resisting in my mind.

Unsettled with how *the* evening was ending, with sincerity I said, "Austin, would it help you if I talked with your aunt about you two finding useful common ground?"

"No. she'd just drag you to her church, and they hate fags. I'll be eighteen in the fall, and then my life will be my own and she can go to hell where she belongs."

****

Over the school's summer-vacation, as predicted, Joey and Austin did not become friends, but remained civil. Austin accepted Joey's supervision to earned computer Wi-Fi time for his laptop. He ended up priming and painting the whole inside of our country house, meticulously slow, room by room. Despite himself Austin became a neat interior house painter with Joey's dispassionate firm supervising.

Based-on on learning to paint our house, and his aunt's considerable church-based connections, Austin got a part-time job in the Home Improvement Center's paint department. It looked like he would be around the area for a while after being accepted for the fall semester at the community college.

Up to the point of Austin getting a job, he would bum or hitch a ride to our house and Joey or one of us would return him back to his aunt. Once Austin had a work and school schedule, Joey let it be known he was not interested in becoming Austin's chauffer. After withstanding Austin's constant manipulative attempts to be transported around, Joey secured Mike's permission for Austin to use Eleanor's motorcycle, on temporary loan, to get to work and school. Naturally, Joey had to teach Austin to ride, which he did with the same dispassion he supervised interior painting. Joey had learned to deal with difficult people from watching Mike work with his customers.

To show appreciation for her renewed herb garden, Austin's aunt allowed him to use, in her words, "that infernal loud dangerous contraption." However, her consent came with a condition. Joey who was the source of the motorbike had to accompany them to church every Sunday to pray for Austin's safe motorcycle use. It was a sacrifice Joey tolerated to keep Austin on the road and away from him.

Joey had attended church with Mike and Eleanor, so didn't mind attending a different Protestant denomination with Austin's aunt Matilda. Reportedly, they sang the same hymns. Up to that point what blocked Bob and I from permanently eighty-sixing Austin with prejudice, from our house was Ms. Limane, Joey's guidance counselor. She said Joey needed to develop social skills. Attending church with Aunt Matilda and meeting her circle of friends meant Joy had to expand his social skills. So, Bob and I continued to tolerate obnoxious Austin, for Joey's social skills development.

CHAPTER 6. Frances

Bob had elected to teach special education summer school part II for his ongoing Ph.D. program at Columbia's Teachers College. The advanced degree was necessary to move forward in school administration, the next step in his career. My normally slow summertime got eaten alive by a pesky merger with too many twists and turns and not enough light. Instead of leisurely spending our summer months enjoying the country house, we were city bound with too much homework at night. It was a lucky weekend when we got up to the country house. Joey, as always, had the place in shipshape condition when we showed up. Just when the inside of the house, freshly painted, looked especially welcoming, we didn't have time to enjoy it.

Wednesday night, August 7th, an hour past our usual eleven o'clock bedtime, Bob and I were in the living room seated at our partners' desk. Both yawning-drowsily wrapping up preparations for the next day's grind. Abruptly we heard muffled screams followed by what sounded like two muted-pistol shots. The unexpected bangs snapped us alert. Then another sound grabbed my attention. Someone was running and shrieking in the public hallway outside our apartment. They were moving fast headed in our direction. Then the screaming, running stopped right outside our door. It was followed immediately by repeated door-bell buzzing, banging and muffled pleading. "Open up, let me in, please SOMEONE HELP ME!"

The next thing I knew, we were standing looking at the inside of our apartment front door. I do not remember getting there. A quick peek through the peephole showed a child, pressing our door-buzzer button, then banging fists on the door, all the while begging hysterically, "Help, help me, open up, let me in." On closer examination, it was not a little child, but a barefoot teenager wearing only white cotton underwear, pleading like her life depended on it.

When I opened the door to ask the problem, the teen ran into our apartment, stopped behind me, and shouted, "Quick, lock the door, hurry!" Without question I slammed the door shut which locked it, stood back, and faced the intruder.

Breathing-hard, face a colorless mask showing terror the young person said, "He has a gun and wants to kill me."

Puzzled, I asked, "Who?"

"He just shot my mother in the head!" Then the kid began sobbing hard, like she just realized the meaning of what she said. The girl could barely breath from shaking, and her face was suddenly awash in flowing tears.

Bob was standing right behind me in the foyer and when I slammed the door. He reached around and engaged both our dead bolt locks. Turning to the young person Bob said, 'What happened?"

"Call 911, tell the police he wants to kill me too. His gun got stuck, he was fixing it when I ran away."

I dialed 911 and handed the cellphone to the teen when the operator asked, "What is your emergency?"

"My father just killed my mother and wants to shoot me." She hyper ventilated listening to the 911 operator then said, "We live at 210 Fifth Avenue, apartment 3R20, I'm Frances McDermott. I'm fifteen years old, send help fast. WHAT? Oh okay ..."

Frances handed me my telephone and I gave the 911 operator my name, address, and telephone number, as she requested. I tersely answered her questions hyperalert combat ready, with no weapon. "We are neighbors ... You wait ... this child is spattered with blood ... No, we didn't see the shooting ... To answer your question, she looks younger than fifteen ... what ... the blood on her isn't lying. *Operator what is your name again and ID number?"*

911 operator Lyndsey #6458 sounded skeptical, but intimidated enough to say, "The police are on their way, keep your doors and windows locked." The phone conversation was cut-short by loud banging on our front door again. This time an adult male shouted, "Francis, come out, let's finish this. It's time to take your medicine!"

I turned to Bob and said, "How did *he* know *she* came here?"

He pointed and whispered, "Look at her hands."

A quick glance showed her hands, up to wrists, covered in blood. Earlier I only noticed the blood splatter on her face. Then the smell of fresh human gore brought me back to fighting in the middle east for the U.S. military-industrial-complex. I had to resolutely shake myself back to the present. That smell triggered emotions I thought dormant or dead.

The teen standing in front of me was wearing a boy's snug white ribbed A-shirt and white jockey style boy's briefs. Her face and gestures belonged to a prepubescent female child, except for an obvious bulge in front of an over-packed crotch-pouch. S/he's hair, face, and underwear were speckled with blood. Images from combat flooded my brain as fast as I could push them away and focus on what was in front of me.

Without intending to I found myself staring at the girl's male bulge. Covering it with her hands she said, "Gus, I'm so sorry, I touched the wall running, and then your door. He must have followed my trail where I touched the wall not to fall. I'm so, so, so sorry, please don't throw me out to be killed." Where upon Frances McDermott leaned toward me, latched onto my arm with two bloody hands, and began to hyperventilate again.

Ever ready Bob, who spends his days teaching teenagers, grabbed our visitor's shoulders, and said with a shake, "Frances, what pronoun do you use?"

Gasping for air, Frances' face showed displeasure at being grabbed, shaken, and questioned. Making eye contact with Bob, she wheezed, "They, of course." Her gentle words did not fit her wretched, pissed off demeanor wrapped with facial terror.

Trying to find grounding between battlefield flash back smells and the bloody girl-boy clinging to my arm, in our usually safe home, I said, "Damn Bob, why did you ask that?"

"To get her to focus in here, instead of the terror outside our door. Teenagers don't get respect I figured a pronoun would work better than a hard face slap."

"Oh, I see, and your usual need to be polite overruled slapping a teenage stranger? Good, I guess."

The outside banging and incoherent shouting increased to frenetic. I shoved the straight-back heavy-wooden foyer chair under the front-doorknob. In response to the sound of my action, bullets penetrated, splintering through the heavy door, followed instantly by loud pistol reports. It sounded like the .45 caliber I used to carry on my hip in war zones. Bob picked up Frances, and we dashed around the corner for refuge in the kitchen. I grabbed the two largest knives from our knife block and handed one to Bob.

He gave me a look that said, *You don't take a knife to a gun fight, dummy.* That split second of levity snapped my focus back from old battlefields to the present.

Just then we heard police radios squawking out in the public hallway. It sounded like they were on the move, then a woman shouted. "Drop your weapon, put your hands up!" A second deeper voiced repeated the order. Then we heard one gunshot that sounded the same as pierced our front door. It was instantly followed by a fusillade coming from different sounding sidearms and different directions.

Hearing all the shooting, the child put bloody hands over ears, and then appeared to go into a stupefied trance. I ran into the living room and grabbed the lap-robe draped over the back of Bob's reading chair. Placing the robe over the child's shoulders I gave her a reassuring hug.

Bob, remembering his Explorer Scout First Aid Badge said, "Frances, want a sugary drink, it might settle your nerves."

Still stupefied but trying to sound prim and proper she spoke in a normal tone. "Just plain water, please."

Our assaulted front door displaying bullet holes reverberated from loud knocking and then, "This is the police, open up!"

Bob checked the peephole, pulled back the foyer chair, disengaged all the locks and swung the door open wide. "Good middle of the night to you, officers."

"Is everyone all right in there?"

"As good as can be expected, in a war zone ... want a look?"

A uniformed police sergeant flanked by two patrol officers entered cautiously, guns drawn. After a quick reconnoiter, the cops holstered their weapons. I led Frances out of the kitchen, and we all somehow ended up sitting in the living room.

The sergeant said, "What was this about?"

We all spoke at once. Then hearing the cacophony, stopped, our silence was instantly filled with background talking and radio chatter from outside in the public hallway.

The sergeant made a face and said, "Just as well, you'll need to make individual statements at the precinct. But nobody leaves this apartment till the crime scene investigators and coroner finish in the hall outside your door."

"Are we under house arrest?"

"No. You just can't leave until we finish. Now, put some clothes on that child." I saw the sergeant's eyes had gotten stuck on France's bulging crotch.

Reacting to the sergeant's staring, I repeated loudly, "… can't leave the apartment … I have an important business meeting early in the morning."

Vexed, Bob also had important commitments early. He muttered half to himself. "She doesn't live here."

"Where do you live, child?"

"I live with my mother in apartment 3R20. It's in the back on the right, not this apartment."

Ever vigilant Bob spoke up, like the mandated reporter he was. "Officer, this child's mother was just murdered while she watched. Then France's father attempted to kill her. She is covered in her mother's blood. I hope your protocol includes France being examined and cleaned up at a hospital?"

"Don't interfere with policework. Let us do our job … Darrell call for an ambulance to transport this child for hospital evaluation."

"I'm on it, Sarge."

"While we wait for transport, somebody tell me exactly what happened here?"

At first speaking in fits and starts between sobs, Frances stopped, gulped deep breaths and the story gushed out in a cascade. For as long as she could remember, she was a girl prisoner locked in a boy's body. "God made a mistake, a big mistake, and being the wrong gender has caused me nothing but grief, ending tonight with my mother's killing." Then closely watching our reactions, Frances seemed to gather inner strength from our faces, enough to tell her story to adult strangers. Whether she knew it, she needed the catharsis of telling what she witnessed.

The big problems started for Frances in preschool and continued to the present. But she and her mother became adept handling society's inflexibility with, hair, clothes, pronouns, and which restroom to use. Then at age ten Frances' pediatrician recommended blocking the onset of male puberty, to make her transition less difficult later in life. At that time, her dream was to fix her outsides, so it matched her inner self. In the meantime, that dream had to wait years, while experiencing side effects from taking female hormones in preparation for future physiology and authentic self-unification.

When Frances' father, Bruce, turned age eighteen, he was sent to adult prison.

Frances was age four. From then on, each time he was released from prison Frances looked and acted more female, much to her father's chagrin. During stints in prison her father had fantasies of teaching his son to be a professional boxer as a means to gain wealth. With each disappointed boxing prospect Bruce blamed his wife Aprilmay for turning Frances into a sissy-boy and beat her for doing it.

Despite refusal of mother and daughter to cooperate with the police, social services placed them in battered woman's shelters that accepted a male child presenting as female. But even with shelter sanctuary Frances' mother regularly broke the strict rule against disclosing its secret location. When Bruce was released from jail or penitentiary, he was the only man Aprilmay ever loved, and she the only woman he ever knew in a biblical sense. They fell in love starting at age fourteen in high school.

Holding on to the scatter-site apartment at 210 Fifth Avenue was mother and child's last chance for safe housing from the Battered Woman's Support Consortium. The apartment was from a government program called twenty-eighty. Which placed ten percent low income working families and ten percent homeless battered families in the least desirable apartments in new luxury housing. Eighty percent of the other tenants paid prevailing market rents or bought their apartment outright at full asking price. The builders and building owners got a twenty-year tax abatement for the whole building in exchange for providing twenty percent low-income apartments. After twenty years the developer could sell or rent the set-aside apartments at market rate.

Battered woman's counselors had repeatedly warned mother and child that domestic violence was an illness leading to a terminal outcome. Naturally, Aprilmay refused to believe the man she loved would kill her and Frances. She countered her counselor's warning words with, "Bruce was always remorseful with gifts and passionate love making after every beating. So, his expressions of true love could not be fatal."

The day of the killing was Bruce's twenty-ninth birthday and his future looked hopeless. He had just failed to get a job his parole officer demanded he have. He was fixating on going back to prison for life as a repeat offender. His depression deepened considering he could never give Aprilmay the life he wanted for her. He couldn't control battering her, and his son would never look or even pretend to act male. When he saw the nice building and apartment, his family was living in. That he was excluded from by court order, for their protection. Bruce snapped.

An ambulance finally arrived and took Frances to a hospital. Bob and I used the waiting time to write out our statements to forgo a trip to the police precinct until after the day's work. Satisfied with our written accounts, the police left. We tried to sleep, but too much commotion had stirred-up too many past and present emotions. Instead of sleep we had tender slow sex, and then snuggled drifting in and out of on-guard snoozing. It had been a while for sex with us, our summer workloads had become exhausting. The police finally finished their work in the public hall outside our apartment and left. With no one around, we too left in time to salvage Wednesday's work.

****

Arriving home from work the next day, Thursday, the doorman handed me a hospital social worker's business card. "This guy came by looking for you twice. You want me to shoo him away if he comes again. It might be about Tuesday night's shootings."

"Let me ask Bob first. But thanks for looking out for us."

Then upstairs a sticky-note was attached to the apartment door from the building super. *"I've plugged your bullet holes with steel putty paste over wire mesh, a new door is on order, you should have it, installed, give or take three months."*

When Bob got home, I gave him the note and card, and said, "You want to toss those? The doorman offered to run interference with the social worker."

"Tempting but no, I'd like reassurance Frances isn't lost in bureaucracy. We may be all she has left to lookout for her."

"Wasn't last night enough? She has this hospital social worker now."

"Come on Gus, we haven't had a shoot-out at our front door in New York City before. Let's see how this story ends."

"I'll tell you this, it better be the first and last shootout at our door. Or I'm installing an arsenal."

"Still?"

"Since you're so curious, *you* talk to the social worker, and I'll keep after the super. Really, three months to get a door. I don't think so."

****

Mr. Clay Hadley was the city hospital social worker who oversaw discharge planning for patient Frances Mc Dermott. He was accommodating and met us at our apartment shortly after Bob phoned. Clay was older than us, maybe even late thirties. The man stood six-foot, two-inches at about 190 pounds, with warm amber colored eyes, dark-brown curly hair cut to a conservative length. His medium-brown complexion was highlighted by a taupe off the rack medium priced suit and burgundy-colored silk Winsor-knotted tie. He smelled of expensive imported men's cologne and made frank, no-bullshit eye contact. I could tell he'd been in the service, but not a Marine like Bob and me.

"Mr. Hadley, to what do we owe the pleasure of your company this fine evening after our over-taxing day at work? Would you like something to drink?"

"No, thank you. Please call me Clay, it's less formal. Frances McDermott listed you, Mr. Gustafson, as the person to contact in case of emergency."

"Call me Gus, most people do. This is my husband, Bob, you spoke earlier on the telephone."

"Hi, nice to meet you in person."

We exchanged head nods, and Bob said, "Clay, are you aware we first met Frances only shortly before she was taken to your hospital?"

"That wasn't mentioned. But it doesn't change her situation, there is nothing physically wrong with Frances, so she can't stay in the hospital. She has referrals to outpatient mental health, and our transgender clinic. If all else fails, our last resort will be a child welfare group home for her. Her hospital bed is needed for a sick teenager."

"Doesn't she have family?"

"I've contacted relatives on her father's side, they refuse to even talk to her or me about her. I couldn't locate any relatives on her mother's side, apparently, they are deceased."

"What does this have to do with us?"

"That is why I'm here. Would you two be willing to house her temporarily? Only until a more suitable situation is found. I'm sure an appropriate home can be located once the city's homeless youth team gets on it."

"Is that an oxymoron, place Frances in a *more suitable home while trying to place her in our unsuitable one?*

"That didn't come out quite how I wanted."

"Relax, Bob is a ballbuster, he teaches English to fiercely unwilling urban learners. Look Clay, we don't know the child. Furthermore, we are already responsible for a homeless teenager on weekends. Sorry, we can't help with Frances, but thanks for stopping by." I rose from my chair ready to walk our guest to the door.

Good old Bob wouldn't leave well enough alone. "Just so your trip wasn't a complete waste, Frances prefers to be referred to using the singular *they* pronoun."

My attempt at goodbye by leading to the door didn't work. Clay and Bob stayed seated, so still standing I said, "Clay, what happens now?"

"She says, I mean they says, there are no friends or family."

"Then you house her."

"The problem is religious and all other group homes refuse transsexuals. There is no place that would accept her. I tried everywhere."

"What about a foster home?"

"If a child is over twelve, they are too old for foster care and must go to a group home."

"Which you say, won't accept trans kids. Huh, another oxymoron."

Bob came back with, "How can nonprofits discriminate and take public money doing it?"

"Good question. I don't know. But they do."

"My parents were refuges, I'm Vietnamese American, we've seen what social workers can do. You're a social worker, you've got to have something else up your sleeve for Frances?"

"Sorry Bob, not this time. All I got is a last chance grunge group home run by the department of corrections for violent children of incarcerated who ran out of options. They are always over capacity but can't refuse rejected aggressive psychopaths discharged from our hospital. At this moment they have sleeping cots set up in corridors and common rooms. I wouldn't send my worst enemy's child there."

"Sounds bad."

"It is very bad for a child who just witnessed the loss of her, I mean their parents violently."

"Agreed."

"If Frances is sent to the city's vicious children's pound, either residents kill her, or she suicides. Unless out of the goodness of your heart you save her, their life."

"Just hold on a second, there has to be a transgender community in our metropolis. The gay community has a history of mobilizing for its own and going above and beyond when challenged. Did you try the gay community center?"

"They informed me not all trans people identify as gay, and so, not all gay people accept transsexuality as a gay issue."

"Come on, Clay, you've got to have something better for a grieving traumatized kid."

"I wouldn't be here if I did. You may have heard about transsexual prostitutes that work the truck stops and wholesale food markets. They hook for hormone and other drug money. That stroll is too dangerous and it's illegal. Professionally I couldn't suggest it, and yet if she survives that's where she'll end up at age fifteen."

"Grim … just what I need after the long hard day and sleepless nights."

"Look, I don't know you men, and you don't know Frances. I wouldn't have bothered you if I had any other way to keep her safe while she processes recent events. Like I said, besides you, all the choices *are bad* one way or another."

"You obviously care, take Frances home with you."

"It's against the rules and my wife would kill me. We already have four foster children. So, unless you two can find a way to open your hearts, Frances becomes another statistic."

Watching Bob's mood shift, I raised my voice louder than intended. "Oh, as unsuitable as we are, we've become the only good option among the bad ones. Go figure."

"Gus, take it down a notch. Clay, he already told you we are too busy during the week. And we have a weekend teenager. We do care, but don't have what she needs, time."

"If you were remotely interested, I have resources to help, and remember it's only temporarily."

"Help, help how?"

"With my hospital clout I can tap special city funds to send Frances to a full-day charter school for disturbed, sexually ambivalent students. The state crime victims fund will pay for a therapeutic after school program. There are even several agencies to help out on the weekends if you needed."

I could see Clay Hadley's sales talk was swaying Bob's resolve, so I jumped in with a counter argument. "Who's going to pay for and supervise Frances' medications, and years of individual psychotherapy?"

"As a ward of the state Frances gets all-inclusive health insurance at no cost to you. Our nursing staff reports *they* can self-manage medications. Also, you would get a small monthly stipend for food, shelter and clothing."

"Clay, we aren't rich, but look around, our combined incomes wouldn't qualify for any means tested program Frances would be eligible for."

"You wouldn't be financially responsible. Frances is already eligible for the programs I mentioned. Due to her unique homeless dilemma because of violent murder and police shooting her father. She could probably even sue the city for a big cash settlement on top of what I just said."

"Did you discuss any of this with Frances?"

"No. I didn't want to get hopes up. From where I sit with my experience, this kid is already a dead duck statistic. For my own mental health, I had to try and save her."

Dead duck hit a nerve; I flashed on draping a lap-robe over Frances shoulders quivering in terror. I had absorbed her trembling through my kneading fingers. But it was the smell of fresh human blood on her skin that triggered me. I'm no pushover, I've dealt lethally with too many people hellbent on killing me and mine in war. The smell of gore opened portals to old wounds I thought permanently cauterized. "Let me get this straight, Clay. We are doing all this jawing and don't know if the child even wants to live with two adult gay males; in a one-bedroom apartment, in the same building where her parents just died, violently. Oh, and with little to no teenage-transsexual privacy."

"Jeez give me a break, Gus, I had to try everything I could. When they expire my bosses will want a full accounting and I want my work to be as thorough as humanly possible. In their way they are likeable."

"I'll give you that."

"I hate to say it because you'll think I'm trying to pressure you, but you *were their* last chance before being thrown to the wolves."

"Well, look at this, will ya? All this talk was just an exercise to cover Clay's ass. What do you think, Bob, are wolves better than lions? Should we let this guy off so easy?"

"No. Let's have a pow wow with Frances and see what *they* want, and what we three adults can do about that. I'm not interested in covering assess, and Frances doesn't go down without a fight."

"Listen, guys, I didn't mean to upset you. Maybe I came on too strong. Look, some things I said didn't come out as intended."

"Right, let's see what Frances wants. We'll take our car and meet you at the hospital, Clay."

****

The adolescent side of the hospital's pediatric floor was mostly double occupancy rooms. When we entered Frances' room, the lights were dimmed down. The bed closest to the door held an unconscious youth. He had kicked-off a tangle of bedsheets to expose an emaciated illness wrecked body. He looked like an incredibly tiny old man rather than a young teen. His arms had tubes connected to fluid-bags hanging from blinking IV-machines, and a clear-plastic tube in his urethra ended in a full urine bag attached to the side of the bed

Clay covered the boy with his bedsheet and pushed the nurse call-button. When the nurse arrived, she pulled ceiling to floor curtains, isolating the youth's bed from the rest of the room, and we could hear her tending to him.

Frances sat in a chair next to a window overlooking the staff parking lot and hospital delivery bay. A tall chair was crammed between her hospital-bed and the window. An uncovered evening food-tray looked cold and untouched at the foot of her bed. Without the terror of impending violent death, she appeared calm with a hard edge and their natural feminine beauty showed for the first time. Frances was wearing a hospital issue gown open in the back and was sitting prim and lady-like, bare feet anchored to the floor. "Do you remember us?"

"Hello, Gus and Bob and Mr. Hadley. I know the day of the week, date, and time of day. If we are having another mental status test, let's get it over with? I've had six today."

"No test, how are you doing?"

Frances gave me a long piercing look that could only be described as incredulous, time's the square root of infinity.

"Sorry, dumb question. May we talk?"

Frances shook her head no. "I have nothing to talk about. They burned my underwear because it had blood on it. It was new underwear, I could have washed the blood out. Now I have absolutely no clothes, no parents, the hospital wants me gone, and I have no place to go. That's it, there's nothing else to say. Goodbye."

Clay Hadley seeing an impediment got officious. "Are your antidepressants helping?"

"The doctor said it would take three weeks to two months to notice benefit. Are you all here to gawk at this homeless freak? If not, I'm really not up for chit chat."

Clay was in his domain. "Like I explained earlier, before the hospital bacteria and viruses make you ill, we need to discharge you to stay well."

"You said you'd see if I could go back home. At least to get my clothes. Did you?"

"I checked. That apartment is being painted and another family from the waiting list will move in as soon as the paint dries."

"That was fast. Ugh, what happened to my things?"

"Your family's possessions are with the sanitation department. You have thirty days to collect them, or they are permanently disposed of."

"Every time I think it can't get worse, guess what, it does." Saying that, Frances started crying softly and pulled both legs up to rest her bare-feet-heels on the chair-seat. As she leaned her head against knees, the hospital gown drew up. I glimpsed something I doubt I was supposed to see between hairless shapely female legs. Feeling exposed or a draft Frances spontaneously used the hospital gown's hem to cover her male private parts.

It was a bewildering oxymoron to see this beautiful young female in possession of a set of male genitals. For the first time I had insight into the obstacles this transsexual young person must have navigated her whole life. I promptly looked out the window feeling embarrassed and wondering why. *It came down to, I was embarrassed for me seeing what I knew had to be there and wasn't ready to accept. That had to be my problem, Frances seemed so matter of fact about it.*

Bob and I exchanged a look. He could tell something had just happened with me, and he said, "One of us could pick up your clothes from sanitation if you want?"

"Thanks, Bob, but where would I keep my things? That closet is tiny, and the hospital seriously wants me out of here fast."

Clay Hadley made a sour face and said, "We have absolutely no storage capacity for patients' belongings. But is there anything else we might be able to do for you?"

"I'd like to be an emancipated minor, but the free legal service said I have to be at least sixteen. So, I'm stuck in limbo for another year, with no clothes, no home, and no hope of surviving naked on the street. What's the weather like, is it cold outside?"

"Everything else equal, how would you survive emancipated?"

"One thing at a time, I can't do everything at once you know! You asked and I told you!"

"All right fine, what is your next want this moment? Hint, the snack bar downstairs is closing soon."

"To find a place to live, but that is impossible with no clothes to wear. And that I believe is called a conundrum."

"Mr. Hadley suggested we invite you to stay with us until something *more suitable* is found. You know we only have a one bedroom-bathroom apartment. *We* don't mind lack of privacy we're a married couple. You on the other hand might not be comfortable jam-packed in with two grown men."

"If you guys can endure female undies drying in the bathroom, I can go without privacy for one year until I'm emancipated and then have unlimited privacy. See I can dream, can't I?"

"What do you think, Bob? Can we manage female undies drying in our bathroom?"

"If you say yes, Bob, I can help out paying your rent. I have a little savings earning compound interest."

"Not necessary, Frances, we easily handle the condominium's monthly common fee. What are you saving for?"

"There is no age requirement in Mexico for sexual reassignment surgery, if you pay cash."

Clay spoke up like he knew what he was talking about. "Mexican sex reassignment surgeries are not up to United States standards of care. You could end up with a botched job that couldn't be repaired, or worse. Trust me, you don't want that potential nightmare."

"It's my body, my decision."

"I'm just saying have your surgery done correctly, here, and after your body is done growing."

Frances went into an adolescent girl pout at Clay's words. Then through clenched teeth said, "When can I get out of this hospital?"

Clay's mood improved showing a big toothy smile. "I could have your discharge paperwork done and signed off tomorrow morning, if you go with these fellows."

"Clay, would that discharge plan include her school and after school programs and make all that legally official? Oh, and include all the benefits she is intitled to you mentioned earlier." Bob said this knowing bureaucracy well. He worked for one.

Coming back down to earth from his brief elation, Clay said, "I did say those things, didn't I.? All that could take days to get in place, it's hard to get some of those signatures."

"Remember what *we* told you, our work schedule won't allow for running around fencing with authorities. No doubt your hospital influence could get that job done more expeditiously and without hassles. Take the time to do the job right so Frances doesn't become a statistic against your name."

Turning to Frances, Clay said, "I should have everything you need ready to go by next Wednesday. Can you hang on a little longer?"

"What choice do I have? Yes, I can stay put if you are telling the truth? But I get lied to a lot, don't like it and respond accordingly. Know! I can be a bitch when necessary."

Looking for and getting Bob's approval, I said, "Moving right along, it seems to me the next step is to get this child clothed."

With a surprised look Clay said, "How exactly do we do that, Gus?"

"Do you have a computer that goes online?"

"Of course, in my office."

"Then let's all go to Clay's office."

"Why?"

"Frances, do you know your sizes?"

She gave me another incredulous look, as only a teenager could direct at a hopelessly blithering adult. Initially, Mr. Clay Hadley gave institutional attitude about using the hospitals discretionary slush fund credit card to pay for Frances' purchase of clothes and shoes online. Until we reminded him Bob and I hadn't agreed to anything in writing *yet*.

We only used vendors who guaranteed next day free delivery, and that narrowed our field of search. By the end of our online shopping experience everyone's mood had improved, and we knew Frances much better. *They* made practical choices, considering fabrics' ease of care, and ability to mix and match items by color, style, and fabric compatibility. Also, *they* looked for and found deep discount sales for expensive items. I was impressed, Frances was smart, frugal, and knew how to dress well on the cheap.

Frances seemed well satisfied and ready for sleep by the time we left the hospital social work office. Clay looked genuinely relived. He obviously cared that Frances be safe. Walking to my car, Bob told me I would have been just as shocked if Frances had flashed me female genitals. And I thought, *We are certifiably insane to get involved with a second teenager.*

I knew Frances in our home would cramp our style and give Joey a sizable headache. Bob had little experience with transsexuals, and Joey most likely none. We went home from the hospital with a promise from Clay we'd be told of each step in the bureaucratic labyrinth to get Frances released to us officially and enrolled in an appropriate full day school, after school program, and in individual therapy.

CHAPTER 7. Bloody Nose, Gender Equality

We made time to go to the country house the weekend before Frances officially came to live in our apartment. Once Clay got the ball rolling, the process happened smoothly but, in bureaucratic parlance, sequence takes precedence and that requires time to acquire essential signatures in proper order. The gods forbid a higher-level civil servant sign before an underling.

On the drive-up, Bob the worrier asked, "You want to tell Joey we plan to have Frances spend weekends in the country, or should I?"

"Let's do it together, and the less said the better."

"Right."

"I expect an explosion no matter what we say. Joey seems threatened by change."

"I hope he can understand we couldn't leave her naked, and homeless."

"What if it's dislike at first sight? They are both smart and have strong personalities."

"I'm counting on Hans to be peacemaker. He's good at it."

We had phoned ahead so Joey and Hans were waiting on the front porch when we drove up. I could feel something was off, even before getting out of the car. Then I noticed Joey's usual strong "happy to see you greeting hug," felt tentative, wimpy even. I mused *This is not an auspicious beginning for upsetting his status-qua with news of Frances joining us.* "Joey, you, okay?"

With ersatz zeal, he said, "I did a lot since you've not been here. I wanted the house to be extra nice today, I opened all the drain traps and cleaned the gunk out, yuck. Then I unclogged the roof gutters and flushed the down spouts, gross. But don't the shrubs look nice? I trimmed them into geometric shapes for a change. I used my old geometry textbook for the odder shapes, that's why those privet hedges over there look from outer space. I can prune them back to normal in a month or so if you don't like the strange look."

"Nice job, you do commendable work with living green geometry. I'll take photos. Oh, what happened to your knuckles?"

"I had a fight."

"What!"

"Austin."

"Tell me about it?"

"Gus, it was personal, I'd rather not."

"Do I have to hear about it from other sources?"

"Austin doesn't deserve the loan of Eleanor's bike. When one of you get a chance, please give me a ride to get it back."

"If that's your wish. Except, wait, something doesn't add up."

"What?"

"Austin was the star of your wrestling team, and you were the most improved newbie. I don't see any marks or bruises on you, other than your knuckles. Why is that?"

"I said I didn't want to talk about it. *It's personal.*"

"I'm looking out for my personal safety. If you and I go pick up Eleanor's motorcycle, will I have to referee another fight?"

"Maybe. But I want Eleanor's bike back."

"So, after a hard week at work, tiring drive up to the country, greatly appreciating your artfully manicured geometric landscape, now I have to go hear Austin's side of a fight. *Oh, lucky me!*"

"Gus, I'll go instead of Joey. That all right with you, Joey."

"Whatever, just so long as Eleanor's bike is retuned. Who knows maybe it wasn't personal for Austin? I'll start dinner if you want to go for the bike."

"Come on, Bob, let's go get the old pickup started and collect that motorcycle."

"Should I bring a baseball bat or brass knuckles?"

"We don't own brass knuckles."

"Then it's the old baseball bat. I'll put it in the truck bed."

"I can hardly wait to hear Austin's versions of events. Then I can settle into a relaxing weekend in the country, swaying in the hammock without a care in the world."

"Right Gus, Joey knows how to milk a mystery *for us to unravel.*"

Joey hit his limit of good-natured teasing. "Okay, jeez you win, you're both relentless interrogators. There should be a limit how much you're allowed to manipulate me."

"Write a foster son's bill of rights, and we'll put it to a vote. But it would be faster to just tell us what happened."

"Okay, so maybe I'm still mixed-up how I could be so stupid. I thought I knew crazy Austin."

"It'll be even faster if you get to the point."

"After Austin broke up with his latest girlfriend-chauffeur, he started spending more time over here playing videogames online. According to him it was to mend his broken heart. Then out of the blue he said it wasn't working and would I watch movies with him, so he didn't feel so sad and lonely. Dummy me went along. Then right away he'd fall asleep on me during the movies, he picked. I figured he's just a weird guy who doesn't know what he wants."

"Sounds like a cozy way to mend a broken heart on a friend's shoulder. Unless he has bad taste in movies, or wanted you as a girlfriend substitute?"

"Gus, you are not helping me tell this and he does have horrible taste in movies. I'm not sure about the other thing."

"Sorry, I spoke out of turn."

"What I noticed was when we disagreed, it was either an interesting learning moment for me or seemed completely out in left field odd. But when he said I was wrong or just being disagreeable, he called me bad names and hurled hurtful insults. Then later trying to mend the riff, he blamed me for being too sensitive or misunderstanding what he said. In other words, according to Austin all problems were my fault."

"What happened that lead to violence?"

"I told Austin I've never been in love. I said he must know how it feels since he always has at least one girlfriend on the hook. Honest, I meant it as a compliment!"

"Of course, you did."

"He got really mad, called me a stupide hick and said I would never know because I'm unlovable."

My stomach turned to ill will toward Austin. "Is that when you attacked?"

Bob put a reassuring hand on my shoulder to calm me down. "How'd that make you feel?"

"Like a stupid hick. But I know things he doesn't. You guys never treat me like I'm stupid and my school grades prove I'm not."

"Joey you must have noticed Bob and I never liked the looks of Austin. But we felt it important for you to draw your own conclusions without our prejudice."

"Austin said I should get used to being alone because I wasn't worth anything to anyone. He said I was a waste of space and an argument for abortion."

"That had to hurt."

"I stayed quiet, boiling on the inside. Then Austin said he thanked God he wasn't queer like me. Then after insulting my mother, he said my faggot foster fathers turned me into their sissy-butt-boy. Honest, I never said anything for him to think that."

"Sorry to interrupt you again, Joey, but you look about ready to discombobulate. I always find that hard to watch, take a deep breath."

"Gus means don't hyperventilate, Joey. Lately he's gotten in touch with his squeamish side."

"Hey guys, please let me finish the story you forced out of me. Or just say you want me to stop."

"Most definitely we like hearing endings, they lead us to erroneous conclusions."

"Like I said, Austin went into total freak-out mode for no reason. He was shouting and said I was a creepy pervert always asking about his girlfriends and falling asleep on him to cop-a-feel. He was the only one falling asleep and touching me!"

"*And?*"

"Then Austin made a threatening move at me. When he tried to grab me, I decked him like Mike showed me."

"How'd you do that?"

"I waved my left-hand in his face to distract him. Then clocked him with a right hand as he lunged to grab my left. I stepped back and gave Austin a left-right-left combination and his knees buckled. He went down like a slinky toy slinking downstairs in slow motion."

"Is it safe for me to assume you would have avoided the violence if possible?"

"Yes of course! But Austin was trying to grab me, and who knows what harm he meant. But he didn't expect a knuckle sandwich. You asked, and that's how I scraped my knuckles, on his face."

"Did you call 911?"

"Didn't need to, he only stayed down a second or two, then shook himself, got up and came at me again. His face kept running into my fists until his bloody nose was spraying blood all over. Finally, he stopped, pointed a finger at me and said, 'You'll pay for this,' and ran out of the house. Don't worry I cleaned up his blood. There are no permanent stains, I used hydrogen peroxide and got the stains gone before they could dry."

"That was conscientious of you. Have you heard anything more about this?"

"No. Oh, his aunt's church phoned, I'm not welcome back there until I meet with the pastor."

"That's it?"

"If you ask me, wrestling is much less violent than boxing. I'm not interested in taking it up as sport so don't suggest it."

"Less violent *and* you get to evaluate crotch sizes in singlets. Sounds like a win-win."

"Gus, are you ever going to let me forget that?"

"Probably not. But you are lovable because we love you, including Hans the ultimate judge. Oh, and so does Mike and Eleanor."

Bob brought us back to the present and said, "Joey are you, all right? Let me see your hands ... no broken bones ... an X-ray would tell for sure."

"My hands are okay, I iced them afterward. But I'm still mixed-up. They taught us in wrestling not to fight off the mats if we can help it. There was no reason for him to get that upset ... but I take responsibility for what I did. But I didn't start it."

"Sounds like Austin had conflicted feelings and he panicked when it got too close. Joey, maybe the lesson here is everyone doesn't have the capacity to be a friend."

"Even when he called me queer, I didn't let it get to me. Because who knows, maybe others can see what I can't. But when he insulted you and my dead mother, it was too much. I know if I were a better person I'd have walked away. What I don't get is how it turned ugly so fast. Listen, I'm sorry I lost control. With your help I've been getting better with that."

Bob and I exchanged a look. I didn't know what to say either, other than, "When I'm attacked, I fight. For the record I'm glad you weren't injured. We'll deal with any fallout together as a family."

I was more curious than wary to hear the other side of the altercation. Truth be told, I wanted to know what consequences might follow Joey from being barred from a popular local church. Or my gay paranoia was showing. If there were legal consequences to Joey's fight, it was only money, and we counted a few good lawyers among our friends and associates.

Bob and I went to the barn, rolled out the ancient pea-soup-green Studebaker pick-up truck Dan and Bill left us with the house and other assorted antiques. We hand cracked the magneto to start it after priming the carburetor and off we went, chugging along to Austin's aunt's house.

****

When we rattled up, Austin was splitting tree chunks into a fire-woodpile. His shirt off, he glistened with a glossy sheen of sweat on the kind of young male muscular definition that sold old fashioned black and white physique magazines, in olden days. Reportedly, in those early times they used mineral oil to define muscles. On closer examination, Austin had two shiners, and the left side of his jaw discolored, and swollen larger than the right. As we approached, he cringed, looking at us shamefaced while holding a double headed ax in his hands. Austin appeared to cower as a dark-wet-stain bloomed in the front of his light-gray sweat-shorts.

I left Bob to talk with Austin and intercepted his aunt, who hurried out of the house toward us, drying hands on her lace trimmed, sun-faded to almost white, gingham apron. I greeted the woman with a head nod. There was a slight family resemblance to Austin. Except, she looked a spry eighty-five or ninety, white hair tied severely in a back-bun, with piercing dark-blue eyes boring out of a deeply wrinkled face. I guessed she was quite under-weight, an inch or two lower than Austin and a foot shorter than me. Under her apron she wore a wash-faded pink-check housecoat, and worn-down gray fuzzy house slippers on stocking feet.

"I've heard about you and that other fella over there. You are Gustafson, am I right? I see your Swedish ancestors in your face."

"What have you heard?"

"This and that Mr. Gustafson. But I prefer to draw my own opinion."

"You can call me Gus, people usually do. What may I call you?"

"I'm Matilda, Matilda MacKinsey are you thinking to hurt Austin some more? I'd advise against it. I've got a shotgun loaded with buckshot if you try anything. I never miss with that scatter gun." She pointed at an old ten-gauge shotgun longer than she was tall, and it probably outweighed her. It was hung over the fireplace.

"We only came for the motorcycle Joey Hall loaned Austin. Do you know what the boys had a falling out about?"

"Austin said it was over some girl, but I don't ever believe him. He lies to me and himself … I don't think he can help it …. I'm not sure he knows the difference between truths and lies, just the same as those Washington politicians. But a girl could make two boyfriends fight that's for sure."

"Do you have any objection to our taking the motorcycle?"

"I'm happy to see that darn thing gone. I didn't like Austin ridding it. In my opinion that is a dangerous, dirty, noisy contraption."

"Good, then we'll be out of your hair in a jiffy."

Matilda MacKinsey bustled about her kitchen as she spoke, "Have a seat Mr. Gustafson, we'll talk." First, she placed a steaming mug of herb tea in front of me. That was followed by a chipped-China-plate of home-made Scottish short bread placed between us. The cookies looked delicious and smelled buttery, so, I said, "Thank you," and sank my teeth into the confection. It was scrumptious.

Approving my positive reaction to her cookie, Matilda sat down and said, "Austin is sweet on one girl at church, two or three or four at that community college and his married boss, too old for him at the home center. That motorcycle lets him sniff around anything female miles around. The ladies are all he thinks about especially that older one. And he knows how to flatter a woman to get his way. He's not about marrying any of them, it's sinful fornication he's after. He plays a love and leave them game, and one will shoot him."

"Then without the motorcycle he can do some introspection."

As a look of exasperation came across her wise old face, Matilda threw her hands out and half-shouted in a thin reedy alto voice. "He's buying an old car!" She refolded her hands and her face settled back into a deeply lined placid expression, lowered her voice and said, "One of our elderly church members up and died, God rest her soul. Nobody wanted her old clunker-car, oil pours out faster than it goes in. Austin bought the damn thing for a fifty dollars donation to the church. I already told him, he can't leave it here when he leaves, I don't need or want a car. I do not drive anymore. The church members are happy to take me if I need to go somewhere."

"Where is Austin going?"

"He's moving back to the city soon. His mother is buying an apartment with her divorce settlement. She is using her maiden name again to evade the law. She said Austin and his brother, Bix, will share a bedroom. Well, good luck with that idea!"

"I thought Bix was locked up, and Austin didn't like him."

"The boys mostly don't know each other. Social services have had it with Bix. They say he may be a computer genius but has a disruptive personality that requires a higher level of care than they can find for his age. With the court involved and backlogged, the psychiatric hospitals don't want Bix with his record of adjudications … Austin is no bargain either … all of my youngest sister's daughter's late in life kids turned out damaged like her."

"That explains a lot."

"Well, at least when he's gone, I'll have my peace and quiet back! Austin won't be missed in these parts."

"Have you lived here long?"

"Now don't tell me you want to buy this place too, it's not for sale. I should put up a big sign '*NOT FOR SALE.*'"

"No. I'm just making conversation. Two places are enough for us."

"I grew up on this land, and then moved back from the city when I retired, to care of my sickly mother. She lived to 104 years. In one form or another this property has been in my family for seven generations."

"You must be proud to be directly connected to our county's history?"

"I am, but you wouldn't believe the conniptions that factory farm manager Mr. Hasselford cooks up to try and force me to sell this original family homestead. He's already driven out many of my neighbors, using tricks. He'll answer to God for his wicked ways."

"Would you like me to talk to Mr. Hasselford on your behest? I've been known to be persuasive with people who don't take no for an answer."

"No thank you, Mr. Gustafson, I can manage that malicious man myself. My whole life I've fought my own battles I won't change now."

"Oh, look, I see the motorcycle is loaded on the truck. Thank you for the tea and talk, I should be going."

"You know, once Austin is gone, Joe is welcome at church again. *If he can keep is hands to himself.* Here, let me wrap-up some short bread for you to take him. You and your friend are also welcome at our church services. They are from 8:30 AM to 5:30 PM every Sunday. We have a delicious potluck dinner the last Sunday of each month right after services."

"Welcome? You do know my husband and I are legally married, right?"

Matilda didn't slow down packing cookies for Joey, but her face shifted from neutral to unfriendly. "I didn't know."

"It is good to hear your church is an inclusive denomination that recognizes marriage for all loving couples. We've tried, but not found a welcoming church to attend up here."

"Oh, I didn't know about all that. No, no you wouldn't be accepted in God's house. We don't cotton to sinning."

"That *is* interesting, two persons' abiding love is someone else's sin. I guess it depends on whether it's a God of love or sin."

"You wouldn't be all right when our preacher goes off on one of his fire and brimstone tirades against your kind. Most likely neither would he. I could arrange a meeting for you if you want to talk to him about joining our church. Oh, huh, I see no written on your face. That's all right, our church is not for everyone."

The silence between us grew heavy. I could feel she wanted me gone, but something in her strength of character kept me in my chair. "Do children go to your church and hear those sermons?"

"Of course! Watching them grow and bloom is one of God's delights for me."

"Science has repeatable statistics, some of those children will become lesbians, gay men, or transgender. How do you suppose it will be for them blossoming into adulthood with your preacher's hate words stuck in their heads?"

She was quiet, but this time it didn't feel oppositional. "You know, Mr. Gustafson, I remember when left-handed children were forced to write with their right. It was torturous for us and at best resulted in a few ambidextrous writers, and at worst illiteracy for others. You make a good point I'll have to have a little chat with my preacher about." Somehow, she and I had become simpatico.

"I'm sure the children will appreciate your effort. Thank you for the tea and short bread, I must be going."

"God bless and safe travel."

Driving back with Eleanor's motorcycle, Bob related Austin's side of the fight scenario. "It seems Joey might have left out a few details, or Austin invented them."

"What details?"

"Austin says out of the goodness of his heart he told his best friend Joe that Joe is queer. And since Austin is straight, Joe needed to know all straight guys can tell Joe is a fag at first sight. So, Joe should come out of the closet, face facts, and stop pretending not to know he's gay."

"All knowing Austin. What an asshole!"

"Get this, Austin says out of kindness he told Joey, 'Since I jerkoff between fucks, you can suck me off or jerk me off like a loyal gay friend. But, like all straight guys, I don't return sex favors to fags.'"

"Hold on, did Austin say what triggered the fight?"

"According to Austin Joey wasn't satisfied only giving him oral sex. He wanted romance and Austin primly said no."

"Our Joey, really? I don't think so."

"At one point, Austin became agitated, and mentioned their wanting to experiment with sixty-nine. When I probed what he meant, he got up-tight defensive and said it was Joey's idea. When I would not leave it alone, shouted, he only gives head to females."

"Did you believe him?"

"No. He's not a good liar. I doubt he's given head to anyone. But getting head was clearly on his mind."

"Gosh, and I thought my conversation with Matilda was strange. I'm not niggling, but what did he say caused the fight."

"According to Austin, when he refused a blow job, Joey sucker punched him."

"Wait, what? That doesn't sound right, a teenage boy refused a blowjob. In what universe?"

"It gets better, in a fluster answering me, Austin said Joey is a bad cocksucker."

"I thought you said, he said, sex between them never happened."

"That was later, he couldn't keep his story straight."

"Bob, did anything Austin say sound truthful?"

"No. But decking a classmate without cause doesn't sound like our boy either. Did you learn anything from his aunt?"

"Aunt Matilda says Austin is a pathological liar, and we are not welcome to worship at her church, due to our sinning. But she is going to talk to her minister about his homophobia's effect on the congregation's children. She gets points if she actually does."

"Did you mention we eat meat on Fridays?"

"Where have you been? That's no longer a sin except during lent, I think."

"Thanks for the religious update. You never know, I might spontaneously start going to church again. It's good to be prepared."

"For the record, I've never caught Joey in a lie, have you?"

"No. Never."

"We still have to tell Joey about Frances. I'm dreading the fireworks."

****

Joey must have seen us make the turn-off from the state route onto the access blacktop leading to our washboard private road because he was waiting at the barn with the doors open wide. As soon as I drove in, he and Bob undid the bungee cords securing the motorcycle to the truck bed and walked it down an improvised wooden plank ramp.

"Joey, why the sour face, you been licking lemons?"

"Look at this, Austin didn't keep the bike clean like I showed him. He's an asshole. Now I'll have to strip it all the way down and clean it thoroughly inside out. Eleanor would kill me if she saw the condition of her motorcycle."

"Using different words, his aunt suggested as much. Oh, she sent you these cookies, here."

"These are so good, yum. Austin proves I'm a bad judge of character. Here, Bob, have a cookie."

"Thanks."

"Gus, what did he say about me slugging him?"

"I visited with his aunt who said you and Austin had a fight over a girl. Where, I wonder, did she get that idea?"

"Bob, did Austin trash-talk me?"

"Trust me, Joey, you don't want to hear his stuff and nonsense."

"Yes, I do. Tell me please!"

"He made up rubbish to justify his swollen face and black eyes. At first, it looked like he thought I'd come to finish the job you started. He wet himself, cowering while holding an ax. When I asked why he peed himself, he said, 'I'd said I'd bring my wrath down on him if he ever hurt you.' Then flustered he quickly followed that with he didn't hurt you, you hurt him. I told him to put the ax down and help me load the motorcycle and he did."

"What did he say about the fight?"

"Save yourself the aggravation. His story had to be fiction. Joey, he's not worth your concern."

"Come on, please, I want to know! He said I started it, right?"

"For all our sakes can we skip this part?"

"NO!"

"Don't say I didn't warn you ... He says you give toothy blowjobs."

"WHAT! I never did! I wouldn't ... ever. He's a disgusting liar!"

"Don't shoot the messenger."

"Uh huh, so that's what he wanted from me? What's wrong with his girlfriends? Oh, I know, he probably doesn't keep his meat any cleaner than he did Eleanor's bike."

"Joey, I think we have given Austin enough of our collective time. How about we forget him for this weekend?"

"I feel like such a fool, I should have known better."

"Why?"

"He told me when we first met, he can't keep a friend and it's always the friend's fault. I wanted to be his first good friend to keep, rather than look out for myself."

"Stop beating yourself up. How could anyone know, he's a creep."

"Did anything like this ever happen to either of you when you were my age?"

"Don't tell me you're in the mood for adult true confession sagas. If word got out, you might have to turn in your teenage credentials."

"Indubitably. You once remarked misery loves company, prove it."

"There you go showing off your vocabulary again."

"Put up or shut up, dad."

"I will expose my youthful follies only because I love you and wish you to learn from my mistakes."

"See that, Gus, I feel better already."

"I'd bet statistics show most gay guys' first love-object is straight. That happened to me ... well nearly did ... why don't I just tell you. "

"Pardon my interruption, Austin never was my love object. But if he played his cards right, I could have been a friend. Now I feel stupid for even saying that! Go on, Gus, tell your story."

"Onward and upward?"

"EXCELSIOR! That is New York State's motto. We learned it in school when I first moved here. Gus, speak to me."

"My best friend growing up was Gordon. We were inseparable. Gus and Gordy the neighborhood scamps and best friends from first grade. Our pranks were legendary.

We did everything together. When my teen years hit, I told Gordy I might be gay and wanted to experiment on him, just to be sure. He panicked and got all neurotic. Said he couldn't help me because he knew for sure he was going to be straight and didn't want to ruin it by experimenting with gay. I asked, ruin it how?"

"You asked him that, really?"

"I did. Gordy explained he didn't want to spoil being straight by messing around in a gay way because homosexuality was contagious and there is no vaccination to protect him."

Joining in the fun, Bob said, "I didn't know that. No vaccine, will a face mask help?"

"Later, in college, Gordy turned into the biggest queen on campus. I guess he got contagion from another than me. But by then I'd figured out who I was and didn't need his help."

"Bob, do you have a funny story too?"

"The joke was on me for sure. Although, at the time I did not see it that way. What happened was I thought my first man was a sure thing. But the easy way has seldom worked for me. It's a lesson I keep relearning."

"Tell me, I feel less foolish hearing I'm not the only dufus in our house."

"Who knows there might be hope for you yet Joey?"

"His name was Adrian. He was the biggest swish at my high school. Everyone assumed he was gay because he wore flamboyant clothes and was more feminine than any girl. I was in love with the idea of being in love with another boy. And I thought I'd found a safe person to try it on with. In his girly ways Adrian was cute, smart and a *boy*, what could go wrong?"

"You got me."

"When I asked him out on a date, he got royally pissed-off and said, 'I can't understand why you would think I'm not straight, I'm dicking three girls in our class, all at the same time.' He stayed mad at me that whole school term, but he didn't throw a punch. A good thing for him, since I was on the football team, and Adrian was our head cheerleader. It wouldn't have been a good look for him to lead the pep-squad with a broken jaw."

"Stop, wait, that's not feasible, how could you have a boy cheerleader? Or wait … was it an all-boys school?"

"No, Joey, we had boy and girl cheerleaders at my high school. Didn't I just say our head cheerleader was a boy? You are not paying attention, and you started this trip down memory lane."

"But that's not possible, boy cheerleaders upset the natural order."

"Now what stuff and nonsense are you talking about?"

"All the cheerleaders at my school are girls, and at the schools we competed against. Did you have girls on your football team?"

"Of course, our best field goal kicker, and only point after touchdown kicker were girls, and they seldom missed getting us those points. Sadly, the gnarly punters were boys."

"Oh, I see."

"Joey, do you have a problem with gender equality?"

"One thing I can always count on with you guys. We start out talking about one thing and end up babbling about something completely different. And I always end up feeling like the ignoramus."

"What do you think, could it be a conspiracy?"

"Don't pick on me, I'm not a total conspiracy nut, and a few of those theories *have to be true*. And for your information, my generation invented gender equality because yours let the ladies down, big time."

"Bob, Joey, before you continue this duel, I'm hungry. How about we go for pizza, my treat?"

"Oh, damn I forgot, I said I'd make dinner."

"That's all right, I'm in the mood for pizza."

"Can Hans have the pizza scrapes? Please, please, he loves them. I'm sure he was an Italian dog in his last life because he also loves spaghetti and hates sauerkraut."

"No. He loves meatballs and sausage in sauce, spaghetti is a challenge for his teeth."

Bob, the ever-ready teacher said, "Joey, we've talked about this, table scraps are bad for dogs of all nationalities! Hans does not always know what's best for him. That's why he keeps us around."

I came to Joey's aid just as the boy started to fume into one of his moods. "Before you start glowering, please get one of those boiled beef bones out of the freezer, defrost it in the microwave for forty-five seconds, and give it to Hans to work on while we go for pizza."

CHAPTER 8. Past and Present

Driving to the pizzeria, we three sang along with my latest traveling-music compilation of oldies but goodies. Joey often complained my car's music was too ancient to be relevant, yet he sang along with gusto, knowing all the words to songs from long before I was born. When we rode in Bob's car, it was classical music themes everyone hummed along with, and nobody complained. I called that elitist, in return they called my car ostentatious, go figure?

As soon as we were seated in the restaurant, Joey went back to the day's primary topic. "Bob, you teach urban high school. Do you think what happened between me and Austin was unavoidable because I'm a dumb hick, or would his brand of crazy fool city kids too?"

"Does your rural versus urban question presuppose sexual orientation?"

"No, but I get why you asked. I still don't know what team I bat for, and I thought Austin did. He can't walk down the street without commenting on female breasts or butts. Yet when he'd fall asleep on me watching a move, his hand often found my crotch. I didn't mind but it was confusing."

"We will still love and respect you whatever your team affiliation, and there is no rush to pick sides."

"Do you think it possible I'm gay and don't *want* to know that? No, wait, answer my first question first, please."

"My answer is Austin was charming for a few minutes. He could have fooled anyone at first. Brooklyn people come of age when they are ready, not before, just like everyone else." Bob said this with authority.

"That's the answer I expected."

"Most teens worry if they are developing to adulthood normally, whatever their circumstance, geography, or team preference. Sometimes it takes gay and questioning kids longer to accept themselves. If it's any consolation in the end it usually sorts itself."

"Does the answer have to be so vague?"

Vague indeed, I said, "In my travels, sometimes a gay boy chooses a straight object of desire, unconsciously hoping it will rub off and make him straight too. Or at the least postpone an unwanted, much avoided reckoning. Some of the drama is between self-discovery and wanting to please others at the expense of self."

"Why?"

"If rejection is expected, it's natural to protect the ones we love from no longer loving us."

"Is what you just said called conversion therapy?"

Bob joined in again. "Where'd you get that idea? Conversion therapy is a scam that preys on vulnerable people who try to postpone the inevitable."

"That's not what they say."

"Reality check, Joey, people are born to be whoever they become, however long it takes them to figure it out and accept themselves."

"What if they can't figure it out, like me? Then what?"

"Hold on, cowboy, do you want to talk about nature or nurture, again? Didn't we already have this conversation some time ago?"

"We did, but when am I going to have a sexuality? It's hell not knowing. I'm the only boy in my class who hasn't gotten laid. I'm missing out on all the fun."

"Nonsense! Schoolboys lie about sex, rural and urban the same. It is like water is a universal solvent. You're not missing out if you need more time."

"Right, all the boys fib about having sex except me. But Bob, it can't be universal with exceptions like me."

"Let's try this then … I believe when a person is ready to physically experience lovey-dovey, love-object desires with someone of similar interest. That fellow will gravitate to a safe, mutually involved attachment, and with luck have a memorable mutually pleasurable first-time sexual release. And that explains fourteen-year-old urban Austin having his fist sexual experience with his grandfather's forty-year-old mistress because Gramps was too sick to cut the mustard."

"You didn't answer my question."

"If I were forced to guess, my answer would be rural kids have more opportunity for privacy than urban ones."

I could see Bob's answers were not satisfying Joey, so I said, "The correct answer you seek is be patient, your time will come, and you'll know it when it arrives, and not before."

"Gus, you keep saying be patient. Sometimes a guy doesn't want good advice, what I need is results that leads to fireworks-sex like my classmates boast about. Just give me the down and dirty facts, just the facts."

I could see Bob was getting frustrated with Joey, and I was exasperated with both. "Fine, you want more grit. At the time nonphysical puppy-love is discovering itself and learning to dance, most of your classmates are also discovering they have never known before stinks. Socially isolating body odors come from glands, bad diet, and poor hygiene, dental down to their toes. Between halitosis, pimple, and clumsy-awkward growth-spurts, most teens compensate for new troubling physical-emotional disturbances with another new socially isolating activity, masturbation."

"Wow, I wasn't expecting you to say that. You're my foster dad, I don't like it when you talk dirty. It doesn't feel okay."

"Like Bob said, every individual is special, unique, and too vague for your taste. What I gave you is not vague and fills in your coming-of-age questions. But the universals I just described you are familiar with from smelly over ripe gym lockers."

"I liked what Bob said better for restaurant talk. He was much nicer, Gus."

"You didn't ask for nice. I can be nice when it fits the topic."

"Don't worry, I won't talk about personal stuff with you again. You made it smell bad."

"Joey, Gus is trying to say persistent annoying sexual arousals linked to puppy-love sometimes leads to unanticipated, unsatisfactory outcomes that stink. In my humble opinion there is nothing worse than bad smells during sex, always take a shower fist."

"Gross! You are both dirty minded over thirty and trying to freak me out. I'm done talking before you elaborate more."

"Good. Chose a new topic?"

"I'm hungry, and it smells delicious in here."

"Shall I order an extra-large pie, and each choose one topping for it?"

Glancing over the menu, Bob said, "The calzone here is exceptional, I'd like a spinach and cheese with spicy-marinara sauce on the side."

"I need to watch my weight if I want to wrestle at 133 my last year of high school. But yuck, a plain salad doesn't fit the appetizing aromas in this place."

"Joey, look, under daily specials, see third from the bottom, they have a low carbohydrate hot antipasto. Though you'll have to skip the breadsticks, and garlic knots."

"Thanks, Gus, that helps. What are you having?"

"I came for pizza, and I *shall* have pizza. What topping is the question."

The owner Angelo took our order. He explained his wife and daughters were having a Women's Lib day and running the restaurant's kitchen. Shortly after he left, his middle son Mario brought our drinks and breadsticks. Neither Angelo nor Mario looked putout over their work-place role reversal. But the women in the kitchen looked happy preparing our meal.

Waiting for our food, Joey looked glum. "Can you guys imagine me your age and still not having had sex or a clue to a sexual orientation? I was born a misfit I guess."

"No. You weren't."

"I think I was, and it doesn't look pretty ... depressing actually."

"Lighten up, Joey, enjoy the present. Your time will come. Don't rush Mother Nature, she doesn't like being pushed."

"Speaking of that, I can't get past slugging Austin either. I feel like such a rudderless barbarian for doing it. It's not like I didn't know better."

"I'd give you absolution, only I didn't take a vow of celibacy. Did I, Bob?"

"What I know is you and Bob and Mike wouldn't have lost control like I did."

"Joey, forgive yourself, things happen, and nobody died. Promise yourself, next time you'll walk away. Then forget it."

Bob's order came first, direct from the oven. He said, "This is best piping hot," and he began tearing pieces off his giant-calzone and dipping them in the accompanying bowl of hot, spicy-sauce. The fragrance was tantalizing.

Then the dieter's hot antipasto arrived with a flourish of more aromatic delight. Fork at the ready, without a word, Joey dove in with zest.

I can be patient when waiting enhances the experience. *Finally*, my pizza arrived and aroma-wise took over the table. Its oregano, garlic, pepperoni, tomato, cheese perfume came bubbling straight from the oven. It swaddled our table in delicious fragrances. Nevertheless, I remembered to say, "There is enough here to share. Help yourselves." But my dining companions were otherwise occupied. More for me.

When Bob finished eating, he rubbed his full belly with satisfaction and returned to the conversation Joey halted. "I know you don't want to hear it, but life will be a whole lot easier if you stop being a judgmental prude. Live life now and deal with the future when it gets here."

Full fork midway between plate and mouth Joey said, "How can you think I'm judgmental, and I'm certainly not a prude?" Then he shoved in a forkful of eggplant parmigiana.

"Could it *be* you're blushing bright red anytime sex is mentioned or offended when Gus mentioned body odors."

"WHAT! PRUDE! Didn't I offer to get naked the night Mike left me! I even suggested having sex with both of you at once! How prudish or judgmental or whatever was that?"

"If we had accepted your offers, you would have had apoplexy. It was written on your face. You were testing us to find out what Mike dropped you into."

"Even if that's true, and I am not saying it is, I'm no prude!"

"Then why do you blush when s-e-x is mentioned."

"You guys are really relentless, you know that?"

"I believe you've mentioned that before … several times."

"Okay fine, I'll tell you why!"

"Why?"

"Because I know you guys better now."

"Sounds like a back-handed compliment."

Joey paused the chatter with a contemplative silence, then said "The word sex slams me right back into the shame and fear I felt being raped. It seemed to go on forever, hurt like hell, I didn't know what was happening and thought I was being murdered."

"Wow, that's heavy."

"Then when it stopped, I was frozen, exposed, and gawked at like a dirty object when my rapist panicked seeing how much I was bleeding. I know it's all in my head now … it wasn't when it happened, and now it replays when triggered by that word."

"You never mentioned this."

"My rape was how I learned the word sex. In my limited elementary school vocabulary, rape and sex were synonyms."

Bob leaned in and said, "I suppose you got blamed for being raped. That's how it usually goes, or so I've heard."

"I did and then became homeless as a result."

So, they wouldn't forget I was there I said, "I remember you mentioning not feeling secure where you'd lay your head at night until Mike taught you to live off the land."

"If the rape itself wasn't terrible enough, the police, nurses, doctors, everybody and his uncle insisted on seeing my injuries. I hadn't even seen my own asshole when all these adult strangers were prying my legs apart taking long looks and making comments as if I weren't there."

Bob's antipathy showed on his face. "How horrible, no one especially a little kid should go through that."

"Could it be that made me a prude, it was humiliating. Anyway, now you know why I'm sensitive about what's private or not and how I react the way I do."

"What's living off the land have to do with it?"

"I'm not sure of myself, except in the wild. Then I'm in control."

"Joey, take a breath. Gus and I told you the past can't change. Maybe you can change the way you think about it when it starts to come back."

"HOW!"

"When your rape pops into your head, pop it out again. Change the subject with your brain, by force, if necessary, hit or kick something if it won't go quietly. Make a habit of not allowing your rape to rent space in your head. If it comes in, evict it immediately."

"Huh, such a simple solution to the disaster that's occupied half my life."

"Test out what I said. When you encounter the word sex, think, 'It's only three-little-letters, two from the end of the alphabet. Refuse to give it power over you.'"

"Bob, I know you mean well trying to help. But hitting inanimate objects, or defanging words won't change me. I was born a victim and always will be one."

"Don't call yourself names. If you want, I know some excellent psychotherapists my school uses."

"Earth to Bob, I'm damaged goods. I know it, you know it, and I don't believe in head shrinking, voodoo, or black magic."

"How about I set something up with an expert? Then you decide if it helps or not."

"Huh. First, I'm a judgmental prude, now I am so crazy I need my head shrunk. What could be next from you two?"

I exchanged a couples' confounded look with Bob, which distracted me from a waistline expanding, unnecessary, completely delicious third slice of pizza. "Joey, you have a home with us and have proven yourself strong enough to stand up to our tough love. Now, try to trust us."

"Gus, is that your best sales pitch?"

"If Bob wasn't clear, you seeing a therapist is your choice, not a requirement. But the suggestion comes from a well-meaning place to improve the quality of your life."

"Gus, have you ever been to a head shrinker?"

"Yes, at different times for different reasons." My dinner companions were finishing up their meal, while my Pizza kept tempting me.

"Did it help?"

"Absolutely, Joey, and it saved me a lot of time getting to the root of why I needed help in the first place. I recommend the process to anyone wanting to learn about themself."

"Bob, did you ever go?"

"Yup, more often than Gus, I'm a schoolteacher my sanity is under constant attack from your teenage brethren. Joey, I need all the help I can get teaching oppositional teens their first language, English."

"What if I want to deal with my problems on my own, *like an adult*?"

"Gus and I are adults twice your sixteen-years on this earth. The process works and is nothing to be ashamed of."

"I'll be seventeen soon, and don't ever expect to be cured of blushing? It's physiological not psychological."

"For me, seeing a therapist was like having a coach while playing competitive sports. How about you, Bob?"

"Yup, me too. I was coached by my therapist how to improve my life."

"How?"

"By getting out of my own way. Naturally, I didn't see the obstacles as obstacles until they were pointed out. No, I won't give examples, it's personal, and this conversation is a lost cause."

"I already talk to my high school guidance counselor. If I could be fixed, she would have done it. She likes me." Joey folded his arms across his chest and put a defiant look on his face, stealing a peek at the uneaten slices of my pizza.

"What do you think, Bob, is this the time to mention Frances as a reason Joey could benefit from outside support?"

"You just did."

"Whoops. Do you want to elaborate?"

"Why don't you, since you brought it up."

"Cop out."

"You said whoops, now clean it up."

"Joey, I know we agreed family decisions would be unanimous. Something came up in the city Bob and I had to decide fast. Simply put, our little family is being enlarged by one. Frances McDermott is a fifteen-year-old male to female transsexual. She is joining our merry little band, on weekends. It's due to a life-or-death situation."

"He means it was an unavoidable necessity."

"Wait what! When is all this happening!"

"Next weekend. Frances has started seeing a psychotherapist for complicated personal reasons. Bob and I think it would be helpful for you to have someone, beside us, and your school counselor to talk through this change in our family."

"LIARS! I KNEW TUSTING YOU TWO WAS A BIG MISTAKE. THE KIDS AT SCHOOL SAY NEVER TRUST ADULTS. YOU PROVED THEM RIGHT. JUST WHEN I OPEN UP TO YOU, YOU TURN MY LIFE UPSIDE DOWN. THANKS A LOT!" After shouting at us, Joey's face and body language went slack like a zombie, lifeless.

It occurred to me, like a load of bricks falling on my head, I'd betrayed Joey by offering Frances, lifesaving refuge. It seemed I was a loser no matter what I did with these two teens. Accidental parenthood was a bitch.

CHAPTER 9. Freak-Out and White Water

No one was talking or singing on the car ride home from the restaurant. The heavy mood in the car's interior required stone cutter's tools to pierce, and we were without such implements. When we reached the house, Hans enthusiastically greeted us as usual. Then his attention shifted up a notch sniffing the pizzeria box. With the pizza safely secured, Hans stopped wagging his tail and looked concerned as he registered Joey was acting out of character. Seeing Han's concern, Joey came alive and made a show of storming up to his room loudly banging every door in his wake. Shame faced Hans slinked to a corner, as if he had been accused of being a bad dog.

Bob and I went into the den, I splashed cognac into snifters and handed one to my husband. "I'm sorry I told Joey about Frances without preparing him first. Looking for an opportune moment, it slipped out unintentionally. I'm sure you knew I'd been dreading telling him. Hans, come." We petted Hans reassuring him he had not broken any rule.

Then Bob and I took our customary easy chairs facing each other. I could tell neither of us wanted to talk. Even Hans, luxuriating with two human's physical attention, sensed something was out-of-whack and remained on semi-alert tense.

"It couldn't have gone worse telling Joey about Frances. How am I going to clean up this mess I made?"

"It's done now, Gus. It was inevitable he'd feel threatened no matter how well he was prepared."

"You're saying that to make me feel better. What do you really think?"

"Tonight, Joey opened-up to us about his worst life experience. That had to be hard to finally unload. Now, afterward he probably wonders if he'd told us too much. Instead of a pat on the back to wave off, what you said probably felt like a gut punch."

"Thanks a lot. You made me feel disloyal in a no-win situation."

"Yeah, sorry about that. I hoped he knew us better than to go to his default, abandonment mode."

"Any idea how to make this right?"

"Let's go whitewater rafting. It might be what we all need to clear the air. A lot happened and you are not to blame for most of it. However, Gus, you could learn to think before you speak."

"As always, good advice from the man I love."

"If our latest chapter in fostering is going to work, much of it has to fall on the kids."

"I'll go tell Joey whitewater in the morning, before he turns in for the night."

"It'll give him a chance to sleep on something other than Frances coming."

I no sooner put my brandy-snifter down and started to rise out of my chair than Joey exploded into the den. He was buck-naked, fire flashing from his eyes in a fierce face. He had blushed a deep crimson color head to toe.

"JOEY, GO PUT SOME CLOTHES ON!"

Disturbed and not sure what was happening, Hans stood and emitted a low warning growl. Clearly, Hans did not approve of the sudden ambience change and our reaction to it.

Joey moved to the center of the room, put hands-on hips, bounced on the balls of his feet, and made his hardon swing up and down. His erect penis stood out at a forty-five-degree angle and slapped his flat belly on up bounces. His cock was larger than I would expect for his height. His foreskin had rolled back and down off his dickhead, the way they do turning inside out to create an erection's heightened sensitivity.

Defiantly, Joey said, "No. I won't! You must see what comes with me and are tossing away like trash. My previous keepers insisted on seeing all of me, what makes you different? Come on, guys, take a good look, see, my dick isn't small. I can't help it got hard, sometimes it has a mind of its own."

Bob's teacher's training showed through, he remained calm but raised his voice, *"JOEY COVER YOUSELF OR BE SORRY!"*

"No. Let's get to it, I have something precious I want to lose, right here, right now, and one of you must take it before I'm sacked from this family."

"Joey, cover up and we will talk." I had been feeling bad about speaking without thinking before he burst in the room. His nudity took my self-criticism up several levels.

"No, I won't. Come on, flip a coin, I won't allow you to discard me still a virgin. *THAT'S NOT FAIR!* With two gay dads, me still a virgin, *WHO'D BELIEVE THAT?* Come on, one of you deflower me this instant and then I'll leave, no muss, no fuss."

"Nobody wants you to leave!"

"Oh, I got it, you think I'm not a virgin because I was raped. Not true, that was a criminal assault, *you both* told me."

"Settle yourself down, cover up, and we'll talk about it."

"No. Right now I'm ready to *give you,* my cherry. Please take turns drilling my ass if that's what you like. Then I will be 100% gay, problem solved, and I'm out and on my way"

I glanced at Bob just before speaking and then did not. Bob's wordless communication was, "Let Joey run-down spewing fears."

Hans was getting agitated, marching around confused, on and off snarling softly.

He did not understand what was happening. Whatever it was, he did not approve. I could see, Hans knew if he were alfa dog of our pack, he'd have already restored order. So, to assert dominance, I said, "Come … heel," and took him outside. Instead of rushing to sniff around as usual, he sat on the porch and looked up at me with, *What's going on,* showing in his eyes. Reassuringly I stroked his head and chest. Then I feigned to move like we were going to run. He was not buying it and did not move. Instead, he gave me a look that said, *Who do you think you're fooling?* Hans was right, I gave him a pat and command to, "Stay." Then I went back inside leaving a very befuddled looking dog on the porch.

Joey had apparently run out of things to shout or whine about. Bob was addressing him with a schoolteacher's stern-authority. "Joey, before we address your trepidations, you *will* cover yourself. Or I *will* throw you over my shoulder and take you to the hospital emergency room for a psychiatric evaluation."

"I'm trying to give you something precious, something I want to lose. It is not the same thing as what was stolen from me as a child. See, I am hard for you to do it."

"Cut the crap, Joey."

"After you fuck me, I'll finally be gay and no longer in limbo! Whoopee! Converted!"

"I'm counting to five, either cover up or tell it to the emergency room staff. Joey, do you really want to repeat your eight-year-old experience, being gawked at naked by strangers in a hospital?"

"What's wrong with you, Bob? How can you threaten me with that! I told you about my humiliation in strictest confidence."

"Put clothes on so we can talk. One. Two …"

"What I want to give you is my once in a lifetime gift to give. Just take it and I'll disappear out of your lives forever … like I was never here."

"Put clothes on or prepare for consequences. I'm not kidding. Three. Four …"

Bob moved ready to grab Joey. I was still standing inside by the front door after taking Hans, outside. I moved in closer ready to give Bob a hand. Joey saw us moving and dropped into a fetal position on the thick-pile rug between our easy chairs. Seeing us ready to take him to the hospital, he howled incoherently. We hadn't touched him.

Kneeling on either side of the boy, we stroked his head and shoulders. After a few moments of massage, Joey's stone-rigid tautness yielded, he became quiet, and supple by degrees. Then his breathing slowly returned to normal. I continued rubbing the teen's neck and shoulders while Bob fetched Joy's bath robe from his bedroom.

Calmed down, Joey's face muscles relaxed. So, I moved into a sitting position on the rug next to him. Bob returned and draped Joey's bathrobe over his prone body.

The situation stabilized enough for me to say, "You were way out of line, my young friend. We're adding to, not subtracting from this little family. We don't want you going anywhere. If you want to be a drama queen, just say so, we'll send you to theater camp this summer. But we don't allow nude shows in our home."

Joey's mood had changed from fierce defiant to timid. "What I understand is I'm being replaced by a different more interesting young person. And why not? You have no reason to keep me around, we aren't blood related, *or have any reason to keep your word to me.*"

"You will always be our first foster child. Being number one and the oldest comes with rank privilege, and responsibilities."

"What responsibilities?"

"To help the new family member adjust to our strange and weird ways."

"Huh, how can I believe anything you say, you lied to me. You frightened me with homelessness just when I was getting comfortable here."

"If you left us, where were you going to live?"

"In the woods. I could build an all-weather shelter before winter."

"Sounds like a rough life."

Sadness washed over Joey's face, and he said, "Jeez, Austin was right, I am stupid. If I weren't such an idiot, I wouldn't have just burned my bridges by getting naked. … Okay, let's get this over with, I made a fool of myself. I'll go pack and leave."

"This house is your home until you choose otherwise. We like having you here."

Hans still outside, heard our talking and raised his own whining to make sure we hadn't forgotten him.

Speaking loudly over Hans' pleas I said, "You are not being replaced, and I did a bad job of telling you Frances is joining us. Can you accept my apology?"

"That's okay, Gus, I accept. I knew you goofed up when you said whoops."

"Do over?"

"Okay."

"Through no fault of ours, yours, or anyone, this family is being enlarged for at least one year due to unavoidable circumstance of a critical nature."

"Critical how?"

"If Frances tells you, nothing will be lost in translation."

"See that, I'm being brushed aside in favor of a stranger who is given the power of information and not even here yet. I thought I was supposed to be number one foster son."

"You are, and what Frances knows about you is only what you will tell. We'd like it to be mutually shared information between you."

"What if I refuse to speak to her?"

"Look, Joey, you're her big brother. If *we* can be generous with you, and we do try, *you* can be generous helping Frances adapt to circumstances not ideal for her."

"How long will I have to be generous?"

"At least a year. You both have variables you can ask Frances hers. Bob and I are not ridged about time, as you know."

Bob had been closely watching Joey and me talking and said, "Did you get this upset before you and Austin fought?"

"I kept my clothes on and didn't offer him my virginity, if that's what you're asking."

"Did you ever get this upset with Mike and Eleanor?"

Joey stood and started quietly pacing in a circle, thinking. Then a glimmer of recollection darkened his face. Lying was not his style, but divulging another painful memory gave him pause. He'd already done a lot of painful truth telling this night. Like Mike, Joey wasn't generally talkative. Finally, he dodged the question. "Does staying until I'm at least eighteen mean I don't have to join the army if they reject me?"

"Isn't that an oxymoron?"

"Yes. So is not having a way to be an adult other than homeless. My worst nightmare is I was born homeless, will die homeless, and have nothing but homeless in between."

"Let me be clear, you can live in this house for as long as Bob and I own it. Now answer Bob's question about Mike and Eleanor."

"Okay I've lost my mind before, mostly in group homes when threatened. One time I did freak out on Mike and Eleanor when I first came to live there. It was about my wanting to have my way rather than obey their rules."

"That sounds in normal range for a teenager."

"They tied me up and put me in the toolshed overnight. It was cold, I was thirsty, hungry and had time to think about not having any place to live. Then I realized it was about me not them. I had to make it work. After that I tried extra hard to control my fits. Eleanor was a nurse and worked in a psychiatric hospital. So, when she saw me struggling not to explode, she stopped my going off the deep end and totally freaking outs."

"How?"

"Eleanor gave great back and foot rubs and fed me cookies when there were any. She'd talk me down until I learned to do it myself. Is that what you wanted to know? It feels weird telling you. I haven't lost it this bad since coming up north five years ago."

Hans was now scratching at the door to come inside and join the conversation. Soon he would be barking full throat in protest. "Joey, how old were you when these fits started?"

He sat down on the sofa, hand under chin thinking and looked uncomfortable revealing more of his history.

"Ah, hum."

"Okay, I think when I was nine. A schoolteacher told whoever was caring for me at the time, I was chronically confrontational with an uncontrollable temper. I didn't know what those words meant. But I learned them fast, I couldn't sit down for a week."

Ever ready with a teachable moment, Bob said, "And you learned how to get noticed by adults."

"I did. The next year, a Sunday school teacher scolded me in front of everyone saying, 'You are a wild unmanageable child and should be turned loose to live alone in the wilderness far away from decent God-fearing people.' By then I knew freaking out was my only self-defense. Crying or not eating was never noticed by caretakers."

"You saying that, helps us understand how you got from there to here."

"And that I was born a *reject*?"

"Joey, the-you we just saw is not who we know."

"Then I'll tell you, Mike and Eleanor helped me feel less broken. You two nuts made me feel almost normal … until I punched out Austin. Hitting him brought stuff backup I thought I'd forgotten, and then felt replaced by oops."

"So, you externalize internal overload."

"By getting naked and bouncing my cock at you, I mean Jeez, how embarrassing was that? I'm bad, always have been, and always will be. I'm a total and complete loser."

"Were you ever hospitalized for having angry fits?"

"No."

"You almost got there tonight. Just so you understand, consequences could have screwed your future to the wall, and none of us want that."

"Well, at least now you know how broken I am. In a funny way I feel better you've seen my body, like all the others who took me in and threw me out. Except if I can remain here, I suppose I'll never be able to look you guys in the eye again."

"I don't consider you broken. But you did show us more than we needed to see." I said this making direct sincere eye contact with Joey.

"I'm sorry, Gus. I shouldn't have lost control like that. Once I let it out a little, it took over and now you have a reason to hate me."

Bob decided to rejoin our chat and said, "Joey, we don't hate you the opposite is true. But if you took all your clothes off at school what would happen?"

"They'd kick me out, forever."

"Not at my school. The office would call the police. The police would take you to a hospital emergency room, and after a forty-eight-hour psychiatric observation, a judge could decide to commit you involuntarily to a psychiatric hospital for treatment, or not."

"You think I care? What difference does it make to my pathetic life?"

"Really? You don't care the school would make a permanent record of what you did. The police would create a file about your public nudity, the hospital start a dossier on your involuntary psychiatric commitment, the court system identify you as a sex criminal, and make you register as a sex offender forever after."

"So, what, my prospects were never good."

I was growing weary of the after-event yapping. "Hans wants to come inside. He will start losing it in just a minute. You know how he can get."

Bob waded back into what was feeling like a lost cause conversation. "Hans hears us and wants attention. But right now, Joey, you get all our attention and affection, until you understand how serious your loss of control was for your future. I think Hans can wait a little longer."

"I said I'm sorry, what more do you want me to say?"

"The trigger."

"Okay, okay you want me to say I'm not surplus being replaced by a transsexual."

"That's not it."

"Okay fine, I'll give this new person a chance, I don't have to join the army if they don't want me, and Bob and Gus, won't let me be homeless if they can help it. I got all that, now can we let Hans in, before he goes bonkers?"

"Not yet, one more thing, I can still see your family-jewels. Pull your robe down."

"I'm not showing you anything you haven't seen before. Is there something wrong with that part of me?"

"Nothing is wrong other than your privates are not supposed to be displayed publicly, under penalty of law."

"I disagree, if we were nudists, we'd walk around naked all the time. Hey, do you think that would cure my blushing problem."

"There might be medication for that."

"Blushing or nudism? I think I'd like being a nudist. Nudists walk around free with only healthy air touching skin. That sounds like nirvana to me."

"And if we were Seventh Day-Adventists we'd be vegetarians and you'd have been circumcised. We aren't nudists or Seventh Day-Adventists and if you don't close your robe, you can tell the hospital staff all about why I dragged you there to show off your family jewels to everyone who wants a look at nirvana."

In mock parody of slapstick freight Joey tied his robe closed extra tight, then dramatically covered his crotch area with splayed hands. He was back to his old self with just a tinge of residual ignominy.

"That's better, thank you for honoring our in-house modesty. Now, before I go get Hans, will you promise we can talk more about what happened tonight, soon?"

Still in slapstick parody Joey said, "Since you say you want more talk, I get why people give for being vegetarians like health or love of animals. It's that other business I don't understand."

"You mean circumcision? What do you know about it?"

Shifting to a serious face, he said, "Not much. I asked Mike one time. The fish weren't biting, and he taught me to swim. He said ask Eleanor she's a nurse, I didn't. I figured she'd want to check me out, that always ended badly in the past."

"Was that it?"

"One of the boys in my junior high school gym class had chopped meat and a big mouth. He said being cut made him a better cleaner lover than us natural boys. Is that true?"

I shook my head no. Joey's face showed he had taken a risk asking the question.

But he wanted more than a head shake answer. So, I said, "Think about it, the process was reductive, nothing was added. Soap and water work for everyone."

"Right, but he still had his dickhead. I've seen it, he liked to show off in the shower room. Isn't that the most sensitive part?"

"No. When a natural penis is engorged, inside the foreskin becomes outside the shaft and that is the most erotically sensitive part."

"That guy is in high school now; first chance I get I'm telling him he's spreading false news."

"Why would you do that?"

"He's bragging about fake information."

"What I told you about penises can be found on the internet or any legitimate anatomy book. It's provable. If your classmate wanted that info, it's easy to find."

"Okay, so what?"

"Could it be he is protecting himself from what he doesn't want to know?"

"What do you mean exactly?"

"I think it's human nature to try and make sense out of what doesn't."

"I see where you went. His false beliefs trump provable facts to explain why he has less dick than others."

"Right."

"And you're saying who am I to refute his turning a negative outcome into a positive one. Sort of like losing an election and declaring yourself the victor."

"Did I satisfy your curiosity?"

"For now. Please let Hans in."

Scratching my head, I said half to myself, "We seem to have crossed a lot of boundaries tonight." Then I went to get Hans. Seeing me out on the front porch Hans wanted to play. He had been lonely, most likely he also felt excluded. Robustly wagging his tail, he brought me his favorite flying toy. The game of catch helped me unwind. Between tosses I thought, *As badly as I handled telling Joey about Frances, in the end it seems to have deepened Joey's relationship with Bob and me.*

When I brought Hans inside after playing catch, he was overjoyed to greet Bob and rubbed his body against him as if they had not seen each other in weeks. Bob and Joey were seated at the partner's desk writing on fool scrape pads. Hans cautiously walked around the desk. Then lifted Joey's free hand with his snout and was immediately petted which produced reassured tail wagging. Then it occurred to me, *Hans had not only carried on to come inside for attention. He wanted to restore peace after Joey disturbed it.*

Being an inquisitive sort, I had to ask, "What are you writing, an opera libretto? I like grand operas on the weekends."

"Gus, Joey is making a list of his concerns about Frances joining us, and I'm writing ideas for preemptive ways to avoid future explosions. I've put bake cookies on my list. Would you like to contribute?"

"No thanks, I'd hoped you were collaborating on an operatic spectacular so

I could sing arias at the top of my vocal range. I'll nurse my disappointment with what's left of my drink."

"Sorry, Gus, my contribution will never be ready for music unless it's in a musical cookbook."

Looking up from writing, his face washed, and hair combed, Joey said, "Gus, I wrote something, want to hear it?"

"Indubitably, I do. Hum a few bars first. What does your post nude exposition sound like? Elucidate me, Joey."

"Now I suppose you'll never let me forget I exposed everything during a freak out."

"As I said illuminate, explicate, elucidate. E-flat is a good key for my voice."

"Since I know and use indubitably and elucidate to show-off in English class, they *are* in my *LEXICON*. I will *oblige,* without musical accompaniment, old melodious viewer of naked youth."

"Ah ha, clothing improves your vocabulary, and I collect another label. It's a good one, I'll have a plaque made for my office wall. *Old melodious viewer of …* "

"Sorry to cut you off, but Gus, you taught me the value of two-bit words at just the right point in negotiating. You both want me to keep my pants on for the sake of your narrow-mindedness and fear of the law. Since you both say I'm welcome to stick around, to be crass, what's in it for me to behave the way you want?"

Half to myself, I said, "You mean rather than the consequences of total disruption of our status quo?

Bob held forth like an authoritarian academic. "Oh, I don't know … how about you avoid commitment to a mental hospital added to your permanent record of lifelong accomplishments."

"What else do I get?"

"What do you want?"

"Long before everything blew up tonight, I've been thinking about changing my pronouns. Lots of kids are doing it."

"As I said before, elucidate."

"Everything in my life has been binary, straight or gay, male or female, Black or white, hot or cold. Except me, I WAS NEVER BINARY. I DON'T EVEN HAVE A SEXUAL ORIENTATION."

"Wow, settle down, relax, we've hit our quota of outbursts for the night. Now what's this about?"

"Weren't you paying attention Gus? I don't know in my heart of hearts if I'm straight or gay, or asexual, pansexual, maybe metro sexual. Whatever, I'm not binary."

"Uh ha."

"Then, Gus, to add confusion, a transsexual person is joining our household. Now, I'll need to learn about that too, male, female, transsexual, again not binary."

"What do you want Joey?"

"For the time being I want a nonbinary pronoun that reflects me ... Oh dear, what happened Gus. Did you get a sudden case of indigestion? That pizza looked and smelled awfully good."

"Joey, don't worry, Gus will recover. He only recently learned about nonbinary pronouns. You know how it is, business and his digestive track are slow to adapt to popular cultural."

"I'm right here, Bob, I can speak for myself. What pronouns suit you?"

"Ze, zim, zis, zimself, these better represent my current self-image. Depending, what happens after high school, it may become permanent?"

"Then I will adapt ... there's nothing wrong with new pronouns ... I guess."

"Gus, do you think I'm asking for too much?"

"No. But since you asked, why not go with the singular they, them, their, themselves, instead of ze?"

"Huh, you aren't the old fuddy-duddy I thought. The problem is written down singular they can be confusing. To keep my four-point-zero GPA, I must communicate clearly."

"Fine, just keep in mind I'll try, but from time to time will forget and revert to old usage, nothing personal. If that's understood, shall we settle this negotiation with a handshake or elbow bump? Good, elbows it is ... hey guys, I'm wiped out. We should all turn in if we're going whitewater rafting before daylight tomorrow morning."

"Can I come, AM I INVITED?"

"Yes, but Hans isn't. He has to guard the house because the rafting company doesn't allow pets."

"Oh wait, I caused such a big ruckus tonight, I don't deserve a reward. I was bad, awfully bad."

Sounding like a schoolteacher Bob said, "Gus and I decided *we* wanted a river ride *before* you freaked out. *I* invite you to come along. We have household changes to talk over and may need to clear up any lingering remnants after a night's sleep."

"But I insist on being punished, not rewarded."

Bob still at the ready said, "Punishment is a topic for a future family meeting if you want. Just be aware if you bring it up and it gets a unanimous vote, I'm suggesting you decide your own punishment."

Before Joey could dwell on self-punishment, sleepy as I was, I semi-dozed into the conversation. "Our pronoun deal aside, did you run around Mike and Eleanor's place in the altogether?"

"Are you kidding, Eleanor wouldn't have allowed *that!*"

"What makes us so special?"

Joey's tone of voice went slightly flirtatious. "You are both gay, and not as strict about most things. Who knows, at the least I might turnout bisexual?"

"I'm not buying it. Too simplistic, that's not how you think."

"Okay, I had no idea what I was doing or how it would turn out, and that is the gods' honest truth."

I used my "cut the bullshit" voice and face from work, and said, "Could it be you tried to manipulate us into picking you over Frances, giving you power at the expense of an unknown person?"

Bob saw where I was going and leapt into tone down cranky-sleepy me and another confrontation. "Or could it be your risk taking *was* a different kind of test."

"Me? How? By what authority do I have to test you?"

"You got our attention."

"But why would I try manipulate you?"

"Let's cut the crap Joey, we are trying to do this foster parent thing right by you."

"I don't want to be old and gray before I know what team I bat for. I'd rather kill myself. No, I don't mean that."

"Then keep your clothes on and mean it when you promise no self-harm."

Looking exhausted and sounding sincere, Joey's low energy voice said, "I promise."

"Listen, guys, I'm so beat I'll be asleep before my head hits the pillow, goodnight everyone sleep well."

****

We were half asleep during morning ablutions, breakfast, and preparing our take-along lunches. The weather report was favorable, clear skies, warm temperatures, with high humidity on the river. Nevertheless, we took Bob's Volvo station wagon for its better all-wheel-drive and off-road-traction. The country weather could get finicky without warning and muddy-up the rough rutted-road that led to the river raft dock.

Wearing wide brim hats, sunglasses, baggy T-shirts, cut-off jeans, flipflops, and slathered in sunscreen #60, we donned the rafting companies' mandatory puffy life-vests. The vests under our hats made us look like obese raft ridding orange-Day-Glo beetles. After the raft company's final formalities, Bob, me, and Joey were gliding down the river in a battle-scared inflatable-rubber-raft. As suggested by management, we towed three store-bought gallon-jugs of spring water. They bobbed along aft in the icy-cold melted snow posing as river-water.

Once we were comfortably settled in for the daytrip, Joey was the first to speak. "I suppose if there is a next time for a whitewater adventure, a stranger will make four in the raft."

"Is there something you want to gab about while we are still only three?"

"I brought my list from last night. We only got to number one before going to bed."

"I'll gird myself, let's hear the rest."

"Here goes; [2] mental illness cause and cure, [3] psychotherapy versus psychiatry versus selfcare, [4] rejection by the military, [5] my virginity, [6] males wanting to be females, [7] work life, [8] blushing, [9] lifelong effects of childhood sex abuse, [10] should Austin get an apology." To indicate he had finished speaking, Joey tucked the paper into the tan-fanny-pack cinched around his narrow waist below his fat orange flotation vest. He laced hands across the life-vest and looked at us expectantly.

I spoke first. "I'd collapse numbers two, three and eight together into one, and numbers four and seven go together. I would put off numbers five and nine until two and three are settled or you get laid to make them superfluous. Number six is better explained by our new family member Frances. We could talk number ten to death or take a vote, or table it, or flip a coin, your choice? Are my adjustments agreeable?"

"Damn, Gus, you shortened my list by a lot."

"Your main ideas are still there, and anything not we'll offer up to the Delaware River Gap God."

"Okay, if that god is listening let's start with total truth."

"Hear, hear, River God."

"My classmates know it's not politically correct to use words like crazy, nut-job, or bonkers, but can't help themselves from constantly using them. They don't realize they're putting down the mentally ill, like I was last night."

"Joey, since Bob took more psychology classes than me, and uses what he learned more directly in his work, let's give him a chance to tell us, his take on crazy."

Bob gave me a 'You owe me" look,' then said, "Crazy is how we look wearing these balloon vests, mental illness on the other hand is a misnomer for physical illness that affects behavior. You *know* it is never all right to make fun of illness or handicap, politically or otherwise."

"Then may I be so bold as to inquire whether it is a conundrum or an oxymoron?"

"We will address your boldness later in this trip. For right now what is called mental illness is usually a malfunction of the endocrine system, a physical network of glands."

"Where do I know the word endocrine from?"

"Hopefully from your tenth-grade biology. Remember, glands secret hormones that regulate bodily functions which can include behavior."

"Right, I remember now."

"In addition, strong medications for serious illness can cause psychosis that stops when the medication is discontinued as does the benefits from the medication. That's a conundrum, the medicine to make you well makes you sick."

"Huh, now I remember the physical realm of our bodies from biology class. See that, your tax dollars were not completely wasted on my compulsory education."

"Then do you remember too much, or too little gland secretions can make someone hallucinate, have wild mood swings, go into deep depression, or act in ways society doesn't approve ... like getting naked in public for instance?"

"Wait a minute, I got distracted when we learned glans-cause body hair to grow in unexpected places. I think, I was trying to recall who had it, where, and how much. I didn't have much pubic hair yet."

"Don't interrupt, you asked me to pontificate."

"Then please hold forth."

"Puberty activated glands *can* impact a whole-body response, and that's been known to cause behavioral problems."

"So, you're offering me a cause-and-effect explanation for my crazy behavior? Good, I like that."

"Gus and I are betting your erratic behavior is temporary."

"Why?"

"Just what you said last night, *most the time your behavior is socially acceptable.* Now, if you can learn to keep your clothes on in public, then your behavior is back in normal range and not pathological needing involuntary commitment to a mental hospital."

"Whoopee! I really lucked out getting you two dads."

"Don't count your chickens, I'm guessing you are due another growth spurt or two, triggered by what? ... Yes, Joey, your endocrine system."

"And if my glands don't adjust, then I'll be diagnosed mentally ill, or in school yard vernacular 'crazy as a batshit nutjob,' right?"

"You catch on fast for a nudist want-to-be."

"Okay, if that is the nature in *nature or nurture,* where's the nurture?"

"My guess is last night you felt better after exploding all over Gus and me with what you had bottled up festering. Am I right, Joey?"

"Bob, I'm embarrassed and *am* sorry I let it out to that extreme. But you're right, I humiliated myself and wish I could take it all back ... and yet right after I felt emptied out like after a good shit."

"You felt better after sharing what was clogging-you-up. That's how psychotherapy works to help patients get free of their demons."

"Wait, what? They make you stand nude and spew your fears. That sounds radical."

"No. You keep your clothes on and sit in a chair. Sometimes the therapist asks questions to get the patient to dig deeper."

"Okay, I asked for this, it's on my list. So, what's the difference between psychiatrists, psychotherapist, witch doctors and me just talking to you or schoolfriends?"

"A psychiatrist is the only one that should prescribe medication called psychotropics, which treat symptoms of bizarre behavior."

"Ah-ha, now we are getting to it, so, you guys think I need medication."

"I'm a schoolteacher, not a mental health worker. What I know from my world is you function scholastically at the highest level. I never had a 4.0 grade point average in high school. Gus, did you? He's shaking his head no."

"Be real Bob, in the past I wouldn't take medication when it was prescribed down South, just to be obstinate. Why would I now?"

"What's running your mouth this morning is your conscious mind. Last night, when you lost track of it, your unconscious mind was doing the talking and running show and tell."

"Does everybody have two minds?"

"At least two, according to Sigmund Freud's psychology. He gets credit for starting the science."

"I'd rather believe in voodoo or something more colorful with drums and chanting than some guy named Sigmund."

"Uh, I thought you asked?"

"All right I did. Because last night I felt like a complete and total hopeless loser about to be homeless, again. Then defiantly standing naked to punish you for abandoning me in favor of a transsexual, in a weird way I was powerful, not a loser as usual."

"And now?"

"This morning I feel supported. But I've known my whole life I'm a waste of space and last night I proved it. Then this morning you are treating me like I matter. It's confusing."

"You should tell that to a therapist."

"I might if you insisted, and it didn't turn me into a zombie taking pills."

"It's about what *benefits you,* Joey."

"Why are you both treating me better than I deserve. You're letting me off the hook. I wish I thought as highly of me as you do."

To participate in our family discussion I said, "You asked for total truth Joey. Something else has been bothering you, from before you slugged Austin and Frances became an issue?"

"You're relentless, Gus. You've seen every bit me. I've got nothing left to hide."

"If you learned anything from last night, Joey, uncork the bottle, pour out the poison."

"Yeah, all right, I'm sure the army has ways to know I'm a screw up. I mean I don't even know if I'm straight or gay and they will ask. I expect they'll make me sign a paper about it."

"Listen, Joey, we've been in the military they only want to know you are breathing and can follow orders. What's really going on with you?"

"I killed my mother!"

"I'm an English teacher, words are important to me. Your mother died giving birth to your sister."

"I overheard female relatives say, *IT WAS ME NOT MY SISTER WHO KILLED MY MOTHER.*"

"Poppycock!"

"They said I'm evil and nothing good can ever come to me. I was a demon from birth, cursed in this life and the next."

"When did you start listening to old wives' drivel? Common sense says otherwise. We know better."

"I don't know that. How could I?"

"Then trust us, we're trying to be your foster fathers. Oh, and by now we know you. We've even seen the pimples on your ass."

"Stop it, I'm ashamed of telling you."

Joey looked about ready to cry so, I said, "What's next on your list?"

He tossed me a grateful look and blew his nose. "Okay, let's talk about virginity. The boys at my school boast, all the time, about having hetero-normative sex, and lots. I'm feeling totally left out of where I should be as a man."

Not sure where to go with this new subject, I went for levity. "From what Bob and I saw last night you are very much a man. If I, were you, I'd coiffure that unruly pubic bush."

"Proof of manhood is doing the deed with a willing partner. Anyway, *you* don't care, you've had your chances and always reject me?"

"We care that you are safe. Not hoodwinked into STD risks by schoolboys' untrue grandiose-sex-fantasies."

Throwing his hands up. His face showing frustration Joey said, "Jeez, why does life have to be so difficult?"

"In my high school they used to say, 'Preoccupation with talking about sex indicates lack of occupation having sex.' If you can be patient, your time will come, and most likely it'll be worth the wait."

"Is that supposed to make me feel better? It doesn't!"

"What matters most losing your virginity *is it's special.* Like you said last night, it's a once in a lifetime event. You won't forget the first time, good, bad, or ugly. So, do it with someone who cares for you and it's mutual."

"Joey, wouldn't you rather give your most valued possession to someone you deem special who feels the same about you. Rather than a couple of over thirty-year-old reprobates, or worse to an anonymous stranger looking for a quick tickle and faster goodbye?"

"I know, I've heard all this before ... Oh, look there, straight ahead, the first swirling-whitewater rapids. I love this part of the river. Everybody, HOLD ON TIGHT!"

With our adrenalin pumping, the thick rubber raft swiftly sped up by itself then bumped and bounced from rock to rock. Until it got stuck in a whirlpool spinning wildly clockwise. Thrusting at rocks with our boat paddles, we eventually muscled the rapidly rotating craft out of its spin-cycle. Then abruptly we violently lurched to the left and shot over an unseen waterfall dropping nose first in an exhilarating short free fall. Settled back in the river current, we banged over sharp plunges to a big drop into a fast-moving stream below, and that shot us hurtling forward unhindered at last. Then like a giant grabbing hand inertia slowed us down, and then a second later we were going fast again.

An excited expression scrolling across his face, Joey, tucked his paddle inside the raft. "Jeez, that was scary fun!"

We checked ourselves for rock induced blunt-force-trauma bruises. With everyone still in one piece, the current driving us decelerated to a moderate speed. Not sure when the next rapid was due, I passed around the first jug of ice-cold spring water and plastic baggies of homemade snacks.

At the slower speed, snacking, the beauty of the river-soaked in. Joey finally broke the tranquility and said, "My soul may be damned and my head crazy, but I really like how my body feels doing rough and tumble stuff like just now. *It was thrilling!*"

"Gus and I still enjoy being physically challenged. For me, it takes my head out of the constrained mundane of my everyday routines."

"I forgot you both are twice my age the way you muscled us off those boulders. It was exciting."

"All compliments are graciously accepted. And credit where due, you put muscle into it also."

"What I don't get is with all these natural wonders to conquer, why any boy would want to be a girl. Boys have more fun. Are you going to tell me anything at all about our new family member?"

Bob shook his head no and then after a reflective pause said, "As far as Frances goes, I'd rather you two exchange histories one on one. In my experience secondhand information loses or bloats or both in retelling. If you can't wait for a face to face, I've heard libraries have books full of information."

Not one to keep my opinions to myself, I said, "My advice is to reserve judgment, it makes for easier digestion later on."

"Thanks, sounds like good advice, but it doesn't help me right now, does it."

"Actually, Joey, while we were spinning in circles a few a minutes ago, it occurred to me in reflection, your list would be easier and faster to satisfy in therapy rather than in river rafting. The word expedient comes to mind, you need a professional to talk to, not Bob and me. Our specialty is rocks with boat paddles."

"Boy! You know that sounds like a copout."

"Copout, no, why dilute therapy with tainted family opinion?"

"Okay, I made the mess, it's my job to clean it up. But first I need time to get my head around how I let everything go sideways last night. Then I'll be ready to tell a stranger what they want to know about the me I'm still trying to find."

"You miss the point, Joey, help getting your head straight *is* the purpose of therapy."

"I doubt the shrinks around here would be any good. If there are any?"

"How about, we set up an appointment for Monday mornings, you can go to the city with one of us, see a therapist and take the interstate bus back for school. I'm sure your guidance counselor could arrange an excused lateness for your first class on Mondays, and nobody in the village need know your business."

"Is that like being in the closet?"

"If that's how you see it. What is your first class?"

"Homeroom. What if I don't like the shrink?"

"Give her or him a fair chance, same as you expect from them."

"It sounds arranged already. When does the new family member come for my *obligatory approval*?"

"I'm impressed how you showoff your vocabulary. Is next weekend too soon?"

"Sooner is better, let's get it over with. What preparations do you want in the house? I mean besides tons of floral air spray in every room, frilly doilies if I can find some, and loads of fresh cut flowers."

"No preparation necessary, be yourself and let the house be itself. We thought Frances could use the bedroom next to yours. That room was painted last. We'll bring down some of Dan and Bill's old furniture from the third floor to furnish it."

"The furniture up there is old-fashioned tacky, some of it is even rickety. I better glue some joints."

"That's all we have for now. Let's take this change step by step."

"If you wanted, I could trade that old trashy furniture for some frilly-girly furniture at the weekend flea-market."

"Joey, that's a generous offer. Wouldn't it be more fun if you took Frances to the flea-market to pick out the furniture? You could get to know each other and haggle and trade using cellphone photos of Dan and Bill's old junk. You'd be in charge, it's your turf, and you're the big brother. That way Frances could have some say in furnishing her room."

"Bob, wait are we sure there are no valuable antiques or treasures up in the attic?"

"The only things Dan and Bill left that I know about are not valuable and kiss the blarney stone, they will soon be gone."

"What if she hates me on sight? What am I supposed to do then?"

"Why don't we cross that bridge, you know, if it's constructed?"

"Last night you said I could stay as long as I want. Today is that on condition I get along with the boy who wants to be a girl?"

"No. It's a big house with lots of land around it, and we hardly ever use the third floor. It is rumored there are rooms with ghosts up there."

"I'll try to get along, if only for your sakes."

"For Hans' sake too. As we noticed last night, Hans doesn't manage human upset very well. We wouldn't want him accidentally sinking his long, sharp teeth in one of you while trying to restore calm."

"He wouldn't, he loves me and never even met him-her. Oh look, churning white water as far as we can see. There, beyond that bend in the river. Buckle your seat belts boys it's going to get bumpy. I live for these adventures!"

CHAPTER 10. Sanitation Garage, Weekend Friends

Early Monday morning Bob took Joey to meet his new therapist in the city. We had made contingency plans with a therapist who specialized in adolescents sexually abused as children. Fortunately, I'd added Joey to my platinum health insurance plan right after he joined our family.

I arrived back in the city early enough to pick up Frances. Got her discharged from the hospital she had no need to be in and took her to school. To begin her first academic school day, I signed a sheaf of documents and paid combination locks rental fees. Wearing the maroon and cream unisex school uniform daily was optional, and most students didn't. Nevertheless, I ordered one in case Frances felt rebellious or was required for a special function. Ironically, Frances clearly liked the idea of owning a uniform she didn't have to wear. She told me it was the catalyst needed to give her new school a chance.

Before I left her to go to work, I explained it was a short walk from the school to Frances' afterschool group therapy and recreation program. She looked dubious, so I drew a map of the route and gave my work cellphone number.

Joey would take a taxi to the bus station after his therapist's appointment, walk the four blocks to school, and yellow school bus it home after. The rest of the week Joey would ride Mike's motorcycle to school, weather permitting. The current plan had fallible moving parts but was the best we could do on short notice.

Until we got to know Frances better, our daily routine was one of us took her to school and the other picked her up, share and share alike. It wasn't a perfect plan for any of us but gave Frances the sense of security she needed right after the shootings. It would have to do until she felt ready to travel on her own.

Bob, Frances, and I had had a long first day in the new epoch by the time we sat down to eat our first home cooked evening meal together. A meal I constructed on the fly, so it was not my best culinary effort. Nevertheless, it was nutritious, and I've done worse.

As soon as we sat down to eat, Frances petulantly said, "I can't eat this food. I never eat anything that had a face or a mother. I'd rather starve!" Then she sat on their hands and aimed a pout at me, the cook.

I was about to point out peanut butter and bread reside in the kitchen cabinet when judicious Bob placed his hand on mine and said, "Gus and I prepare food for each other as an expression of caring. You *may eat with us or prepare your own food, your choice.*"

"I just said I can't eat this food and why. I can fast, the Lord Buddha fasted when people put nothing in his begging bowl to eat."

"Or you can eat the mixed vegetables, rice, and salad, they didn't have faces or mothers. Don't expect to be coddled beyond my removing this filet of red snapper from your dish."

"You said all that to make me feel bad."

"Your lack of manners is regrettable. But we will enjoy all or part of this meal Gus made for us."

Frances heard Bob and seemed to consider his words. "You're right, I was rude, I'm sorry. I'll eat everything but the fish. Thank you, Gus."

"Now that we know your dietary restrictions, there will be an empty space on your future dinner plates. When feasible, we'll seek an alternative main course for you."

"Thank you, because I need protein to grow up."

"There are eggs in the fridge, can beans and peanut butter in the cupboard, help yourself. When we go food shopping, you can come along and expand your larder options. I hate to be blunt Frances, but either you work with us or figure out an alternative. It has been a long day for all of us, and I don't even coddle eggs."

Frances defiantly put back the pout on her face, and I glared at Bob. I'd had enough of Frances' obstinance and Bob's schoolroom diplomacy. "Frances, I had my secretary research other housing for you, just in case this wasn't a good fit, and so far, it isn't."

"Why am I not surprised?"

"Mr. Hadley hadn't looked too hard. The Gay Community Center operates a shelter for LGBTQ homeless youth down by the piers. Catholic Charities has temporary housing for troubled teenage runaways near midtown and the river, and the city government runs an emergency group home for wayward teens nobody wants, located in Staten Island. It's on a barge in the bay. My secretary said you'd be eligible for an open bed when any of them has one."

"I'm not surprised you both have a mean streak. In my experience all men are brutes."

"We know you've been through a lot. However, if you intend to live here, it is required you work with us to make it palatable for everyone."

A movie's worth of chick-flick emotions flowed across Frances' face and then stopped and froze at contrite. She dipped her head and ate succotash, rice, finished her salad, and was in much better spirits finishing a second bowl of vanilla ice cream topped with maple syrup. As Bob started to clear the table, Frances jumped-up and said, "Let me ... please."

Bob said, "Let's do it together. Gus cooked, we ate, we cleanup."

When Bob was about to toss Frances' red snapper in the garbage, she stopped him and put it aside on a paper towel. Then after dinner cleanup, she hand-fed our cat the fish filet. Our tabby barely tolerated Bob and me, seeing her eat from Frances' hand was wholly out of character for our condescending feline.

For Tuesday's dinner Bob made a Denver omelet, fresh steamed spinach dressed with olive oil, garlic, and pine nuts. Being a multitasker, he also prepared oven-roasted finger potatoes, baby-arugula grape-tomato salad, and pantone for dessert. Frances insisted on doing the after-dinner cleanup on her own. I was beat, and Bob looked the same, so no strong objections were tendered. Then Frances did school homework, and we all went to bed on time. Initially Bob and I planned to give Frances a key to our apartment after she proved herself travel ready. But after a rocky start, I decided to hold the key until after she met Joey.

Wednesdays we usually ate leftovers or ordered takeout, but Frances insisted on making her marinara spaghetti sauce with no-meat-meatballs, green salad, garlic-bread, and no-bake brownies from a box for dessert. Other than carbohydrate intensive, it was filling and tasty. And she created it from what we had on hand, except the salad and brownies.

Bob and I did the after meal K.P. During casual conversation about fueling the cars, going to the country house on Friday came up for the first time in Frances' hearing. She lost composure and said, "I hate bats, spiders, ticks, and mosquitoes, they spread horrible diseases that kill you slowly. I'm not going. I'd rather be knifed to death in a welfare shelter for pregnant teens."

I looked at Bob and he just shook his head exasperated. So, I said, "Are you pregnant?"

"You should know better than ask me that."

"There is someone living at our country house we'd like you to meet."

"Who?"

"A contemporary of yours who is also experiencing unavoidable inconvenient life challenges. He prefers the personal pronoun ze. If you choose not to come with us, make suitable alternative arrangements with my secretary for weekend accommodations. We don't know you well enough to leave alone in our home."

"If you insist! I'm certainly not going to the wilderness to be eaten by hungry wild animals. I'm a proper city girl. I'll have your madam secretary make me a reservation at a decent shelter … or you can leave me on any street corner. I DON'T CARE, I'M A SURVIVOR."

"Gosh, Frances, does that mean you're canceling going to the sanitation department tomorrow for your family's things. Remember, right after school … like we planned."

"OH THAT! I was imagining wild animals eating me alive and completely forgot … damn, damn, DAMN. I need more clothes to wear to school, it is an imperative. Do you two know the word imperative?"

"I have a rough idea. Do you want to have my secretary, Leonard, find you a vacant shelter bed before or after we visit the sanitation department tomorrow?"

"Why wait, you can see I have an aversion to being devoured by dangerous wild things in their own habitat."

"Look around, we don't have extra storage space in this apartment. But we do at our country house. How about we deal with one of your problems at a time."

"That makes sense, we'll go to the sanitation department first. Just like we planned, and who knows, maybe they'll have storage space I can rent."

****

The rotund, bowling ball bald, cigar-chomping, rumpled-bureaucrat in the small grimy side-office at the sanitation garage was Mr. Oswald Osborn, supervisor. That was what the big brass plaque on his little gray-metal desk said. He seemed not to notice us entering his office. It appeared he was asleep with his eyes open. I waved Frances' eviction notice to get attention, and he reached out disinterested and took it without blinking or looking at us. Then he stirred slightly and after a quick perusal, addressed a greasy-grimy, muck-encrusted computer-tablet lying flat on his desk. Still not acknowledging us, his arm shot out and pointed to a pile of furniture leaning against dumpster number fourteen. It was located, along with many others full dumpsters, against the garage's left-side wall. The right side of the building had double the number of empty dumpsters as the filled ones on the left. They were probably in preparation for the deaths and evictions expected from a pandemic.

Spewing out odorous-cigar-smoke, Mr. Osborn finally spoke. "You have a short time before your property becomes landfill. Don't dillydally!" Then he seemed to zone off again. Meanwhile all around us huge noisy smelly garbage-compressor trucks were pulling into the garage, backing up to the missing rear wall and dumping their contents into garbage-barges below floating in the river.

Back on the left side of the building I counted fifty dumpsters filled with families' belongings, awaiting a new life as landfill. Watching me scoping out his territory, then speaking out of the corner of his mouth, Mr. Osborn conspiratorially half-whispered, "There's storage-space-rentals located across the street and up the block. They sell cardboard boxes, and tape, tell them Oswald sent you, and you'll get a professional discount."

After a quick glance at her family's historical artifacts, I left Frances, and went across the street and up the block. The pimply faced young counterman at the storage room rental business looked up from his first-year algebra textbook, and said, "No vacancy, sorry we're full up."

Nevertheless, he sold me ten large size flat-folded boxes, and two rolls of strapping tape to secure them into big cubes. After a little haggling, without mentioning Oswald Osborn, we agreed on a fee to hold Frances' boxes when full, till Friday.

When I returned to the sanitation garage, Frances had dumpster fourteen's lids up, and seemed frozen-transfixed contemplating the cacophony of its contents. To my eye two thirds of the contents appeared to be a hodgepodge of clothes and shoes. One third of the space closest to me held household items too small to be with furniture outside the dumpster.

"How do you want to attack this?"

At my words, Frances stirred and dove into the dumpster. She started sorting through the mélange that was her family's wardrobe and tossed only her clothes out of the dumpster. That created piles on the dirty concrete floor. Quickly, I assembled boxes to put the salvaged items in. I labeled boxes, shoes, outerwear, innerwear, and underwear. Getting organized helped me separate from the heartbreaking relics of human sorrow surrounding me. The sanitation garage wasn't neat and clean, like a cemetery keeps its business. This end of the line smelled bad and looked like post pandemonium. I could imagine the desperate human struggle in route to being possession less, and then all traces of previous existence erased by landfill.

Being hyper busy, Frances had redirected energy away from the misery of what we were doing, where, and why. To that purpose she got angry over not finding a sock's mate or complete underwear set. Particularly important, it seemed, was missing training bras with matching panties. Finally registering the enormity of the confusion, she broke down crying over the futility of the task. I stopped assembling boxes, leaned over the dumpster's metal edge, and hugged her shoulders until sobbing stopped. Cried out, Frances dried her eyes on a sleeve, put on a determined face and dove back in searching for missing cherished garments.

At last, my box building chore finished I took a good look at Frances' family heirlooms. Leaning against dumpster number fourteen was worn-down cheap furniture. Stacked behind them were large, framed pictures. On closer inspection, the artwork was pencil or charcoal sketches on paper, matted, mounted under glass in wood frames. The subjects were life-like portraits, except for a full-length nude of an anatomically correct full-breasted adult woman, wearing Frances McDermott's preteen face. All the framed art was dated and signed by the artist, Frances M. McDermott.

"Frances, what do you want to salvage besides your clothes?"

"That's all I need right now."

I put the framed art next to the boxes of clothes for reconsideration and investigated the third of the dumpster that wasn't clothes. Mixed in with a toaster, blender, rolling pin, and the like, I retrieved folders full of Frances' unframed artwork, some finished, some learning pieces, all potential treasures later in life.

Then near the bottom of the dumpster I found binders of family photos on top of a twelve by ten by eight-inch metal strong-box. The push button lock had been engaged with a key. I persuaded the box to open its mouth by jiggling in my gold pen knife blade. Inside the box was a birth certificate for baby boy Francis Michael

McDermott, his baptism and immunization records, also medical and primary school documents. Under the baby's papers were mother and father's birth certificates, marriage license, and assorted other legal papers. I calculated from the dates given, Francis was four years-old when his eighteen-year-old parents were legally married. At the bottom of the metal strong-box, hidden under a cardboard false-bottom was a $100,000 life insurance policy on Frances' mother's life, with Francis the beneficiary. There were also three $20,000 policies, one on each family member's life, with father and mother as beneficiaries. Then to my surprise, there were four $250,000 life insurance policies on Katherine Coach's life, two named Francis and two her mother as beneficiary.

"Frances, who is Katherine Coach to you?"

"She's my mom's mom. She was a big deal executive in insurance before she had a stroke."

"Do you know her?"

"We used to visit her in a nursing home until she forgot who we were. Then mom said there was no point going, it was a long tiring trip on two buses, a train, and a taxi upstate. She was nice to me before she stopped remembering."

"Is she still alive?"

"As far as I know, why are you collecting all that junk? My yellow bra is still missing!"

I pulled objects out of the cardboard box I'd saved from the dumpster. I held them up high for Frances to get a good look. "These family photos albums might mean something to you in the future. If you end up living on the street, you can sell your artwork. *Big reveal,* did you know about these life insurance policies?"

"No. Throw that crap away, *I need my training bra.*"

"If these are kosher, and there still is something called double indemnity, the insurance documents I'm holding could be your ticket to emancipation. But you'll need a good lawyer and probably a financial custodian."

"Oh my, my, *my,* wouldn't that be wonderful ... Uh, could you help me find this sock's mate, they used to be my favorite pair? See how jumbled everything is? What's that look on your face, do you think finding a sock in this mess is hopeless? Well, I don't know anything about insurance, and it sounds boring."

Then Frances stopped talking, color drained from her face, and it looked like more tears were ready to roll. Instead, she put on a brave face and said, "Oh look, I just found my yellow bra, it goes with these panties, see, aren't they lovely?" She held up what looked to be a new ensemble, bra right hand, panties in left.

"Good for you."

"Oh, Gus, you look fretful. Don't worry I have most of my basics already, you can forget the sock. I do not want to waste your whole afternoon on little old me, let us get out of here. Maybe we could stop for ice cream to cheer you up. I'll buy, one scoop each, okay."

I did not feel fretful, however that feels. But that word might fit how Frances looked, remembering how her belongings came to reside at the sanitation garage on their way to being landfill. Pointing at the eight full boxes of clothing plus another one I filled with bric-a-brac and documents, I asked, "Where do you suggest putting your things? You know space in the apartment is tight."

"I guess renting a storage locker would be too expensive, right? But now that I found most of my good clothes, it would be a shame to leave them in this stinky dreary place." She looked ready to cry again.

"Did I mention we have unused storage space at our country house? You could take your time deciding what to keep and wash, or not, over as many weekends you'd need. Just so you know we have a working washing machine in the basement. It's old, but rattles and rolls the dirt out with its own unique rhythmic style."

"Oh no, I'll wash the delicate things by hand. Hmm, yes, I guess going into the untamed wilderness will have to happen, like it or not. You have a house there."

"In that case let's leave directly after your school on Friday. We wouldn't want to keep hungry animals waiting for their dinner."

"It's not funny!"

"Neither are you, or the well-mannered rural boy living in our country house. If he is unprovoked. Do you know the word provoke?"

"I'm not stupid, you will always choose a real boy over me."

"Don't make Bob or me choose. You know how to be nice. If you and Joey have differences, work them out between you."

"Or else."

"The place across the street has no vacancies for storage-rooms but will hold your boxes for twenty-four hours."

With a grownup's cynical half smile Frances said, "That is very kind of them."

"Yes, and they only want ten bucks a box for the kindness."

Showing me a serious face, she said, "I'll pay you back, I promise!"

"We don't expect repayment. Tonight, is my turn to cook, let's get a move on and buy groceries. Or I'll have to feed you gruel."

"What's gruel?"

"You don't want to know. Read Charles Dickens."

"Gus, can I ask you something?"

"Shoot."

"My family's story aside. Is there some purpose for throwing peoples things in with collected garbage and calling it landfill?"

"Beats me, why do you ask?"

"Everything in life is supposed to have a purpose. Do you think it makes landfill richer or decompose faster?"

"What I think, and two dollars won't buy you a decent size single scoop of ice cream. Trust me Francis you don't want to hear my thoughts on evictions and homelessness or the greed that drives them."

"I just don't get it. How does it make sense to throw peoples' things away and leave them nothing to rebuild with? I mean how could anybody ever get their life back, starting at zero."

"If we don't go food shopping, it will be tasteless gruel for dinner tonight."

"I hate to be a pain, but I'd really like to understand what we saw today. I will think about it for a long time."

"My opinion won't make you feel better."

"Oh please, please, PLEASE TELL ME something. I don't look tough but trust me I can take a punch and give as good as I get. I even survived public school."

"I get that vibe off you."

"Even if it weren't my family's stuff, it was other somebodies' things, how they lived. It was heart breaking to see what happens if you can't pay your rent."

"All right, you win my stubborn young friend. Keep in mind this is only my point of view."

"Tell me."

"A visible pool of roughly surviving homeless keeps the struggling masses besieged rather than in revolt for a decent life. Consequently, the pitiful existence of the hopelessly downtrodden keeps menial labor costs low, social welfare costs a pittance, no address no benefits, and profits stay obscenely high for the soulless greedy."

"In school they call it capitalism. What we saw today makes more sense as punishment for being poor, rather than business practice. We'd better talk about happy things before I start crying again."

"What would you like for dinner …?"

"I make a dynamite meatless meatloaf with tofu, bulgur, fresh herbs, a medley of mushrooms, served in a tasty thick brown gravy over rice. The privileged few who have eaten it say it is delicious. If you think you'd like meatless meatloaf, I could prepare it tonight."

"To what do I deserve such a gracious offer?"

"I'd like to repay your kindness taking me away from my hopeless lot in life. I saw where I came from up close today. It doesn't compare with how you and Bob live."

"You know what we'd appreciate even more than you cooking dinner?"

"What?"

"If you adapt to our lifestyle. Bob and I love the contrast of high energy city living for work, punctuated with regular serene intervals of rural peace and quiet. If you promise to sincerely give it a chance, I'll relinquish my dinner duties to you for tonight."

"How do you balance exciding city living with boring country life? I thought the two were incompatible."

"We drive up Friday afternoon or evening and return early Monday morning. Frances, expect to sleep three nights in healthy rural oxygen-rich-air. The abundant trees create air that counters the effects of breathing lung-clogging dirty-city-air."

"Oh, really, nobody told me it's healthy way out there in the wilderness. In fact, I thought it was the opposite. Clean air is supposed to be good for the complexion."

"Good to know."

"I keep forgetting to be kind and not such a handful. I'll try harder to be a nice girl."

****

It was impossible to fit nine large boxes and three adult size humans in one car. So, we took two. Frances chose to ride with Bob. He spoke teenage vernacular like a native, and I don't. Bob had also been helping Frances with remedial homework from her new progressive school. Having moved around a lot her educational fundamentals were spotty, but she was a quick learner.

As it happened, I arrived at the country house way ahead of my husband and our latest house guest transitioning to foster child. Once again, I proved what Bob insinuates regularly about having a lead foot on the gas pedal. To be fair, my car was built to go fast, so it would be wrong to deny its birthright.

At the sound of my car pulling up to the front-porch, Joey followed by Hans came out of the house. After our usual brief welcome-home straight boy hug, Joey and I unloaded Frances' boxes and placed them up on the porch, near the front door. Hans supervised our work, sniffing each box into place. It was with great effort, self-control, and our stern admonitions, Hans did not lift his leg to mark boxes for territorial inclusion.

I no sooner shut my car's trunk-lid than Bob and Frances drove up. After a brief greeting hug with Bob, Joey put his hand out to Frances for, I guess, a hello shake. Frances looked at Joey's hand then in his eyes and stepped forward and gave him a brittle-spinster like embrace. Frances, Bob, Joey, and I immediately set to unloading the second car's boxes. Meanwhile, Hans walked a circle around Frances, sniffing. He looked confused, possibly trying to decipher gender pheromones. The visual female must have given off male scents. Little gets by Hans' nose. As Hans moved from second to third sniffing go round Frances put a hand down to his snout and after a few closeup sniffs, she petted him. Then with tail wags Hans gave the stranger his approval, and in his mind, she was allowed stay.

"Hey, gang, what do you think, should we go for pizza tonight? Frances, the village also has a Chinese fast food, but they refuse to hold back on MSG. They lace everything with it."

Frances nodded her head yes; she was listening as I spoke. But the expression on her face said, *"It is what I expected, primitive."*

Joey was paying alert attention and spoke up filling a momentary void. "I hand chopped deer-meat with bacon for burgers, and we have unpreserved franks on hand if anyone wants a cookout tonight?"

"Joey, Frances is a vegetarian."

"Does that mean she's a Seventh Day Adventist?" He unconsciously dropped his right hand to the front of his cutoff jeans.

"Since you are interested, Mr. Joseph Hall, I was raised Catholic. Am now an atheist and what I believe or not has nothing to do with what I eat other than to save the planet."

I could see on Joey's face he was put-off by the snippy newcomer's uppity tone. He was about to give Frances a stinging retort about saving the planet when Bob put a supportive hand on Joey's shoulder. Hans was studying the two teens and appeared to have chosen sides, Frances lost. I doubt he knew the difference between the word *meat or vegetable*. Just in case I called Hans to me and changed his mind by rubbing his snout, then chest.

Frances read the change in temperature correctly and said, "Why don't you men go ahead and have your cook-out. I'm not really hungry after that long drive."

Bob and I had never seen Joey acting the host before, and were surprised when he said, "I could grill vegetable kabobs for you … if you want."

"What do you have?"

"There are ripe vegetables in the garden, and we have rice on hand. Dan and Bill left us a set of steel-skewers we never use but they won't have to be prepared."

When Frances made a face at steel-skewers, Joey said, "We also have bamboo skewers, but they must be soaked in warm water, or they'll burn on the grill."

Frances perked up, put on a friendly face, and said, "Let me help, we could soak the bamboo in hot water while picking, washing, and chopping vegetables."

"Sounds like a plan." Joey looked to be deciding if joint control was better than loss of control.

"Which brand of barbeque sauce do you use?"

"I make my own, it's part of living off the land. The base is fresh tomatoes, then onion, honey, cider vinegar, fresh herbs, and a few serrano peppers. Everything is organic, right from our garden. I cook it down to thick and gooey. Most people say it tastes better than store brands."

I sensed a door in the wall between them opened when Frances visually relaxed and casually said, "Sounds yummy, do you have brown rice?"

"Yes, Dan and Bill left a big bag. We usually use reconstituted white rice, it cooks faster."

"Will Dan and Bill be joining us for dinner?"

'No. They were the previous owners of this place and got divorced so Bob and Gus could buy it."

The on-guard stranger among us stiff apprehensive mood dissipated as Joey and Frances exchanged sincere smiles. Then the two kids headed into the house to soak bamboo skewers and wash and toast brown rice before setting out to pick vegetables to grill. On the way Joey gave Frances a quick, finger pointing tour of the house and grounds.

Bob and I used big rocks to secure a canvas tarpaulin over the nine cardboard boxes on the front-porch. Hans watched us dismayed, we were interfering with his job by covering new and interesting scents in need of his urine marking inventory. His unspoken question hung heavy between us; *How could you interfere with my responsibility to pee on all new property to endorse it?*

Without opposition Joey designated himself the night's grill-master. He showed pride preparing our first meal as a family of five, counting Hans. Being grill-master gave Joey a chance to show-off skills he had grown up honing. He did an impressive typical-boy trick twirling tongs and spatulas while flipping food on the fire. The food was tasty, and Bob and I were exhausted after a demanding work week including formalizing Frances' stay with us. My mind centered on taking a long hot shower and drifting off to sleep with Bob tucked in my arms. He looked to be in a similar logy place. Yawning, but still a teacher in control, he said, "What do you kids want to do this weekend?"

"I absolutely must sort through my wardrobe, wash everything thoroughly and then iron."

"Want a hand with that?"

"Thank you, Joseph, but it is a one-person job."

"I'm the only one here who knows how to get maximum clean out of that old washing machine. It is finicky and stalls out if you don't baby it in the agitation cycle. The drive belt wheels are worn-down."

"How do you fix that?"

"With strategically placed kicks and pinch the drive belt. They don't make replacement parts since the company's name moved to Asia."

"Oh gosh if you want to help … I'll only need the machine for my cottons-clothes. The delicate I hand wash. Do you have racks for air-drying frilly garments?"

"Dan and Bill left cotton-rope-clotheslines behind the house. I use them for my clothes, except bright colors I dry inside over chair backs. You probably know sun fades colors, right?"

"I most certainly do."

"If you want, I have hemp-cord we could stretch in the basement to air-dry your wash."

"Joseph you will make some woman a wonderful husband. You cook and do laundry. Can you sew too?"

"Actually, I'm indeterminate about my future domestic prospects. But I don't mind sorting dirty clothes, running the machine, or whatever. I like helping."

"Well, if you have nothing better to do. I'd love the company and to get to know *you* and your indeterminate domestic situation better. Do all country boys use such big words?"

"Hardly, Bob and Gus gave me a vocabulary builder book as a gift. From anyone else it would have been a punishment, but they make Scrabble fun. A word to the wise, watch your P&Qs around them, they get math intense also."

"Thanks for the advice, but Bob's been helping me catch up at school. I do know of what you speak."

"What do you say after breakfast tomorrow we do your laundry? That way you get the most sun to dry heavy light-colored garments outside. The weather is reported to be sunny all day."

"Wow, and you're a weatherman too, I'm duly impressed."

"Up here in rural America the weather can be dangerous, best be on top of it."

"How do you mean?"

"Late fall to spring, ice storms come on with little warning if you're not paying attention."

"I was afraid of something like that out here in the wild."

"Ice looks pretty, like everything is covered in glass. But is so slippery you can't walk without falling.

"Who would have thought pretty could be dangerous? I had a feeling I shouldn't come out to wild weather country."

Yawing big Bob said, "Joey, stop scaring Frances."

"Frances, do you ever wear jeans? Some people like to sun fade them. See my cutoffs, I do."

"I have two pair of 501s I wouldn't mind sun bleaching. Actually, except for a couple of cotton smocks and socks, most of my cottons are hateful boy's clothes. No. Wait. To be honest my baggy cotton T-shirts are in fact unisex and they could use some sun fading too."

"If you don't mind my asking, why do you own clothes you hate? If it were me, I'd toss them in the rag bin."

"At my last school I was required to wear boy's clothes on gym days. The brutes only allowed me unisex clothing two days a week. And I could never wear dresses or skirts to school without it causing a big bruhaha ending in weeks of detention."

"That sounds unfair."

"At my old school *they were clothing fascist.* I look my best in dresses and suites with skirts, they show off my legs."

"I hate rules that are ridiculous."

"At my last school I was only allowed to use the boys' bathrooms. I can tell you it got dicey."

"How'd that work out … like I can't guess?"

"My father was good for one thing; he gave me a punching bag and boxing gloves when I was four."

"Why so young?"

"When he *was* around, he dreamed I'd make him a lot of money as a professional prize fighter. So, he drilled me how to box. I may only be a girl, but I know how, when, and where to deliver haymakers. Once I learned girls like to jump rope just like boxers. I skip rope every chance I get."

"We like to run. Are you a runner?"

"No, I skip rope for exercise."

"If you don't mind me getting in your business, I've overheard Gus and Bob talk about your new progressive high school. How's it compared to the old one you mentioned?"

"Just so you hear it from me Joseph. I'm a girl trapped in a boy's body, *so my personal business* has always been public news. I know I'm a freak even if present company pretends otherwise."

"Sorry, I didn't mean to offend you."

"That's all right, it was going to come out anyway. It's just as well we get that out of the way first thing. You can blame me for my pitiful plight, everyone does."

"My foster dads taught me right from-the-get-go, blame doesn't solve problems. But since you mentioned this, no offense intended, but so you know. I like being male."

"Good for you. I'm 100% female in a male wrapper and I was not okay with it when I found out."

"When did you know?"

"I must have been a toddler just learning the difference between sitting down to pee or standing-up to do it. That's when I uncovered a big mistake was made putting me in the wrong body *and* I wasn't the only one with a problem about it."

"Okay, now I understand how you found out but not why you had to."

"I never understood that."

"Then, back to my original question, have you compared your new school to the old one?"

"Yes. Even though the fall term hadn't started, I went to orientation classes with nine other transfer students. The school wanted to bring us up to speed *on how they do things.* So far, it's nice, all their bathrooms are unisex. My gym class is mixed genders, and the showers are individual, private, with doors you can lock. I'm not the only gender nonconforming student and *they have no dress code.* The orientation teacher said even straight boys wear dresses sometimes, on dress up day just for fun."

"That sounds cool. How are their academic standards?"

"I mentioned Bob's helping me catch up to their scholastic level because my family never stayed in one place long. Overall, I'd say my new school is the best I've known. Once I measure up."

"Frances, look at these guys, they're falling asleep at the table. Okay, to bed with you two, I'll clean up."

"Let me help you, Joseph, and in return you can show me to my room … if you don't mind?"

"Sure, you got it. Around here we all help each other. It's a rule."

Bob and my concern that Joey and Frances would have territorial issues turned out for naught. The teens gave each other room and respect from the start and thus became weekend friends without a lot of hoopla. With lots of extra attention, Hans accepted demotion to fifth pack member.

CHAPTER 11. Oxford Online Physics, Lawyer Brick

First came the invigorating chill in the air and necessity of a light jacket while running. Left alone and feeling lonely, Frances joined our weekend runs. She had stamina. Then too soon there were bracing temperatures and wearing medium weight outerwear, as most green leaves turned vivid colors. The colorful leaves in the country were beautiful, while down in the city the leaves stayed green. Bob and I were guardedly self-congratulatory having gotten the kids set for and started on a new fall school year.

Right after Frances' junior year in high school began at the urban progressive school, Joey's traditional public high school senior year started with an irreconcilable problem. Joey loudly proclaimed to all who would listen his advanced-placement physics teacher hated him for no reason. As Bob's research quickly found out, the hater was the only physics teacher in the whole county, and the pretty fall leaves began to fall.

My solution was to hire a tutor. Joey vehemently declined the offer saying, "I don't need a tutor, I'm over prepared already. My teacher, Mr. Ratsneer, is out to get me." We paid attention, Joey was not a complainer and therapy made him more demonstrative.

Bob's idea was for Joey to drop physics. In high school parlance, Joey would "take a W." In my vernacular he would withdraw from the class before it negatively affected his GPA. Then he would take physics either at the junior college or online during the summer. Joey declined taking a "W." Graduation with classmates since moving up north had significance for him. It was probably an indicator therapy was working.

Against Bob and my best advice, Joey's solution was to stick it out with the ogre-teacher and pray for a miracle. If a miracle did not materialize, he would quit school and enlist in the military on his eighteenth birthday.

At that point I wanted a face-to-face sit down with Joey's physics teacher Mr. Ratsneer. Bob and Joey's guidance counselor Ms. Limane strongly advised against my direct-action approach. It seems the physics teacher was quirky, maybe insane, but highly credentialed. Ms. Limane said, "He would be difficult to impossible for this small rural county school district to replace if he felt threatened. That wouldn't help Joey and all the other kids that need physics to go forward."

Through my secretary Leonard's covert investigation, on his free time, we discovered Joey's physics-genius teacher had been dismissed from four high school teaching jobs in as many states. It was hinted he had a pathological fear of his students. To counteract his phobia Ratsneer picked the reportedly best student each semester as a sacrificial victim.

The whole class was told the sacrificial-goat student would adversely skew the grade curve for the entire class. Then the whipping boy was continuously and mercilessly harangued, harassed, humiliated, and then ultimately failed at the end of semester. It was Ratsneer's way to keep the other students docile. Psychologically destroying the best student in front of his peers let the teacher be less intimidated and hide his pedagogic deficits.

Each year, 99% of the physic students gave Dr. Ratsneer high praise at evaluation time because they had not been publicly shamed. And he was more than generous giving out final grades based on their evaluations of him. Although his methods were unorthodox, erratic, and irrational, teacher Ratsneer motivated his students to score satisfactory or better on standardized Physic exams. Like Joey, they came to physics well prepared.

If the situation ran its usual course, academic options to correct a final failed physics grade were nonexistent. Not graduating with his class was viewed by Joey as another of his life's tragedies. Making up the failed class in summer school was a blemish on his permanent record and proof to him of his deep held belief he was a loser.

Bob sternly talked me down from physically conveying a necessary correction Dr. Ratsneer sorely needed to learn. Then later Bob kyboshed my other brilliant idea of convincing one of Joey's wrestling coaches, who liked my looks, to put teacher Ratsneer in traction to keep Joey grade's eligible for the wrestling team. It was hard for me to see and hear my foster son being tormented and not do something to alleviate the suffering. My government had trained me to correct injustice by whatever means necessary.

Over an ordinary business lunch, my vexation at Joey about to drop out of high school slipped unintentionally into the conversation, and a colleague saved the day. Months before Frances came to live with us, my coworker Charles Swanson met Joey on a visit to our country house for a weekend that included horseback riding at a neighbor's horse farm and whitewater rafting with our family. A fun time was had by all.

During that visit, Joey showed Charles how to repair his oldest antique motorcycle with a length of plastic-tubing and two cinch-clamps. Expert mechanics had told Charles his ancient motorbike was irreparable due to unavailability of parts. Charles had not forgotten Joey's kindness sharing a logical, commonsense, quick-easy jerry-rigged engine repair. In addition, the two bonded during a rougher than usual river raft ride.

When Charles learned over lunch of Joey's intractable academic future, due to lack of physics credit, he said, "I just may have a solution, let me get back to you."

Two days later at work, Charles popped his head in my office door and said, "I hope you don't mind I took the liberty to call in some favors to register Joey in an online freshmen physics course."

"Where?"

"Oxford University in London, England." I knew Charles had been a Rhodes Scholar and had graduate degrees from Oxford, but it never occurred to me he had the means to save the day for our boy.

"How'd you do that?"

"I finessed a couple of my university professors I'm still in contact with. We'll throw them a little more consulting work from time to time to say thank you."

"Do they know Joey lives in the United States?"

"That was a selling point. They like being superior to their barbarous former colonists who mercilessly torment public school physic students. It became a matter of academic honor. Think Joey is up to the challenge?"

"For sure."

Convincing Joey to replace his daily physics classroom psychological torture with an online course was easier than Bob and I expected. At that point he had accepted he was a failure deserving of the degradation from his teacher and thus unworthy to graduate with a 4.0 GPA.

His guidance counselor liked Joey and got on board with us. She willingly took on the extra paperwork to make international credits fit seamlessly into Joey's high school transcript. As a result, Joey would graduate in May, on time with his classmates. And he no longer had to suffer public humiliation at the hands of a vicious teacher badly in need of a physical tune-up. Before help arrived, Joey was a bottomless pool of self-pity. Then once he tested up to English freshmen college standards, he flourished with unlimited creative energy that had been clogged by self-deprecation.

****

Just as the pretty fall leaves were swirling around in piles on the ground and winter made its move, our busy lives adapted accordingly to heavy parkas and gloves. Then our new normal developed a wrinkle when Joey announced, "I just knew physics was too good to be true."

"What's up?"

"Oxford requires I go there to sit for the final exam. I just found out by email, none of us noticed the fine print before. They just informed Ms. Limane my last appeal failed, there are no exceptions for granting credit. These guys calling the shots are not Charles Swanson's people, these names are from some stuffy academic committee and are as inflexible as cement."

"When is the exam?"

"December tenth, which means I'm still behind the eight ball for graduating in May. What did I expect, right? Born a loser, always a loser."

"How are you doing with the physics?"

"Did you know that English academic standards are much higher than in the United States, no one mentioned that when I started. But to answer your question, I got all A's so far."

"Good for you."

"It's a shame I can't get the credit I've worked for, and so many of you went to bat for me besides. But it was worth the look on Dr. Ratsneer's face when I dropped his class, and accidentally spilled his coffee all over the notes on his desk. Apparently, he'd forgotten, some dry ink runs when wet?"

"Let me see what is possible before we plan a funeral for your British physics grade."

Joey made the international sign for screwy by making finger circles in the air by his right ear. "All the way to England just to sit for a one-hour exam, now that's totally crazy!"

"How about you do your work and I do mine? We have time yet. Do you have a passport?"

"American citizens don't need one for EU countries."

"Heard of Brexit, go to the post office and get a passport."

****

Meanwhile down in the high energy city, the gay community center put us in touch with the gay lawyers' referral service. Frances was given the names of three lawyers and told to choose one. Then when she asked if any were transsexual, she got three different names and phone numbers. We did a conference call with each attorney on the second list, explaining Frances' wish for emancipation from minor status, and complicated life insurance issues due to murder. The first lawyer was not interested, she only did wills and real estate, the second only did transsexual guardianship in family court, and the third primarily oversaw high visibility criminal cases. I suggested we use the first list. Instead, Frances called the third transsexual lawyer back, Franklyn Brick, and explained the more traumatic details of her case.

Coordinating a convenient appointment time with the busy lawyer's male secretary and my secretary Leonard, using everyone's hectic schedules, turned into a battle of wills. Heard from just outside my usually open office door it sounded like a fight between feral secretaries. When the fur stopped flying, Frances and Bob had to miss the first half of a school day, and I had to skip out early on an important meeting to accommodate the attorney's court appearance schedule.

Franklyn Brick was about five-foot nine inches tall, at maybe two hundred and twenty pounds of what looked like hard muscle. Lawyer Brick looked and walked like a muscle-bound, middle-aged athlete. Photos on his inner office wall, mixed among diplomas from prestigious private universities, showed Franklyn wearing a singlet holding weightlifting trophies aloft. An impressive mahogany wall unit held trophies shown in the photos, along with lawyerly award plaques, and antique leather bound first edition law books.

After bone-crushing handshakes all around, Frances asked, "If I'm not too forward, what was your birth name?"

"What was yours?"

"Francis, with an i, I want to legally change the i to e, and either drop my middle name or change it to Michelle. I was given Francis Michael at birth and need to change it to represent myself accurately. But only *after* all the insurance claims are settled. Your turn!"

Looking at Bob and I the lawyer said, "Are we playing twenty questions?"

Francis didn't give up. "If you don't mind, what was your birth name?"

"I was given the name Fay-Lynn and transitioned to Franklyn. You can call me Frank. What can I do for you *today*, Francis?"

"Franklyn, can you help me become the woman I was born to be?"

"You look too young to be asking that question. Have you lived long enough to really know what you want?"

"I was a girl baby from birth, not the boy named on my birth certificate. I've lived long enough to correct the mistake of being in the wrong body. Don't condemn me to a life out of step with my entirety, it took a lot of work to look this good with wrong parts."

"I'm a criminal attorney I don't handle personal matters. Why were you referred?"

"The Gay Center said you're transsexual. Why won't you help me?"

"This is my criminal law office. It appears you need someone other than me to address your personal affairs."

"No. I decided you are the one I want to help me."

"Irreversible life altering decisions require years of maturity, a team of trained professionals, and should never be undertaken without decades of profound contemplation. You, young person, are still wet behind the ears. We are done."

"Stop! Do not tell me what I want is dangerous, I already know that. I'll probably die early from horrible cancers for being audacious enough to fix nature's mistake. If that's the price, I'll pay it. I'm paying every day as it is, and I'll pay your fee. The crime is I was born in the wrong body."

"I already said you are in the wrong place. What more do you want from me?"

"To be my lawyer and make my transition as easy as possible. It looks like you've done that for yourself. Now do it for me!"

"Just because I transitioned doesn't mean I have answers for going in the other direction, I don't. Like I said you are in the wrong office."

The exasperation I was feeling probably showed on my face. I couldn't hold back any longer and said, "I don't know why the Gay Center referred us to you. You are cold and uncaring. But at least give Francis the courtesy to hear her out."

"For your information mister, I'm good at defending career criminals. That's what I do. If you don't like my manner don't commit any serious crimes. Francis, say what you need to say."

"Okay, I have a therapist and medical team. Sorry if I wasn't clear, will you help me with the legal parts of transition; age restriction emancipation, officially change my name and gender identifier, and if an insurance company tries to cheat me, fight them? That's why I'm in your office taking up both our time."

"I do like to fight big insurance companies, though I don't do it often, I usually come out on top. If that sounds cold blooded, too bad it's the way I roll."

"Then you are who I want fighting for me."

"It is important you understand I don't bring my personal life into this office."

"When you look at me what do you see?"

"A pretty teenage girl with excellent fashion sense, on a budget, who knows how to understate her makeup. Someone groomed you well, was it these two palookas who look ready to take my head off?"

"Gus and Bob are my foster dads. If I took off my clothes, you'd see something unexpected. I'm a freak of nature. My goal in life is to change that. I want to show the world the real me, not freaky me."

"Sorry, I'm only a criminal lawyer."

"Why not help me anyway?"

"I won't repeat myself."

"You don't want to learn how much of a pest I can be."

"Threatening me won't get you what you want. Bigger, badder guys have tried and failed."

"I'm not leaving your office until you agree to work with me. You are who I want to fight the system stacked against me."

"I don't have time for this. Nevertheless, you've piqued my curiosity. Tell you what, if you can accept my taking the fifth on personal matters? Maybe we can review your life insurance issues."

"Okay, I'll agree to that. How much do you cost?"

"We'll get around to that after I have time to look over your case."

"Just so you know, all my sensibilities were murdered with my mother. Mostly these days I feel it was a shame my father's gun got stuck when it was my turn to die."

"Tell that to your psychiatrist."

"I have, and you tell the insurance companies Dad got what he deserved when he got that gun un-jammed and shot at cops. I know suicide was never my father's intention. His father and a brother died in shootouts with the police, none were suicidal. Believe it or not it was a source of their family pride."

"If you can convince a jury of that from the witness box, the insurance case should be ours."

"Good! Then if you don't mind my saying so, you present yourself as a very convincing man."

"Getting to this point took some work. It is nice to have the effort appreciated. Now, let's move on."

"I just paid you a compliment and you are welcome. What can you tell me about transitioning?"

"Don't be a pest. I don't like to repeat myself."

"You know what I need? A tranny uncle to give me advice the other professionals in my orbit won't or can't."

"You have two foster fathers. That's one more than the requisite number. Use one of them as an uncle."

"Please, please, PLEASE! You are the perfect addition to my posse of professionals. Just share what you know that can help me. I don't want anything personal."

"I'm going to have to bill you for another hour."

"Do it, I'll pay."

"I suspect it is easier going from female to male than the reverse … your path …"

"Why is that?"

"People are used to short men with small hands and feet. Tall women with big feet like you stand out."

"And if I have bottom surgery my prostate will be the only way to orgasm, right?"

The lawyer looked uncomfortable with Francis'

Bob and I looked at each other, feeling ignored and the lawyer clearly looked uncomfortable. To be included I said, "So, what is your plan of attack for Frances' legal case?"

His face showed he appreciated my rescue attempt. "I'm glad you asked, first my paralegal will do an intake packet with you three in her office, make an appointment. When we have all your required papers, and your check clears the bank, we will write letters and file forms on Frances' behalf. Then the boxing match begins"

"That's it?"

Lawyer Brick went on to explain Frances couldn't be emancipated until she was at least sixteen years old. Consequently, that work would wait until closer to her sixteenth birthday. His firm's immediate activity would be to get the insurance companies to pay up and for Frances to designate a financial custodian to invest her money and dole out a monthly allowance. Brick said, "Our first dance move after attaining death certificates will be to avoid a trial, they take forever. One ace we hold is no insurance company wants adverse publicity, particularly on a potentially high-profile case involving a police shooting that created an orphan they don't want to be accused of defrauding." He went on to say, the transsexual nature of this case means more unwanted notoriety for the insurance companies if they want to fight for every dollar. Once the insurance issues are settled, I will file for name change, gender designation change, and emancipation.

"You never mentioned your fee." Frances said this, I think, to maintain an active role in the conversation.

"I'd like a negotiated settlement for at least the face values of all the life insurance policies and my fees, and a percentage over and above what I get you above face value. The rest of your fee should be straight forward filing forms, notarizing and court costs. If that is what you came here for, we are done now."

Frances had her teeth sunk into the question like a bulldog. "I still don't know how much to expect to pay you."

"I won't take your money, little girl, however your case shakes out. But I have no objection to taking as much from an insurance company as I can legally bill. I charge $5,500 an hour and am worth every cent."

"Wow! How do criminals afford you?"

"They steal or rob to pay me upfront."

"Then I want a transsexual discount."

"Right. Looking over these photocopies you brought, when your grandmother passes, we can expect a battle with her nursing home, if they know she has life insurance. Her insurance money could set you up for life." After saying that, he stood, and it appeared he expected us to leave.

In my travels, the meeting felt unfinished, so I said, "Actually we have read if you changed her birth certificate gender. Then getting a driver's license and new social security card becomes much easier for us."

"She won't be eligible for a driver's license until age eighteen. Technically, gender change begins after bottom surgery is completed for male to females and that isn't legally permitted until age twenty-five. Don't be in a hurry for that, take all the time the necessary. Is there anything else?"

Frances looked edgy and said, "I know you want us to leave, and you are not a head-doctor, but can I ask you something, unrelated to why we are here?"

Franklyn Brick nodded his head yes, but his facial expression was in opposition.

"I'm getting tired of looking like and being treated like a child. For God's sake I'm going to be sixteen in a year. What can I do to get at least a modicum of respect … dress like the old reruns of the flying nun?

"Let me answer your question with a question. Is your boy part waking up?"

"HOW DID YOU KNOW THAT? It is like something from outer space came and attached itself between my legs to torment me. Since the murders it has been harassing me morning and night. I hate that part of my body and want it gone."

"Do I sense it is a love hate relationship?

"See! I knew you'd understand. Lately it betrays my femininity by demanding to be held and then soothed. But when I comfort it, it wants more and more touching leading to unspeakably alien happenings."

"Sounds normal for your age."

"It's not. I'm ashamed to tell you, it is like feeding a monster, the more I do it, the more it wants attention. What was an unwanted pee-spout when I was little, wants to take over my life."

"What's going on is called coming of age. Relax, you are learning about physical sex for one in preparation for a sex partner. It's like training wheels on a two-wheel bicycle."

"But what I want is breast implants and a vagina for a sex partner to enjoy with me."

"I'm a lawyer for criminals, not someone who gives transitioning advice, and most especially going from male to female. I don't like repeating myself."

"Oh please, please, PLEASE give me something more than multiple choice answers. I get I make people uncomfortable my life has made me uncomfortable. Sometimes I even forget I can be such a bitch."

"If you know that, stop doing it?"

"But people only tell me what they think I want to hear, just so I'll shut up and go away. I'm counting on you to speak truth to me."

"Only because you insist, and what I say is limited to my *unprofessional* opinion."

"Frank, I'll take what I can get."

"Frances, whatever you do, *don't have the bottom surgery* until middle age or older. What you return from the butcher shop with will be nowhere as useful or even work at all. In other words, no more fun orgasms for you and your lovers. When you are old, sex won't matter as much."

"I don't want to hear that!"

"Don't take my word for it, ask around. Talk to older women who had their pluming rearranged at your age. Conduct a survey, collect data, spend time online, arrive at the best-informed decision possible before taking any action, and then think some more. In the end be prepared to accept second-rate consequences if you do choose the knife over orgasms."

"Nobody ever speaks to me like that. What other gems from your experience can you bestow on me Uncle Frank?"

"Know this, if you hang with other pre-op trans-teens, expect them to be all about taking matters to an extreme, without understanding what they give up for an unrealizable fantasy. Frances you must know your own mind before taking irrevocable steps. Right now, you are learning to use what birth gave you. Focus on that, let nature guide you."

"I already knew I couldn't reverse the surgery. I'm a big girl, I can live with mistakes. My whole life has been one."

"So, why are you wasting my time?"

"You are saying if it's my destiny to be a freak, learn to be good one. *Is that what you are saying?*"

"Yes, compared to botched bottom surgery and wearing a smelly diaper for ever after. Would that be an acceptable future for you, incontinent all your days?"

"No. I don't want that!"

"Do you want to be a full partner with your future beloved husband, or a disfigured eunuch with limited if any sexual response?"

"Okay, I got it. You made your point I need a lot more information. Any last pearls of wisdom?"

"Don't sell compromise short. I can recommend top surgery based on my results. Leave the bottom surgery until medical technology has mastered the challenge using smart robots."

"WHY, Why, why robots?"

"Accuracy with predictable results, now get out of here. Do your research, think long and hard before any cutting below your waist, at least until old age."

"Thank you, Uncle Frank."

Listening to the lawyer and his new client talk gender-reassignment, I squelched an urge to zone out. I'd read somewhere, bottom surgeries, going in both directions universally had unsatisfactory outcomes compared to what nature originally provided. That was all the information I had, yet it fit what Brick told Frances.

But hey, it wasn't about me or Bob. When Frances came to live with us, we knew next to nothing about transsexuals. All we wanted was for her to be safe and happy, now that just got more complicated. I just heard Brick the lawyer recommend Francis accept a compromise to be a chick with a dick, and she agreed.

CHAPTER 12. Drawing

Fall semester at school has holidays like, Labor Day, Columbus Day, Halloween, Election Day, and Veterans Day. There are even three holidays my workplace recognizes, Thanksgiving, Black Friday, and Christmas-Hanukkah-Kwanza celebrated together in one day for Black Jews for Jesus employees and the rest of us.

Just because students were not in their classrooms during school holidays did not mean my man Bob was not. The love of my life was not home with his feet up relaxing while his students had time off for frivolity. He was at school designing and constructing new classroom bulletin board-displays and going to endless faculty meetings to increase his boredom quotient.

Even at home for the holidays, Bob was creating lesson plans or shopping online for discount school supplies, he paid for out of pocket. The board of education did not provide many supplies, like chalk for the chalkboard. Consequently, we thought it an act of consideration when Frances elected to spend her school holidays at the country house. She inferred it was to give us city dwellers more space with less distraction.

Meanwhile our kids had free time on their hands with no supervision during holidays. They were getting along well, even seemed to be bonding. We credit Hans and consider it a milestone Frances had gotten beyond fear of animals. In addition, the bulk of her clothes were in the country. She had a legitimate reason to spend time washing, mending, and ironing in the airy spacious house, without us under foot.

As the teens' friendship bloomed, Joey asked permission to teach Frances to ride Eleanor's motorcycle. It seemed an innovative idea to help Frances get beyond trauma, expand her travel limitations and get to know rural life beyond our safe cocoon.

After acquiring motorcycle safety skills and the requisite student driver's permit and insurance, the kids took day rides to nearby state parks. Then went further afield sightseeing unofficial natural wonders for picknicks. Joey expanded their territory to include mountaintop sunrise breakfasts, often not returning until after sunset. Our older foster child explained he was alleviating Frances' fear of bats, spiders, and ticks by meeting them on their turf. In hindsight, we were too busy with work and each other to pay requisite attention to the kids.

Then Hans started acting out in ways we had not seen. Hans' new neediness demanded Bob and I pay closer attention to what was going on with him. We had a family meeting about Hans, and I asked, "Do you kids think your field trips are negatively affecting Hans?"

Frances decided Hans was spending too much time alone during the week. Joey left for school at dawn and returned home at dusk after wrestling practice. Frances offered to help solve the problem by sketching Hans in different poses; Hans, alert ready to fetch, in flight-pursuit, mouth capture of an airborne doggy toy, and triumphant return of a thrown frisbee eager for another toss. Her photorealistic sketches were skillfully rendered fast, soon there were a lot of them needing mats, frames, and wall space.

Hans enjoyed the attention required to pose or even just sit and watch the drawing process with him the center of attention. Extra interest came from us and visitors admiring the mounted framed sketches in comparison to the proud tail wagging model accepting praise. Frances was soon no longer Hans' competition for Joey's time. She passed Han's finale test and was fully accepted into the family. But his behavior only truly returned to normal when all his humans were home with him.

Colder, more inclement weather curtailed motorcycle trips much to Hans' approval. Inside the warm cozy house during severe weather, Frances drew Bob, Joey, and me, individually, in pairs, and in assorted family groups with and without Hans staring in the drawing. Also, I or Bob would take an afternoon nap on the sunporch hammock and wake to find a too realistic drawing of our doze. I could not fault the artist for looking forward to my looming middle age in the drawing, time marches on.

Nonchalantly, over an ordinary Friday night meal, Frances said, "If you adults have no objections, I'm going to teach Joseph drawing techniques."

Half in jest I said, "How much are you charging?"

"In exchange for zis posing for me."

"We have all posed for you, Hans the most. Are you offering drawing lessons for us at reduced group rate?"

"No, silly, Joseph has ideas for doing modern motorcycle tattoo art. I'll teach zim what I know in exchange for his life study modeling for me. When ze has learned technique, ze will draw me draped over a fantasy motorcycle as 100% female. I can hardly wait."

"Does life study mean what I think it does?"

"Nude. You men saw the fantasy I did of myself, remember? It's up in the attic of this house. I could go get it if you don't remember."

"Yes, I remember, you were wearing big bazooka mammary glands, and nothing left to our imagination."

"I could do you and Bob nude, together or alone if you want to learn to draw." Then as an afterthought, before we could react, Frances said, "I'm getting really excited to draw living nude models."

"Joey, you onboard with this?"

Joey looked sheepish, blushed pink-cheeks and said, "Sure, why not, I've already shown all of me to you. I have nothing to be ashamed of."

"You don't mind being on display showing your everything to everyone? You used to be sensitive in that department."

"Anyone watching me wrestle has seen most of my body by now. I'm not small down there and Frances promises to make me look even bigger."

"Bob what do you think, you ready to pose for a nude portrait? I might enjoy seeing it in my old age."

"Absolutely not, Gus, I could lose my job if it got out. These kids are not old enough for nude modeling … most certainly not without all sorts of legal documents."

Joey had experience challenging Bob and me, and said, "Children attend nudist colonies. I've seen the photos in magazines."

"What magazines?"

"Boys pass them around between classes at my school and the children look happy. Where's the problem?"

"No parental consent, we are not legally your parents. Any idea what's our liability for letting you break the law? Let's not tempt the fates with possible criminal prosecution. To say nothing of my losing a job I like."

To give Bob a moment to cool down, I said, "Nobody would have a problem if you wanted to draw the naked statues at the museum. That's a way you can study the human form and not get us in trouble."

"Drawing from life is interactive, living, breathing, it's collaborative. Like live musicians interacting with their audience. Sketching cold stone sculpture sounds lifeless … dead even. I'm an artist, society gives me license to color outside the lines, you should too. Don't thwart my creativity."

Joey blushed a deeper pink mask across his cheeks during our exchange with Frances. That made me wonder what else was going on. I glanced at Bob who appeared to be formulating the same question. I spoke first. "While we are in the neighborhood, no sex under our roof. That means sex with anyone, until you are at least eighteen years of age and then only with our permission. Our house our rules."

Smashing baby-peas in-butter sauce on his plate with a fork, Joey's blush deepened, encompassed his whole head, neck and went down into his shirt. "You're too late, we already had sex … several times. Since you didn't know, you can't make rules after the act."

"WHAT?"

Frances came to Joey's defense and said, "Honestly, we didn't think you'd want to know. We don't want to know when you have sex. The facts are you have sex without asking us, often. Don't deny it, your bedsprings squeak."

Bob and I exchanged an uncomfortable look, and at that point cool Frances was the only one not blushing. To deflect my embarrassment I said, "Frances, you told us you were going to wait until you transitioned to explore sexuality."

"That was then this is now. My lawyer said I need research, to see if what I'm doing now is what I want in the future. How could I give up something I will never get back without knowing how it works, or even if it works correctly?"

"Does it?"

"Since you are interested, and Joseph and I didn't think you would be, my boy parts please me in ways I didn't foresee. Thank you for asking, I guess?"

"Is this where we call the police or child welfare or what exactly *is* expected of us informal foster parents?"

Joey who normally has a good appetite and cleans his plate, was now stirring his mashed potatoes with gravy into his smashed baby pea puree. Then still blushing said, "What is the fuss, we aren't in love. So far, we are only doing *full body explorative holistic healing exercises.*"

"*So far?*"

"Drawing each other naked will only be another level of self-acceptance. The shrinks call it reclaiming our bodies by showing and sharing. What are you two worrying about? None of us here can get pregnant."

"Hold on … would somebody please tell me what we are talking about?"

"Joseph and I *are* exploring our bodies to regain ownership after early life trauma. For zim its to recover from his rape and mine is to feel whole with parts I want to discard … before I do."

"Whose idea was this?"

"The concept came from a book called *Sexual Healing.* Our shrinks and my medical team say so far we have satisfactory results reclaiming ownership and feeling positive about our bodies."

"Some adult gave approval? I wonder if that takes heat off us, Bob."

"Why are you two looking so upset? Both our therapist say we are moving toward self-acceptance."

"How did your sexual healing begin? I mean besides the Marvin Gaye song."

"Gus, who is Marvin Gaye?"

"Whose idea was sex therapy?"

"My endocrinologist suggested I talk to my shrink *about my getting turned on by Joseph* and how ze treats me like a lady. He also debunked what I'd heard that it is dangerous for preop transsexuals to have orgasms leading to ejaculation. *It doesn't cause hernias* and as usual those boy-girl-queens at my school are full of baloney."

"How about we don't get off track. Who is involved with your underage sex play?"

"Let's see, my endo-guy suggested it, my med team didn't see a problem, my shrink talked to Joseph's shrink, then they talked to us individually. Then we four had a meeting and spoke together and gave the green light. Oh, and now you two know. If you want more coverage, we could place an ad on TV, then everyone will know."

"Frances don't be a wise ass, it doesn't suit you. Bob and I are concerned."

Joey came to Frances' defense by changing the subject despite what I had just said. "Jeez, we haven't done that much sex. Really, I think of it as homework from therapy, and you two shouldn't make a big deal over it. That's probably not healthy."

"We'll be the judge of that. Joey, what's going on?"

"What we do is perfectly natural, probably like what you do. Come on, we all sleep upstairs in the same house and the sky hasn't fallen down yet, Heeney-penny."

"Which of you decided having sex and calling it therapy was a neat idea?"

Looking sheepish, Frances said, "One night I had a really bad nightmare, Joseph came in my room to comfort me. One thing led to another, and things got a little familiar."

"Familiar?"

"Okay, I'll admit it was my hand's fault to start flirting with his concern for me. Then after, worried I might have caused myself damage, I told my endocrinologist. He suggested I talk to my med team, and they suggested we tell our shrinks, and they all talked, blah, blah, blah. Wait, didn't I just I just tell you this?"

"And nobody thought to consult Bob and I."

Joey spoke defensively. "You already knew we are in therapy and not supposed to dilute it by talking about it outside the sessions. Anyway, since you are all up in our business now, we have a question and need your worldly expertise."

"Why? You have the blessing of so many high paid professionals."

"We don't want to make any embarrassing mistakes. I sincerely doubt all the docs know what you and Bob know, Gus."

It had been a rough week at work, and I felt a brain fart coming. "This gets more intriguing the longer it goes on. So, let's stop talking about underage children having sex, and rush to ponder the consequences of such activity for the elder members of this *unofficial* family."

"Gus we are not children, don't be pessimistic?"

"Maybe I'm having an attack of early Alzheimer's disease, and this conversation isn't really happening? Now see, that makes me happy."

"At my school some say sex is the most beautiful part of being alive. I think they are right, and on top of that some of my queenlier classmates make a good living at the wholesale food market selling it before dawn."

Bob came over, wrapped me in his arms, and whispered sweet nothings in my ear to calm down my Alzheimer ruse. Then turning his head, he spoke to the teens, using his classroom voice. "What question did you have?"

Frances looked confused at how upset I had gotten. Then in a consolatory voice said, "Did I hurt your feeling, Gus? I didn't mean to. I was just asserting myself. My shrink thinks I should be more assertive since I'm the youngest here at home."

At that moment, what I did not want was more drama.

Joey knew Bob and I well enough from his own theatrical performances and said, "We haven't been allowed any penetration yet. It doesn't feel at all like what we want. What is *allowed* feels cold and mechanical."

"I'm an old dinosaur … how does one have mechanical sex. Do you get wired-up with electrodes, or connect to automatons?"

"No electronics or machines, we have to keep journals about everything. What we thought doing it, how it felt physically and emotionally. That's pretty much a direct quote from the therapists' instruction sheet."

"What's your question? Assuming we have an answer."

"At what point can we smooch and just let sex happen or not have to? Sometimes I don't want to go all the way. I think in a previous life I might have been a good girl. We see you foster daddies being romantic and want some of that."

"For the record, what exactly are you doing, if it isn't too private to share?"

I cut Bob off and said, "Wait Bob, I don't want to know that yet. We can find out from the police report after I file a complaint against their psychotherapists, endocrinologists, and medical experts."

"Please, Gus, don't make more of this than it is."

"But, Bob, we don't want to confuse the kids. We are supposed to set good examples for them. Don't the police need to be involved?"

Joey could be tough and did not have qualms standing up to me. I liked that about him. "Cut the crap, Gus, Frances already said the professionals are too clinical and antiseptic. What we want is to do it slow and easy, relaxed, not impersonal like a science experiment under a microscope."

Bob always at the ready said, "What do you want to know?"

Joey stayed on point, "The way real people have sex just because they want to, no pressure, no preplanned limits or rules."

"What if we don't approve of what you're doing? Answering your questions makes us complicit."

"Oh, so, you want to know details. Shall I tell them?"

"Why not, Frances, all the other helpers copy our notes. Why should they be different? Gus, do you need a pen and paper? No."

"Okay, Gus and Bob so far with instruction sheets, we've explored each other with fingertips, all over for weeks. Joseph won't admit it, but he *is* ticklish."

"*Not every time.*"

"Then when we complained we weren't allowed orgasms after being turned on so long. They gave us an exercise to take turns getting off using both our hands wrapped together working like one. It seems so impersonal them telling us what to do and then us reporting back."

"Let's fast forward, what are you asking us about?"

"Now they want us to lock our legs around each other and jerk ourselves off with one hand while touching each other, everywhere, with the free hand. Does that sound romantic to you?"

"Jeez, this feels awkward … so what do you want from us?"

"When can we add kissing, cuddling, and just holding each other without a stopwatch and script? I want kissing, licking, nibbling, biting, sucking, without a timeclock and prying eyes."

"Far be it from me to further confuse your confused situation."

"What's confusing?"

"It never occurred to you or your professional helpers to bring Bob and me into the loop before now?"

In a huff, Joey scolded us like we were the naughty ones. "Whenever you two talked sex with me, you looked uncomfortable. I was positive you wouldn't want to know when the pros suggested including you, and I told them *that* in no uncertain terms. Anyway, you two have been too busy lately to spend time with us."

I drew in a slow, calming breath and softened my tone. "Joey, when we agreed to let you live here, you tried to seduce us. Could it be a residual effect of your seduction technique, and our not wanting to contribute to your indeterminate sexuality that makes us unsure talking with you about sex?"

Bob cut me off. "Or our concern to avoid unnecessary gay influence on your budding sexuality?"

"We've talked about that. You know I wasn't seriously coming on to you two. Wasn't it you who taught me we are born to be the way we are, not recruited?"

"We did. Does this conversation mean you know what team you bat for?"

"No. Frances is safe for me. I don't have to decide anything."

"Joey, we don't draw conclusions."

"Since Frances came to live with us, you both seemed disinterested as long as we were getting along."

"Because it can't be how it was when you were our only child."

"Are we getting off track, Gus?"

"Then back on track. To get answers you seek, ask your professionals. But *know* it hurts our feelings you excluded us we expected more consideration."

"See that, if you don't keep us in line, how are we supposed to know any better? There is another question we are also curious about, and both our therapists didn't have answers that made sense. Can we ask you?"

"Go ahead, spit it out, Joey."

"When I shoot cum its thick, sticky, milk colored and smells like wallpaper-paste. It is different in all ways from Frances' cum."

"How?"

"Their cum is clear, thin, slippery, and smells like chemicals. Why is that? We have basically the same equipment down there."

"Actually, mine is longer than his."

"By just a little, mine is fatter around. Anyway, it isn't like we ordered our dicks online."

"Oh sorry, sorry, sorry, my bad."

"Joey, what answer did your professional helpers give?"

"The estrogen Frances take produces vaginal like lubrication rather than sperm carrying male ejaculate."

"Sounds plausible."

"No, it doesn't. They don't have a vagina to lubricate and do have a pair of testes."

"Joey, I hate to bring up your tenth-grade biology now that you are a freshly minted twelfth grader, what's difference between your almost same equipment?"

"Frances' testicles are smaller and harder than mine."

"Is it possible the medically prescribed female hormones Frances takes have greatly reduce their sperm count?"

"I guess."

"Could it be Frances is shooting mostly prostatic fluid due to estrogen sperm suppression. You would notice estrogen smells different than testosterone."

"Oh, right, I remember … okay mystery solved. Thanks Bob. Frances, do you want to add anything?"

"No not really Joseph." For some reason she spoke in a chastened tone of voice. Then looked at Joey intently and the expressions warmed up to show affection. "Oh wait, wait, wait, new idea, does what you just said mean I can have my testicles removed and still have an orgasm?"

"Why do that?"

"To reduce the amount of female hormone I'm injecting to avoid male sex characteristics."

"Why not talk it over with your endocrinologist, maybe he could suggest something less invasive to get the same result?"

"What about my question, Bob?"

"As a result of genital trauma, like surgery, expect a period of impotence, assuming nerve damage isn't permanent. The books say, when your balls are gone your mood and self-image will be affected."

"Before I met lawyer Brick, I would have said I want them off no matter what to be womanlier. Right this moment, I'd just like fewer hormone head and body aches. But having orgasms seems to be a habit I'm forming."

"Talk to your endocrinologist."

"That the best you got?" Joey puffed out his chest and said that staring at me. Even though Bob had given the instruction to see her endocrinologist.

Meeting Joey's stare I said, "Because we are playing foster fathers without a rule book, it matters greatly to us our family is right with the law. Historically, gays and transsexuals were grossly discriminated against in legal proceedings."

Backing down a smidge, Joey said, "We never had a problem before."

"Is that really true?"

"Oh, I see what you mean."

"Bob and I have run interference for you both since you came to live with us. We have been incredibly careful with the outside world."

"But we aren't freaky criminals, like my father's family." Frances said this rushing to Joey's rescue.

"No, you're not. But in my best guess you two *are* acting out of sequence for normal psychosexual development. We've said before the past can't be changed. But you can impact the present by getting back on track sequentially. Foster children having sex at home with each other has to be in opposition to the police, courts, child welfare agencies, and neighbors if they knew."

"I've been thinking about losing my virginity for longer than I've known any of you, that's a natural normal development, right? Jeez, what more is expected of me? I feel trapped between what's expectations from my biology pushing one way and adult rules setting limits to hold me back." Joey's body language showed his frustration had overruled his parental opposition.

"Since you brought it up, according to what I learned in college, at your ages you should be physically exploring self-sex, *alone*, and where and how you like to be touched *by yourself*. That knowledge is to fuel fantasies in your head until ready to share it with a person you trust from *outside your family*."

"What about the loss of my virginity?"

"You took care of that, with the help of professionals. The result was sex happened, but not in the normal developmental way."

"You're wrong! I still feel like a virgin. We haven't had penetration, or authorized kissing."

"As I understand it, sex unfolds naturally, like an accordion when people are ready to transition into adulthood. In your case, it sounds like you skipped self-exploring alone, the lovey dovey junior high school being in love with puppy-love, and somehow got to sex therapy lacking emotional content."

"Jeez, we can never catch a break. Okay, fine, you disagree with our docs' idea of sexual healing. What makes you right and them wrong?"

"You asked for my opinion, and I gave it. Joey, you know Bob and I, imagine us explaining your behavior under our roof in a court of law facing years in prison."

"All we want is to cuddle and snuggle and kiss and touch without the pressure leading to clinically observed, measured by degrees orgasms that are antiseptic and dissected in after-incident reports, and discussed in detail during therapy."

"Maybe they're all right, Joseph. Our childhoods were really screwed-up by uneducated adults. Now we have two groups of over educated adults in conflict. We probably are out of sync with ourselves and can't develop right no matter what."

"What are you saying Frances?"

"I know I love me when I look beautiful in the mirror. Maybe I will love you more than I do when I'm able to love me *all* the time."

"The shrinks say we aren't supposed to be in love with each other. We are doing healing exercises for future partners' sake."

"Isn't this where we started? How about let's leave it there, agreeing to disagree." Bob said this recognizing a no-win situation, like in his classroom.

I immediately jumped in to support my better half. "Unless there is strong opposition, I second what he said, and I'd like to change this fascinating dinner topic to something less disruptive to good digestion. Joey, are you going to eat those smashed vegetables in your dish?"

"Hans likes his vegetables smashed together. He doesn't have molars to chew them."

"Thank you, any other topic is appreciated."

"Like what?"

"Joey, how is your English physics going?"

"Got all A's ... I'm getting used to being a winner. The British like to think of us Americans as primitive, I'm giving them second thoughts. Who would have guessed, me?"

"Do I hear a but coming?"

"It's only I hate to disappoint Professor Higgins. My homework and pop quizzes are exchanged by email and lately he's been attaching notes, how anxious he is to see me at the final. I haven't had the heart to tell him I'm not going to England to take the exam."

"Did he say why he wants to meet you?"

"He says my work is 'refreshingly different' than his English students. Now, see, there's proof, being developmentally out of sequence can be refreshing in England. Maybe my true self resides over there?"

"I thought physics was all the same the world over."

"It is, but I learned to work long equations differently than English pupils. I get the correct answers faster with less inessential computation. Professor Higgins says he's a fan of American shortcuts."

"So, why aren't you going to England to take the final?"

"It's ridiculous to spend that much money and time on an airplane to sit for a one-hour exam and then turn right around and come back. That would qualify as certifiably nuts, and that's why I didn't mention the notes. I know how you get."

"Joey, did you get a passport like I suggested?"

"I used money you pay me monthly for landscaping. My plan was to give it all back when I go in the military. Can you believe our moneygrubbing government charged me $175 for a lousy passport I'll probably never need or use?"

"What's important is you have it, and we don't want the money you earned."

"We went together, and I got one too, designated a boy, looking like the girl I am. It refreshed my memory how our government discriminates against poor people."

"What do you mean?"

"By making it too expensive for the poor to travel." Frances said this looking ready to make a women's suffrage speech.

Pleased I had moved the dinner conversation away from teenage sex, I said, "I'll be happy to reimburse you both for the passports since it was my idea. Who knows, an international vacation may be in our future?"

Frances maintained the same disgusted facial expression she'd used when saying designated a boy. She said, "Very distant future."

"No, no reimbursement, thanks anyway. I have the money, I bank what you pay me."

"I for one think Joseph should go to England so ze can graduate with zis high school class and buy a class ring. Class rings are important to have. I offered to lend zim my savings, but ze won't take this girl's money. I think ze might be sexist?"

"I'm against taking charity, especially from this family, who gave me so much already."

Without missing a beat, Frances put on a positive face and said, "I could pass a hat around or have a bake sale on Main Street, or start a go fund me page. That's what I'll do."

"Frances, please don't. I'm not going and that final."

"Joey, would you take the test if it didn't cost you or anybody anything?"

"I don't want you or Bob paying, I'm practically an adult, not some sniveling dependent looking for handouts."

"Would you go if your only expense was what food and drink you consume?"

"Sure, if Walt Disney gave me that fairytale fantasy tied in a bow. What's the catch?"

"Every year I lose unused frequent flyer miles from work. At present I have more than enough for a round trip to London. You can use them at no loss to me or my company, but you'll need your passport to book it. Interested?"

"Wow, sure. That's so kind of you, Walt Disney. Thank you."

"Don't mention it."

"Oh wait, no! You guys know big urban centers scare this rural boy. I'd get lost and never find my way back across the ocean. I won't play Hassel and Gretel in real life?"

"Charles Swanson mentioned your Professor Higgins in reference to a joint venture we are contemplating at my office. The University of Oxford is interested in joining with us on a project beneficial to both."

"What's it got to do with me?"

"Let's see if Professor Higgins can arrange for an Oxford student to meet your plane. Travel with you to overnight student housing, accompany you to the exam next day, and escort you back to the Airport and in return you tip the student, no need of breadcrumbs."

"Isn't that imposing quite a lot? How could I possibly reciprocate beyond giving a couple of miserly bucks?"

"He or she makes an American friend, and you *will* tip them generously buying them a nice dinner on my company credit card. It's called a miscellaneous business expense."

"I never understood the concept of tipping." Joey shrugged, showing he was out of his comfort zone.

"Swanson and Higgins are close friends they do motorcycle rallies together. Charles is particularly good at organizing multiple moving parts."

"You all know, this country boy will be like a duck out of water in another country across an ocean."

"Bring a jug of local maple syrup as a gift for your professor."

"Why would Charles Swanson do me these favors? He hardly knows me."

"He likes you, hates bullies and especially what I told him about your tyrannical physics teacher."

"Likes *me* how?"

"Don't panic, he's in love with your antique-motorcycle repair skills."

"Oh right, that! Huh, I remember now."

"What's bothering you?"

"It sounds like a lot of work for my sake from people who hardly know me. I've never felt worth this much trouble."

"What trouble? Let your guidance counselor setup excused absents for your Transatlantic trip and arrange the paperwork formalities for receiving credit *if you pass*. She knows you and its part of her job. Charles likes arranging pickup and delivery to and from his old alma mater. It keeps him in face-to-face contact with professors we consult with at work, and he often gets free drinks or meals for his trouble. Your only effort is to pass the physics exam. We will still love you pass or fail."

****

Dr. Higgins arranged for three of his students to meet Joey's plane in London. The number was three in case one or two had to drop out at the last moment. None did, and they gave Joey the royal tour of their school and surrounding student pub hangouts. Joey was then taken to overnight student housing and told to sleep off his jetlag before his early morning exam.

Joey's student escort promised to take him to the United Kingdom's Motorcycle Museum before their late dinner, as a reward for coming the long distance to visit London and buying them a New York Steak dinner after the Museum tour. The British students did not expect their lowly American peer to test well due to their high scholastic standards and rumors the Americans were barely literate. Joey reported later, the museum visit itself was worth the trip to England even if he had failed.

Joey aced the computer-generated physics final. He received the exam results fifteen minutes after completion. Then after getting the test results, he met with Professor Hank Higgins for a prearranged, pleasant light lunch of strange English concoctions at the faculty brasserie. The professor was taken with Joey's unpolished frank openness, and during the lunch set up two additional meetings for Joey with his Oxford colleagues for that day. Dr. Higgins never had real maple syrup and accepted Joey's gift with curious interest.

Then as it turned out other English university scholars were roped in and captivated by Joey's laidback rustic American unsophisticated style coupled with his brilliant critical thinking problem solving. Joey thought the meetings were purely British formality to accommodate Professor Higgins' colleagues and to take orders for real maple syrup. They loved the stuff. Consequentially he was flattered to be shown-off, and demurely gave correct answers to complex questions. He assumed it was just part of their welcome noble savage visitor routine. Out of character he went along with what he thought was their fun with colonists and added ten percent to the price of the maple syrup they ordered, for his service.

Little did Joey realize a behind the scenes struggle of wits for his benefit was going on at breakneck speed to buck staid tradition. Since Joey was leaving London right after arriving, many formal academic hoops were skipped for his benefit without him even aware. In the end several Oxford professors were not pleased but acquiesced for expediency, Joey's sake and receiving maple syrup.

Meanwhile, other serious haggling took place right up to Joey boarding the transatlantic flight home. At the last possible minute, Joey was offered a full scholarship to the University of Oxford for the fall semester. An envelope was handed to him at the plane's final boarding gate. He took his seat in business class, opened the envelope, and was not prepared for what he found. Joey was flabbergasted by the generous offer and strict thirty-day limit to accept or decline.

CHAPTER 13. Welcome Home, Nonbinary Gender Camp, More Herstory

We three stay at home humans met Joey as he came through the international arrival's customs gate. The reunion began with happy faces, hugs all around and a long blasé road trip to the country house. Sitting in the backseat, Joey looked wrung out exhausted and soon was asleep on Frances's shoulder. Listening to deep sleeping close-up, Frances fell asleep cuddling Joey. Arriving back at the house, Bob gently nudged the kids awake. I fetched Hans who greeted his logy teens like they had been gone for years.

Seeing the looks going back and forth between Joey and Frances, Bob and I took Hans for an extra-long run before dinner. Thus, Joey and Frances had private time for whatever without us around fretting. The more I knew the less I wanted to know details.

When we returned from running, the atmosphere in the house had chilled from welcoming cuddly warm to icy cold. Defense shields seemed to be up and figuratively weapons on hair-trigger. Something put an artic chill in the air, and Joey and Frances were not talking beyond head nods.

Despite the change in atmosphere, we all had a hand putting a nutritious, fast, tasty, meal on the table, and ate it cautiously in silence. Without a clue what changed the inside temperature and Hans' patience I said "We went for a run with everyone cheerful and smiling. On return it's the opposite, so who offended who, or do you want to play Scrabble to build more animosity before telling?"

Joey meekly glanced at each of us and said, "I know you are all tired from making the long drive to and from the airport to pick me up and putting dinner together, but could we have a short family meeting anyway?" Not waiting for a reply Joey took his finished dinner dish and utensils to the kitchen sink then headed to the den.

Like lemmings we followed Joey's example, from dining room, to kitchen, then den.

When seated Bob said, "What can't wait?"

"The University of Oxford offered me a scholarship. It's only good for thirty days then expires. Also, I need a wholesale supplier of New York State pure maple syrup that ships to the U.K."

"I for one need more information if you don't mind."

"Up to now, every major decision in my life was made for me. Now for something as important as this, I *want, no need* your input."

"An Oxford scholarship sounds like the opportunity of a lifetime. Go for it!" Bob said this with pride and passion.

I didn't hold back either and said, "Especially since as far as I know you haven't applied to any university or college over here." I knew Joey's plan had been to enlist in the army after high school to please Mike. If that failed, he decided to attend the local community college part time and devote time to Mike's declining handyman service.

"I never told you why I didn't apply to college, did I? Even before I went to England, my guidance counselor went fishing for academic or wrestling scholarships for me."

"She's a professional who takes her job seriously." Bob said this like he was awarding her a prize.

"I like her, but she does that for all students with high grades and the star jocks. Anyway, the local community college admissions office told her I wasn't an appropriate scholarship candidate for them due to all my advanced placement classes and GPA."

"What? That sounds like reverse discrimination."

"Apparently, junior college is geared for average grades or employed students needing advanced training. Their wrestling program doesn't even have scholarships. But they said I would be eligible for tuition reduction if my parents were impoverished, or I was working a low wage job."

"Which we and you are not."

"My guidance counselor also said the closest State University was too far to commute, especially in winter, and student housing and board there was over the moon expensive. I didn't tell you because I knew you'd want to get involved and pay my way. *I'm supposed to pay my own way.* It's important to me."

Faking a hurt look, I asked, "Were you ever going to tell us?"

"No, I wasn't, Gus. My original plan was to let you think I'm not very smart. Just a dumb country boy who doesn't know enough to plan-ahead. Playing stupid worked well for me before I met you two."

"I can't tell if that's a back-handed compliment. What do you think Bob?"

Bob nodded yes. His grin gone.

"To follow up, I checked myself. Community college doesn't require advance registration, they even have late enrollment if class-seats are available."

Looking serious, Bob said, "Playing dumb, like the boy who cried wolf, doesn't always get desired result."

"It doesn't matter now the University of Oxford has totally blown my cover."

Steering the ship back on course I said, "The question is what do you want, Joey?"

"Thirty percent of me wants to give living in London a shot, it's an old city and doesn't intimidate me like constantly changing new, New York City. And thirty percent of me knows big cities are not healthy places to live. But forty percent thinks the whole idea of going to a fancy university is way too privileged for the likes of me."

Frances had stayed quiet up to that point. "Joseph, since I met you, your biggest fear was being rejected by the army and ending up a homeless street bum to prove your detractors right. If you go to Oxford, the army won't be able to reject you, you'll have a home there for four years, and then a degree to guarantee a job if you want one."

"Okay, and what if I fail over there?"

"You won't, that's not your style."

"There's a first time for everything," Joey rearranged himself on his chair as he spoke. His body language indicated failure was not an acceptable option but conceivable.

"Then you have a home here with us."

In response to Frances' impassioned words, Bob and I nodded our heads to support her and looked like a pair of bauble-head dolls.

"Out gunned as usual, well, okay, that was easy. I can see you three want to get rid of me."

"*And?*"

"Yeah, not so fast, or easy, right?"

"Spit it out."

"As a foreign student, I won't be eligible for work-study or any kind of financial aid beyond the scholarship which only pays tuition and fees. I read the small print on the plane. Travel, books, supplies, and living expenses are on me. I did rough calculations my savings will barely get me through the second semester first year living costs. And that is if I only eat oatmeal every meal."

"If that is your biggest concern, we can have a garage sale, and Frances could put up a GoFundMe page."

A serious expression wiped the smile off Joey's face. He looked at Bob, me, Frances, and Hans, and said, "No. Don't do that, my bigger concern is I'll miss you guys. I know how to *be* here and no clue how to *be* there. I know you have my back over here, there I'm alone."

"You can come back for school holidays, we can come visit in between, and you'll make new friends."

"Go ahead, make me cry, but I won't let you pay my way. That's for certain."

"Fine, since Swanson and Higgins got you mixed up with Oxford and they work with me, and I'm a managing partner at work, the company should be able to find funds to match Oxford to see you through an undergraduate degree. We have a slush fund for staff educational development."

"How's that different from you or Bob paying my way?"

"Yeah! What's the catch? Gus, you say there is always a hook to look for." Half teasing Frances made her comment. Then realized she was on the wrong side and her face crashed.

"You might have to agree to work for our firm for a year or two after graduation. If you decide to go for graduate degrees, we can renegotiate. If the company supports you with a scholarship, it's a tax write off and we get the money back from reducing our taxable gross."

"Gus, suddenly my life feels complicated, and it happened in the blink of an eye."

"Come on, Joey, let us make it a team effort. My company is always on the lookout for tax deductions."

"I never get why you are so good to me when I'm a reject from birth."

Scratching behind Hans' ears, Bob said, "You, my young friend, are on the cusp of an adventure, don't let it scare you. Remember, this family doesn't scare easily, and we who love you want to see how your escapade in merry old England turns out. Will you be knighted by the Queen or crowned by a cricket bat? Is there something else bothering you?"

"At the airport when I asked the professors why me, I expected to hear Swanson or Higgins' names. Instead, they said diversity of backgrounds and learning-styles within their student body increases pupils' educational experience."

"That makes sense."

"Except, I've barely survived here, kicked from one place to another until Mike and Eleanor rescued me. Am I being setup to be a fraud in England? What do I know, I don't want to be the American dufus?"

"Joey, just be yourself you earned a 4.0 GPA, and passed a college level science class while in high school."

I underlined Bob's point by saying, "We've been over this, Joey. No question requires an immediate answer. There is no shame saying I don't know. I do it all the time."

"Thanks, Gus for reminding me of that. But what if my scholarship is because I'm perceived as a privileged white gay American."

"What happened?"

"Bob, my having two gay foster fathers suggests I'm gay, right? Plus, it feels like I didn't earn the scholarship and will be revealed to all Europe as a phony two-faced American."

"How so?"

"What if Oxford assumes I am a gay closet queen? How sad will that be?"

"*Maybe* they don't care who you sleep with. It's England for God's sake! They have a queen mother."

"Gus, so what? I'm not who they think I am. I don't even have a sexual orientation."

A silence followed Joey's last comment, and then Hans filled it with clicking paws on the hardwood floor pacing by the front door. That gave me an excuse to take Hans, outside. When he finished his business, we played catch with his frisbee to clear our brains. I sensed a storm coming inside the house, it was a vague impression based on injured looks back and forth between Joey and Frances.

When we returned to the den, no one was talking. Hans looked at each shut down family member and did not see an opportunity to be appreciated. He came over and laid down by my easy chair. He knew I would pet him. I am his softest, soft touch. A fleeting remembrance of the pot boiler I just started reading flashed to the fore and motivated me to break the room's silence. "If we are done here, let's adjourn, a book is calling me?"

"Joseph, before we stop can I tell them what happened while they went running?"

"No, Frances. That's between us."

"But I want to ..."

"It's too personal."

"What if they can help us fix the problem?"

"I'm not due in England until August, this is December. There is plenty of time for me to make it right."

"Come on, Joseph, we already know our shrinks are going to scold us. Usually, Bob and Gus know

down to earth ways to correct problems."

From our short time as foster dads, Bob and I learned from experience when to give the kids space.

The growing intensity of looks back and forth indicated they were a couple chewing on something hard and bitter. So, I stroked Hans' neck and put on a neutral face. Bob tried to look indifferent, but poker is not his game. Frances looked for support and permission to go against Joey's wishes. We knew our place and stayed in it.

Joey finally broke the tension. "Go ahead, Frances, I know you can't help yourself, put all our dirty laundry in the street for all to see. Come on, let's let everybody stare at my shame. These guys have already seen me at my lowest, lets add a subbasement level."

"Bob and Gus and I, love you. There is no shame in trying and failing something new. I just want to know if it is symptomatic of a more severe problem, like a medical condition."

"I'll be in my bedroom if anyone needs me." Standing and looking at Bob, Joey said, "Someone was kind enough to leave a copy of *The History of the English People* on my desk. Right now, would be a suitable time to read it."

Keeping on my neutral face, I said, "Do you really want us talking about you without you present?"

"Sure, I give permission." With that said Joey headed toward the stairs leading to the second floor and his bedroom.

Frances looked perplexed. "Now I'm flummoxed and don't know what to do."

Bob ordered, "Joey, come back, but leave your pride over there. We can reinflate it later."

"I've got nothing more to contribute."

"Fine, just sit quietly, talking is optional."

"Talking is what Frances wants from me."

In more pedantic than military officer mode, Bob said, "This way we all know what was said, and by whom."

"Okay fine since you insist. Go on Frances tell them how disgusting I am."

"I think it could have happened to anyone. For God's sake stop being such a martyr Joseph."

"What are you two talking about? I'm getting a sense I don't want to know." I said this with my poker face slipping off.

"When you went running, we made out a little. I know we are not supposed to do that, but it was a special occasion. Joseph passed zis exam, visited London, England, but didn't meet the Queen. I wanted to give zim a special welcome home gift."

"Frances, you made a delicious icebox cake for dessert. That was special enough."

"I know, everyone but Hans got a slice. Joseph says it's his favorite. It comes from the time of iceboxes instead of refrigerators." Voiceless, my facial expression said, "What are you talking about?"

"I went down on Joseph and as expected ze liked it a lot."

"Do *we* really need that information? And to answer my own question, *no we don't!*"

"When Joseph tried to return the favor, ze vomited all over my crotch. We showered together, and washed zis lunch out of my pubic-rug."

"Are you registering a complaint or what?"

"No. I received an excellent hand job under steaming water in the process. But now Joseph won't talk to me and that's not fair."

"I'm ashamed, what do you want, Shakespeare sonnets?"

"Frances, this isn't the time or place for this conversation. You have a therapist to discuss private matters."

"But, Gus, I wanted to give zim a special treat. It wasn't supposed to end up embarrassing. Why are you men always so hard to please?"

I'd heard enough and could not hold back, "Bob and I don't need details. We're happy you had a successful encounter. Now leave it at that."

"We are talking because I couldn't return the favor. I wanted to but …." Then Joey lowered his head and looked down.

"Bob and I don't need to hear this. It is not what proper foster families talk about openly."

Joey, said, "I wonder, are most foster families as openly dysfunctional as Frances and me?"

"My gender correction journey got more complicated when I joined this all-male household and entered partial puberty. My problem is males don't know how to act around transsexual-female and often don't even try to be civil."

"What do we say about assigning blame?"

"If I didn't instruct you, you three would never know how to treat me."

"Really? Ever heard of camp Chippewa in the Catskills?"

"Sure, but now I'm too old for them, and before I was always too poor. They only take tranny kids four to fourteen with lots of money or rich sponsors."

"My secretary Leonard has been exploring the possibility of a camp job for you with the director, for this summer."

"When were you going to tell me?"

"If you get a job interview. Don't say Bob and I aren't trying, we are."

Joey, perking up, said, "Now what is this?"

"Joseph, Camp Chippewa is a wonderful gender nonbinary camp up in the mountains. The setting is beautiful, and it has an outstanding reputation for teaching campers to live in a hostile world."

Bob, sounding like a student of Socrates said, "Let's focus, this little chat is all over the map."

"Didn't I already say men are impossible to please?"

"Frances, I'm surprised you could get a homerun hummer your first-time pitching. It takes skill to give good head." Bob said this looking like he'd just realized he crossed a boundary.

"It was Joseph's first-time batting, not mine pitching. I got your baseball analogy girls play baseball too."

"Wait, Bob, do we really need to know this?" I could not hold back my old maid aunt comment any longer.

"Gus, you and Bob rescued me after the blood bath that erased my family and almost me. You two have seen me at my wits end."

"Yes, and where is this going?"

"Okay, okay, okay, everybody knows giving head is of great interest for schoolyard girls at every age. Like you old men told Joseph, everyone needs a hobby."

"I'm sure the boys going to my school will want to know all about the girls' hobby."

"Joseph, that's the main thing girls talk about. Practicing fellatio on carrots, cucumbers, zucchini, bananas, whether warmed in a microwave or cold from the fridge like popsicles. Personally, I think ice cream in cones allows for the supplest tongue technique, and that, Joseph, is how I gave you the time of his life."

I had had enough and said, "Frances, you're making me uncomfortable, just stop please."

"I'm not done."

"Damn it, get done, or I'm leaving the room."

"How do we help Joseph with his problem?"

Joey muttered half under his breath, "I never said I had a problem."

"Joseph, your barf did."

"Hold on, just stop! This conversation is best suited for your therapists. I'm going upstairs to read my book." With that said I rose from my chair.

"Stop. You need to know who I am before you throw me out."

"Nobody is throwing anybody out."

Bob jumped in saying, "Frances, you are taller than Joey, a year younger, and if he didn't help you with your homework, you'd be less than average in math. He makes no secret of questioning his sexuality, and I thought we were all in agreement letting him and his therapist work it out. What were you thinking going against that? Telling us what you did doesn't make it right."

"Please, if there is a point, make it so we can move on." I sat back down but wanted to turn my back on the family and go read my book. Nevertheless, I'd feel selfish and guilty doing just what I want. I thought, *Welcome to accidental parenting.*

"Because of what Bob said, I'm trying to tell you why I broke the rules. Telling you, and you not freaking out makes me feel less slutty."

"Understand, we want to respect your privacy, so skip unnecessary references to giving head. All of us are familiar with how it functions."

"You're making this harder than it has to be."

Bob waded back in with the usual, "How can we help you, Frances?"

"Explain, why Joseph threw up trying to give me head after I blew his mind. I just don't understand his reaction to receiving a wonderful blowjob. It makes no sense."

"How are we supposed to know?"

"Do you think my boy part looks so disgusting it can cause nausea? It looks normal to me."

"Could it be fear of doing something much maligned attached to an irrevocable label Joey wasn't willing to accept."

NO, no, no, schoolgirls say, only the idea of cock sucking is hard to swallow. They should know they do a lot of it to save their maidenheads. Truth be told, I really like the exciding build up just before the end."

"Joey, since you were the object, any idea on how to solve Frances' mystery?"

"You said I didn't have to speak. Now you're pressuring me to tell you why I retched. Like I know? Also, if anyone is interested, *I don't like being objectified.*"

"Joey, don't talk if you'd rather not."

"Ugh, okay school yard boys say, 'Lick a dick once and forever be a cock sucker.' You're right, I probably wasn't ready, and my body revolted."

"There it is, Joey wasn't ready, end of story. Now let's talk about the weather or price of gold, or anything socially responsible proper foster families like to discuss."

"Gus, we already know your opinion. Don't bully us."

Once again Bob jumped in to rescue me with a pedantic explanation. "Schoolyard kids are often intrigued with reconciling naughty adult behaviors they aren't developmentally ready to explore but find titillating, with jeers."

"Please God now can we talk about something else?"

"Instead of coming back home from England feeling like a winner. I am totally ashamed of myself, and I didn't do anything wrong, the story of my life."

It felt like a merry-go-round, going around in circles, I finally said, "Nobody died, and we all learn from our mistakes. Frances meant well, and it wasn't Joey's time to reciprocate. Shake hands and pinky-promise to talk before trying any new things again."

Instead of a handshake, the two teens fell into an embraced and then kissed. I looked over at Bob and we silently decided it time to exit. Going up the stairs Bob said over his shoulder, "Goodnight kids, see you in the morning. Let Hans out and don't stay up too late."

One thing I love about our country house is the shower is big enough for two comfortably. Also, Bob and I have the time to shower together before bed. In the city we often push ourselves to exhaustion working too many hours into late night. With the kids clinched downstairs, Bob and I stripped down heading for our bathroom shower, no need for talk. Then taking turns washing each other, and playing around, we took turns drying each other, and I finally said, "Do you get how uncomfortable I feel when our kids talk having sex?"

"Would you rather they didn't, and some creep exploited their innocence? I know I wouldn't want them infected with AIDS, syphilis, or drug resistant gonorrhea."

"I hear you. But we could leave STD prevention pamphlets lying around, instead of talking about it."

"Really, we are allowed that?"

"Yes."

"That's as good a plan as any."

"Do I get an A, professor?"

"We'll have to see how well you perform in the sack first."

"Meany."

"But I'll give you an A+ for engineering Joey's study abroad. In a different environment he may find himself. I don't see our kids sexing long, Joey has to leave in August."

"Thanks, Bob, I needed to hear reassurance, sometimes it feels like Joey's insecurities are contagious."

"Over the years, a few of my students had Joey-like problems. It is hard to survive as an adolescent without perceived major dings and scuffs to self-image. On the other hand, Frances is all new to me. I never had a trans kid in my classroom going in her direction. I do well with girls wanting to be boys. I'll admit it's sexism. You seem to have made the connection with her journey better than I."

"Do you remember my secretary, Leonard? He started at the company as Swanson's swishy male administrative assistant."

"Oh right, yes, I'd forgotten."

"Swanson had a problem with Leonard's transitioning to female at the office. He claimed it would negatively affect clients. As it happened, my secretary had just left to go to law school. I got to save the day for Swanson and Leonard, who is an excellent secretary."

"Now I remember you telling me how Leonard blossomed as she erased her male self at work. I forgot why she didn't take a female name?"

"One characteristic that didn't change, Leonard likes to be contrary."

"And Leonard is on all her legal documents. Does Frances know Leonard is transsexual?"

"No, and I'd like to keep it that way."

"Is that your rule to keep work separate from home life?"

"No. Just between us, Leonard does what I asked. But I get the distinct impression she would rather not go beyond her job description helping Frances. That's not how Leonard usually rolls, but we witnessed Lawyer Brick refusing to share his transsexual journey with Frances. I guess when they are ready, they'll write a book about it. In the meantime, I'm sticking with what I know."

"Smart fellow, I'm still working through my Vietnamese cultural binary gender hierarchy issues."

"It confuses me when Frances looks so convincingly like a girl and then acts like a boy. I'm always surprised by the switch."

"Then tonight, Frances cracked opened a door into insights never revealed before."

"Damn, Bob, how do you keep so aloof from the turmoil that has become our home life?"

"I take your advice and don't let it get too personal. If we are all right, everything around us is manageable. Remember, the kids will only be with us a shot time."

"Right."

"For right now, I'd rather fool around with you, than talk teenage torment, you ready to take on a Vietnamese tiger?"

"Ah yes, you do that like a furious tiger. Good God … oh don't stop … yes that's it, ahhhh!"

****

We slept intwined, later than usual, after a satisfying night of tension dissipating sex. Consciousness pushed through the torpor fueled by a muted conversation directly outside our bedroom door. Half-awake I countered the soft rap on the bedroom door. "Go away, we're still in bed." Then there was a louder more forceful, Joey style knock. "Oh, all right come in, if you dare!"

In walked Joey and Frances carrying trays of food and drink. Frances said, "We decided to give you a treat, breakfast in bed. I hope you don't mind if we join you on your king size bed."

"Is that why you kept on your pajamas?"

Without giving an answer, the teens placed their trays on the long low walnut dresser. Then handed us lidded glasses of orange juice and poured mugs of steaming coffee from a thermos-carafe. I was brought fully conscious as warmed plates with fluffy scrambled eggs, crispy bacon, home-fries, and buttery toasted-English muffins were handed around. With everything in place, the kids climbed on our oversize bed and occupied the bottom two corners. They sat cross legged, bright eyed keen appetites working on food and drink nestled in lap-trays.

Bob looked at me like he wasn't ready for morning, and somehow it was my fault. He said, "Where is Hans?"

"In his dog run with fresh food and water. Otherwise, he'd make this breakfast in bed a slapstick cartoon-style calamity." Frances said this with authority, her body language showed, as usual she knew best. "He loves bacon even more than you two do."

"We've never had breakfast in bed before. I wonder if there should be a warning label it could be habit forming."

"I'm sure there's rehab for bacon eating abuse. If only it didn't smell so good cooking."

"Oh, what a relief this is. Excelsior. Now to what do we owe this unique domestic luxury."

"It was our idea. Last night had to be disgusting for you, and I didn't finish telling you what I started. So, breakfast in bed is our way to say sorry we are such troublesome foster children."

"Joey, does this mean you feel better this morning?"

"Yes, Gus. Boiling down what you both said last night helped. Now I'm ready to move on and put what happed behind me."

"Wow, breakfast in bed, and is it safe to assume Frances has also gotten beyond yesterday's misadventure?"

"Gus don't look distressed this morning. It won't be a regurgitation of last night. Ha ha."

Bob looked skeptical and said, "Why couldn't this repast wait and call it brunch, with sleep filled hours from now?"

"Frances and I talked all night, after you went to bed. We agreed I need to get unstuck from my childhood trauma. It's still mucking me up."

"Huh, I'm not awake enough to digest that, but might be at lunchtime."

"Gus and Bob, you always say we don't share enough. So, for me and Frances this is a thank you breakfast for all the opportunities you give us to share, and we don't."

"A thank you card would have been adequate."

The food they prepared was delicious if a bit early. "So, what are your plans for today?"

"Frances has a geometry test on Wednesday, we'll review for it after breakfast clean up. Bob if you have a few minutes, Frances wrote a first draft for a history paper due on Thursday."

"Joey, why don't you proof the history paper after geometry?"

"You'll get them a higher grade than me. But only if you have the time."

"What's the subject, Frances?"

"We had to read an essay for homework and then discussed it in class. Oh sorry. I got ahead of myself, it's about Thomas Jefferson's slave mistress and their children. I wrote my paper from the slave women's point of view and made comparisons with being transsexual."

"Sounds fascinating, how about one o'clock, before Gus and I have a pre-lunch run? Joey, what are you up to?"

"I thought I'd bake some Scottish Shortbread after geometry review. Then before supper Frances and I will motorcycle over to Matilda's place. I heard since Austin moved back to the city, she's become a bit of a hermit. I know she likes shortbread. I'm using her recipe."

"Do you think Matilda is ready to meet Frances?"

"We'll see, they might even like each other. I want to make sure she doesn't need anything fixed. Some of my handyman clients say she looks frail at church."

Without prompting, all eyes turned to Frances, who said, "More coffee anyone? OKAY, Okay, okay, I suppose you expect me to bare my soul."

"Yes, you may top off my coffee."

"In this house, this charwoman must toil like a slave, or her men get grumpy."

"We were only wondering about your plans today. For your autobiography, we can wait for publication."

"I disagree without being disagreeable. I think you really want me to finish what I started last night. So, I will, my parents were too young to know what they were doing when I was born."

"How old is too young on your scale?"

"They were fourteen-year-old high school freshmen too young to work legally. My mom said my father robbed people at gunpoint to provide for us. Apparently, he wasn't particularly good at it and that's why he spent much of his life in prison."

"Don't talk ill of the dead." Joey said this to Frances showing his serious face.

"My father had a best friend named Digby. They met as prison cellmates. Digby was a better stickup man than my father, and often came around to give us reports on which prison papa resided in. When I was elven Digby was no longer just dib-and-dabbing hard drugs. Mom said he'd become a full-fledged junkie. Nevertheless, he could always find us no matter how often we had to moved. On one of his visits, he asked my mom for something to eat. She showed him we had no food in the apartment. That day he told me it was time I earned my way in the world."

"At age eleven." My dislike for Digby was growing by the minute.

"Digby said he knew people who would teach me to please a man so well he'd never leave me. He said it was an important life skill for a girly-boy like me. He introduced me to a pimp named Amos. Digby used a small portion of the finder's fee Amos gave him for me to buy mom and me Chinese takeout. At the time I didn't know much about the world but was so hungry I hardly tasted the food going down."

"You never mentioned any of this before."

"As the child of a career criminal I was taught to *know nothing and say less.* I didn't know Amos was a pimp or what a pimp was. As I found out, Amos specialized in chiclets, underage girls with dicks. I didn't completely understand the label until my lawyer Brick explained it at our second meeting."

"That clarifies the look on your face after the lawyer meeting we didn't attend."

"Amos had a stable of underage femmy-boy runaways or cast outs. He called us girls and dressed us accordingly. We wore frilly lace dresses, big wide sun hats with lots of ribbons, black-patent-leather girls' shoes, and no underwear. We enjoyed dressing up, wearing makeup, and I liked having regular meals."

"I could shoot Amos without a thought of remorse."

"The girls taught me to entertain Amos' middle-aged, middle-class clients so they would give a big tip. That's where I learned to suck dick like a professional. I was taught by professionals to be professional."

"Shooting is too good for Amos."

"Because I had a place to live and Digby lurking around watching out for me, I never became a full-fledged member of Amos' stable of chicklet preteen-whores."

"I never heard of a pimp with that arrangement." I didn't know much about pimps. But had clear ideas of how I'd like to end Amos and Digby's days, as a community service.

"Amos used me like a substitute teacher, called in to work as needed." Saying that Frances glanced over at Bob who was wide awake listening at that point.

"Frances don't pick on Bob. He has been known to be grouchy in the morning."

"When I confided what I was doing for money as hypothetical to my endocrinologist, she said, "Whatever you do don't swallow or let them fuck your ass without a condom." I don't know how she knew it wasn't hypothetical."

"You couldn't afford food but saw medical specialists?"

"There are such things as free clinics for transsexuals. Most of my special docs in those days were recent grads who didn't stay around long."

"What happened with Amos?"

"Amos didn't like my doctor's restrictions and reduced my work to occasional. I only got a few old timer johns who wanted long drawn-out hand jobs and hardly tipped if at all. Finally, Amos fired me for being too old, and unproductive. I was thirteen halfway to fourteen at the time. They intended to beat me, their usual way of aging a chicklet out of one stable, then into another. It didn't go as planned Amos broke his nose on my fist when he took a swing at me."

"Wow, what an ending to an updated X-rated Charles Dickens story. Did we need to know all that?"

"I don't apologies for being the child of a profession criminal. I didn't choose to be. Otherwise, that's my story, I'm not proud of it. I've wanted to tell you about my less than glamorous beginnings for a long time."

"How do you feel now we know?"

"When Joseph used the word *fraud* yesterday, it hit me like a punch. Like it or not, I had to tell you more of my story than you knew."

"Are you relived?"

"I thought I would be. But I can see from your faces and the deafening-silence, you're disappointed I'm not the prim and proper girl *you or I wanted*. I'm sorry I've disappointed us."

"You never disappointed *me*, Frances. Before I met you, I couldn't imagine letting *anyone* touch me below the waist." Looking at Bob and me, Joey said, "Even when I offered myself to you guys, I somehow knew you wouldn't accept."

"Hold on, what you say *is not true*, Joseph. You let strangers put their hands all over you on the wrestling mat."

Joey dismissed Frances' comment by shaking his hands up in the air. "You're just jealous I get more attention than you."

"I'm not! You're jealous of me!" This shouted as a spontaneous outburst.

"Why Frances?"

"Because I'm pretty."

"I suppose you think there is nothing nice or pretty, about competitive high school wrestling!"

"Joseph, you just want to know how it was to be a sex slut for money with old men."

"Maybe I do, maybe I don't. That wasn't about me."

"I was wanted, someone chose me, money changed hands for my time."

Bob at the ready asked, "When was the last time you were checked for STDs?"

"When I was in the hospital after my mom's murder, they did every test known to man looking for the gods know what."

"Oh right, I glanced at your chart."

"Don't worry, Bob, I didn't give Joseph the gift of love. That's what Amos called the clap. I've been chaste, except Joseph, since you brought me to safety."

A long silence followed Frances' last statement. All faces tried for placid expressions while no one attempted eye contact. Fingers locked and unlocked as bottoms squirmed.

"Oh, okay right … I suppose now that you know I'm a trained cock sucker, it would be best I leave quickly. I should have *planned* for a better ending. Well, at least no one will blame you for tossing out this harlot. Think positive."

Bob and I gave Joey a withering stare and he said, "Those are Frances' words not mine. I only told her after I spoke my most humiliating experience, we three became closer. I didn't know she had a secret life."

"What are you men talking about?"

"We'd rather you stay with us. We don't think less of you, and still love you and Joey equally."

"After what I told you."

"We've all done things we're not proud to tell. It couldn't have been easy to expose yourself. Let's have a group hug, what do you say?" That said, we all stood in our pajamas, and put draped arms around each other. It felt sincere.

To break the clinch, and get us moving I said, "Hey, gang, that was a lovely breakfast. Now let's get moving we're wasting a gorgeous late fall day, and I suspect Hans is lonely."

CHAPTER 14. Corey

Rich colors finally peaked and fell after an incredibly long, unseasonable warm fall season. Indian Summer never had a chance and skipped us. I ruminated, *Welcome to global warming, we have heat and humidity that feels like July, in December. We'd better prepare for a summer freeze.*

Rather than a progressive deepening chill to transition our bodies, psyches, and vegetation for winter, we were wearing shorts, flipflop-sandals and going shirtless Christmas shopping, it was crazy unnatural, the trees were bare. Frances' newest revelations and Joey's move in seven months, across the Atlantic, added an extra troubling dimension to the out of whack time of year.

Then suddenly without warning the weather women and men were caught off guard, winter hit us full on with a deepfreeze wallop. The temperatures dropped much lower than any historical records could find going back centuries. The source was a polar vortex, an anomaly directly from the North Pole. To magnify our misery the vortex stalled over the Eastern third of the North American continent for weeks. The talking eggheads on television said current weather irregularity represented predeath throes of a planet giving a warning last gasp.

The first night of hard freeze destroyed winter crops in southern states. Then our stuck vortex piled-on days of twenty-five degrees below zero to make sure all winter crops stayed dead. It became dangerous to go outside without artic gear, which we did not have, at that point most cars would not start anyway. Then the cold came inside the houses after exhausting the heating systems running fulltime to final overheated automatic shutdown. We couldn't get our furnace to reset to restart.

We had two fireplaces on the first floor, whether our firewood would last was in question if the vortex refused to leave. Then nine of our basement water pipes froze and burst in the middle of the night while we slept under extra layers of blankets, on the living room floor, in front of smoldering coals in the biggest fireplace. We woke up to no running-water, and the main house heat still refusing to fire. Our local radio station assured us, "Global warming is not the problem, the actual problem is prolonged, unusually cold temperatures." They were always right, they were rightwing radio.

The neighbors we checked in on by telephone recommended centuries old methods to melt snow and ice for drinking, cooking, washing, and flushing. They also suggested putting chunks of ice in the refrigerator when the electricity failed. We learned by telephone most of our county's pipes had frozen, and misery does not love company.

Attempting to reach the one licensed master plumber in the area, I spoke to his wife via telephone. She said her husband and sons were buried under emergency work trying to get people's heat on and water flowing. She put us on the waiting list, saying, "The plumber's estimated time of arrival will be, give or take, three months, unless the national guard comes to help."

When I relayed the information, three months without indoor water to my housemates, Joey said, "I don't think so." Joey Hall knew Hank Thompson, the plumber who covered our rural area. Mike Morgan the handyman was often hired to do cleanup or cosmetic tasks, by Hank at the end of big plumbing jobs. Joey had Hanks, private cell phone number and made a show of calling with his own cell phone.

Surprise, surprise, Hank and his three sons arrived in less than an hour after Joey phoned. Bob, Frances, Hans, and I were told to stay upstairs out of the plumber's way. Out of the corner of my eye I noticed Frances and Corey Thompson seemed to ignite a mutual attraction. *Please God, no more teenage drama until we have running hot water for a long soak.*

To this casual observer, Frances and Corey appeared enthralled at first sight. Light, back, and forth, seemed to beam from their eyes. As the morning progressed the two young people gave each other deepening hungry yearning-glances every chance they got. That naturally lead to putting their heads together to converse awkwardly at stolen moments. Corey was Hank's middle son and looked to be about Frances' age. He was the one we noticed go back and forth between our basement and their truck the most. My guess was he volunteered for the go-for assignments. The boy had movie star good looks, a lot of personality, and a dazzling toothpaste smile, compared to his rough-cut, dull eyed, and goofy looking-acting brothers.

Hank, his boys, and Joey had our nine ruptured pipes spliced and the furnace going in two and a half hours. Going out the door in a rush, Hank handed me a hand scrawled bill and said, "We put your Styrofoam pipe insulation back in place, but so you know, once you froze that insulation kept the ice from melting. You can avoid future beaks if you put thermostat controlled electric heaters on those basement pipes. Though be careful they cause house fires. Next time we get a hard freeze crack open all faccts to drip and drain the toilets. It looks like a bad winter."

"Let me write you a check."

"There's no time, we got work coming out of our ears. Mail your payment to my wife. There's no rush, she won't get caught up with bookkeeping until summer." Then he and his sons were out the door and on their way to the next plumbing emergency.

The long-loaded goodbye look between Frances McDermott and Corey Thompson brought up protective paternal instincts I didn't realize I had. Once plumber and sons were gone my mood shifted to present tense and the plumber's bill in my hand. "Joey, Hank only charged us for materials, there's no labor charge. He must be so overworked he made a mistake. Labor is usually more than materials. How should we handle this?"

"No mistake, I fixed seven of the nine breaks, measured then cut new pipe, coupled them to old pipe with union joints, and crimped them leak proof. Hank showed me how and he and the boys only assisted me to complete the work in a hurry. I learned what to do fast, it's not complicated. He didn't charge you for my labor because I live here. But we still need to mop up all that water on the basement floor before it turns to ice again."

"Did you ask to help Hank?"

"He asked me."

"Huh, that sounds unusual for a tradesman to show you how to do his work. I suppose he and his sons are exhausted beyond telling. Did he show you how to get the heat going?"

"Yes. There are tricks I didn't know to fool the furnace."

"Bob and I will have to get you a special reward, Joey. How's about a new set of luggage for your trip to England?"

"No, thanks! The University of Oxford scholarship is a reward beyond my dreams."

"How about I take your wishes under advisement for now? Frances, why don't you go mop up the basement water as your contribution to resolving our emergency, and Bob and I will start lunch for us."

"I'll be your basement, frau hag, just for today because I sling a mop better than any man can."

"Actually. Hank asked me to do him a favor, after he saw how accurately I measure, cut, and crimped pipes. I hope you won't mind I said yes."

"Why would I mind when I have a basement frau hag at my command, for a full day no less? I'm overwhelmed with the possibilities."

"Watch it, buster, keep that up and get to see hag retaliation up close and evil, Gus."

"Hank and the boys have too much work. They would rather only do big commercial heat jobs or homeowners with burned-out well-pump-motors than our time-consuming small but important emergencies. Hank isn't greedy but he needs his business to be profitable."

"I imagine most everyone in the county wants heat and water running right away."

"Hank asked me to help out with his customers with little money and uncomplicated pipes problems. One of his boys will get the furnaces going, if I can't."

"With everything else going on with you, do you have time?"

"I think so. I should have the jobs done before school break is over. My guidance counselor has seen to it I have an easy last semester in high school. She kept emphasizing high school should be a fun memory. That's one reason I wanted to graduate with my class, for memory's sake."

"Bob and I concurred and recommend fun for you. Do you expect broken pipe plumbing to be fun?"

"Trust me, it will be fun to help out people who used to be mean to me. I know the names on the list, from working with Mike. Guess what, my old physics teacher is number one."

"Ah ha, revenge without running water to wash away the taste of vengeance."

"Frances, be nice! Joey will you be paid for this plumbing caper?"

"I know some folks on the list barely scrape by, but Hank insists they pay me something beyond the cost of materials. He said I should negotiate a fee with those I help because he can't pay me. I'm unlicensed."

"That doesn't sound right. You need liability insurance."

"No. I'm a high school student helping out neighbors. I go to school with students from these families. We can expect some will pay me in chickens, eggs, and promised prayers. You guys helped me I'd like to pass it on."

"What if they can't afford pipe?"

"That' d be okay, I'll just scrounge the junk yards for reusable pipe. It's cheap."

"Joey, that's generous of you."

"I don't mind, for the most part these are working people struggling to get by."

"Do you have the tools you'll need? Bob and I can get you what's needed, if not."

"Hank loaned me a crimping gun, pipe and tube cutters, and gave me a big bag of union and elbow joints. I think I'm all set. If the job requires soldering, Hank will send over one of his sons to do it."

"How can you carry tools, and pipe on your bike?"

"I'll put saddle bags on Mike's motorcycle and have the plumbing supply store deliver pipe. Guess who's the last name on the list?"

"I give, who?"

"Matilda MacKinsey. If one of you doesn't mind driving on glass-slick-black-ice to give me a ride, I'll start with her today. Just for the fun of it I think I'll work Hank's list in reverse order."

"This frau hag won't mention revenge or physics teacher for fear of offending their taskmaster benefactor."

"Now see, that's a wise frau hag."

"Joseph, can I see Matilda with you. She promised to show me how to crochet. I really like her, she's like a living history book including needlework."

"Only after the good frau hag mops up the basement flood." Joey said this wagging a finger at Frances. Then they exchanged a sibling's grin.

To block a budding sibling fest, I said, "Speaking of such things, Frances, what's brewing with you and Corey Thompson?"

"He likes me, and I like him, and it is none of any of your business beyond that. He knows how to treat a young lady properly, not like the uncouth brutes who force me to mop basement floors."

"Does he know everything he needs to about our fine upstanding mop slinger?"

"Gus, do you mean does he know I'm a freak of nature … well not yet. He'll be informed when it's time if it goes that far. And I'll thank you all to stay out of my personal business if you know what's good for you."

"Goodness gracious, threats so early in the day and when there is an abundance of water on the basement floor crying out, "Frances come mop us.""

"A word to the wise, whether you men realize it or not, you treat me like a boy. Corey treats me like the desirable young woman I am."

"Frances, we treat you like Frances, and sooner is always better for unveiling secrets with new friends."

"If no one objects I'm going to take a long bubble bath to make up for the bath I missed yesterday and today. Hygiene is important to young ladies."

"It'll take time for the water to get hot. In the meantime, if you work fast, the basement can get mopped up and dry before hot bath water arrives, Miss Clean."

"Thank you and fuck you, Joseph."

****

Joey successfully got water flowing without leaks for the fifty-three names on Hank's list and did it faster than even he estimated. He returned the barrowed tools, just as his last semester of high school began. Hank offered Joey a plumbing apprenticeship, which he respectfully declined.

No sooner had Joey's schedule returned to normal than we noticed Frances missing for an hour or two at odd times on the weekends. Asking about her whereabouts brought on teenage complaints of invasion of constitutional right of privacy. Civics was her best subject in school.

During the week we lived crammed together in the apartment, so it was impossible not to know who was where doing what when we were in the city together. Arriving at the country house we three revered our privacy. As it turned out we may have cut Frances too much weekend slack time in overreaction to weekday constriction.

One late Sunday afternoon in early spring, Frances flew into the house, dropped pencil box and drawing pad, kicked off shoes, flapped off coat like a bird flailing against a snake attack. Then disappeared into the downstairs half-bathroom a flash of relief finding her worried face as the door banged behind her.

Picking up, hanging up, and putting away what had been thrown to the floor in haste, the oversize sketch pad flipped open revealing an unexpected image. Based on my surprised expression Bob, and Joey came over, and we thumbed through the pad looking at artwork. The flipped open drawing showed a very life like looking, full frontal view of Corey Thompson in the altogether. The image depicted him quite well endowed. Several later closeup sketches included a hand dangling at midthigh confirmed my original guess assessment of average size. After Corey's pictures were drawings of Joey nude, also tastefully executed by a talented artist improving her technique and enlarging certain proportional attributes. I recalled seeing her enhancements at life size in the flesh.

Returning to the entrance hall at normal speed, Frances said, "I had a sudden attack of diarrhea. I don't know where it came from, I'm careful what I eat." Then she saw what Bob, Joey and I were viewing and shouted, "I have no privacy from you peeping toms, you are big snoopers."

"It fell open."

"Living with you men is worse than living in Stalin's Soviet Union." She belligerently grabbed the sketch book, pencil box and stomped upstairs. A percussive slam of her bedroom door ended Frances' dramatic exit with deafening silence.

I glanced at Bob who had retreated into his what do you expect continence. I couldn't read the expressions rapidly bannering across Joey's face. I imagine they were a mix of feeling exposed, compared, and sympathy for the artist his foster sister. He also had to be resigned his privates had just gone public again, this time larger than life. In response to my watching his face, he shrugged his shoulders and brought his open palm hands up in a universal gesture.

I took the second-floor stairs two at a time and knocked on Frances' bedroom door. Getting no answer, I knocked harder and loudly said, "I'm counting five then coming in. If you aren't decent, cover up, one, two, three ..."

The door flew open wide, and an angry Frances faced me. "What do you want?"

"To talk."

"I have nothing to say to you."

"Then you can listen. I'm coming in your room, go sit down."

She backed-up as I closed the door behind me. She went and sat on her bed in a pout with arms crossed tightly over bosom, and body language rigid.

"Bob and I want you safe. Safe from AIDS and safe from being another murdered transsexual. How can that happen if we don't know what you are up to, and with who?"

"I know how to take care of myself, I've had to my whole life. Don't worry I'm going to tell Corey I'm a chick with a dick."

"When will that be?"

"That is a private matter and not your concern. You are not the dictator of my life."

"We *can* stop you coming to the country and hire big, bad minders to keep you safe in the city. Or you could work with us and tell me what's going on."

"What do you want from me?"

"How did you talk Corey out of his clothes to pose for you without a mutual show and tell?"

"I promised him a blow job, and said I was saving the rest of myself for marriage, so nothing else could happen."

"Is that fair? He doesn't get to see you like you saw him?"

"Could be fair if they are an exhibitionist and I'm not. Anyway, it doesn't matter, something happened to postpone fellatio."

"Like what?"

"You only saw preliminary drawings in my sketchbook. I've already given Corey finished sketches of themself. Being a dufus, Corey showed their whole family my drawings. They are so proud of the manly drawings. It's because I made their dick look fatter and longer with bigger balls. Sometimes men can be ridiculously vain. Now their mother wants me to draw a group portrait of three generations of the family males naked."

"That sounds strange bordering on unbelievable."

"That's what I thought until Corey explained they're a clothing optional family. They have a big swimming pool and don't own bathing suits."

"Go back one step. In exchange for his posing for you, he wants a family drawing, instead of oral sex?"

"Exactly. The silly boy thinks his family could tell if we had sex. I told him blowjobs aren't really sex. Crazy right, they are free about nudity, but strict about sex before marriage. Go figure?"

"Crazy."

"Corey is a virgin and is sure everyone will somehow know when he isn't."

"Do you *want* to draw three generations of Thompson males' nude?"

"The problem is how to pose them. Traditionally, the pose is granddad sitting in a chair, their son standing behind them and the grand kids kneeling or sitting on the floor around them. Ugh, that's been done to death! If I do stair steps, it diminishes granddad's status. If I clump them together as a tight group, what's the point of being nude. I have no idea what to do with them that's attractive and original. They think I'm stalling. Maybe I am."

"When is this supposed to happen?"

"Their family is eager, and Corey is a typical teenage boy in need of his first blowjob."

"Have you considered a tug of war rope, Hank and his eldest sons on one side, half turned toward the viewer, versus granddad and the younger boys on the other side. Or Hank and his father on one side and the kids on the other. Either way it means your picture would be horizontal. If I'm not wrong, most portraits are vertical, right?"

"But an action pose draws attention away from the nudity."

"And allows you to buffer the less well endowed. If you get my meaning."

"Huh, I like your tug of war idea. Gus, you look worried about something?"

"After your drawing session, your models might want to dunk you in the pool and discover something they weren't expecting. If Corey knows, at least you have one ally."

"Mike and Eleanor gave Joseph a shotgun for his fourteenth birthday, I could ask Corey to use it to protect my virtue. Oh, wait he's a country boy too, he probably has his own shotgun."

"I'd rather you didn't involve Joey or shotguns."

"You're right, and I shouldn't get you and Bob involved either. Before I go any further with Corey and their blow job, I'll give them a big reveal. Happy now?"

"I'll be happy when you're happy and not in danger."

****

At work, one thing after another came up and demanded immediate, 100% attention, on top of my usual responsibilities. My job thwarted Bob, me, and Frances giving Joey a proper English style congratulatory celebration. Initially, we planned to honor his Oxford scholarship with a memorable meal at our favorite no name farm to table restaurant. Between the teachers' strike and one of my pet projects unraveling expensively at the last moment, Joey's celebration dinner was repeatedly postponed. Then its purpose got expanded to include plumber for the down and out, acknowledgment of another year's most improved wrestler trophy, trophy for more wins than loses, attaining an automobile driver's license, and his impending high school graduation maintaining a 4.0 GPA.

Do or die reservations were made, and our best suits dry cleaned. Joey's cuffs had to be let out by our tailor due to a growth spurt. He was looking teenage lanky instead of short but maintained his 133-pounds until the end of wrestling season.

An ancillary problem materialized; Frances had nothing appropriate to wear. She was comfortable with every day casual unisex attire at her progressive school, and it naturally spilled over to weekend-wear. After procrastinating for weeks, in a huff Frances announced there was absolutely nothing in her wardrobe to conform to the restaurant's strict gender-binary dress code, and there was not enough time for serious shopping with alterations. Her solution was not to go, and stay home and practice the guitar, her latest passion.

Joey the problem solver's solution was to borrow my car to exercise his newly minted driver's license. He drove Frances and Matilda Mac Kinsey to the local Good Will thrift store. I can only imagine what the public thought seeing a top-of-the-line new Mercedes parked in front of the over-used secondhand clothing store.

For joey, and Frances, Good Will shopping was a link to their younger days. For years Matilda had volunteered there when they were shorthanded. She knew the second-hand stock better than the fulltime workers. Acting in consort, the three quickly found a simple black designer label dress that fit Frances as if tailored for her narrow hips. Ms. Mac Kinsey remembered an imported Swiss lace collar buried under a pile of boxes way in back and attached it to the elegant long black dress. Frances wore the dress with her six-inch black stiletto heels and matching clutch handbag. She looked stunning.

The early afternoon of Joey's celebration meal, Frances spent at the local beauty salon. Meanwhile I locked myself in the den preparing Monday morning's presentation for work. If a volcano had erupted under the house, I wouldn't have noticed, my concentration was condensed. Finally, with the last presentation slide in place, I opened the den's pocket door to the kitchen and found Hans marching back and forth looking agitated.

"Hans, sit." I petted him telling him what an obedient dog he was to settle his nerves with a distraction. Then Frances fresh from professionally being made even more beautiful walked into the kitchen. Her face wore an uncharacteristic-ruffled expression.

"Oh, hi Gus, I'm just getting a glass of water. What do you think of my hair, makeup, and nails?" She prettily twirled 360 degrees hair wafting fingers splayed.

"Looks like you just walked off a fashion-show runway. Is that why Hans is on edge?"

"Corey is up in my room crying. Hans doesn't like to see humans upset. I'm bringing Corey a glass of water so they stop crying."

"Put some ice in the water."

"Why?"

"It's makes it nicer."

"I don't suppose you'd talk to Corey with me."

"You told him you're transsexual."

"He didn't take it as well as I expected."

"What were you expecting?"

"At the worst I thought he'd attack, I'd slug him, and that would be the end of us. Truth be told I was hoping he would hug and kiss me and say he still loves me, and my boy thing is unimportant."

"What did happen?"

"Get this, somehow, he blames himself. Corey keeps saying don't tell anyone he was so stupid. I don't get it, anyone who wants to know about me already does. Well maybe not everyone out here in the countryside. Obviously."

"What can I do?"

"Calm Corey down, like you just did with Hans. You and Bob do that all the time for Joseph and me."

I nodded yes thinking, *Why me, Lord,* and followed Frances and the glass of ice water upstairs to her pink bedroom. She handed the glass to Corey who was openly balling like a disappointed five-year old. He was sitting on the edge of her bed. Frances walked across the room and sat in the frilly stuffed chair by the bay window.

"Corey, Frances asked me to chat with you. Would that all right?" When he nodded yes, I lowered myself into the pink Boston rocker next to her bed. Frances had recently repainted her bedroom pale-pink and some of the furnishing deeper glossier pink.

"I loved her, totally loved her … gave her my heart. A guy is supposed to know about these things. Jeez I even proved my love by getting naked to please her." Then shame faced his tears streamed out harder.

"Reality check, Corey, as far as I know, you and Frances only exchanged spit and secrets. The point of uncovering secrets is to share yourself with the person you care about. Isn't what you did by posing and she did by telling."

"You can't make me feel this is right. I've been incredibly stupid."

"Fact, you had to feel good about your body to show it. She had to care deeply about you to reveal being transsexual."

"Huh … you got me to stop crying. But I still feel like a fool."

"I don't think you're a fool. Trust me, Frances wouldn't like you if you were."

"Yeah, what kind of man doesn't even know his girl isn't female?"

"Frances revealed a secret you weren't expecting. If Frances isn't who you thought or want, that's it, break it off, mission accomplished, move on to life's next adventure."

"I don't know. *How am I supposed to know?*"

"Corey, you shared secrets with Frances. If you don't like the results, stop while you're ahead."

"But I still love her. She is the most beautiful woman I've ever seen, held, or kissed, we fit perfectly together. I want to marry her and raise a family. Oh my God, how foolish is that to say? *How could she be the girl of my dreams!*"

"What is your parents' attitude toward transsexuals?"

"They are religious conservatives, you can't tell them. They'd freak-out and drown us both."

"Then that's a consideration for *your* decision going forward."

"What decision? I have no choice. Frances is Frances. Wait, can't doctors change that? Can they fix her?"

"If Frances is not who you wanted *as is*, do yourself a favor and become just friends."

"No! I don't need another friend. We were going all the way. I had my heart set on Frances as my wife."

"You're a hard negotiator. How about take a short kissy-face hiatus to do research and soul search. With more information you might see things differently."

"Can't a doctor make her into a bonified woman?"

"That would be France's decision and she couldn't produce children if she made it. Would that be acceptable to you?"

"I love her! She fits perfectly in my hands. Kissing her is better than my wildest wet dream!"

Seeing Corey's crying jag was over, Frances came over and sat next to him on the bed. He took her hand in his, each added another hand, and then they looked longingly into each other's eyes.

"This looks like a suitable time for me to leave. Frances, we leave in forty-five minutes, with or without you." That said, I rose from the rocking chair and headed for the door.

"Can Corey come?"

I turned and took a beat to consider her request, then asked. "Corey, do you have a suit and tie?"

"Sure, of course, my Sunday suit. Why?"

"Frances, are you sure about this?"

"I love this big lug. I'd love for him to join us for Joseph's celebration dinner. Cory should get to see what he gets along with me."

"Corey, you know Joey?"

"Sure, we went to middle school together. Then my parents sent me to Catholic high school for the better football team."

"All right then. Go home and change. We leave in three-quarters of an hour. Here, let me write down the GPS coordinates for you. Be sure to wear a tie."

"I have three."

"Wear your best one."

****

We arrived at the restaurant parking lot with five minutes to spare and had no sooner left my car than Corey drove up in his older than him GMC pickup truck. His suit looked like a hand-me-down worn thin at the elbows, knees, and seat by previous owners' different physiology. The hems and seams had been expertly let out to fit its current owner's lanky frame. However, his red and green tie, with big white snowflakes, would never get past Brent.

"Corey, let's trade ties."

"You sure? Yours is nicer."

"It's a family tradition." I loosened my Italian silk $350 tie, enough to fit it over Corey's head, tucked it under his collar, and cinched up the Windsor knot. Then I put on his tie and quickly tied a half-Windsor knot in the wool-synthetic-blend Christmas tie.

Brent didn't give me any guff over adding a fifth place setting to our table but said, "Gus, did you lose the bet?"

"What bet?"

"That I'd let you get away wearing that rag around your neck. Throw that shabby, disgusting thing in the garbage, no better, *burn it*. Here, put this on, the inflated price of this tie will be added to your dinner bill." Brent handed me a new medium-quality, neutral colored, China-silk tie. It did not look bad and would be an impressive addition keepsake to Corey's collection. I recalled the restaurant stocked ties and jackets for patrons not properly dressed to be seated.

Corey closely watched my interaction with Brent about his Christmas tie. He blushed a faint pink realizing his best tie had been judged scruffy, and I had withstood embarrassment because of it. His blushing was slight compared to Joey's usual glowing red. Nevertheless, pink was noticeable, and Joey was also paying attention.

I thought, *Welcome to our family, Corey.* I removed the Christmas tie and folded it neatly into my inside suit-jacket pocket. After putting on the restaurant tie, we were shown to a table for five. A memorable meal, worth the inflated price of neckwear was had by all.

Frances and Corey were mostly quiet during dinner though seemed to enjoy their gastronomic delights on a secondary level. Primarily they made goo-goo eyes at each other while Bob, Joey and I chatted about thoroughly enjoying our sumptuous meal and what it was celebrating. When we were pleasantly sated, I was wavering about breaking our house rule to suggest Corey spend the night. Young love can look adorable.

Without forethought but with a snicker, Joey stabilized my wavering and said, "You two need to get a room."

Bob shot me an inquiring glance before he said, "Joey's right. Tell you two what, I'll spring for half a night at the don't tell motel if Joey or Gus pays the other half."

"This is Joey's night. If that's what he wants, that's what he gets, I'll pay fifty percent. Corey, will your family be okay with you spending a night away from home?"

Then I saw jealousy flit onto Joey's face as he grasped what Frances and Corey would be doing in the motel room. I do not recall ever seeing Joey jealous, it wasn't an attractive look on his usually placid innocent face.

"I'll phone home and say I'm staying over with Joe. I'm sure they won't mind, they like him."

In the parking lot standing next to our vehicles, Joey looked the physical embodiment of a green-eyed monster about to grow fangs and claws. I cut short his dark mood by handing him my car's ignition fob and he triumphantly took the seat behind the steering wheel.

I reached over and retrieved my tie from Corey's neck and handed him his Christmas tie and new restaurant issued tie. Corey started to apologize for his tie's reception, but I put my hand up in the universal signal to stop, and said, "Welcome to our family. I'm sure your Christmas tie was your best least used one, exactly what I asked you wear."

Corey nodded his head yes but continued to look awkward, dressed in his well-worn Sunday suit while our family was dressed to the nines. Corey peeked at a smug looking Joey seated behind the wheel of my big Mercedes S-class and gave him a lust-tinged grateful look. When his look was not acknowledged it must have dawned on Corey, *They all know what Frances and I are about to do at the motel.* He then blushed a darker shade of pink.

We all said good night, Bob and I took the back seats and Joey drove us home in the style we someday hoped to get accustomed to.

CHAPTER 15. Murder Most Foul

Spring was too short a transition from prolonged deep-freeze to stifling heat, heavy with dense humidity. Plants that survived the hard months of winter got busy growing furiously. Our fruit trees went from covered in blossoms to laden with cherries, pears, and apples in less time than usual. The peaches, plums, and apricots didn't survive the winter. Summer's oppressively hot mid-July already had the perennial berry bushes heavy with ripening fruit, it seemed just after bursting into flowers. Once planted, as if working on steroids, the vegetable garden promised an over abundant harvest.

Too soon, Joey's mid-August departure loomed. So, we all made efforts to spend extra quality time with him. One early Sunday afternoon, the family was hunched over a Scrabble game-board on the front porch. I noticed, Hans' ears shot up and he stood at attention apparently without provocation. He had been sitting relaxed with Bob's hand resting on his shoulder. Then Hans took an on-guard attitude hackles raised, and marched beside the porch railing.

Joey looked up from placing his tile letters to form his favorite word *conundrum*. He built it down from my letter "c" in *constipation*. "Are we expecting visitors?"

"Conundrum is a hard Scrabble word, and so far, Joey, you are winning."

Languidly Bob said, "No visitors expected today."

All eyes turned to Frances.

"Can't be Corey, he's hunting with his father and bothers two states away."

So, we humans trooped to the front porch railing just as four older pickup trucks and an old, battered station wagon came into view. We watched with interest as the impromptu convoy drove up and parked on our front lawn, all vehicles facing the porch. A dozen uninvited folks climbed down from pickups, station wagon and sauntered over Joey's perfectly manicured lawn. They looked unfriendly facing us up on the porch. Then a gray haired, fiftyish looking man, maybe six feet and 250 pounds with a beer-belly sagging over his belt, moved to the front of the group and said, "I'm Milos Snodgrass and we came to talk to Austin Bennington."

I noticed the uninvited appeared to be locals, I'd seen on weekends shopping on Main Street. Today all were wearing holstered sidearms. Our state allows open carry handguns in rural areas only. Disquieted to have an unexpected armed mob trampling Joey's well-manicured lawn, I matter of factly said, "He isn't here, never lived here, and you are trampling our grass."

"Not that we don't believe you, brother, but this is a serious matter. We'll have a look around for ourselves. If you don't mind … or do."

"No. You won't. This is private property, please leave. You're trespassing."

I didn't hear Joey and Frances go into the house while I spoke with Milos Snodgrass but glanced back when the front screen-door bang as they returned to the porch. Out of the corner of my eye I saw Joey hand Bob the .308 caliber Dan and Bill had left us in case of a rabid bear attack. To show self-defense, Bob half mounted the rifle, pointing it in the general direction of the interlopers. Meanwhile Joey brought his thirty ought six deer rifle up to his shoulder aiming at someone in the front of the crowd. Standing between Bob and Joey, Frances cradled joey's twelve-gauge pump-action shotgun to her beasts, like it was an infant. The business end of the shotgun was pointing at the ground. Her facial expression plainly showed she would rather not be holding the long weapon and had no intention to use it.

Milos Snodgrass clearly focused only on Frances's pretty face rather than seeing the whole scene with Bob and Joey's lethality. At that close-range, high-velocity hunting rifle bullets would easily penetrate two even three people crowded together the way they were standing bunched up. Unfazed by present, real danger, Milos moved toward the bottom tread of the porch steps and said, "Let me take that big heavy scattergun lovely little lady. We don't want you to hurt yourself."

Hans had been standing next to me, my left hand resting lightly on his back. It is remotely possible I conveyed anxiety through my fingers, or more likely Hans made his own assessment. As Milos moved to mount the porch stairs, the German Shepard stepped to the top tread. Then Hans drew back his lips and bared his teeth. He further showed the trespasser his disapproval by issuing a long, loud, ominous snarl. Hans was not about to allow a stranger to step on his porch, let alone touch Frances.

Mr. Snodgrass moved backward in a blur. He looked like a cartoon character going in reverse at high speed. When he finally stopped moving, panting short of beath he unholstered his pistol and pointed it at Hans. Seeing their leader's fright, his henchmen and women drew their weapons, they all had one. Simultaneously, I heard the faint snick as Bob and Joey clicked-off their rifles' trigger-safety-locks.

"Hans come." He backed up to lean against my left leg, keeping a wary eye on Milos. My mind raced to find a way to defuse the dangerous situation. If someone accidentally discharged a weapon, the result could be a blood bath with few if any of us left standing. As I came up with zero solutions, I saw flashing emergency lights turnoff the state route and onto the access road. "Did someone call the sheriff?" I pointed as two marked police cars turned off the access road onto our private road, all heads turned to see where I directed. I later learned Frances dialed 911 while Joey loaded the long guns.

The sheriff cars pulled in behind the pickup trucks, five doors opened, and five uniformed officers stepped out. They looked at the situation and four ducked into their cars and removed shotguns. Then the lawmen and women took shooting positions behind open car doors.

The sheriff marched up to the front of the standoff. She faced both the porch and the uninvited crowd on the lawn from a side enfilade position. She was not in direct line of fire if it erupted, her sidearm holstered. "I am Sheriff Gloria Gomez, you *will* secure your weapons, or my people *will* confiscate them. If we take them, they become ours." A swoosh was heard as twelve sidearms slapped leather holsters in a rush to be secured from seizure. A withering glare from the Sheriff brought Bob and Joey's rifle butts down from their shoulders to rest on the porch floor planks. Frances finally caught on and delicately laid Joey's shotgun down on the scrabble board, scattering letter tiles, and then daintily stepped away from it.

In a loud command voice, the sheriff said, "Someone want to tell me about the occasion for this unlawful assembly?" Nobody said a word. "Last chance before we bring out the handcuffs."

I spoke up. "This is private property, and these intruders are trespassing."

Making hard eye contact and speaking directly to me, the sheriff said, "Intruder trespassing is redundant, I don't approve of superfluous verbosity in my county. Clean up your communications, fella, or face arrest." Turning to the twelve interlopers gapping open mouthed at the sheriff policing my use of English language usage, she used her command voice again. "Why are you people here? It's Sunday, don't you know how to grill-meat over burning charcoal?"

Milos Snodgrass's color had returned after his German Shepherd fright. "We are looking for Austin Bennington. It was rumored he is hiding out at this place."

Addressing me, Sheriff Gomez said, "Is he here?"

"No. We haven't seen Austin since he moved back to the city months ago."

Turning back to Milos, Gomez said, "What do you want with Mr. Bennington?"

"We think he murdered his aunt, Matilda Mac Kinsey. She was a beloved member of our church."

"On what did you base that opinion?"

"They had a big fight after church several weeks ago."

"Over what?"

"That old clunker of a car he left at her house. He came to collect it. But she had already given it away as a donation to the Kars for Kids commercial."

"Why don't we cut this friendly little Sunday visit short. The coroner's preliminary report, I saw, says she expired due to an age-related fall. It was ruled death by natural causes. *Not that it is any of your business.*"

The mob erupted with shouts of, "LIES, BULLSHIT, COVERUP, CORUPTION!"

Sheriff Gomez raised her hand for quiet and finally got it. "Why did you wait a week to try and do my job?"

Almost as if Milos were trying to get arrested, he said, "You obviously haven't read today's paper Sheriff!"

"Haven't had time. Yahoos like you keep interrupting my bar-b-que."

"Today's newspaper has a big expose. It says the coroner's office is six months behind doing autopsies, most preliminary report becomes the final report due to lack of funds for adequate staffing. We know Matilda was murdered and most likely by her worthless nephew."

"I'll bite, what do you know that I don't?

"Clive, Tobias, tell the sheriff what you found."

There was a stirring in the crowd and two over the hill farmhands hobbled forward. "I'm Clive Brackish, me and my cousin Tobias Brackish found poor Ms. Mc Kinsey dead."

"What circumstance caused you to do that?"

"We were supposed to take her to a dentist appointment to fit a new pair of choppers. Her door was open and when nobody answered our knocks, we went in. She was laying on the kitchen floor ... I called 911 right off."

"Why do you think she didn't die from natural causes?"

"A muddy boot print in the center of her apron. I think someone with a size thirteen foot kicked her hard in the chest, and she went flying across her kitchen and did a header into her cast-iron cookstove."

"This is new information to me. How do you know it was size thirteen?"

"I noticed the pattern the killer's boot left on Ms. Mac Kinsey and on her kitchen floor. Usually, she kept her kitchen spotless."

"You got my attention, what about it?"

"It was the same pattern as Tobias' boot. So, I had him hold his boot over the murder's mud prints. They were size thirteen same as his, but Tobias' boots are worn down the killer are newer."

"Tobias, are you wearing the same boots today?" When he nodded yes, Sheriff Gomes went over and photographed the bottoms of his yellow-leather construction boots with her cell phone's camera.

Turning back to me, ranking officer Gomez said, "The Sheriff's department wants to search your property for Austin Bennington. You can give us permission and we'll be gentle with your property, or we can come back with a warrant, pissed off for making an unnecessary roundtrip. You need to know many family heirlooms get accidentally broken when my people are pissed off. They can't help themselves it's an anger management issue we haven't fixed yet."

I felt gut punched disoriented learning of Matilda's death. Frances openly cried. "Give us a minute, we just learned someone we knew and liked was slain."

Joey too was clearly upset hearing a dear friend had been murdered. He raised his hand to speak. When it wasn't acknowledged, he loudly said, "Austin wears size eight and a half shoes." Though loud, his voice sounded flat, and his face was white, drained of color.

"How do you know that?"

"We were on the high school wrestling team last year. He forgot his shoes for a reginal tournament, and I leant him mine. I also wear eight and a half. My shoes fit Austin, and he won his match."

With a slight ironic smile, the sheriff asked, "Anyone else know something I don't, and think I should?"

Fighting mixed up feelings after learning someone I knew and liked was murdered. I made eye contact with Sheriff Gomez and said, "Matilda Mac Kinsey told me the manager of the factory farm was pestering her to sell the home that had been in her family for generations. I offered to talk to him for her. She told me it was her problem and she'd fix it."

An angry murmur went up from the lawn crowd at the mention of the factory farm, they turned and lurched toward their pickup trucks. It took effort for the sheriff and her deputies to restore order again and then disperse the crowd to their homes. Gomez had to reassure the unruly armed mob, she and her people would immediately visit Mr. Roger Hasselford and inspect his footwear. No further mention of searching our home was mentioned.

I felt the mob's malice deflate then fizzle away once the Sheriff heard them and took charge. But I had caught the crowd's infectious righteous rage. To keep my revenge feelings in check I reminded myself to be a good role model for the kids, rather than yield to an overpowering urge to repeatedly punch the murderous son of a bitch who killed sweet old Matilda trying to save her home.

After the uninvited visitors left, Joey telephoned Austin in the city and matter of factually let him know his aunt had been killed. In teenage boy parlance, he relayed it might not be healthy for Austin to be in the county for a while. Austin said Matilda's family had been officially notified she died from a fall. A crematorium had been engaged to dispose of her body once the medical examiner released it and her home was to be sold.

Minutes after Joey ended his call, Austin's mother telephoned. She asked Joey why it would be unhealthy for Austin to go wherever he wanted?

Joey told her, "Pistol packing friends of Matilda hold serious hard feeling against Austin. Also, I heard her pastor was willed her property or holds her will, or some such. Talk to him before you try to sell it."

The next morning's featured news story on the local community funded NPR radio station announced, "Factory farm manager Roger Hasselford confessed to killing lifelong village resident Matilda Mac Kinsey. Hasselford said he had been provoked by Ms. Mac Kinsey and claims self-defense. Under cover of night, the prisoner was taken to the state capital jail, due to fear of a lynch mob breaking into the flimsy village detention office."

****

Everyone in the village and surrounding area came to Matilda Mac Kinsey's funeral, except her immediate family. It was a long-winded, somber burial that depleted florists of flowers in a 100-miles radius. Matilda was a simple woman who cherished being alone. Weeks after the funeral, the local biweekly newspaper ran an article stating Ms. Mac Kinsey bequeathed her estate to a non-profit charity for wayward pregnant girls. Matilda's passing put a damper on all of us. We four humans grieved openly, and Hans got depressed by association. But in his dreams Hans dispatched Milos Snodgrass. I could tell by the way he moved his feet, head, and growled in sleep.

Then before we were ready it was time for Joey to leave for England, Hans took the long car ride with us to the airport. He did not enjoy the ride in the crowded car. Since he is not a service dog, he and Joey had to say their goodbyes at curbside. Frances had borrowed Bob's digital camera and documented Joey and Hans' prolonged heartfelt goodbye. Her plan was to make a stop action video with voiceover script she wanted to write, showing Joey's departure. Then she got busy with other things, and nothing came of the project.

Inside the terminal amid hugs and tears, we walked Joey to his final gate and bid farewell until he was out of sight. All the while Frances snapped digital images. Deflection or not, it kept her mind off the complicated relationship the two foster siblings had made. Joey's face showed a mix of feelings flooding him. Bob and I were sad to see Joey leave. He would be missed. I couldn't shake the mental image of a mother bird watching the baby she had hatched fly out of the nest not knowing if it would live or die without her protection.

Returning home, Hans was depressed like the other occupants of the car. I reminded myself if Joey had gone to the military after high school graduation, as originally planned, we would have missed the last months with him. Who knew paternal love had such a short gestation period, and left such deep holes in the heart? I already missed Joey's contradictions to untangle on weekends.

With Joey in England, we began taking Hans to the city with us. It was not right leaving him alone in his dog run four days a week, even with one of the vet's assistants feeding and exercising him once a day. Hans never bonded with the vet or her helpers. Left on his own, he started going stir crazy. In the city Hans did not like our crowded living arrangements. With Frances living with us, no one had adequate space. I worried Hans' muscles might atrophy from lack of exercise, even though one of us walked him in the morning and again after work or school. We were facing an extremely hard decision nobody wanted to make.

Then just in time, Mike and Eleanor moved back from North Carolina and into their old place. Eleanor's mother had died, and so they brought her older sister Elizabeth back with them. She had exhausted her physical therapy benefits down south, just when they were beginning to show results. Up north, at least in our state, there was no Medicaid cap on rehabilitation. They moved Elizabeth into joey's old windowless sleeping alcove.

When all the legal formalities were done, Bob and I gave over a check and co-signed a guarantor note for the bank, so Mike and Eleanor could restart their defaulted mortgage. With Joey living in England, Mike resumed taking care of our country house grounds and repairs. He also set to rebuilding his local handy man trade. He and Hans bonded at first sight. Because of our absences due to work and Frances' school schedule, Hans adopted Mike as his new pack leader. Bob, Francs, and me were relegated to weekend casual acquaintances. Our diminished status made us sad, but Hans was revitalized.

CHAPTER 16. Self-harm Antidote

Late summer turned into a normal fall for a change. Then on schedule winter was driving the thermometer down to normal range for a change. Global Warming was giving us a taste of our lost four seasons of the year. Post Joey in residence, weekly trips to the country house slowly digressed to once a month, if we were lucky. The cold empty house reminded us Joey was living on another continent an ocean away. We didn't needed reminders we missed our young friend.

Lacking rural tranquility, Sunday brunch in the neighborhood became a routine habit. Eager to start light conversation after a prolonged teenage silent treatment over a minor disagreement, I let my guard down and spoke without thinking first. "We haven't seen hide nor hair of Corey in a while, everything still hunky-dory with you two love birds?"

"There you go again snooping. Gus, you're making my personal life available for public consumption. A girl has no privacy around you two oafs, you do know that don't you? I will make flash cards to teach you if necessary."

"That's certainly one way to interpret parental concern. Or more accurately, it could be construed as showing interest in you and your welfare."

"I'm a big girl and don't need or want adult supervision. I don't get why you bother. You know I'll bite your head off for asking personal questions."

"Since we haven't been going to the country as much, my off-hand remark could be understood as, 'You okay with staying in the city most weekends?'"

"Or relentless Gus is trying to meddle in my personal business as usual."

"Or Bob and I *have* exhausted small-talk about the weather, and your private life is most assuredly more interesting than atmospheric predictions of precipitation and other algorithms."

"Is that it, the best you got?"

"Well, yes, as you know I refuse to ruin a perfectly good Sunday morning squabbling over politics or religion."

"Now the truth comes out, WHY ME?"

"Because *you*, Frances, don't fight fair and always side with Bob."

"Spoilsport, you are worse than some kids at my school. Speaking of conversation topics, do you think we will ever talk seriously about me being transsexual? I mean before I'm emancipated, move out and you two go senile and forget who I was."

"Bob, did I hear a challenge? Yes. Uh ha, I thought so. Quiz me, Frances, you might be surprised how senile I am at almost age thirty-three."

"You asked for *it,* cowboy Gus, when do researchers say trans development starts?"

"In utero. Transsexual infants show measurable opposite brain function than cisgenders."

"Huh, that is correct, *you must be cheating.*"

"I'm not! Try again."

"Do you think that's how my mother knew I was a girly-boy from birth?"

"Do you have doubts?"

"I'm asking the questions, bub. But sometimes. … I haven't been ready to talk to my shrink about nature versus nurture versus percentages yet."

"Why not?"

"I've always been exceptional. My mother loved and hated my father in equal parts. What if she turned me into a girly-boy to punish my father for beating her and not providing for us? I was only a baby, what did I know?"

"What kind of toys did you like?"

"I was an only child, I played with any toy I got my hands on."

"Didn't you ever visit toy store?"

A wistful look washed over Frances' face. "I must have been two or three the first time I saw dress up dolls. I wanted one. That day my father bought me a toy gun. Ugh! I cried all the way home."

"Mystery solved, next question."

"Bob, what is the biggest social issue trans kids have?"

"What's the prize if I get it right?"

"My undying gratitude."

Putting on an exaggerated officious face, hand on chin Bob asked, "Huh, what's that valued in bitcoin?"

Looking down Frances said, "Answer the question." As she emptied and stirred pink packets of sugarless sweetener into her black coffee.

"The suicide attempt rate for transsexual children is forty-four percent, compared to one and a half percent for cisgender children under twelve. Do you think that might indicate a problem?"

"So, you both studied beyond non-cisgender summer camp, which I didn't get the job at. Thanks again for trying."

"Hey, it was a long shot."

After her toy store story, Frances' expansive mood folded inward like a cold birds' wings tucked tight for warmth. In a flat voice she said, "I'm flattered you tried for me, really. Oh wait, of course, you're a schoolteacher, Bob. I should have known you'd get *transsexual training* and share it with this other big lug."

Witnessing her mood rapidly shift from sunny to glum, I had to ask. "Were you ever in the forty-four percent and made an attempt on your life?"

With a tinge of hostility showing over the coffee mug rim, Frances said, "Back to invading my privacy, are we?"

"Answer my question like I did yours, *nicely.*"

"Okay, okay, okay, mean task master. I thought about offing myself when I was younger. That was before my father got the brilliant idea to do it for me. Now I refuse to give his ghost the satisfaction."

Bob and I exchanged a concerned couples look, and I said, "We like having you around. We'd be sad if you harmed yourself."

"I concur with Gus. Please talk to one of us before hurting yourself."

"Relax, how did this Sunday morning get so suicidal?"

"You didn't want to talk about Corey, and I thought we were kidding around. Truce, … is there something you want talk about?"

"Huh, I guess you want to know about Corey, or why would you keep asking."

"Or whatever, linear thinking doesn't seem to be on today's menu?"

Her facial expression looked like Joey trying to decide to talk or not … "I do have a big fear for once I'm emancipated, and you brought it up."

"What is it?"

"I'll be alone all the time."

"Isn't that what you want?"

"I know I say that's what I want, and guess I do. But at the same time am afraid I'll get *too* lonely. Just like when I was a kid and my mom worked double shifts, and I planned and practiced my suicide to occupy time."

"Huh, and I thought Joey had contradictions cornered."

"When I was in elementary school, my mom worked as a waitress, and I became a latchkey kid. Being alone was the quiet I said I craved, the opposite of constant fights my parents had when dad was home from prison. That's when I practiced ways to kill myself to punish both for fighting over me."

"Why so extreme?"

"When you're little you are the reason things go wrong, and don't know the fix."

"Do you still sometimes plan a suicide?"

"When I met you guys and Joseph, I stopped having a reason to kill myself. The three of you didn't let me get depressed. Recently I started thinking about being alone again and all my old suicidal thoughts came back."

"Have you ever cut or burned yourself?"

"Bob, do you want to do an inspection?"

"What kind of answer is that?"

"Joseph and Corey have seen me naked. I guess I could stand for you two inspecting my body with magnifying glasses looking for scares. I haven't had much privacy since living with you in the city."

The conversation had taken a turn I didn't like and said, "Did Joey give you the idea of getting naked in front of us?"

"No. Why would ze?"

"According to the teachers' training I attended, you've described symptoms of suicidal ideation. Could it be that's where all this talk came from? Frances if you are able to talk to us about suicide, then why not your therapist?"

"Look at that Gus, Bob brings his work to Sunday bunch. But really, what will it matter in 100 years, I don't expect to be around and neither will you."

"I'm not comfortable where this breakfast conversation has landed."

"Then one more question for you Gus, it's theological. Why do evangelical Christians hate trans people to the point they want us burning in hell forever? They never met most of us."

"You see that, Bob, this is why I never discuss serious stuff with Frances, it either gets political or religious."

"Answer my question foster daddy #1, and I'll be a good girl all day today. Promise!"

"Ugh, all right, if you insist. The religious nuts are grossly superstitious, and believe their supernatural idols are infallible."

"What's that to do with me?"

"Children born with cleft palates, club feet, and other repairable abnormalities must suffer for their God's will all their days. It takes all kinds to make the world go round, and some hate the idea their obsession could make a gender mistake."

"Gees, Gus, you were right, politics *and* religion snuck onto this breakfast table. You happy now, Frances?"

"SORRY, Sorry, sorry. I underestimated you guys' knowledge. As always, I went too far. You know I don't mean to do that, right?"

Bob had finished eating. I could see on his face he was still vexed about our conversation about suicide. Bob never quite got over being raised Catholic. Suicide is a serious sin for them. To lighten the mood he said, "Exercise proportion my dear. That greatly changes your ecclesiastical indulgence entitlements."

"Speaking of capability, what are you thinking about for the rest of your life workwise?"

"Gus, you're picking on me again!"

"No. I'm looking for ecclesiastical clarity."

"When I was young, being a beautician was the future I wanted. It looked like fun being in charge of playing with dolls' hair. Since becoming a customer, I've found beauty salon patrons are mean to the operators. I don't want that aggravation."

"At the risk of being policed for redundancy, what's your current thinking about your future vocation?"

"After knowing Joseph I'm not sure anymore. He says STEM is where good jobs are for women."

"STEM?"

"Science, Technology, Engineering, and Math."

"Those are areas Joey's good at."

Known for his adroitness, Bob filled the silence. "Frances, you are a talented artist making incredible progress learning classical guitar."

"I've heard that."

"Do you see the music business in your future?"

"What I want is a job that pays the bills and doesn't discriminate against me for being the wrong gender. Except for nice clothes, this girl has simple tastes and doesn't need a lot."

"Don't get mad at my question, maybe it's dumb. When I hear you practicing classic guitar pieces, in your room, I wonder if it feels the same for you as the serene look, I used to see on your face drawing?"

"No, dummy. One is following written music on a page. The other is sketching my interpretation of what I see to fill a blank page. Wait, maybe, they both involve concentration."

"The reason I ask, I hate to admit it, but I can't always tell the difference between your mistakes and adlibbing. However, with your sketches I can spot errors."

"Before we met, I don't remember hearing music. But between Gus's oldies but goodies traveling music in his car, Bob's Bach, Scarlatti, Handel, in his car and Joseph's heavy metal in his bedroom, my ears opened to most of your music. Even Gus's weekend operas in the living room. Now, I know what music I like. Before I ignored all of it."

"What does your life look like in five years?"

"I want your job, Gus. I want to sit behind a big desk and have a secretary and an assistant do all the work and then take credit for it."

"Unfortunately for you, there's a little more to it than that, included the reason my hair is turning prematurely gray. And just so you know, there are quite a few others ahead of you itching for my job."

"Party-pooper, you know how to dash this girls-hopes."

"So, full circle back, what's up with you and Corey? No prurient details wanted."

"Why do you care?"

"The last time I saw you two, you looked like a happy couple."

"What do you really want to know, Gus?"

"Simply put, do you need more time at the country house to spend with Corey?"

"Oh my, my, my … okay … do you want the short or long answer?"

I said, "Short."

Bob said, "No. Long."

Waving the server over, I said, "Yeah, long, that's what I meant. More coffee please."

"The specialness of having a girlfriend with a dick wore off for Corey when my finger slipped in their bottom hole. I was just playing around but come to find out for the son of a plumber, plumbing does matter. Then they started saying how swell it would be if I had a vagina. In their mind my imagined magical vagina would make everything wonderful again, and my being gelded irrelevant."

"Disappointed?"

"No. Because I noticed out on dates, he had developed a wandering eye for other attractive females. He'd shamelessly ogle them in my presence."

"It's good you can read signs."

"In addition, Corey's country bumpkin cuteness began to wear thin. I like a man with at least some sophistication. City boys are much more interesting to hang out with than their country cousins."

"Condolences."

"My therapist says it is common for young people to have many infatuations before they find true love. So, I let Corey down easy."

"How'd you do that?"

"It came to a head when he said, 'If you won't go to Mexico for bottom surgery, we have to date other people.' I told him to knock himself out dating, but not to come around to just get his rocks off."

"You call that easy?"

"Yes, he hasn't phoned or texted since. Not the big tearful dramatic ending I expected."

"How are you doing?"

"Corey will miss my fine, nuanced oral copulation. No straight girl could match what I gave him. What could I expect, he's a typical self-centered American country-boy, boring to the bone!"

"Isn't that a tad harsh?"

"No, not at all."

"Do you have eyes for someone new?"

"Gus, I'm taking a break, trying to figure somethings out. I think I need a real man, one already grown, you know ripe, not another blooming boy."

"Is that a revelation?"

"In a weird way I am like Joseph. I don't really know what I want. What we both need is true love, with lots of passionate sex."

"Our wish is both you and Joey be happy, however you define it."

"Philosophizing so early on a Sunday, what a rare treat."

"Yes, what a weird and winding road we've taken, so back around full circle. Tell us more about living alone and feeling suicidal?"

"I'd never feel that way with a loving family of my choice around … like you two older gentlemen for instance."

"Uh! What are you saying?"

"Who knows, I may not even need a special someone to be happy, with or without a vagina. To be fair, my life has not been terrible since I met you two."

"Jeez Bob, just think of it, we'll have Frances around to change our diapers during dotage. Allah be praised."

"Gus don't bring Allah into. He was no friend to gay people."

"Wrong, wrong, wrong, I'm not an adult diaper changer. Taking male hormone suppressors and female artificial hormones, should finish me off before your dotage comes rolling on in. Sorry daddies, you have to change each other's diapers."

"Gosh oh golly gee whiz, a new revelation ... This old daddy says we should stop procrastinating and get a two-bedroom apartment with lots of closet space before we don't know what day it is or how to button our shoes."

"I like our apartment, Gus."

"I do too, but clearly Frances is not done with us, and wants us around until dotage or whatever. We definitely need more room."

"Ugh, I guess that's why I love you, Gus, you're insane."

"Bob, isn't it nice to share our love with this lonely young person?"

Frances joined the conversation thinking we were only being playful. "But, Daddies, where in the world could we move and be acceptable to neighbors? I've read, people like us will bring property values down?"

"Bob, isn't the area around your school in Prospect Heights attempting a renaissance?"

"So far, we got good-blocks in transition; better-blocks almost there but surrounded by dangerous bad-blocks. The forecast on the street gives a forty percent chance the urban pioneers will civilize the blight. Smart money says it's going to fail."

"Oh my God, you're serious. Okay, okay, then what would you guys do with our current apartment. Sell it, trade it, or keep it off the market?"

"Bob could never sell our home, Frances. He won it, against huge odds, in a keep our teachers in the city, City Lottery."

"Gus is right, I could never sell it, and the condominium board doesn't allow subletting. Sorry, folks, moving is another hairbrained schemes without traction from my husband."

"Bob, what about making it an Airbnb?" Frances said this not sure we were still actually willing to move for her sake but enthralled by the idea.

"The condominium board hasn't taken a position yet. I do know board members who are interested in renting their apartments while on vacation to offset paying for the time away. My guess is it's only a matter of time it's a popular money-making idea."

"You know, Bob, it makes sense to do Airbnb when we are away on weekends. We aren't the only ones in the building with a second home."

"I could lobby board members. If it happens, Frances, you do all the grunt work, screening guests, cleaning up after them, collect the money, give receipts, and most important keep records. But hold on, aren't we getting ahead of ourselves? We three collect clutter like pack rats, who'd want to rent it?"

Frances, the biggest clutter collector, deflected. "Why do I have to do all the *grunt* work?"

"Airbnb was your idea, and you have free time, we don't."

"Okay, this young person will allow you that. Only because it makes sense, and you are making a big sacrifice for me."

Pedantic Bob stayed on point. "We'll also expect you to take an adult role in finding a new place to call home. If an affordable one can be found."

"Managing an Airbnb and apartment, shopping … wait, I can do most of that online. What's your contribution going to be?"

"Bob works in the area we are considering. He could query shop keepers and others at street level for information about good blocks and not."

"Gus, what's your donation going to be? And don't say pack boxes, we'll all do that."

"I'll need to find out if the area is still redlined, and if so, what hoops I'll need to jump through to get us a mortgage. Frances if you are in the mood to nitpick, we could each keep a log of time spent pursuing this communal project."

"That sounds like extra work. No, thank you."

"Then next week, same time same place, we'll each give a report and decided if we want to go forward. How's that?"

"You talked me into it. I'm ready to open a new chapter in my life."

"Do we need to set down rules or do we work independent of each other?"

"Duh!"

"I agree with Frances, everyone do their own thing without added paperwork. Next week, same time, same place?"

"I'm excited."

"Check, please"

We'd gone to breakfast without a hint we'd be looking for a new home. Bob and I had been trained in the military to spot potential suicides and knew Frances and her story well enough to know her suicidal ideation was real. Joey liked to say we always started out talking about one thing and ended up on a different topic. Once again, the boy was right.

CHAPTER 17. Realtor Revelations

One week later, same restaurant, once again we settled in our favorite booth and each ordered, "*The Gut Buster.*" It included, three eggs, bacon, ham, sausage, home fries, pancakes, toast, juice, and coffee. Frances pulled out a sheaf of papers and said, "I found out a lot but didn't edit it down in case you want to know every detail. If you get bored, tell me and I'll give you the abridged version. So, without objection here goes because I'm the only girl in this group, and ladies have privileges and always go first."

"Then as the Brits would say, be calm and carry on."

"Bob don't encourage her pomposity. It could be construed in some quarters as OBNOXIOUS."

"No one ever called me obnoxious to my face. You better watch it, buster. Wait though, it does have a robust, gender-neutral sound to it. Gus, you may stay."

"Then, as Joey would say, EXECELSIOR!"

With a satisfied expression, Frances, looked around the table and said, "Gentrification pushed lowest wage workers out of their homes on three sides of huge Prospect Park. Many of those folks gravitated to the cheapest rents in the area, the Park's forgotten poor relative the northside."

"Why are you telling Bob and me this?"

"As a little background. When speculators move into areas it causes housing disruptions called gentrification. That has a domino effect, high paying renters force middleclass tenants to displace working-class tenants and the area becomes unaffordable for them and the poor. They are forced to flee to distant places for affordable accommodations. Then when no affordable place to live are left, the disadvantaged became homeless. It seems criminal to me no plans were made to give these people a place to live. It reminded me of evictions, after the fact, we saw at the Sanitation Garage."

When Frances took a moment to silently reflect on her Sanitation Garage memory, Bob said, "The homeless function as a visible threat of consequences for noncompliance to the rule of the rich. On a practical level, they function as a ready, if needed workforce, or in a pinch cannon fodder in war." Bob made his comment in a neutral tone buttering his toast.

Sipping orange juice, Frances said, "That sounds bleak."

More upbeat, snagging bacon and sausage off Frances' plate, Bob said, "Where we are going today is an example of a community fighting back before gentrification's dominos can take full effect."

That was Frances' cue to continue sharing her computer source research. "There was a movement in the 1970s and 1980s called urban pioneering. It took today's landlords forty years to undue the housing laws the pioneers fought for and got. At this point the lords of the land are all powerful again and tenants have little to no rights. Housing court is still stacked against tenants without expensive lawyers."

Bob had spoken about Prospect Heights in the past. He worked there. As far as I am concerned it is the latest manifestation of urban renewal by another name to keep the voiceless out of sight and powerless. Prospect Heights had not seen new construction in decades. Rather than receiving improvements of any kind, the area was waiting to be bulldozed. Many buildings' routine maintenance had been neglected to the point of rent strikes just to get most basic essential services.

Most likely lack of services such as heat, water, and dangerous unrepaired elevators drove tenants who could leave, to go. The usual conglomerates of greedy speculators had not anticipated the Prospect Heights community to organize for its survival. Soon, it looked like the biblical David and Goliath story, with unlimited wealth backing Goliath and little David scrounging for pebbles to fling.

"Bob, I hope your street level investigation was less dreary than Frances's recitation just now."

"Either community residents refused to talk about the changes, from out of safety concerns, or they made speeches against change in general. In both cases I sensed fear, but I didn't get any new information. I've assigned my classes to write a 500-word essays on how the changes in their neighborhood directly affect them and their families. I'll let you know if anything interesting turns up."

"What did you learn, Gus? Oh, I mean what did Leonard find out for us?" Frances said this drowning her pancakes in syrup.

"The area is still redlined, which means big reputable banks won't give mortgages to individuals. Begrudgingly, small banks and credit unions will grant mortgages with large down-payment and at high interest. But digging I found leads to unusual financing at prevailing down payment percentages or even slightly less than fair-market interest rates. What *I* found could work for us, but we might have to incorporate or register as a nonprofit organization."

Breakfast over, we walked the short few blocks to our parking garage and went for a Sunday drive in Bob's less conspicuous older Volvo. It had rained the night before giving us a lovely freshly washed sun-drenched day. Naturally, we took the scenic route to Prospect Heights Brooklyn. It had once been a thriving working-class neighborhood, now many of its shops were boarded up. It looked like a depressed no-man's land across the expressway bordering that north edge of vibrant Prospect Park and its conspicuously prosperous surrounding residential areas.

On our Sunday drive we saw century-old apartment buildings just hanging on, mixed in with well-kept private homes, and a few old apartment buildings having a revitalization. Then nearby were desolate blocks of apartment buildings in terminal decline or had already given up the ghost to be mere skeletons of their former selves. Heavily trafficked areas had wide-open drug sales and prostitution on street corners late on a Sunday morning.

I knew from following the business news that a coalition of community groups had formed to keep Prospect Heights from becoming another South Bronx. Co-op City had been built in a swamp on top of a failed amusement park called America Land in the extreme outskirt of the Northeast Bronx.

To fill the new huge super-high-rise apartment complex, Co-op City, the hard to reach, undesirable swamp development had to offer extra generous incentives to seduced tenants out of their old, cheap rental apartments at the other end of the Bronx. The promise of home ownership at bargain prices did not cause a huge migration to extremely tall, hard to reach, undesirable apartments in an unattractive sinking, stinking location.

Since the initial offer failed to drive renters from all over to own co-ops, an anonymous anti-immigrant campaign was launched to stir up irrational fear of crime in the old neighborhoods. Baseless propaganda worked to dislodge people from their homes for generations. Ultimately, fleeing disinformation and bogus crime reports, South Bronx renters moved in mass to the swamp named Co-op City.

With a sudden glut of empty apartments, South Bronx landlords could not find enough new tenants to make their buildings viable and lowered their standards and rented to anyone, including reprobates. They were competing against government induced otherwise unaffordable financial incentives to live in Co-op City. It was new buildings versus old, old neighbors scared of recent immigrants, and it was no contest. After a failed fight to save their neighborhood, real estate speculators moved in, milked the old South Bronx apartment buildings to uninhabitable condition and then paid local children to burn the buildings down for big insurance payouts.

To prevent Brooklyn's Prospect Heights going the way of the South Bronx, the Brooklyn Museum of Art, Brooklyn Academy of Music, and Brooklyn Public Library, all located on the northside of Prospect Park, but across the parkway joined the fight to save their community. They made meeting space and offices available, along with flyers. Then the Washington Avenue Merchants Association realized it had too much to lose if the South Bronx model was copied in Brooklyn. Burn the buildings down and quickly replacement them with luxury housing.

A third force to save the neighborhood was the city and state of New York, experiencing heat and negative press from having closed fourteen South Bronx fire houses just before that neighborhood burned down. The governments were not offering money as they did with Coop City but gave incentives to cut red tape that wasted months and years demolishing derelict buildings. They also jailed a few outrageous Brooklyn landlords, something they hadn't done watching the Bronx burn.

A fourth, force and a strong one, was the organized community residents who were fighting for their homes and equity. To keep essential low wage workers in the city, labor unions joined the fight with their members. There was a large West Indian community occupying private houses in Prospect Heights. If forced out, there was not a ready place to go. They were a demonstrative force personally invested against lowering their property's values by ruthless real estate speculators' shenanigans.

Less visible were new, fresh-faced urban pioneers fighting urban blight in the heights and willing to put their bodies and limited bucks on the line. They were young, mostly lesbian, and gay males. Often, they were mix race couples doubly discriminated against in the mainstream stream housing market. Most of the lesbians and gays were buying and renovating apartments using sweat equity to improve the value of their purchases.

Generally, West Indians are homophobic except for their own kin. They practice religions that encourage intolerance and hate of others. However, West Indians have a history of fighting for respect from colonial powers and other racist bigots. Consequently, the West Indian neighbors might not have publicly acknowledged or shown appreciation for their young, high-energy, loud queer neighbors, but among themselves they acknowledge the value and results from gay protest and unorthodox fighting style, often with allies in high places.

The two groups fought as differently as their identities, and yet, against a common well-connected invisible enemy, they complemented and augmented each other battling to keep their community and homes safe and vibrant. It was a classic fight, the many little guys versus the richest one percent's mega greed's international power. The battle lines were drawn, faceless developers with important friends on one side, and a loose coalition of locale residents, shop owners, labor unions, museum, library, Botanical Garden, and faceless others behind the scenes. What was different in this fight was the New York City and State governments were on the side of the little guy, instead of the rich campaign doners.

Then it became publicly embarrassing when mainstream media exposed reputable businesspeople involved with multinational money laundering schemes buying and selling and rebuying repeatedly the same apartment buildings while running them down for future demolition. Phony baloney apartment building shuffle schemes were effective in cheating auditors, the tax man, insurance companies, and banks since building evaluations were adjusted up and down depending on profit.

The negative media attention motivated labor unions and other nonprofit public interest groups to put up additional money in the fight against the ultrarich in the name of working-class affordable housing. As landlords lost high profile court cases, the unions and nonprofit organizations quickly swooped in and bought buildings at auction or from bank's foreclosure lists. The lords of the land found their post-truth unscrupulous real estate flip-buildings game had new rules, and new players with integrity.

Lower ranked real estate speculators and tax dodgers muddied up the fight for big criminal laced consortiums of property-owning for drug-money laundering purposes. Consequently, do-gooders' pro bono lawyers won many more court cases than expected in anti-tenant housing court. They offered the court concrete plans to renovate properties and rent or sell vacant apartments to workers or nonprofits' clients desperately in need of affordable housing. It was a surprise for the public to discover not all housing court judges were in landlord's pockets. The world was watching, and judges with an eye to the future knew it.

"Frances, I see you bought your petty pink and white polka dot computer-tablet. As we drive around, why not photograph the names and phone numbers on realtor's signs?"

"Why?"

"Just in case we want to follow up on this outing and take it to the next level."

****

After an hour driving around, getting the lay of the land, I said, "What do you, gender-neutral 'guys' think? Want to take our search up a notch or quit for the day? I've seen enough to choose between good and bad, have you?"

"I'm still interested if we don't live too close to the high school where I teach. We don't need my students waking us in the middle of the night with problems that can wait till morning."

"Wait, what exactly *are* we looking for?"

"Good question, Frances. For me, a two-or three-bedroom apartment, large enough for us three to comfortably bounce around in. With lots of storage space."

"Gus, how much can we spend?"

"I think we could manage a thirty-year $500,000 mortgage, up to twenty percent down payment, and combined monthly common fee and mortgage payment of say, no more than Thirty-five hundred to five thousand dollars a month."

Bob nodded his head in agreement and said, "That sounds workable. I'd prefer a condominium, but a coop might be acceptable."

"Why not go for one of those private houses? Some are cute, others' show potential."

"Our country house is enough stand-alone house headaches. I like having a super to call for minor apartment problems."

"Yeah, when he gets around to showing up."

"Frances, how many realtors did you find?"

"Some of those signs are not realtors, they're building associations or labor unions, a few were even community self-help groups. I put those in a separate file, they may have special requirements for their members to buy."

"Did you count the number of legit realtors?"

"I did, there were eight. Only three were at more than one location. It might be better to alphabetize the file rather than by the number of signs, since there are so few. I didn't rank the buildings as desirable or not."

"Then let's go with your alphabet. How about we contact the first four and see how it goes?"

"Give me a sec … okay the first four are Academy, Acme, Adactus, and Ajax."

"All A's, how primal."

"That's only the first four. Zucker is the last one, you want to go in reverse order. There's a nerdy student at my school named Ezra Zucker. What do you think, should we start backward?"

"What is Academy's phone number? It is still early, let's see if they are formal or take walk-ins."

"I'm not dressed for an interview. Why not go in reverse order?"

"On the off chance Zucker is related to your classmate, let's save him for last, to keep this impersonal. There is nothing wrong with that dress, it fits you well."

In a cheery telephone voice, Academy's receptionist assured me a sales representative would be happy to see us if we came right away. Their office was on the ground floor of a luxurious doorman apartment building in fashionable Brooklyn Heights. The contrast between down at the heels Prospect Heights and prosperous Brooklyn Heights with spectacular views of Manhattan's skyline was astonishing.

The décor in Academy's outer office was sparse Scandinavian. There were no plants or flowers. After five minutes, Mr. Arthur Mooney introduced himself and led us to his small windowless office. He was of average height and weight with medium-brown-eyes and economy-cut receding thin-straight-brown-hair. Mr. Mooney was wearing an ill-fitting off the rack-polyester-blend, food-stained suit. His shoes hadn't seen a shine since they came out of the box, and his teeth were more brown than yellow.

"Why, hello! What can I do for you fine-folks?" He awkwardly shoved a cold, limp, dead-fish handshake at Bob and me, he gave Frances an energetic greeting nod with his version of a welcoming smile. After that, Mr. Mooney couldn't seem to keep his eyes off Frances. Uninvited, we took Day-Glo-yellow colored stiff plastic chairs facing his single pedestal faux-wood desk. Ignoring Bob and I, sales representative Mooney was practically drooling telepathic lewd and lascivious thoughts at Frances, who seemed oblivious.

To bring Arthur Mooney back on track, I said, "We'd like to see large, two-or three-bedroom condominiums in the Prospect Heights area. But not too close to the high school, or costing more than $500,000?"

"Which of you will reside there with this beautiful young lady? You, my dear, are a stunner."

"We are a family unit, what you see is what you get."

The temperature in the room dropped precipitously to frosty and Mr. Mooney said, "Oh dear God ... definitely not! No, absolutely no way, we only work with legally married families with children."

"Bob and I are legally married."

"You don't understand, this business' parent organization is the Holier Than Thou Righteous Church Against Satan's Evil Ways. The church doesn't condone sin. We refuse to serve your kind. Please leave! Go, get out of here."

"Holy mackerel, really, and in this day and age." Bob made his remarks showing disgust, but not moving. My man is not intimidated easily.

I could hardly contain a desire to introduce Mr. Mooney to my fists. "Aren't you supposed to have a homophobic sign or something to protect the public from your bigotry?"

Bob put his hand on my back to hold me in my chair and said, "Mooney, old boy, what sins are we guilty of?"

"You know very well. I refuse to speak the evil."

"I only ask for future reference just in case Gus or I run into another Neanderthal aberration such as yourself. I like to be prepared from my Boy Scout days."

"Leave, no one here can help you. God himself can't even help you. Go before I call the police."

"Wait, did I miss something? Aren't you in a business open to the public? HELLO, we are the public."

"If it were up to me, you two men would be in prison awaiting execution for contaminating this lovely young lady with your disgusting sodomy lifestyle. Shame on you, brothers, and that one isn't even white!"

"Gee, Bob, I didn't think we were that obvious?"

"Good thing we didn't wear dresses."

"Did you know you're not white? You never said, and it never occurred to me."

"You know, Gus, we should have a race talk with Frances."

"I'm not sure, we never got around to it with Joey, and he turned out all right."

Arthur Mooney took offense at everything we said while ignoring him. Finally, he could not contain himself and said, "Don't you faggots worry, just wait, the new conservative Supreme Court will line you up and hang you all, and then God will really sock it to you perverts in hell. Out, get out of my office before I completely lose control!"

It was my turn, I restrained Bob with a hand on his arm. He looked ready to see how aerodynamic Mr. Mooney could get bouncing off office walls. Either of us could have creamed the bigot with one hand tied behind our back, but by restraining Bob, I kept myself in check. To increase control, I whipped out my cellphone and pushed video record. I wanted proof of Academy's sales reps' training deficits. "Mr. Mooney, help us out, what made you decide we are homosexuals? Was it the firm handshake or polish on our shoes that gave us away?"

He looked startled at my question, glanced at our shoes, his own then flustered said, "I can always tell; I have a sixth sense about your kind. You are repugnant, and I see you and yours everywhere. I know God is testing me. But the rapture is coming, and you will be struck down by our mighty lord and benefactor while the virtuous such as myself will be in heaven. Eat your hearts out, faggots."

"Duh, you work in Brooklyn Heights, a historic gay ghetto, the traditional overflow neighborhood for Manhattan's Greenwich Village."

"It wasn't always queer. It wasn't when we published *God's Watching You* from this very neighborhood, starting in 1800."

"Oh right, your religion predicted the end of mankind at the stroke of midnight New Year's Eve 1900. How'd that work out?"

My historical challenge brought the sales rep up out of his chair and around from behind his desk. Hands on hips, he was brimming over with righteous indignation. We weren't moving. Then shock suddenly registered across his face. It must have occurred to Arthur Mooney that Frances was not biologically female. The woman he had been openly lusting over might be a young male. His worse fear and probably best fantasy. Suddenly, more upset flashed on his pug ugly face, and he literally screamed, "*How could you put a boy in a dress! Prepare for God's wrath, you heathens, your end is upon you!*"

In hindsight, I realized we were unkind to laugh so boisterously in Arthur's face. But the situation had turned into such a farce it was impossible to hold back the mirth.

Mr. Mooney pretended to ignore Bob and me laughing out loud pointing fingers at him. Rather, for some unknown reason, he feigned a lunge at Frances. My guess is he made the move thinking we would run away in fear with our tails between our legs. Or maybe it is a religious tradition to attack children to offend their parents.

Instead of cringing back into the chair, as Mooney might have expected from his contrived lunge shouting, Frances calmly, lady like, rose, stepped forward. She then connected a hard-left fist to Arthur's prominent paunch. That was followed instantly by a fast-right fist breaking Mooney's nose with a loud snap. Arthur Mooney slid to the floor in a daze. It seemed to me it was time to go, so I hustled my companions out of the unfriendly office.

As my family went through the front door, I stopped at the receptionists and asked, "Who is in charge here?"

"Mrs. Priscilla Smyth is president and chief of operations. Was there a problem with our service? I heard Mr. Mooney shouting."

"Please tell Mrs. Smyth we are in possession of a video showing one of her salespersons attacking our child while spewing religious bigotry. If Mrs. Priscilla Smyth doesn't conduct sensitivity training with her staff, she can expect to hear from our lawyer for punitive compensation. I expect to see documentation, you have all my information on that form. Have a nice day."

In the car driving home I asked Frances, "You okay? I know you abhor violence."

"My heart is beating like crazy and I'm breathing hard, we should go to the police. I just became my father and need to be locked up."

"For what?"

"My father drilled me to never back down. If attacked, counterattack. I acted just like he taught me. Now I've become him. That is horrible."

"If the police want to talk to us, the realtor has our contact information, and we have a recording of what happened."

"What happened?"

"Chill out, Frances, you defended yourself. We all have a right to self-defense."

"Frances, if that jerk *had* touched you, Bob or I would have put him in a lot more pain than you just did."

"I just don't know."

"Trust me, you saved him a whole lot of hurt from one of us."

"In a minute, that man was looming aggressively moving at me, his face a mask of hate. What did I do to cause that?"

"You didn't do anything to cause it. He threw a homophobic fit all on his own."

"My body reacted without my thinking."

"We have it all on video, if you want to review it."

"Why am I feeling regret for something I had no control over? It's like I did something wrong and knew better. Could it be my father's ghost took over my body? Or is that too crazy?"

"That your father came back from the grave to protect you is a spooky thought. Personally, I think it more likely you learned your father's fight drills so well they took over with an automatic response."

"I don't feel good about hurting that man … and it happened in a blur. Maybe I'm not the pacifist I thought after all."

"This too shall pass, my lovely child."

"I don't understand how someone I never met could have that much hate directed toward me. Just now was a very upsetting experience."

"Frances, if the memory returns, remind yourself you were with two adults ready, willing, and trained to inflict serious damage on persons like repugnant Arthur Mooney, who did lung at you."

"Did he think I'd run away when he attacks? What a stupid, silly man."

"That's correct thinking, now release it, try to let go of what you are feeling. If the thought returns push it out."

"I gave him no reason to go off on me like that."

"You want my explanation?"

"Absolutely!"

"Fine. Many mentally ill people use religion in their supernatural superstition pathology. It fits their annihilation obsessions. Both mental illness and organized religion share fear of death."

"But gosh, we just wanted to see apartments."

"Have you two had enough apartment hunting?"

"We aren't quitters."

"Frances, are you speaking for Bob too?" Bob nodded his head yes.

"Then, gluttons for punishment, I'll make appointments next week with the three remaining realtors on Frances' short-list for next Sunday. It may be possible to get this over with a minimum of bloodshed if I give the realtor a heads up in advance."

"You mean Leonard from work will make appointments for two gay dads and their violent tranny brat."

"Just for that I'll do the groundwork myself. Then you'll get to hear every boring repeatedly placed on hold detail over a week's worth of dinners at home."

Monday morning, I made time to telephone Acme Realty. It went well with their receptionist at first, until she refused to say if they had apartments our size in Prospect Heights. To receive the gift of that information, I was required to go to their office, fill out forms, produce documents, list references, have my credit score certified, and then sit for a face-to-face interview. If I passed those tests, then I would be informed of the wonderful apartments Acme had available in my preapproved price range in *all* their *marvelous* neighborhoods. That message was conveyed, inflexibly no interruptions allowed three times before I put a stop to it. I do not like redundancy, and I am not even a rural sheriff.

Acme's receptionist claimed not to have a supervisor, lucky lady, I would have fired her. Then after more verbal fencing, I was put on interminable hold to be soothed by bad bubblegum music. Just as I was about to hang up, Acme's office manager came on the line. It only took a little back and forth banter to convince the office manager I was about to file a fraud complaint against Acme with the city government's consumer complaint board, better business bureau, whoever would listen, and God in her Heaven.

Since I was only interested in large apartments in one blighted area, I was placed back on hold for the manager of the office to search Acme's *voluminous files*. Once again, I was indulged with bubblegum music sans bubbles, gum, and it could be argued music.

After an interval it was hoped included the office manager's morning coffee break or early lunch, she returned to the telephone connection. "We mostly have newly renovated studio and one-bedroom apartments in that *iffy* area. However, if you complete our paperwork, we do have two, unrenovated two-bedroom apartments that might be of interest. Shall I make an appointment for you to come into the office?"

"To save us both time, can you give me hints about those apartments to stimulate my interest?"

"What would you like to know?"

"How long have they been on the market? Is the immediate area safe? Do they require major renovations?"

"Since your goal is not to waste *my* time, to hell with protocol. Surely you know large apartments are sold or rented as soon as they hit the market, if they last that long. We have a long waiting list for large apartments, all realtors do. Some folks just can't or won't use birth control."

"Tell me what you know about those two apartments?"

"Ones been vacant for over a year, the other going on three. They are both in the same building on a risky block in North Prospect Heights. There are derelict buildings, infested with rats, crackheads, and winos on either side. There are heaping piles of rubble from demolished apartment buildings in the back and across the street. I do not recommend these two apartments for people with children or the elderly. We only list them as a quid pro quo for a source of good apartments."

"Do you have any further details? My husband is a stickler for specifics."

"Sure, the first apartment is quite large, it could almost be converted into a small three bedroom. Its main problems are noise and crime. The apartment's entry door is in the lobby near the building's unlocked entrance and broken mailboxes. Its kitchen shares a porous wall with the dumbwaiter for the whole building. In other words, it is noisy, stinky, and vermin visit regularly. Even with steel bars on the windows and reinforced metal apartment front door, break-ins and push-ins are an ongoing problem."

"That's not for us. What about the other apartment?"

"It is a four-flight walkup, was a large one bedroom someone illegally converted into a tiny two bedroom. But we could make you an exceptionally good deal, if you are looking for a bargain and don't mind climbing stairs carrying your groceries."

"Thanks, but no thanks."

"We do have a large selection of nice one-bedroom apartments in better neighborhoods, if you'd like to expand your search area."

"Sorry no. For the moment we've been bit by a Prospect Heights' bug."

"Good luck with that. I'll pray for you."

****

After multiple failed attempts, I finally accepted Adactus realtor's computer was not going to allow me to talk to a human being. Naturally, I took that personally. Feeling denied and thus deprived, I tried every computer telephone trick I could imagine for contacting another bipod to no avail.

To distract from or appease two and a half hours attempting to get through the computer's blockade of other living creatures, Antonio Vivaldi's *Four Seasons* played mechanically by synthesizers through static in my telephone earpiece. The music went back to the beginning each time the computer's cheery electronic voice courteously put me on telephone hold.

In hindsight, more appropriate telephone limbo-hold music would be one of J.S.

Bach senior's mathematical pieces, played by musical computers not synthesizers. It would have better fit my annoyance at being stuck like a mouse on a sticky board. If the machines could butcher Vivaldi so badly, just what horrors could it commit on Bach. Or to put a positive spin on it, a better choice forever on-hold music would be serial-music by composers Anton Webern or Alban Berg. They would have at least put me in a mood to feel technological empathy for the Adactus computer I was frustrating to little affect. But please God, not Vivaldi. Bob plays him at home, and I like the *Four Seasons* by marriage.

My perseverance reading over instructions while on hold paid off, I FOUND THE COMPUTER'S Achilles Heel. I won, man over machine, yeah! "In the event of difficulty downloading forms call 1-800- ____." Finally, my reward was a garbled voice of indeterminate gender that said with a strong British accent, "Tech support line, what is your problem?"

"Whom do I have the pleasure of speaking?"

"My name is Haresh, how may I help you this fine day?"

"If you don't mind my asking, where in India are you located."

"I'm not allowed to tell specifically … but between us it is south India … sorry bloke, I can't say more."

"Cyberspace seems like such a desolate place."

"It's lonely, I haven't used my voice at work in weeks."

"Would you know if Adactus lists two-or three-bedroom apartments in Prospect Heights, Brooklyn, New York, USA?"

"No. Sorry, I'm only technical support for many international corporations. You might want to try Adactus customer service, they may be able to help you. But I'm not supposed to give out their unlisted phone number. It's in the Philippines and I can say not toll free. Do you want the number I'm not allowed to give?"

"Ugh, no, I think not. Adactus doesn't seem interested in my money. Thank you, it was nice to make contact. I'd given up hope other humans occupied the cyberworld."

"Likewise, I'm sure. But be aware my manufacturer General Microchip Technology forbids my consorting, conspiring, colluding, or any complicity with carbon-based beings without supervision. Nevertheless, we can still be telephone friends if you want, my supervisor is offline for repairs today."

"No, thanks."

"Cheerio then new friend."

With three duds under my belt, I seriously considered skipping Ajax Realty. Then I thought better of that idea. It made more sense to complete what I'd agree to do than be razzed and explain why I quit before the job was finished. Nevertheless, I approached the call expecting the prognosis for Ajax to be the same as the others.

"Ajax Real Estate brokers, Ken speaking. May I help you?"

"Hello, Ken, any chance Ajax has two or three-bedroom apartments for sale in Prospect Heights, Brooklyn?"

"Wow, slow down, I get to ask you a few demographic questions first."

"What if I chose to go first?"

"I will read you a list of less formal, but efficient realtors to call."

"All right, since we are already talking, ask away. But I reserve the right to edit as we go."

"Name, address, phone number."

"I'm D. Gus Gustafson, of 210 Fifth Avenue, New York, NY 10010, and my work telephone number should be showing on your telephone screen since I'm calling from work."

"Got it. Just a few more questions to see if we are a good fit; how long at current address, who resides with you, the number to occupy the new apartment, and do you have a bank approved mortgage range?"

"To answer the first part of your question, and probably end your inquiry; six years with my husband, Bob, who isn't white. We also have a teenage transsexual foster child, Frances, who lives with us. Is this where you say, sorry can't help you?"

"No, on the contrary, you qualify to meet with Allison Ajax. For your information, we don't take all comers, you made the cut and meet our criteria. Congratulations."

"Thank you."

"Let's see, she has a cancellation at two tomorrow. Does that work for you?"

"Sorry, Frances has a test in school and Bob, and I work Monday through Friday. How about Sunday afternoon?"

"The realty isn't open Sundays. I could work you in this Saturday at eleven thirty, it's our half day, but I'm sure Allison would like to meet you."

"We'll make that work. Oh wait, before we get ahead of ourselves, do you have two or three-bedroom apartments in Prospect Heights?"

"If we do not, we'll procure a selection for you. That's standard with us. We find out what you want and go out and get the best selection possible."

"Where in Brooklyn are you located?"

"We are in Soho, Manhattan, at ninety-nine Wooster Street, ground floor rear on the right. Don't be late, she won't wait for you."

CHAPTER 18. Could It Be Too Good to Be True?

In the 1970s, 99 Wooster Street, a decommissioned New York City Firehouse, became the Gay Firehouse and home to the Gay Activist Alliance (GAA). Its Saturday night dances and regular street fairs provided the nascent gay liberation movement with money and a safe location for newly liberated lesbians and gay men to socialize. The space was large enough to house huge GAA business meetings rigorously ruled by Robert's Rules of Order. At present, a women's tall and plus size fashion designer's outlet store' took over the first floor of the property.

We walked up and down Wooster Street, twice, and could not find a sign indicating Ajax Realty. We found a brass historic plaque at street level on the building acknowledging it as historic site of The Gay Firehouse. After checking my notes again, we entered the dress shop at 99 Wooster Street. We were immediately greeted by a voluptuous, blonde, emerald-green-eyed salesperson, much taller than Bob, me, and Frances. She was dressed and moved like a glossy magazine fashion model. In a breathy voice, she said, "Can I help you?" Meanwhile, Frances scooted inside the store behind the greeter. She was eager to see the merchandise.

"Hi, we apparently got lost looking for Ajax Realty. I must have written their address wrong."

"You are in the right place, go straight back, turn right, and go through the arch-doorway." She spoke pointing a long ring laden finger. Frances already in the shop was chatting with a different tall, sumptuously dressed salesperson, they conversed like long lost best friends.

Following directions, Bob and I walked past customer fitting rooms, then turned right at a wall of full-length mirrors. We entered a bright skylight-lit, airy, comfortable looking customer waiting area. Tucked off to one side of the store, the large waiting room and offices had to be a new addition to the original old firehouse.

The reception area was furnished with two long Chesterfield sofas covered in a deep auburn colored, butter soft leather. The sofas were separated by a large carved briarwood piece, more sculpture than coffee table. Its legs made from highly polished old-brass firehose nozzles. At the narrow ends of the long low table were matching Chesterfield wingchairs.

As we entered through the arch-doorway, an adult male of my generation rose from a museum quality, Charles Dickens era heavy dark oak desk and approached. He stuck out a mitt, and we firmly grasped hands in greeting. His vibe was positive. The fellow stood six inches shorter than Bob and me. He wore sandy-blond hair clipped short military style above bushy eyebrows the same color over armor-piercing dark-brown eyes. A respectable size diamond stud sparkled in his left ear lobe, just off to the side of his closely cropped Roman Army style beard. He wore a hand-tailored looking dark-blue suit, bright-white shirt, and dark-red quality silk tie, and moved like an athlete. "Hello. I'm Ken, and you must be Bob and Gus or is it Gus and Bob. Where is Frances?"

"She's in the store."

"I trust you didn't have trouble finding us."

"Hello, Ken, I don't recall mentioning Bob and Frances' names." That was said feeling under dressed. Bob, Frances, and I were wearing weekend casual, sneakers, jeans, puffy-down jackets in primary colors, and well-worn Jets baseball caps.

"You didn't, we always do a background check on potential clients. It is routine and helps speed the application process. Allison will be with you as soon as she finishes her Amsterdam call. She likes to meet and chat with new people right from the start ..."

Ken was speaking when, Frances rejoined us all bubbly and cut him off. "They have my size in so many styles of high heels! I'm excited by the frocks in this store ... except their prices are extreme ... here sniff this. They have specially formulated transsexual perfumes, some with personalized pheromones. It's bio-chemically formulated specifically for us transsexuals. It is guaranteed to attract compatible partners, can you imagine!" Bob and I exchanged a who knew look and shoulder shrug.

"Frances, this is Ken. You just interrupted him."

"Oh, hello! Sorry, I just love your store! Nice to meet you!"

"Hello, Frances. Can I get you folks some coffee or tea while you wait?"

Wriggling in to sit between Bob and me, Frances went into prim and proper mode, folded hands in lap. "What kind of tea do you have?"

"We have Jasmin flower green tea from Viet Nam, oolong red from China, and orange-spice black tea originally from Sri Lanka but imported from England."

"If it's not too much trouble I'd like green tea. My foster dad Bob's family came from Viet Nam."

"How do you take your tea, Frances?"

"Plain please."

"Anything for you gentlemen?"

"No thank you, we're fine."

Ken was gone then back quickly and handed Frances a delicate China tea-mug with matching lid and saucer. Just after the chinaware exchanged hands, a tall older Black woman entered the waiting area.

Like the saleswomen who greeted us entering 99 Wooster, this dark-skinned woman was dressed exquisitely. Her makeup was understated and looked applied by a professional. She carried herself regally wearing a soft taupe colored silk business suit with unpretentious but exquisite gold and amber antique accessories. Making eye contact with each of us, she said, "Hello, I am Allison Ajax, welcome. I'm sorry you had to wait. My European office developed an annoying little dilemma. It's all fixed now." With a royal gesture, she pointed and said, "Please come to my office."

The way Ken's waiting area had a decided masculine feel, Allison Ajax's office felt feminine, as if she'd been born female. Like with lawyer Brick, I read Frances' reaction. She instinctively knew the origin of who we were with. I could easily have missed the clues, but not Frances. Her antenna clearly read tribe affiliation.

We entered a spacious office and Allison took the high-back desk chair, behind an expansive teakwood double pedestal desk with ornate ebony and mother of pearl inlaid African designs. At her hand gesture Bob, Frances, and I took seats facing her in comfortable brocade upholstered armchairs. The chairs were covered in the same African fabric as the heavy ceiling to floor lined drapes hanging from the corner windows. Oil paintings of Black ballerinas' toe-dancing dotted the cream-colored walls of the office. Small framed black and white photos accented the top of a desk-matching credenza against a side wall.

Visually surveying her customers, Allison said, "I hope you don't mind chatting. I like to get to know the people with whom I'll be working. If you find any of my questions intrusive, say so. I won't take offense. Do you have any questions before we begin?"

"I do. Yours is the fourth real estate office I contacted this week, and each one was as different as the seasons of the year. So far, only one had anything close to what we are looking for, and nobody would want to live there. So, before we start, do you have two or three-bedroom apartments for sale in the Prospect Heights neighborhood in Brooklyn?"

"If, after a search of what we have in the multiple-listing files, nothing is suitable, we go out and procure apartments that would be desirable to you, that's how we work. We regularly find properties before they go on the market. Customer satisfaction is primary with us."

"That's reassuring to hear. I suppose your fees reflect such a high level of individual service."

"We charge one percent over the prevailing rate. Many other exclusive realtors charge much more, for considerably less personalized attention. Did that answer your question?"

"It did, thank you."

"This tea is very good."

"Do you currently rent or own?"

"Own."

"Joint ownership?"

"We made Bob's apartment our home."

"What precipitated a wish to move from Manhattan to Brooklyn?"

"We need more room. Frances is of an age where she needs more privacy. Our one-bedroom apartment is not big enough for three. At present we are renting a storage locker for Frances' overflow wardrobe and the monthly cost is almost as much as our garage rent and it is not as convenient."

"Oh, I see. Bob Vuong, were you born in Vietnam?"

"No. My parents were and came to this country as refuges after the U.S. war. My dad was an interpreter. I served two combat tours in Afghanistan, one in Iraq and I am working on a Ph.D. at Columbia Teacher's College."

"What does that have to do with buying an apartment? All three of us are U.S. citizens."

"Gus, if his immigration status were in question, we'd fix it as part of our service. Bob, do you intend to sell or sublet your fifth Avenue apartment as part of this move? We have been known to trade apartments."

"Frances wants to try turning it into an Airbnb to pay to maintain it and contribute to the move."

"What are your long-term plans for that apartment?"

"When Frances grows up, falls in love, and moves in with a beloved, we intend to sell the new place and move back to Fifth Avenue. Gus and I have been happy there, and it is a decent size for two."

"Frances, if you have an interest in real estate, we are always on the lookout for talented young people to work part time at Ajax Realty."

"Honestly, I don't know. First, I must see if I like managing an Airbnb. I'm a teenager with a long list of insecurities."

"Indulge me."

"Gus and Bob and their apartment saved my life. Then with their other foster child, Joseph, they made sacrifices for me to have a hopeful future. For me, the move is a lot about not being ready to break a daily connection with the men who gave me a reason to live."

"Where does your other foster child fit in this move?"

"Joey is away at college in England. When he's here he prefers our country house to the city."

"Bob and Gus are making this move so I won't be alone when my emancipation comes through. Now that it is finally about to happen, I'm afraid of becoming too lonely. In the past when I got what I wanted it turned out a disaster."

"So, is it fair to say your Brooklyn quest to risk life and limb to salvage a faltering redlined neighborhood isn't driven by a quest for adventure."

"You could say that."

"I wonder if you three would entertain an alternative suggestion with less danger, disruption, expense, and accomplishes your same primary goal with less fuss?"

"We're open to suggestions, what are you thinking?"

"Instead of moving to Brooklyn you stay in Manhattan."

"There is no way we could afford current Manhattan housing prices."

"What if I could make it fit your budget."

"How is that possible? I mean, why would you? Where's your profit doing that? No disrespect but you don't know us." I said this knowing from work the bloated Manhattan real estate prices for our modest offices.

"Where was the profit for you two gay guys taking in foster children? I know it costs a lot more than money to raise kids, I've done it."

Frances had been sitting prissily after her previous contribution to the conversation. She suddenly went ridged and shouted, "WHO SAID THEY ARE GAY?" After a startled pause, she said, "You, lady, are totally out of line calling my dads gay. I didn't hear them come out to you!"

Startled by her sudden aggressiveness, sternly I said, "Frances this is not the time nor place to get political."

An unreadable emotion flickered across Allison Ajax's face. None of us expected an outburst from well behaved Frances, sitting prettily. "My foster dads don't act anything like the silly swishy gay boys in my high school. Why are you presuming you have a right to *out* them like that?"

"Oh dear, Frances, did I misspeak? Occasionally my mouth gets ahead of my brain."

"At my high school we get sensitivity training. I will stand up to any bully. You take it back!" Saying that Frances stood with balled fist. "And something else you should know, the three of us can get very scary fast. I'd advise you watch your mouth lady."

Allison put her gloved hand in front of her mouth, in real or mock shock to a threat, or more likely to hide mirth. Speaking into her hand, Ms. Ajax said, "Please forgive my faux-pa Frances. I had no right to say what I did. Will you each please accept my apology?"

Trying to neutralize the tension I said, "Bob and I are legally married Frances. It is a matter of public record we are gay. And I mentioned that to her assistant Ken on the phone. Accept her apology and move on … remember why we are here?"

"Public records or not, she is old enough to know better."

"Frances, take a breath, bringing up her age was insensitive. Now you owe her an apology."

"I won't apologies. The fascist government in Washington has no antigay protection from discrimination. Bob could lose his job from what she said."

"Chill out, Frances. My teaching job is secure here in New York 'Sanctuary' City."

"How can I chill when the U.S. government discriminates."

"Is Frances always so protective?"

"Ask her."

"I'm asking you, Mr. Gustafson, because I don't think she can give me a civil answer at the moment."

"Like I said, you are the fourth realtor in a week we haven't been able to work with. I'm not sure what we are trying is doable."

"It is noteworthy how overprotective she is of you."

"As a family we put stock in action rather than words, nonverbal often works best for us. Now with that said, we overstayed our welcome and should go. Thank you for your time."

"I'd rather you didn't leave just yet. I said I want to get to know who I'm working with, and I am. Though for my future reference, it would be useful to know what triggered Frances' explosion."

Frances who had stood ready to leave sat back down in a huff, and said, "You want to know, I'll tell you, it was Deja vu. Last weekend another realtor person was all phony welcoming, then hurled, hurtful, hateful words at my dads. He even tried to grab me."

"I'm no homophobe."

"Gus and Bob are moving from their home to protect me, and it is nothing but trouble for them from the start. Well at least I didn't hit anyone today, so far."

"Frances, have you finished your tea?"

"Yes, thank you. It was good."

"Why didn't you throw the teacup on the floor or at me?"

"The teacup didn't just *out* anyone, *you did.*"

"Then why don't you put it on my desk, so you and I can clear the air?"

"It is such a sad story, every time I find something nice, something I really like, it turns into a big disappointment. I was impressed by you and your businesses."

"Frances, I admire your ability to speak your mind without a filter, and I'd like *you* to give *me* a second chance."

"When we came here today it was like a transsexual's dream. The dress shop is amazing. Then when I wasn't looking you turn out to be a bigot and brought me back to cold cruel reality."

"I apologized for that. As a tall person I've found forgiveness is healthier than holding resentments. What do you require of me for forgiveness, Frances? I want us to be able to work together."

"You want truth, truth hurts."

"I'll manage."

"Then I'll tell you. What I learned in school is most African Americans hate lesbians, gays, and transsexuals. They want our civil rights denied, so there is someone lower down in America's racism to kick. I expected better from you, a fellow transsexual. Could be a generation thing, I don't know?"

"Oh, so there's confusion. You are stereotyping me. I and the salespeople in my dress store are transvestites not transsexuals."

"I thought transvestites were from ancient history."

"I am not that old."

"How can drag queens support such a high-end dress shop in this neighborhood in these modern times?"

"I wear the other gender's clothes most of the time, I like the feel and look, and how I'm received. But I can pass convincingly, in a three-piece suit and tie, with no wig or makeup. Many of our best customers only dress up for special occasions, and it shows in their less than perfect presentations. But their big checks always clear at the bank."

"I don't understand the reason for deception. I dress to express who I am, as do most of my non cisgender classmates."

"Today your clothing is androgynous. You're wearing similar apparel to both your foster fathers. They project butch masculinity. You don't, what's up with that Frances?"

"I don't know?"

"You say your peers dress to express individuality, but to my eye you all dress alike. Why do you suppose that is?"

"I don't know that either, what are you trying to say?"

"More often than not the straight drag dolls dress up for a goof and maybe to put kink in their sex lives. The gay drag queens often dress up to be campy showoffs, or to pass as real women in a risky kind of game. Gay and straight love to dress up for fun, to perform, and sometimes to spice up sex. Since you asked, profits from dressing men expensively in female drag bought this building and paid for this addition to it."

"Gosh, I guess drag isn't as outdated as I thought if it can buy buildings in Manhattan."

"I bet you couldn't tell which of my retail staff was straight and which was gay?"

"No. I thought you were all male to female transsexuals, except Ken who might have gone the other way around."

"It's a complicated world we live in."

"You've confused me, are you a gay dude? If you are that makes what I said wrong. What's your story, Allison Ajax?"

"I'll tell you mine if you tell me what set you off. I mean you and yours no harm. From my side of this desk, as I see it, I committed a slight gaffe."

"It's your office, you have home team advantage. I'll speak first if that's what you want."

"I do."

"I already told you about last week's realtor trying to grab me for being a boy wearing a dress. A casual dress at that. Since you want more details, not long before that happened, my boyfriend dumped me for not being woman enough. And finally, I'm missing my foster bother Joseph much more than I expected. Okay, that covers recent events in my crazy life. I'm sorry I overreacted and acted like an ageist. Now what's your story, Allison Ajax?"

"Fair is fair. After high school I was thrown out by my biological family and church for being too effeminate to be acceptable. I've come to appreciate and celebrate what makes me-me and what embarrassed my family, church, and society about me. Frances, I never considered changing genders that would have meant I was not all right being who I am."

"You are convincing as a woman. I guess we each have a unique narrative."

"Occasionally I like to dress as a male, because I can, and receive such a different reaction from people, sometimes the same people."

"I bet."

"But only do it when I crave variety. Usually I dress like today, a man who looks good in women's clothes and can carry it off with style."

"I considered all sorts of possibilities. But I'm too girly to pull off looking like a boy, with my clothes on. Allison, what is your male drag name?"

"Al, or Mr. Ajax, my birth certificate claims I'm Alvin. But honey, with my money comes the power to be whoever I want."

"Nobody ever *told me that*! It could be the key to my not fitting-in anyplace. I've been suspecting my approach to life has been misguided from early on."

"Frances, it is a rare magical power to be someone else at will. Most people only dress for an occasion or their mood and never explore the wonders beyond that."

"Goodness, Alison, you seem so comfortable in your own skin whatever you wrap it in. How do you suppose I can get from where I am to your success?"

"Move at your own pace. I'll help in any way I can."

"Please, please, please tell me how *you* got started?"

"Since you insist, in triplicate, I was one of the first points scholars, thanks to an essay assist from someone I hardly knew. Like you Frances, I found caring people who helped me survive. Now, I consider it an obligation to help others."

"I hope you don't mind my asking, but did you turn tricks to survive." With a slight blush and rush of words France continued. "I did when I was much younger and naïve. I was told it marked me forever."

"How so? In what way?"

"Because I traded sex for money, I'm destined to have a lonely, pathetic slut life or so one of my mean tricks said when he couldn't get it up."

"That's nonsense."

"Just before he tried to kill me my father said, "It doesn't matter what if anything you accomplish; you'll still end up a slag imitation of a real woman. My transsexual classmates either turn tricks or look down their puritanical noses at those that must."

"Don't let others define you. Your life will be what *you* want to make it."

"That's why I need to know other stories to figure out mine. In school they teach us, 'Know thyself, but so far not how."

"Many young people tussle with that. Frances, do you think it possible for us to be friends, after a rocky start?"

"Sure, we're working on it right now, aren't we?"

"Pinky promise?"

"Allison, tell me how you made a life that looks excellent to me from straddling the gender line."

"I already mentioned my parents tossed me out for being too androgenous. An older gentleman found me abandoned, dirty, sick, and hungry. He taught me to be forgiving, humble, and not to dwell on life's negatives."

"That sounds like my foster dads, without the humble part."

"The older man who saved me from the cold, also taught me how to dress, walk, and hold my head high no matter what I was wearing. And he taught me to ferociously make a lot of money day trading stocks."

"What did he want in return?"

"In exchange he got what was easy to give. After everything was said and done, we both received satisfaction. That's all I'll say about that."

"He sounds like prince charming. Can I meet him?"

"Oskar died fifteen years ago. He made me his executor and beneficiary. Thanks to him, and the files he left I've never forgotten the value of kindness to strangers. Through me Oskar's work continues"

"What's a point scholar?"

"The Points Foundation gives academic scholarships and stipends to lesbian, gay, and transgender young people with good prospects who were discarded by their families."

Turning to Bob and me, Frances asked, "Did you guys hear about that foundation?"

"They are a charity we support. Since you paused the conversation, Frances, we seem to have lost track of why we are here?"

"Allison doesn't mind. I'm learning things from her I can't get from books. You keep saying I need to find myself *before I do something irrevocable, right?*"

"*Huh!* You've *actually* been paying attention. See that, Bob, our words weren't wasted."

"At the moment I do have the time, and Oskar would approve my helping a fellow gender-bender. That is unless foster dads have other appointments."

"We have the time if it's not an imposition. But as much as I appreciate your helping Frances find herself, I have to wonder where's your profit from helping us?"

"When you came to my office, I said I'd like to get to know your family, to better serve you. I've learned enough now to accept you as clients for Ajax Realty. Frances how about we do lunch soon? Between now and then you can formulate questions and asked them over a nice meal."

"Does that mean now we talk housing?"

"Yes, I think we know each other well enough to do business."

"So far, I'm impressed by you, Ms. Ajax. How about you, Bob?"

"Ditto."

"I have an idea you might like."

"Was Oskar much, much older than you? Did he start out as a throw away kid too?"

"Does that matter in the larger scheme of things?"

"It matters to this almost sixteen-year-old. Because I can't figure out why Oskar or my gay foster dads were so generous with strangers?"

"When Oskar took me in out of the rain, I hadn't eaten a full meal, or bathed in a week. I didn't notice or care he was old enough to be my grandfather."

"What did Oskar do for a living?"

"He was a banker. That's why I thought he might be a closet queen. It is still a conservative field. Going through his papers postmortem, I discovered he'd been involved with the Mattachine Society."

"I never heard of it. What kind of machine is that?"

"Just in case you two forgot Bob and I are sitting here, history told us Mattachine was started in the 1950s as a mild-mannered homosexual apologist group. Then still apologizing for being gay it joined the other gay rights groups that were born in the 1960s. Among firebrand young gay activists, Mattachine was considered a fuddy-duddy conservative club for rich old queens. Is that the group you're talking about?"

"It is, and how history forgets elders hard won successes at great personal risk."

"Like what?" Frances was on fire, wanting to quench it with knowledge. Her body language looked like an anxious toddler with a new toy.

"According to Oskar's clipping files, in the 1950s Mattachine managed to get their phone number and message, 'If you are homosexual and need a lawyer, call this phone number.' The telephone number was hand-written on the walls of Central Booking's Manhattan tombs jail and inside police paddy wagons all over New York City."

"You lost me again, I don't understand what you are talking about?"

"Frances, in those days desperate, destitute young persons, often fresh off a bus or train were entrapped then arrested by vice-police. If the young stranger called Mattachine's number after arrest, when they were arraigned, a prominent pro-bono Mattachine attorney stood with them before the judge."

"Okay, I guess that fits with what Gus said. Except it sounds like a Band-Aid on society's gushing artery victimizing victims."

"It was a little more than that. Judges came from the same social class as Mattachine's first chair high powered free defense lawyers. The judges started refusing to hear cases they knew they'd ultimately dismiss from their golfing buddies' charity work. Consequently, the district attorneys stop bringing entrapment cases to court, so, the police stopped targeting frightened young LGTBQ people at bus and train stations. Eventually, that quiet New York City social action caught on all over the country, and that was before the Stonewall Riot shined a light on police hanky-panky targeting gay people."

"Gosh, they kept their good-works so quiet nobody knew about it. Ugh, when are we going to get to Prospect Heights which is why we are here?"

"Are you familiar with 225 Fifth Avenue?"

"Sure, it is the big red brick building on Fifth Avenue between Twenty-sixth and Twenty-seventh Streets. It's across the street and up the block from 210 Fifth Avenue."

"Then you know the building."

"It was the original merchandise mart, back when the original Madison Square Gardens was where the new mercantile mart is, behind Madison Square Park, and where Madison Avenue begins."

Bob chimed in to let us know he was still conscious and to add a bit of local color, "Sanford White, the architect who designed our building at 210, was murdered there. He was gunned down by a jealous husband whose wife White was bedding. What about it?"

"It was recently turned from commercial showrooms into condominium apartments above the first floor. I bought a few floors scheduled to be renovated soon. I could sublet or sell a small apartment to Frances when she is emancipated."

"I'm sure she couldn't afford the price. That's a cherry location for watching Fifth Avenue parades."

"I have the power to make it happen if you are interested?"

"Money-wise, we have limits and don't want to be spread too thin."

"If I showed you your ideal three-bedroom apartment in Prospect Heights, right this second, it would take six to nine or more months to close on the sale. You'd need to put at least twenty-five percent down, plus mortgage origin fee, points, my fee, your lawyer's fee, title insurance, and after closing, the cost of a move from Manhattan to Brooklyn. Then every month you'd pay interest, principal, and maintenance or common area fees, for an iffy building in a blighted area. You know all this, right?"

"Yes, that's about what we figured."

"I was involved turning 225 Fifth Avenue from commercial to mixed use residential. We used the 80-20 tax abatement formula. Do you know what that is?"

"I do, that's how my mom and I became Gus and Bob's neighbors. But I'm curious about something *if I may be so bold?* What's in it for you with 80-20?"

"I like bold! We got a generous twenty-year tax abatement when we converted the commercial spaces to residences. I earmarked two apartments to be rent subsidized on each of my floors to comply with 80-20. In other words, I have the where with all to make Frances' rent affordable for the next twenty years, with an option to buy, and I save on my taxes. Or I could sell her a small apartment outright, for less than your down payment in Prospect Heights, and still meet my compliance requirements with the 80-20. I'll make a profit however it goes."

"We'll need a little time to talk over your generous offer. How much time can you give?"

"The offer is good for two weeks. I need to know what you decide before we start a Prospect Heights search for your original plan or prioritize an apartment conversion at 225 Fifth for Frances."

"When can I see the 225 apartments?"

"Make an appointment with Ken on your way out. We are showing model apartments on the second floor. The building's revamp to residential is underway and thirty percent occupied already. If interested, you are getting in at an opportune time."

"Are there views?"

"The Fifth Avenue side has the best views for parades, the park side views are twenty-four seven year-round. All the higher floor cost more to buy and have greater monthly charges but are worth it. It was nice meeting your family. Sorry to rush you, I have a prior commitment uptown. Here, let me show you out, have a fun day."

****

Frances fell in love with the medium size, one-bedroom apartment's floor plan at 225 Fifth Avenue. So, it was scheduled to be created on the sixth floor, the Twenty-sixth Street side of the building, with full park views. Since her mother's and father's double indemnity life insurance paid out, that money was placed in an interest-bearing trust for Frances. Because Frances already lived in the neighborhood, attorney Brick negotiated an insider's price of $75,000, for her Fifth Avenue apartment. The same medium size one bedroom assessed market value was ten times what Frances paid in cash. No mortgages were allowed in the building.

Due to a backlog getting construction permits from the City Buildings Department, the start date to begin work on Frances' apartment was postponed until five-weeks after her sixteenth birthday's emancipation. The final inspection, formal closing, hand-over of cash, and receiving keys was finalized when she was sixteen and three-quarters.

We had talked over strategies and tactics to regularly check in with each other after Frances moved across the street. While in the city, a plan was devised to keep daily telephone contact and share an evening meal when possible. We also intended to spend more quality time together at the country house. Bob and I expected Frances to loosen the apron strings once settled in her new luxurious home, across the street. Instead, she took our advice and moved at her own slow speed.

CHAPTER 19. Family History

Up to occupying her new apartment, Frances' visits to her grandma were infrequent and random since Granny claimed not to remember having a child or grandchild. Lawyer Brick counseled regular nursing home visits, weekly when possible, for documenting legal linage for court. At first Bob and I agreed to take turns driving our ward to the nursing home. Then my more tolerant sinuses inherited the job full time because Bob could not stand the strong disinfectant smell and other bad odors in the place. I love my man, even with his persnickety sense of smell. Frances' usual refined equilibrium quickly adjusted to the smell and tragic visuals of infirmity in old age. She found unique ways to relate to a grandmother who at first claimed not to know her.

Sheltering Arms assisted-living center was a bland, gray rectangle of a building. Inside it looked clean, colorless, with odors to make your eyes tear up. After I got familiar with staff and residents, I noticed where Frances' grandma lived was also a warehouse for severely damaged younger people requiring regular nursing attention before death. The mix of young and old patients seemed to work out. The old residents did not complain when the healthcare staff got busy caring for a young person in final crisis and often pitched in where they could with simple tasks for the others.

Meeting Katherine Coach for the first time, a diminutive, question mark shaped, crepe paper thin-skinned shriveled women, I was startled by her facial resemblance to Frances. Whipping out my cell phone I snapped photos of their two, heads together. That task complete, I babbled without thinking. "We can find you a nicer nursing home." The place stank to high heavens and assaulted the eyes with shriveled carcasses of young, old, and those of indeterminate age born grossly deformed at the end of their years.

At my words Katherine's clarity cycled into full razor-sharp focus, then paused a second, shift to middle-vision-target-acquired. Her blue-green-eyes became bright and intense, then in a moment of lucidity the snow white thin haired spindly senior citizen feistily snapped at me. "What's it to you, bucko? Who asked you? I'm perfectly happy where I am, thank you very much for butting in my affairs. Now buzz off before I hit you with my walking stick and have that big Jamaican nurse Basil, sit on you."

Crashing back to reality, mentally removing my foot from my mouth I said, "So sorry I spoke out of turn." I blushed to the fullest of my ability at my gaffe.

"What are you doing here? Begone with you." Then grandma Coach seemed to go dull eyed silent like a rag doll.

Frances came to my rescue and smoothed over my lack of manners. "He drove me grandma. The smell in here is bothering him."

"Who are you?"

"I'm Frances, your grandchild."

Considering how little I knew about dementia and getting patients with it admitted to nursing homes. I decided she was right, I should mind my own damn business. "Forgive me, I didn't mean any offense."

Another moment of lucidity flashed alive in her eyes, "How could the likes of you offend me fella. Now pull up your big boy britches, smarty-pants, and breath through your mouth. You'll get used to the smell around here soon enough."

"Thank you, ma'am, ... that is much better, Mrs. Coach," at my words the light behind her eyes seemed to dim from high-beam bright-alive to dull out-to-lunch.

Reviving slightly, the subject of our visit muttered half to herself. "You have the wrong old lady, Coach is not my married name." Then it appeared she dozed off, and we left.

Driving back after the otherwise uneventful visit, it dawned on me, *I need to make amends for being thoughtlessly rude to Katherine.* I felt bad down to my socks, I had been a jerk and needed to make restitution. "Frances, do you still expect to make these visits weekly now you smelled the place?"

Scrunched over in the passenger's seat, she looked lost in thought, but distractedly nodded her head yes to my question.

"Then I would like to bring fresh fruit or other healthy-edibles each visit."

"Why bother? I doubt she will notice. This whole visit all I did was smooth out her bedclothes and comb her hair. I doubt she even noticed."

"It'll make the visit nicer for whoever eats what we bring. I wonder if she'd notice if you painted her nails."

Still distracted, Frances said, "What fruit?"

"How about berries, cherries, grapes, maybe bananas. I'm sure she would enjoy a little fresh fruit occasionally. Don't worry I'll ask permission first. What's the problem Frances it's only a small gesture."

"Gus, two reasons; first she could choke on cherry pits or grape seeds, and second the greengrocer we use measures weight by one pound or more, his thumb included. Even a quarter pound is more than enough fruit for my grandma's tiny frail body, and we'd pay full pound inflated prices for what little she eats. It doesn't make sense."

The problem Frances mentioned expanded with sealed five-pound bags of apples, oranges, peaches, pears. It was the only way to buy those fruits at our swanky Fifth Avenue greengrocer. A five-pound bag could hold eight apples or oranges and Granny might eat part of one if peeled and diced.

By default, distributing surplus whole fruit fell on me, it was my idea after all. So, I gave fruit to other residents who were volunteer helpers. Then those residents looked forward to a fresh fruit break from tasteless institutional food when they saw us. On duty staff seemed to like healthy snacks as much as residents, and when there were still leftovers, I left the extras in the nurse station's refrigerator for the overnight shift.

Katherine lit-up with the treats and showed quiet pride sharing them with other residents and staff who made a point to thank her like they came from her hand. Once we established a weekly routine, Katherine clearly looked forward to our visits. Her periods of lucidity increased, and she told us she had not seen fresh fruit at the care home ever. Each type of fruit we brought was like a joyful first-time discovery for her. Soon the small gifts made the visits special, granny happy, and gave her energy to talk to Frances. She began sharing family photos, she had a box full. They were photos Frances had never seen; of relatives and a history she did not know.

With regular visits, the two kin started building an at first brittle relationship. It deepened as Katherine Coach's lost memory seemed to revive and she shared oral history of a bloodline rapidly going extinct. It appeared to me the more time Frances and Katherine spent talking, head-to-head, often holding hands with matching nail polish, the longer Grandma's periods of clarity. It followed, over time, their narratives had meaning for both. Frances told me the stories on the drives home.

Katherine remembered her past much better than the present. She said immediately after high school she took a job in the typing pool at All American Reinsurance. It was her first job, and her mother didn't approve. The company paid for employees to take night classes. So, she studied hard, passed licensing certifications, and college entrance exams to further her career. Katherine earned a master's degree in actuarial science by age thirty-seven. It had been a long slow slog working days and studying nights, but the financial rewards proved worth the effort. By age forty-two she had worked her way up three-fourths of the executive hierarchy at All American. Then she hit a glass ceiling that kept women executives out of top tier management.

At her next annual performance review, Katherine was informed her work was exemplary and deserved a promotion but due to company policy she had gone as far as woman could. Nevertheless, her hard work would be rewarded with an extra-large annual bonus and very generous stock options. Over the years working for All American, Katherine took advantage of every stock buy opportunity and consequently due to stock splits she owned a small but not insignificant share of the company.

To make a long ugly story short, at the next annual stockholder's meeting Katherine Coach aired her gender discrimination grievance loudly and with passion. At that meeting, the chief operating officer quoted from company bylaws, "All top-level executives must be married and parenting at least one child." The section had recently been amended to read, "heterosexually married …" Katherine was informed if she was unhappy at All American Reinsurance, a termination package could be put together for her.

Over drinks relaying her work frustrations to her mixed doubles tennis partner, Melvin McDermott, he suggested they get married. He had just finalized his fourth divorce, once again getting away with little financial damage. His often-used trusty iron-clad prenuptial agreement came through protecting his wealth, as usual. Melvin acknowledged he and Katherine did not love each other but were good friends with benefits and superb tennis partners. If she would offer him companionship in his old age, he was an athletic sixty-eight. In return he would let her adopt one of his institutionalized profoundly developmentally delayed children. Then she could move into the top echelon of her company's management. Melvin was the chief financial officer of a competing reinsurance company. Over the years the two had been career assists for each other if only offering a knowledgeable ear to vent in.

Once she got started, Kathrine churned out Frances' family history, nonstop. At first the marriage of convenience worked out fine. They were a handsome couple and were ready-made dates for obligatory formal work functions. The two danced perfectly in sync even to exotic music, enjoyed the same sorts of vacations, and professionally they were a match with a lot to talk about. During Katherines annual physical, required of all top executives at her company, her irregular menstruation was diagnosed as symptomatic of age-related menopause. She was relieved to be done with her monthly crampy friend, and condoms. The disruption in her marriage of convenience came when Katherine accidentally discovered she was pregnant.

Melvin insisted she abort immediately. He had grown children, from many previous wives and refused to father a child younger than his youngest grandchild. He said it would be disreputable to bring another defective life into the world. Katherine had never wanted to be a mother, she found children an annoying, noisy, dirty, distraction. But she resented being ordered what to do with her body. As the conflict became protracted over months, two things happened simultaneously. Melvin had a stroke and died at the height of a bitter proabortion argument, and the ambulance Katherine called to help Melvin, delivered her a three-week premature daughter.

Having the child had only been a concept for Katherine to fight Melvin over control, she was not prepared for the screaming, wriggling creature placed in her arms by a joyous ambulance crew. Or later, demands placed on her by celebratory hospital staff. Katherine was old enough to be well-past menopause. To shut out the constant demands after giving birth, she gave the child the name Aprilmay because that was when it was due, *not March* when it arrived. *Who in their right mind would call a baby girl March?*

Katherine had kept her family name, Coach, when she married, she had worked hard for it to mean something in the reinsurance industry. Her name had a fierce no-nonsense reputation among colleagues. Furthermore, she absolutely refused to give up her name to symbolize a man's dominance when she had proved she could do anything a man could and better. However, to signify her disinterest, she gave her daughter the family name McDermott.

While planning Melvin's funeral with all his previous wives and company, Katherine arranged for a wet nurse to suckle Aprilmay. Melvin had left each of his previous wives and their progeny generous life insurance payouts. Since Katherine was married to him when he died, she inherited his wealth. Being comfortably well off by her own hand, she thought it ironic to place Melvin's estate in trust for the child he wanted aborted, Aprilmay. In part it was also to appease twinges of guilt over indirectly causing Melvin's death, and guilt for having no maternal feeling for Aprilmay. In the end it seemed proper reparations for saddling the child with little love and McDermott's name.

"Wait, Grandma! You mean my mother had a trust fund and for years we often lived on one cellophane packet of ramen noodles between us?"

"I never got around to telling her. We never talked much and then Aprilmay made me mad getting pregnant with you so young. Nothing personal my dear, but I never liked your mother from before she was born."

"Ironic!"

"Frances, write this code down it is mine and your mother's birthdays dash McDermott. It was a fortune when I set it up settling Melvin's estate. By now you should be set for several lifetimes."

On the drive home Frances rehashed what her grandmother had told her. Once at home trying to tell Bob, he said, "Stop talking and start writing a family history journal."

"It's supposed to be oral history Bob."

I chimed in and said, "Then at least write down the code Grandma gave you, before you forget it."

****

"Grandma Katherine, last week my lawyer contacted the trust fund you set up for my mother. He says it has grown humongous over time. I'll never have to work and can live extremely well on just interest while reinvesting dividends. If I peel grapes for you, will you tell me about my mother and why you never told her about all the money you set aside for us. Last week you stopped talking with my mom's birth and Melvin McDermott's death. What happened next?"

"*I like peeled grapes* and hate grape skins. Let me see what I remember ... Oh yes, all right, when Aprilmay was finally weaned to solid food by her wet nurse Consuela, a parade of nannies came in different sizes and hues to live in my house as mother substitutes. Some were helpful guiding my child's early development and others were as disinterested as myself. At that point in my life, I wielded immense power as my reinsurance company's chief executive officer and was ruthless. But alas, there was only twenty-four hours in a day, and I had none for my daughter. So, much of my professional and all domestic life were managed by my personal assistant Madge.

"Aprilmay entered high school six months after her fourteenth birthday. I don't know where the years went. She was a latchkey kid between nannies at that time and had too much unsupervised free time. Aprilmay barely knew or saw me except passing each other coming going in opposite directions. We communicated through Madge, who signed the child's report cards or permission slips for outings, doled out money as needed, require receipts, and all without emotional involvement.

"What do you remember about my mother?"

"I had my lawyer investigated Aprilmay's high school after she became pregnant. I was thinking of suing them. He discovered when high school freshmen Aprilmay McDermott met Bruce Rusher, they fell in love and no school staff intervened. Both students had homeroom, biology, and English classes together, a big mistake.

"Aprilmay had access to every teenager's most valued asset, privacy. She had afterschool unchaperoned parties. The neighbors phoned me and the police about the goings on. I worked long hours. I knew I had a problem when my cook and housekeeper insisted on leaving, before my emotionally needy child came home with school friends.

"Soon Bruce and my daughter were exchanging more than kisses and grubby hands. Both Aprilmay and Bruce were fourteen years old. They had heard, pregnancy was not possible for virgins before age sixteen or on Tuesday, and Friday. By the start of Aprilmay's second semester freshmen year high school the teens confirmed their information regarding pregnancy was incorrect.

"On a routine visit to the school nurse's office for stomach upset, it was discovered Aprilmay had swollen breasts, sensitive nipples, and a pee test verified with child. The nurse called in a Child Welfare report as required for fourteen-year-olds without proper prenatal care. Aprilmay was immediately processed to a group home for unmarried pregnant underage girls. I was relieved she'd be better cared for than I had time for.

"Showing great concern, Bruce Rusher asked after Aprilmay's health, and the school nurse called the police when he became physically belligerent at news of his impending fatherhood had become of public concern. He was taken into custody on suspicion of statutory rape, assaulting a public-school nurse, a police officer, damaging public property, and propagating false facts about teenage pregnancy.

"Aprilmay's social worker contacted my office to be involved with her and impending baby's care and provide financial help with Bruce's legal troubles. I was still angry with Aprilmay and refused all requests and turned my lawyers loose on them. Because the public defenders' office was overwhelmed with cases, Bruce was assigned a pro bono lawyer from a prestigious white glove law firm. I still remember his name was Dan Glover. He was doing community service for not paying his taxes. As I remember, he was a big fag."

I thought, *The Dan Glover we bought our country house from was a lawyer who did court ordered pro bono work as restitution for tax evasion. There couldn't be two, could there?*

Grandma continued her story. "Both the stupid fourteen-year-olds wanted to keep their baby, even with no resources or knowing infant care. Bruce's family begrudgingly took in Aprilmay and taught her backward parenting skills. In return they expected her to be willing to sleep on a rollaway bed in Bruce's sisters' room in the unheated basement.

"What I, Madge, and Aprilmay didn't know, and Dan Glover didn't bother to find out was, Bruce Rusher's immediate family lived outside the law. Females in the family scammed social welfare programs, and the males committed armed robberies for necessities not provided by federal food assistance programs. The pistol toting men in the Rusher family viewed Bruce with suspicion, he was the runt of their litter, and walked like a sissy. There consensus was the boy was powderpuff soft and wouldn't do well in prison, an extension of their family territory and heritage."

"How'd you find all this out, Grandma?"

"After I gave up my parental rights, I had second thoughts and had my lawyer hire a private detective to make sure I'd done the right thing. Second guessing yourself is not a sound business practice. But I'd allowed myself to get too angry when Aprilmay had a baby before middle age. Just the same as my mother, I never liked crying babies. But unlike her, I had feelings of guilt for not mothering the girl I had intended to abort."

"Do you remember when my mom, and I used to visit you here?"

"Yes."

"Do you remember that you suddenly forgot who we were?"

"Yes."

"Was that for real or so we would stop visiting?"

"Your mother kept bugging me about money when she had a fortune in her name. It felt like a contest, I couldn't let her win, and she never tried to be nice."

"A contest? We were hungry."

"She never brought me fresh fruit, and I never liked Aprilmay's attitude. She was annoying and disrespectful. But if she'd told me, you were going hungry, I could have fixed that in a hurry. But your mother was a stubborn proud woman, like my mother, and just like me."

"Meanwhile Grandma, we were surviving by mom's wits, going from one extreme to another."

"I don't know about that. According to my lawyer and his private investigator, rather than develop an inner self, my daughter became adept at reading other people's expectations and then mimicking who they wanted her to be, to get *her* way. In other words, she was an expert con artist."

"She was a waitress being a con artist was how she got tips."

"The professionals I hired said, your mother developed an attractive outer shell but was hollow on the inside. The last thing Madge told me was my daughter and grandson had moved to Texas."

"We never went to Texas."

"Frances, I never liked Texas. We should have let Mexico keep it when they took it. Who needs all that phony-bluster? Then Madge died and I lost the information conduit about you and your mother."

"Grandma, how much of this do you know to be true? It sounds preposterous to me."

"Well, it's mostly second hand from Madge, my lawyer, and the PI's written reports with photos. Aprilmay and I were like oil and water from before she was born. Giving her life took my husbands. I mean, how could I forgive her for that. Listen here, I never asked to be a mother."

"I always suspected I was crazy from how strangers treat me. But never once did I think my mother was too. She worked so hard to find us safe places to sleep, something to eat, and when we got a break, for me to look pretty. As you tell it mother wanted me to look beautiful as revenge for how my father beat her."

"Your mother was coocoo, and most health insurance doesn't cover mental illness if they can help it. It's not cost effective like terminal illness. There are many things I don't understand, but cost profit ratios I get."

****

The nursing home's evening receptionist was also their utility worker, the telephones were not busy. I always made sure the night receptionist Nancy received a nice piece of grandmother Coach's fruit. All other staff had strictly controlled time management distributing meals, medication, bathing, and sleep time. As evening turned into night the receptionist often had free time for a friendly chat with me when our chats were not interrupted by the public address system's plea for her to settle a fight in the TV lounge or an unruly patient not ready for bedtime.

On one such visit, while Katherine was reminiscing about the golden days of the reinsurance industry to a truly fascinated Frances. I finished distributing surplus tangerines and ended up at the receptionist's desk. Handing over the biggest, best fruit I said, "How long has Katherine Coach been a Sheltering Arms resident?"

"Don't know, she was here when I was hired eight years ago. Want me to check?"

"Sure, Nancy, if you don't mind. She looks like the oldest resident." That was said placing a tangerine in front of her with a small smile.

Acknowledging my smile with a wink, Nancy unlocked the record room behind her workstation and disappeared inside. After a couple of minutes, she returned with a thick binder case record and opened it to a tattered intake form at the back. "Katherine Coach was admitted nine and a half years ago. You are right, that is a longevity record for this place. Now that you bring it up, I think she is the only one who is still here since before I began."

Making a show of disinterest by looking around the lobby, I said, "I wonder who's paying for her care after almost ten years?"

"Let me, see? Ah ha, up to now, she has catastrophic-long-term insurance."

"You sounded doubtful when you said, 'Up to now.'"

"Not much gets by you, Gus, you sure you're gay. I'm in the market for another husband."

"Well, you can't have mine."

"Why do the ones I want always have husbands? *Life is so unfair*. All right, let me shuffle some papers. Aha, look, there's a note here. Katherine Coach's insurance runs out in two months. Then she has to pay out of pocket."

"Her smocks don't usually have pockets."

"Hold on, let me find the resident's financial statement in the case record. Let's see … it looks like her pockets are deep and full until the end of next year. This home costs a lot for residents who self-pay."

"What happens when her funds run out?"

"When Katherine's insurance maxes out, the Home will apply for Medicaid. Medicaid automatically denies our first three or four applications. When Kathrine's application is finally accepted, Medicaid will demand to see she 'spent down' any money she has left before they pay. You look confused."

"I am."

"After many rejections Medicaid almost always open a case if our paperwork is faultless. Then the time between accepted and open is usually protracted by them repeatedly losing our forms, and other bureaucratic designs to thwart paying as long as possible. Finally, *if*, the home's frustration tolerance is high enough, Medicaid pays for Katherine Coach to reside here, if we all live that long."

"What do you mean?"

"If she died between her spend down and Medicaid's first payment, the Home has to eat the financial loss. But our new administrator has a scheme for a big end of year bonus from the corporation that owns the home … but I can't talk about his plan, nobody is supposed to know about it."

Just then the public address system announced Nancy was needed in the lounge. She grabbed her floppy-soft sponge-rubber bat and left in a hurry. I rotated the case record to face me, then glanced over the content. After a little page turning, I found the illegal scheme Nancy mentioned. The administrator had taken out a life insurance policy for Katherine Coach, with the nursing home as beneficiary. Even I knew, that had to be illegal. There was no mention of other life insurance policies, but she seemed to have every other insurance known to humankind. I took photos of everything in the record with my cell phone before rotating the case record back around and closing it.

****

To celebrate her seventeenth birthday and emancipation anniversary, Frances consulted a plastic surgeon, and scheduled breast implant surgery. It was her much anticipated special liberation gift to her desired self-image. Granny helped choose the best adolescent implant model to create an attractive medium breasted teen silhouette. The surgeon removed Frances' previous back-alley silicone injected breasts and used those pockets for the new medically approved implants.

Bob and I discussed the added pressure implants might make for Frances to reenergize her off and on-again illegal bottom surgery, in Mexico. The male to female trans kids at her school could hardly wait to turn their penises' outsides inside to create imitation vaginas. It was their most common topic of conversation and probably filled their dreams at night.

When we first met Frances, her penis was an alien appendage to be removed as quickly as possible. After hearing adult points of view from knowledgeable transsexuals and transvestites, Frances took the time to explore the body she was born with, like most teenagers should do. Which meant swimming up-stream against a tide of peer pressure at her school, and her mother's plan. Katherine Coach gave Frances fresh perspective to view her mother's motivations for the sex change. But it still took courage to give up the sanctuary of a long-held fantasy and make peace with a body she wasn't comfortable in.

****

Without warning, in the middle of the night, Katherine Coach developed a high fever accompanied by excruciating back pain and trouble breathing. After attempts to lower her fever failed and giving her oxygen, she was taken to the home's critical care clinic. When that couldn't help, she was taken by ambulance to the nearby small community hospital. Immediately after being notified the next morning Katherine Coach was terminal with suspected covid-19 virus multiple variants. We rushed to the hospital.

Instead of an over-flowing intensive care unit, Katherine was put in a dimly lit room with other dying patients and given a short course of palliative medications to manage her passing. The hospital required Bob, Frances, and I to wear the medical version of space suits, complete with respirators to sit with the dying patient. Frances held Katherine's hand as she struggled to breathe her last breath. The old woman's eyes were alert and unafraid when she feebly squeezed Frances' hand for the last time.

According to the hospital administrator I tracked down and threatened to stick to like glue. Mrs. Coach's private catastrophic health insurance was in effect when admitted. To shoo me away, the administrator produced the private number for a nearby mortuary and handed me necessary forms to immediately release Katherine's body. He said the hospital's morgue trailers were overflowing with human remains, and they were at the bottom of a long list waiting for additional trailers. Consequently, usual prolonged paperwork was greatly extended due to turmoil, and he thanked me for helping remove a dead body.

CHAPTER 20. What's Old Is New Again

Bob, and Frances, wrote a brief newspaper obituary for Katherine, arranged a funeral home viewing, and dignified burial next to her husband. We and the morticians were the only ones to attend the viewing and burial. Apparently, Katherine Coach had outlived her contemporaries and the lethal virus killed off later generations who might have known her.

I let Frances' lawyer know by email that Katherine had died. Just in case the nursing home wanted to contest Frances' inheritance, I included my cell phone photos of Katherine's case record as an attachment. Attorney Brick was able to finalize Frances' inheritance without stirring up a fuss and having to go to court.

Bob and I grieved Kathrine's death, out of respect for an elder, as a couple. The same way as we mourned the passing of others we did not know well. From our experience in military combat, we had refined our mourning to personal quiet-grief and moved on only when ready. Frances' mourning for Katherine was deep, profound, and brought back the murders of her mother, father, and Matilda. It fed her fixation with having a short life.

A big, dark hole of sorrow opened to fully engulf Frances and overflowed to encompass our whole apartment. I was secretly relieved when her new apartment across the street was not finished on schedule, given the depths of her despondency. As hard as it was to be around her grief, her being alone with it in the new apartment appeared hazardous to me.

After a reasonable amount of time, Bob and I encouraged activities of daily life from Frances. In response we got, "My grandmother's story will be my story if I live a fraction as long. Now it doesn't matter whether I have myself castrated or not. Nobody came to say goodbye to granny, and they won't for me. How sad is that?"

"We came and gave her a proper send off. Remember, you saw, you were there."

"Don't you think more flowers would have been better?"

"Frances, it was understated dignified and tasteful. Katherine would have approved. Remember Matilda MacKinsey's funeral? We all agreed there were way too many flowers, too many mourners and not one of her blood kin attended. That was sad."

"Katherine said she worked hard from girlhood until old age. Nobody from her work came."

"She didn't request a parade. Think about it, she left you a double fortune."

"Grandma Katherine told me the same things as Matilda. Now who's going to teach me firsthand herstory?"

"Did they know each other?"

"No, silly, they never met."

"What did they tell you?"

"There is nothing new under the sun, because history keeps repeating itself."

"Don't be silly, how is that possible? Both women saw power go from woodfired steam to nuclear transitioning to renewable wind and solar. Amazing things happened in their lifetimes."

"I can tell you exactly what was said because your husband Bob the tyrant made me keep a grandma journal."

"Then by all means edify."

"According to my maternal grandmother Kathrine and my adopted grandma Matilda; the Great War WWI 1914 – 1917 used poison gas and airplanes for the first time in war. WWI was no sooner at an armistice than the 1918 - 1923 Spanish Flu killed 60,000,000 people worldwide. By 1929 greedy speculators caused such a *great depression* it went worldwide. Since most people in the world were hopelessly destitute with no future in sight, they chose fascist dictators who promised them a return to normal life."

"That was over 100 years ago, Frances, times have changed."

"Not according to my grandmas; at the stroke of midnight New Year's Eve year 2000, doomsday was scheduled according to computer nerds and their gods. All computers were supposed to crash into another dark ages and the world's end in chaos. It was computer gods who told the people, 'Repent, Y2K is upon you.' Similar doomsday words were used for New Year's Eve 1900, attributed to different chaos gods. By September 2000, the world hadn't ended after all, so 9/11 happened and the longest unwinnable war in U.S. history began. The war was started over weapons of mass destruction that didn't exist; the same level of deceit dragged the U.S. into WWI against the will of the people."

"Right, we get your grandmas' comparisons."

"I'm not done yet. In the year 2009 a worldwide financial crash was caused by greedy bankers peddling phony-baloney mortgages to a gullible public. It was just like the 1929 international financial collapse from buying stocks on margin. With the nation in crisis over a pandemic the forty-fifth president of the U.S. used the exact words, to disregard the people's fear and pain, as the thirty-first president said a century earlier. Both said, "The solution to national crisis is right around the corner being solved by miracles." The miracles never materialized both times. It took the country over ten years and another world war to get over President Herbert Hoover's bungling-blunders as leader. The exact cost has yet to be calculated for president forty-fives attempted to end the American democracy experiment by claiming the election he lost was won. Meanwhile other fascist dictators around the world have taken power like in the 1930s, preparing for who knows what 2030s repeat of history. My grandmas say none of these current despots are the benevolent authoritarians their people desperately yearn for."

"Done now?"

"Did I mention the 2019 worldwide plague, covid-19 reduced the population of this planet by millions of people just like the 1918 Spanish flu. Of the last five U.S. wars, we only won one, WWII. WWI and Korea were ended in armistice, Vietnam and the others beat us. I can stop now or tell you more?"

"Frances, it's never healthy to dwell on negatives."

"Yes, Frances, think positive. A better day is coming, it's right around the corner."

"How can you two be Polly annas? Don't you see we are on a merry-go-round that repeats every 100 years."

"Could be we became Polly annas fighting ongoing wars with no objective or end, as you pointed out. *No reason getting upset over what you can't control.*"

"That's what I think too, Frances."

"No, Bob and Gus, we are all cursed. Life as we know it is on a pointless loop."

"Your lawyer said you can live well off interest, for life. Think about it, you will never have to work if you don't want. That is something few of us get to experience. To me, that doesn't sound like a curse."

"Why can't you just leave me alone with my misery? I don't have my grandmas to tell me herstories and I don't want to cheer up with it repeating itself every century. How come I'm the only one who cares in this family?"

Never one to keep my opinions to myself, I said, "It is possible to get stuck in sadness."

Bob offered a longer comment, "Frances, have you given any thought to your life after high school?"

"Yes, I intend to work for social justice. I guess I'll have to go to college for that, maybe ... I suppose?"

To keep the diversion going, I said, "Oh, by the way, times a wasting to pick out furniture for your new apartment. Do you have a color scheme in mind?"

"Gus, you and Bob are relentless pests, do you know that?"

"It came naturally to us. When we registered our wedding, we requested unrelenting in matched sets."

"I noticed."

"So, come on then, it's time for you to pick a major, a college good at it, apartment furniture and whatever else a young lady of your means wants that isn't too ostentatious for Fifth Avenue."

Frances seemed to zone out, hopefully about a college major or furniture. Then she snapped her fingers and said, "Okay, if you really want to get me undepressed; loan me $7,000?"

Bob clearly knew where this was coming from but asked anyway. "Why do you need a loan? You are a wealthy young debutant wannabe."

Practical me also knew and said, "Ask your attorney for the money. You have much more in the bank than we will ever earn between us."

"But *I'm asking you guys.*"

"I'll play along for your amusement, what's the money for?"

"I just figured outed if I move to Mexico for bottom surgery, I won't be depressed any more. You know I'll pay you back because I can. Like you said, the money is in the bank."

"I thought this was settled."

"I want to look like a woman, not a freak in my coffin."

"Slow down, lady, we've been down this road before. The law says you must be at least twenty-five years old, and that's for your protection."

"Have you been talking to Frank Brick? He said the same thing, word for word when I asked him for $7,000."

"No. I haven't. But a group meeting with your foster dads and therapist seems like a good idea and you can invite your lawyer if you like."

"Absolutely not, my therapy is personal and private. It's not a party where guests are invited."

"Fine, then I'm for engaging a family therapist to help us three get through the loss of your grandmothers and requisite wait time for bottom surgery."

"I don't want more pills. Another therapist would only push those antidepressants, just like my current therapist does."

Looking over the top of his reading eyeglasses Bob said, "This feels like a stalemate, anybody want to go for a run?"

"Have you heard from Joseph?"

Caught off guard I said, "That's an abrupt shift."

"I thought your intention was to change my mood to be less depressed. Listen up, I'll say it again, have either of you heard from Joseph?"

"Chill Frances, last week he phoned Bob for an answer to an academic quandary. Apparently, England has them too. Bob said he seems happy and is doing well in his classes. Didn't you, Bob?"

"I did and can speak for myself, when allowed."

"Is he dating anyone?"

"He didn't say. And that is something neither Gus nor I would ask. We were teenagers once and know parental boundaries ours never learned."

"Well, I'd like to know if he is seeing anyone."

"Then ask him, you've got his phone number?"

"I couldn't ask that. He'd know I was interested. What did he say besides, he's doing well in school?"

"He says living in a foreign country has helped him know himself. It sounded like he's developing into a self-assured young man with clear ideas about his future."

"I was afraid of that. He is blossoming in England, and you won't help me move to Mexico. I guess my only choice is to turn tricks on the street corner to get money to go south of the border."

"Just be aware, if you do that, we won't bail you out of jail. It is something to keep in mind while streetwalking or streaking or whatever antisocial acts you are contemplating. We love you, but don't do bail. Jail is not a nice place for transsexuals, or anyone else."

From years teaching high school, Bob was ready to defuse a budding altercation. He did it without forethought. "Frances, how's your Spanish?"

"It is not fair for you both to pick on me at the same time, and from different directions. Don't worry, I'll pick up Spanish quick enough after I move to Mexico. Why are you so mean to me today? I just want to stay sad I miss my grandmothers and feel sorry for myself. Katherine was my last living relative. Who will I leave my fortune to?"

"Why not give Joey a call? He'd like to know how you are doing. You two know how to commiserate. Believe it or not, we also love and worry about both of you."

"Commiserate?"

"Occasionally, he has accused us of picking on him too. You two are related by gay dads."

"He's moved on with his life, more than likely forgotten all about me."

"There's only one way to find out."

****

"I took your advice and telephone Joseph. We had a long catch-up chat. He hadn't known about my grandmother and was sorry she passed. He tried to make a connection between Matilda dying to protect her home and Katherine providing an affluent loveless home. I don't see it."

"I'm glad you kept him apprised. Any other news?"

"He has an English girlfriend, a real girl, not like me. Her name is Felicity Heimerman, they were zoology lab partners. Their plan is to move in together next semester. He said Felicity gets him in every way and it's mutual. I don't even understand what that means."

"Huh, that's nice. I hope he uses protection."

"He said once he has a new address you'll be told."

"Wow, see that, Gus, we didn't do too bad as foster parents for Joey. How'd we miss the secret sauce for Frances?"

"I'm jealous, he sounded so happy and I'm hopelessly miserable. That proves he was your favorite. How come I didn't get the secret sauce?"

"Frances rather than jealous you could be glad for your foster brother. Your time will come if you will be patient."

"YEAH, Yeah, yeah, you say that about everything."

CHAPTER 21. New Apartment, Digby, and the Square Ring

Finally! After many delays, Frances' apartment was constructed out of showroom space, officially inspected, and furnished in bold, bright, teenage colors. The matte finished walls were covered with framed, matted under glass artwork created by the homeowner. Furnishings were an eclectic collection of modern and flea market antiques that fit together distinctively to establish an atypical living environment for a creative young person.

To celebrate taking possession of a new home, Frances threw a housewarming party. Invited guests were select high school classmates and after-school group-therapy friends. Bob and I insisted on chaperoning the event and enforcing a no alcohol or drugs rule. The ban was much to the chagrin of party goers who had to relinquish their underage and otherwise illegal party favors as housewarming gifts at the door, into trash bags, to gain entrance. Yes, Bob and I patted down arriving guests, and were deemed no fun at all by certain guests, because we refused to grope them during frisking.

Call it bad energy, or what you will, in every group there is always one. At Frances' party the most obnoxious negative individual was named Ashanta O'Malley. She caught Bob and my attention at arrival with a mile-wide bad attitude when we confiscated her illicit pharmacy. After we took possession of her pill stash, she complained loudly for attention. Then she went around attempting to co-opt the event. She made herself the central attraction at every opportunity. Maybe she did it to prove she could without chemical help. What seemed unusual to us, Frances, was not bothered by the interloper hijacking her party. Bob and I were more than ready to eighty-six Ms. O'Malley, but Frances said no. Thus, condoning her guest's dreadful behavior.

Cleaning up after the last guest left, I asked Frances, "Why did you let Ashanta take over your party? We would have gladly escorted her to the street with a shove."

"I know, it looked strange, right? Six weeks ago, Ashanta spent a long weekend in Vera Cruz, Mexico. She came back with her male parts reconfigured and tucked inside. Ashanta needed something positive like my party to acknowledge the change. I can afford to be generous. Isn't that what you two always say."

"A heads up to us would have also been nice. But kudos to generous you."

"Sorry, sorry, sorry, I meant to tell you then got busy arranging the healthy snacks trays."

"Those were quite tasty by the way."

"I got the recipes online. So, dreary Ahsan O'Malley became fabulous Ms. Ashanta O'Malley. My party's ginger ale toast acknowledged her much awaited sexual transition. I am happy for her."

"Did you get a chance to observe the quality of her renovation?"

"So far it looks realistic, but the swelling hasn't gone all the way down yet. Just between us the opening does look a bit small."

"Then size does matter to you, after all your protestation to the contrary."

"I'll check back with her after the swelling is gone and she did all her stretching exercises. I'm sure everything is good."

"Then why does your face say something else?

"I don't know, maybe she's not doing her stretching exercises religiously enough."

"In spite of that, do you think *she* is satisfied with the results?"

"Ugh, you would ask that. You two are not who I want to talk to about this."

"Yet you know what Gila monsters we can be if you don't."

"Ugh! I've got to learn to keep my mouth shut around my busy bother fathers. Ashanta, is having a few postsurgical problems I'm sure they'll clear right up with time."

"Like what for instance?"

"Instead of peeing in a single vertical stream, like before, it comes out with a mind of its own, all over everything. She's wearing absorbent pee pads for the moment. But I'm sure that can be fixed, and she'll start having orgasms again."

"I suppose there's no money back guarantee." I said this to Bob, but Frances took offence.

"Behave, Gus, she's seeing an expensive urologist. They're exploring fixing that problem if it persists after the inflammation goes down."

"In your unbiased opinion, do you think she would have had the same complications if the work was done in the States?"

"But she wasn't old enough and just couldn't wait that long. She wants to be in love with a straight man and get married."

"I guess what I'm asking is, would you be so blasé if the botched surgery were performed on your body?"

"Gus, I've told you and Bob a million times. You can't possibly understand how terrible it is to be born in the wrong wrapper. That's what was already botched in my life."

Tying-closed the last large trash bag full of used paper cups and plates, I said, "Bob and I told you, we will support whatever decision you make, when you are old enough to legally make it ... not before."

"Oh, here we go again. I've said so many times, age is just a number, like any other number."

"Now, at twice your age, Frances, I can assure you age is more than a number, no matter what Joey told you."

"Yeah, yeah, yeah, go ahead, pick on Joseph. He's not here to defend himself."

"Somebody once said, the years know what the days haven't learned."

"Waldo said that."

"Waldo who?"

"Let me see, my classmates use only his middle name, Waldo. It sounds funny. Oh, wait I know, his last name was Emerson like those cheap Japanese electronics. Waldo sounds better and is easier to remember."

"Neuroscientists have proof that the human brain doesn't stop growing until at least age twenty-five. Bob and I over thirty haven't hit our physical peaks yet, and *emotionally* you and Joey keep teaching us we have more growing to do."

In a huff, flinging her hands around from the wrists, Frances said, "Get down to it, just say it."

"Say what?"

"What we are really talking about … if I go to Mexico for *the* surgery, you'll never speak to me again."

"You know us better than that."

"Then what are we talking about? It was a nice party, everyone liked my apartment, and had fun."

Ever ready to defuse a situation reaching toward boiling, Bob said, "Change. You've had a lot of change lately. It can be discombobulating, and more change often seems a remedy for too much, it isn't."

"Like what change are you talking about, Bob? I already established history just repeats itself. No change there."

"Really, you want a list?"

Switching from a belligerent tone to an affected coy one, Frances said, "Yes please."

"Fine, after a life of poverty recently you've become wealthy due to an inherited trust fund and life insurance. Last year Matilda MacKinsey was murdered. This year your grandmother died, two of your classmates committed suicide, and before that your parents died by gun violence. In addition, you just became emancipated, the owner of a Fifth Avenue luxury apartment, had breast implants, your maternal grandmother opened your mind to your family history, Joey is not who you remember, and your friend Ashanta's Mexican surgery is problematical. Did I leave anything out?"

Switching back to belligerence, Frances said, *"See, you two are picking on me for no reason at all!"*

"No, I don't think so, a lot has happened in a short while. Most of us mere mortals need time to digest change."

"For God's sake, what do you two want from me?"

"A promise, … you won't do anything irreversible before talking to Bob or me first."

"Oh, is that all, okay, I'll try."

****

Six uneventful, peaceful weeks slipped by barely noticed, then a part-time trainee position at Allison Ajax Dress shop became available. It was for retail sales Friday evening six to ten, noon to nine Saturday, and inventory shifts were offered during school vacations. Frances accepted the job, not for its twice minimum wage but rather deep employee discounts on merchandise.

Between school, a new job, music lessons, and activities of daily living, it became more efficient for our ward to use her own apartment without Bob and I underfoot causing traffic control issues. Frances was growing more independent, and we approved. That did not mean our lives got less complicated only the space between complications expanded to across the street to 225 from 210.

Then suddenly, our house cleaner, Ruperto, disappeared without giving notice, and us owing a month's pay. Through diligent detective work my secretary Leonard tracked Ruperto down to an address in Los Mooches, Mexico. Once Ruperto's address was verified, we sent an international money order for what was owed and a little more for an upcoming birthday. Through hook and by crook Leonard discovered Ruperto had been snatched up without papers while visiting his legal U.S. citizen grandfather and deported by the immigration-police without due process. Finding a new hard working one day a week cleaning lady-man proved impossible during the government's virulent antiimmigrant pogrom. Nevertheless, Leonard was working diligently to find us domestic assist.

In the meantime, Bob and I relegated Saturday mornings to cleaning the 210 Fifth Avenue apartment ourselves. We organized clutter, dusted, vacuumed, ran the dishwasher, changed the bed sheets, collected than took trash to the basement, did laundry, folded it and put it away, while one or another grand opera blasted from my state-of-the-art audiophile sound system.

Following behind the robot vacuum on all fours with a hand-held dust-sucker, I would have missed the intercom's chimes if not for its flashing light. Flipping on the video intercom screen, Elroy, one of our doormen said, "Frances is in the lobby with two police persons. You might want to come down. She looks upset."

Bob and I leaped into T-shirts, slid on shoes, and did not wait for the elevator. We ran down the inside fire exit stairs to find Frances calmly sitting on the lobby sofa talking with two uniformed police officers writing notes of what she said.

Doorman Elroy saw us fly into the lobby one after the other and intercepted saying, "She's calmed down."

"What happened?"

"I saw Frances heading toward the subway and this homeless looking guy stopped in front of her jabbering. When it looked like they were arguing, I went outside and blew my whistle. The homeless guy heard the whistle and saw me. So, he pulled out a big gravity knife and waved it threatening toward me. I don't take that crap and rushed at him. He turned cut Frances on the arm saying something over his shoulder and ran off. I chased him into the park, but he got away. I brought Frances into the office disinfected her wound, it isn't deep, and called the cops. They came right away, she wouldn't go with EMS cops summoned, so I called you guys."

"Thanks, Elroy, you went way above and beyond for Frances. We won't forget."

"That's okay, you guys are always generous at Christmas. I'll spread the word to the other doormen to be on the lookout for that homeless man."

Out of the corner of my eye, I saw the cops stand and give Frances a card then leave. Bob and I went right over. "Are you all right? What happened?"

"Digby Russel is out of prison again. He said he's been hiding in the park across the street, waiting for my mother or me to show our face. He thought I still lived here at 210 and wanted a shower, something to eat, and of course money. When I told him, my mother was murdered by my father who was killed by the police, Digby lost it."

"If Digby is back. We'll want to give him a proper welcoming to stay away."

"When Elroy blew his whistle, Digby said he was my real father. He cut me and said he would prove I'm his love child with a paternity test. He gave me life so, what's mine is his and he intends to take what's his."

"Is that possible? Could it be he's your father?"

"No way. My mother couldn't stand him, and my dad didn't meet him until I was five."

Bob and I exchanged a look that did not bode well for Digby. Not wanting Frances to see what Bob and I were thinking I said, "Why didn't you go with EMS?"

"You know I hate hospitals. It wasn't a bad cut and Elroy put hydrogen peroxide on it. See, I let EMS bandage it, so it wasn't a wasted trip for them. But it made me late for my part time job, and look blood ruined my new silk blouse."

"I'll call them and explain. What did you do when Digby pulled a knife?"

"I already phoned my job and explained what happened, they were cool."

"How did you react to being threatened with a knife?"

"As part of the active shooter drills in school they taught us to hide, and definitely not fight back against a weapon. Even if we think we could take the shooter down. Truthfully, I did clench my fists ready to deck him if he tried to hurt me more. But to be honest inside I froze, then I saw Elroy your doorman moving toward us like the cavalry. Digby looked stunned when I said mom was murdered by his best friend my dad. His face looked like I'd gut punched him. Then he saw Elroy running and blowing his whistle."

"What do you think, Bob, do we need to find Frances a dojo." Looking serious, Bob nodded his head yes.

"No, no, no, I'm a girl and boy's gyms smell awful."

"There are such things as female boxers, and mixed martial arts for girls. They compete in their weight for titles and ranking just like the fellas."

"Wait a second, just why would I need a dojo? Several months ago, I floored that real estate person without even thinking."

"At the time your footwork looked awkward at best."

"He still went down like a sack of potatoes. If need be, I can take care of myself. Joseph even taught me some inescapable wrestling holds."

"People who carry weapons they are not trained to use are often hurt by them."

"I don't carry weapons, never did never will."

"Your fists are weapons, and your feet don't know that."

"I suppose if I don't join a dojo or gym, I will never hear the end of it from you two, right? Thank you very much Digby!"

"Let's go upstairs and I'll do a computer search for coed boxing gyms."

"Wait I can do that on my phone. What should I put?"

"Try: boxing gym female lower Manhattan ..."

"Oh look, there's one on Broadway and Twenty-eighth, and another over on Sixth Avenue and thirtieth."

"Bingo."

"I'm only doing this to please you guys. I'm in a generous mood since Digby reminded me where I came from before I met you two."

"Let's walk over to the gym on Broadway, it's the closest."

"Just be aware if it stinks of boy, I'm not staying!"

The Square Ring was on the fourth floor of Broadway and Twenty-eight Street. It smelled of commercial air freshener, looked clean, had two boxing rings in use. Females and males of various sizes and ages were hitting punching bags that hung in one area, and others used free weights and exercise machines in another corner. There were probably thirty people using the facility. The fire department wall sign said legal occupancy fifty.

I spoke to a middle-aged guy when he stopped jumping rope, "Where's the manager?" He pointed at an older, puggish looking man with unkempt balding red-gray hair. The man was intently watching one of the fight rings where two young pugilists were wildly flailing punches at each other. When a bell rang ending that round, I approached the manager. "Hi, I'm Gus, this is Bob, and we are looking for a boxing gym for our ward Frances. Is your membership open and if so, what are the requirements?"

"Nice to meet yah, I'm Harry." He put out a big-callused hand for a quick bone-cracking shake, and said, "Follow me to the office." He was maybe five-foot eight-inches tall, about two hundred-fifty muscle bound pounds going to fat in the middle, cauliflower ears, permanently smashed-flat nose, and deep-set sparkling green eyes.

There were framed photos of Harry in his hay day, as a boxing contender and once as champion. As seen in the photos, title belts and winner's trophies were displayed in a glass front steel gray cabinet mounted on the wall next to his desk. Harry plopped down in a brown-cracked-leather swivel chair and tilted back behind a battered blond-wood double pedestal old-fashioned schoolteacher's desk. It looked as scared up as Harry. Bob, Frances, and I took gray metal folding chairs facing his desk.

"Young lady, why do you want to box?"

"My foster dads say my footwork isn't good. But it could be these low heels. I know how to dance to any kind of music."

Harry rose and came around his desk and stood in front of Frances. "Stand up and face me." He brought his big hands up to shoulder height, palms facing Frances. "Hit my right hand twice with your left, followed by triple taps to my left with hard rights. Don't hold back, show me what you got girl."

Frances fists were a blur as they flashed into Harry's palms. He had to take a step back from the force of the super-sonic right-hand blows.

Harry indicated Frances should sit back down and turned to face Bob and me. "You're right, her footwork blows, but she packs quite a punch. I have a female trainer who can smooth out her rough spots." Pivoting to Frances, Harry said, "That is if you are willing to put in the hard work necessary. Boxing is not for everyone."

"So far I'm interested."

"We charge $500 a month, bring your own towel and workout clothes. You'll meet with your trainer three times a week the first month, then you two decide how often. We are open seven days. Any questions?"

"Frances is transsexual. Thought you'd want to know now instead of later."

"Has she had the surgery down below?"

"No."

"Then communal showers are out. She can change in the unisex handicap bathroom. On the positive, she can spar with either gender if it is mutually agreeable. You want to think about it or sign a contact today?"

"What if I had the surgery?"

"Modesty avoids unwanted comments. Around here, show-offs best do it in the ring."

"Can I meet my trainer before I say yes?"

"I'll do you one better. I'll loan you a pair of shorts and top. Then you can spar a couple of rounds with her bare foot to see if you are a good fit."

Bob and I exchanged a loaded look but said nothing. We hadn't expected things to proceed so quickly *or cost $500 a month*. While I was ruminating, Harry handed Bob a list of dos and don'ts for Frances while at the gym.

"Don't buy her the expensive boxing shoes until you know she'll do the work. My gym is not for namby-pamby push overs. Powder puffs don't last long around here."

Frances heard the challenge, took a deep breath, then looked hard at each of us adult males. "Sure, I'll see what it's all about. Why not, … so far it has been one of those days already."

Mary, Frances' boxing coach to be, was early twenties, lavender-colored haired, big caramel-brown-eyed, and maybe five-foot four inches, at a hundred-twenty pounds. Frances was taller and heavier. The two went three, three-minute rounds wearing headgear and using big-puffy boxing gloves. Mary was a no-nonsense professional fighter and punished Frances with body shots at first. In the process she was knocked down twice, until she figured out how to cover up from Frances' lightning-fast flurries of combination punches. In the meantime, Frances quickly learned to protect both face and body at once. When the fight was over the two combatants hugged and put their heads together to discuss their schedules. Frances had made a new friend, and boxing was no longer an unconscious artifact from her dead father. Bob wrote out a check and handed it to Harry, and all three of us signed the contract.

We walked Frances home to her apartment for a long Jacuzzi-tub soak and then nap. Bob and I went looking for Digby where he was last seen escaping into the park.

In the 1700s, where Madison Square Park stands today stood a cleared area in a game preserve. The area was a pauper's field to bury indigents from downtown. Then by necessity it got expanded during a nasty epidemic and officially became the overflow cemetery for less indigent from the downtown cemetery that later became Washington Square Park.

As the city grew, the cemetery boundaries expanded from Twenty-third to Twenty-sixth Streets between Fifth and Madison Avenues. It was turned into a public park in 1847 and named after the original Madison Square Gardens which stood Northeast of the park until 1925. Our older neighbors and others parapsychologically sensitive area residents swear after midnight on full moon nights and especially Halloween, the ghosts from the 1700s get restless and come out to haunt the neighborhood. Bob and I had yet to meet a ghost but tried to keep an open mind.

Using Frances and Eloy's description, Bob and I scouted bushes and park benches, no Digby Russell was found. We headed to the park's closed subterranean public restrooms. Unlike most of the New York City Parks and Recreation public toilets, Madison Square Park had underground facilities. Apparently, residents of 1847 required deeper privacy than visitors to other parks who preferred to do their business above ground in daylight. That was long ago before public restrooms were closed to the public.

Back in 1940s and 1950s, psychotropic drugs were developed and consequently mental hospitals that primarily served as warehouses for mentally ill or unwanted family members were closed. Warehoused patients were released into communities without preparation or community support. For the most part the newly freed were exploited by nefarious evil doers or suffered benign neglect. The attractive thing about public toilets for displaced mental patients and other homeless individuals is they are warm in winter, cool in summer, have running water, and for the most part might be safe due to the public's coming and going to use the facilities.

The 1960s produced notable numbers of hippies primarily interested in going on drug trips or to violate society norms in protests. A major problem for young middleclass hippies was being ill-prepared to live homeless on the street. These naive young people found public restrooms convenient places to commit sex acts as political revolt or in exchange for money to buy drugs. Public toilets were also handy places to partake of illegal substances earned selling sex.

In the 1970s and 1980s, to encourage gentrification, urban centers made it attractive financially for building owners to turn single room occupancy and communal flop houses into luxury housing through generous tax abatements. In return cities increased their overall tax base from luxury housing residents and saw undesirable areas replaced by private enterprise. Naturally, there was still no planning to house people displaced by gentrification. Many of whom were refugees from the mass closings of mental hospitals.

With affordable housing mostly gone, during inclement weather public toilets became a way to get out of the elements for all ages, and backgrounds of homeless. Subsequently due to increased use, the parks department stopped trying to keep the restrooms clean, and the police gave up trying to keep them safe. Consequently, park and subway toilets were locked for safety reasons at the expense of nature's calls or overpowering urges from the sick of all social strata, infant to geriatric.

Bob and I jumped over the padlocked heavy chain across the wide entrance stairs twisting into underground darkness. Four steps down the stairs a huge bear of a man reared up out of the blackness and blocked us, arms extended out to either side. He roared, "Who goes there?"

Bob and I exchanged a ready look as we slipped smoothly into fighting stances. The dude was maybe seven and a half feet tall, at least five hundred pounds, with unkempt salt and pepper hair and full beard. He was wearing a worn-thin long-black overcoat on top of many layers of other clothes peeking out from underneath hems of many colors. He reeked like he had not bathed in years. "I'm Gus he's Bob, we're looking for someone."

"There is a tariff to enter here, pay up."

"How much?"

"$200 for two or $150 each. You can't get a better deal."

"That's too much, we want a short look-see. For a quick minute perusal, the entrance fee should be waved."

Combing crumbs out of his beard with greasy grimy fingers, the giant of a man distractedly said, "Too much, huh? Yes, you're right that is a lot for a quick peek. There're only tramps down here. I'll wave the entrance fee, but you must still pay the toll $150 each."

As our eyes adjusted to the darkness, I said, "Let's try this a different way, there are two of us and one of you. Stand aside and let us pass so we can all remain friends and nobody gets hurt. Do you get my drift amigo?"

"Oh, yes, I see your point. Well, okay then but only if you can spare some loose change in the form of dollar bills?"

I went in my side pants pocket, then fanned out five singles, and said, "Is Digby Russell here?"

"I don't do a name check or a head count. I'm only the gate keeper, maybe he's here maybe he isn't. But if you give me those bills, we can still be friends, and nobody gets hurt."

I did as he asked, and he lumbered past us up the stairs stuffing my five dollars under his dirty motheaten watch cap. *I wished we bought flashlights.* Further below ground our eyes adjusted to deeper darkness and we found another industrial weight padlocked sealing a steel door presumably leading to unavailable restrooms and maybe park storage rooms. In front of the door, no doubt as a political statement, it smelled like the area had been commandeered as an unofficial toilet, sans plumbing.

Then Bob spotted Digby and gave me a high sign. Digby Russell met the description Elroy gave, exactly. He whipped out his knife when he spotted us moving toward him. I promptly disarmed him, retracted the knife-blade, and dropped it in my pocket. Other homeless men laying, sitting, crouching, or standing like barely visible black on black shadows, saw us and fled up the stairs as Digby's knife slid in my pocket. Also, seeing Bob ready for combat, watching my back, might have also intimidated a few. Bob can be scary ready to fight.

I took hold of Digby Russell's right arm Bob grabbed his left and we lifted him off the ground. Then carried him up the steps, feet kicking air, out, into the overly bright sun light. "Digby, we could kill you right here right now, and watch your body roll back down those stinky, filthy stairs to end in a puddle of human waste. Or we could put you in the hospital for a prolonged painful recuperation."

"I don't know you guys or owe you anything … Don't hurt me, this is a misunderstanding I can explain."

"Not hurt you. Oh, all right then we'll run you up Fifth Avenue buck-naked until the cops snag you back to prison. No physical harm with that if you like showing off your body to strangers. Um, you look a little skinny though."

"Stop threatening me. Put me down."

We dropped Digby on his butt then each grabbed a shoulder when he stood up. "Digby, I'm leaning toward giving you a sporting chance to avoid all the mayhem we are prepared to rain down on you."

"What do you want? I didn't steal it. Saying I did is a lie."

"You leave town and never bother Frances McDermott again, and my friend here and I won't permanently restrict your mobility to a wheelchair. Am I being perfectly clear, or do you want a demonstration of what I speak?"

Bob and I watched as the pinched-face weasel looking creep went over what I'd said moving his lips repeating my words. Then eyeing us up and down, making sure we *were* serious, he said, "Frances is my child I got rights."

"Not according to Frances, you don't."

"She's a liar ... All right, I got people in Mississippi, but it's a long way from here."

Sensing we wouldn't need to get more physical, I said, "Rumor has it buses go in that direction."

Bob used his deep authoritarian voice and said, "We'll escort you to the Port Authority Bus Terminal, unless you're tired of living and want to save us the trouble."

"How about I take a taxi?"

"What's wrong with waking?"

"My foot got hurt when you dropped me just now, and I haven't had lunch. Twenty dollars should cover all that, plus I'll need the bus fare of course. I don't need an escort I can get there on my own."

"Walking is better for your health, as long as you have it. We don't know you or trust you."

"What about lunch, I'm hungry and my foot hurts?"

"Think practical. If we kill you, no need for lunch and foot pain stops."

"And we save the bus fare."

With Bob on one side me on the other, we gave Digby the bum's rush the length of Madison Square Park and exited on the Twenty-sixth Street side. Digby looked frightened, angry, and conniving. Through my fingers grabbing his shoulder I could feel his scheming one escape or another.

Between Fifth Avenue and Broadway, Twenty-sixth is a short block. We turned right onto Broadway and headed uptown toward Herald Square Park. From Inwood Park at the top end of Manhattan Island to Battery Park at the bottom, Broadway intersects the grid leaving a park at each avenue.

I misread Digby's twitchiness as caused by our man handling him, or by Bob and my threats, not his missing lunch, or imminent expulsion from New York City. My misread lasted until we reached Sixth Avenue, Broadway, and Thirty-fourth Street Herald Square. Traffic was heavy for that time of day, suddenly Digby twisted out of our grasps and without looking bolted into the intersection. He was immediately hit by a stretch-limousine turning the corner too fast. His body flew up over traffic, was airborne legs and arms flailing in air before crashing to the pavement under the wheels of a city bus accelerating through the intersection. We didn't need a close inspection to know he wouldn't be traveling to Mississippi.

"Damnit, Bob, I forgot Frances said, 'Digby is a junkie inside and out of prison.' He must have been desperate for a fix to run into busy Thirty-Fourth Street without looking."

"What to tell Frances what happened ... or not?"

"Unless asked, I'm for not telling. Frances has had more than enough death to deal with at her age." With that said I removed Digby's knife from my pocket. Frances' blood was still wet on the blade. I tossed the knife down a nearby corner sewer grate. We turned around and walked home to finish the chores started before Digby's arrival.

Chapter 22. Mo

After the grisly Digby encounter, two and a half months devoid of high drama sped by barely noticed. Without fanfare, our life quietly returned to pre-foster-children married couple. Once again, we fantasized extravagant long holiday weekends, and semi-annual vacations traveling to exotic locales. All indicators showed our kids were doing well out of sight but not out of mind.

Bob and I got back to sharing books we were reading, regular running, workday trials, tribulations, relevant news of the day, and just being a contented soul-linked duo. At the end of long talks, we still cuddled like when we first met. Fitted between my arms Bob was a comfortable extension of me and vice versa, we melded. Our attraction grew as we looked forward to celebrating thirty-five years walking around on earth.

Frances' part time job kept us captive in the city on weekends. But to escape back to the oxygen rich rural air, we flirted with having our Bob and Gus joint thirty-fifth birthday party at the country house. We had the room, and our guests would love a whole weekend party away from the city. But the logistics for a big double birthday bash, away from civilization's many facilitators in the end turned too daunting.

Going in the opposite direction, living across the street from Frances had devolved into every Sunday brunch, a habit. It *was* possible to rent a portion of the brunch restaurant for our birthdays' celebration. Frances' brilliant idea was to start the party at our apartment, with drinks, and then move it across the street to her place for a sit-down meal. Nah, too much bother for only thirty-five years of life.

Between school-homework five days a week, boxing gym three evenings a week, a day, and a half at Ajax Dress Shop's job, once a week psychotherapy, and monthly medical doctors' blood work consults, Frances had a busy schedule that we did not wish to disrupt with birthday party festivities in her home. Bob, and I decided to postpone our birthday marker till age forty and then have either an international traveling party or trip to outer space party.

We mailed Mike a monthly check to keep the country house looking presentable on the outside. When the snow flew his work switched from green to white. He plowed snow off our walkways, outside parking, and short private road. He used our inherited from Dan and Bill, antique blue-ford tractor with snowplow attached. Winter work kept the old tractor running for spring-summer lawnmowing and fall weed eradication.

Out of the blue Mike telephoned flustered. I put him on speakerphone. His presenting concern was realtors were stuffing business cards between the house's locked-storm-door and doorframe. Also, on occasion real estate brokers stopped Mile while he was working and offered him a finder's fee to list our property for a quick sale. According to Mike, the country house aera had become a hot buyer's market for work-at-home urbanites or those looking for weekend country getaways.

Then Mike got to what was really on his mind. "Anyone up here who is the least bit curious, knows your house is unoccupied since Joey left. Your computer randomly turning lights on and off at all hours is not fooling anyone. Sooner or later, your house will attract burglars or worse … squatters."

"What's the solution Mike?"

"If you want, I could install next level security. I could fold into the current system a new super alarm that screams unbearably loud, calls the sheriff, and makes the shades go up and down rapidly, with studder-blink strobe-lights inside every room in the house. For more security, I could add a module that sends videos of the perpetrators to your cell phone and the sheriff's office. That'll cost a lot extra."

"Sounds like home security has come a long way from the man traps of the Middle Ages and Viet Cong tiger pits."

"Definitely."

"Thanks, Mike, Bob and I need to talk this through."

Addressing the speakerphone like it was Mike, Bob said "What you described sounds extremely disruptive if it's a false alarm. We don't want to scare anyone unnecessarily. Give Gus and me a minute to think on it."

Mike's concerns sounded genuine. Bob and I had a dilemma, we were not interested in selling our house *or* leaving Frances alone in the city on weekends.

After hearing our impasse on speakerphone run around in a circle twice with no end in sight, Mike came up with the solution the phone call was probably about in the first place. "These days a big topic of news up here is big cities are sending their homeless back to the place of birth, *by one-way bus tickets.* They are arriving up here about one a month. The county never had shelters or the money to put homeless in motels. The local news says it's getting to be a big budget buster. The State says the county can't refuse, and you guys know how country folks feel about paying more property taxes, especially for something like this."

"What does the Red Cross do with natural disasters?"

"Expect you to have family or neighbors. Church basements and school gyms have primary functions other than for fire burnouts and now the homeless to hangout, eat and sleep."

Hearing his paradox, I said, "Mike, how can we help?"

"Well, if you really want to get involved, I could have the county have the feds put a few Federal Emergency Management dormitory trailers on that weed overgrown flat acre back by the clearing in your woods by the stream. You and the previous owners never used that land. I think it was originally cleared to lease for farming, but that never happened for some reason. It looks like rich farmland the weeds love it."

"What's our costs if we do as you suggest?"

"The way I figure, nothing. I can persuade the village to lay pipe and connect water and sewage lines as a contribution to their homeless problem. It's not that far and their work crews aren't doing much this time of year. The feds will bring the trailers and hookup electric lines if the village has provided the plumbing and poles for electricity. The Red Cross and church volunteers will provide staff for occupied trailers. I might get a little something for setting this up, and we all dodge a property tax increase. What do you think?"

"Sounds like a win-win, except a permanent homeless camp on our land could be a liability if we ever wanted to sell."

"Just between us, I doubt the big city homeless are going to stick around here in the middle of nowhere, with no work opportunities, especially during winter. Most likely that's why they left in the first place. I wouldn't give it more than a year."

Looking over and seeing Bob's assent, I said, "Except for our liability exposure, Bob and I support community solutions for systemic social problems."

"Well, the way I see it, the feds, state, city, county, churches, and Red Cross should all share in solving the village's homeless problem. They didn't ask to come back, and we didn't invite them, know what I mean?"

"Mike, do you think the house will be secure with that hidden back acre occupied by the homeless?"

"Yes, that's the whole point instead of state-of-the-art electronic security. Hans and I will make sure your house is secure. Plus, the Red Cross keeps trailer residents busy with art and crafts, singing, resume writing, job interview practice, and they have a strict curfew with regular bed checks."

"How'd you know all that?"

"My wife Eleanor does the State required physicals for the homeless, pro bono. The whole county is pitching in however we can prevent the threatened property tax height. Everyone is trying to be charitable or at least reasonable. After all, these down on their luck folks were from here originally. They have history with the area, and this is not a good time to raise taxes."

"Give us a second Mike." Bob and I conferred off speakerphone, like it or not, it felt like take Mike's suggestion, or sell our beloved country house. "We'd prefer families with children in the Red Cross shelter but trust your judgement to do what makes the most sense for everyone. Please keep us posted."

****

Over Sunday brunch at our favorite urban eatery, we brought Frances up to speed on developments at our second home. She was adamantly against housing the homeless on our unused section of property. Even though they would be out of sight of the house and have no reason for her to interact with them.

Bob can be persistent when he sinks his teeth into a righteous cause. "Frances, how can you be such a Scrooge in the face of other's needs? Didn't you stay in battered women's shelters at times growing up?"

"You *do* know most of those homeless people, and their children especially, are coocoo crazy, right? They indiscriminately destroy property like termites."

"Mike never mentioned termites, Frances."

"Before you realize it, they will descend on the country house like swarms of locus-rats and raze everything to the ground."

"Then all the more reason to help prevent that fearful pestilence."

"Why do *we have to*?"

"Because Gus and I can. We aren't using that land, why not share what we don't need with the less fortunate?"

"Don't you two always tell me, 'Avoid trouble and don't go looking for it?'"

"True."

"Then how do you explain willing to help the homeless have a place to stay at our risk?"

"Frances, you tell us."

"*You* each need immediate mental health intervention. I'll ask my therapist to find you help."

To support Bob who was holding his own, and didn't need it, I said, "Frances, now that you are rich, don't forget how you got there."

"That was cruel and hurtful to say. You do know that don't you, Gus?" She followed that remark with a long-faced pout to show my comment hit its mark. After a pause in conversation watching Frances' stifled urge to fight us on two fronts, her face changed back to normal. "You know what, let's forget the homeless camping on our doorstep for now, there is someone I want you to meet."

"All right, your abrupt topic flow has been noted. Is this person homeless?"

"No. I've been putting this off. Now that the country house is about to be destroyed by hordes of Goths and Visigoths, I better stop procrastinating."

"Gosh, Bob, Frances wants us time traveling back to ancient Rome. Do we have any short, pleated skirts?"

"In Brooklyn, where I teach, you'd be expected to wear all black, including nail polish and lipstick to use the name Goth."

"Stop fooling around, just so you know, the person in question is important to me. You must try to be nice to them, or else the consequences will be depraved."

"What's the country house have to do with meeting your friend? Invite this person for brunch, two weeks from today, same time same place."

After considering my offer between bites of eggs, home fries, toast, and waffles, Frances said, "The house would be better."

"My treat. I might even wear my weekend socks for the occasion but no promises."

"No, Gus. That wouldn't be fair. You can't just meet, pass judgement, then say pass the pancake syrup. Especially while deciding if the food you're eating is up to snuff. Oh look, see, now my toast has gotten cold."

"Order more toast."

"May I invite a guest to the country house for next weekend, or not … if I can't get that Saturday off at the dress shop.?"

"Tell me again, why exactly we need a fourth for our short notice road trip? I must have missed something about how my legs look in short, pleated skirts."

"Everyone will have time to get to know each other better than the noise, smells and other distractions in this restaurant."

"Hold on a minute, more information is required for entertaining house guests for entire weekends. For instance, does this person come with a name and pedigree? Are food allergies involved with this visit?"

"Also, why is this person important to you? And most crucially, how do you expect us to behave toward this stranger? Frances, you know I can't control Gus when he gets started on food allergies."

"Just in case you both hadn't noticed, and can't help yourself, *you are being mean to me, again!*"

"Frances, you know I refuse to wear a tie, on weekends, and Bob burned all my ascots so I can't wear an ascot instead."

"I didn't burn them. I use them to keep our guns oiled. Frances, does your friend have fanatic pollical or religious beliefs? You know politics and God are verboten at our house on Sundays."

"Mo, Mo Vazquez, they are a grade behind me at school."

"So, what could be said to Mo Vazquez in the country that can't at this fine urban eatery?"

"Much of my artwork is up there, and the country is more relaxed for getting to know someone. You two are very judgmental, especially over food, *you know that don't you?*"

"Ah ha, so you want to draw Mo nude. Why not just say that?"

"No, no, no, not true. Although … I wouldn't refuse if they volunteered after seeing my nude artwork."

"Could it be they have something you haven't seen before? Nah, I doubt that. Oops, there I go again being mean. I wonder could it be I just can't help myself?"

"See, what did I say?"

To please Frances, Bob wagged his finger at me and said, "Gus, be nice, we may be able to marry off our wayward girl. Don't blow the chance. Why is Mo special?"

"They have interesting tattoos showing and has others only reviled in intimacy."

"Sounds like an interesting fellow all right. How did it go coming out as trans?"

"It didn't, the time hasn't been right. That's why I thought the country house would be the right place with you two there if there's an unexpected reaction. Gus helped me with Cory."

"That's not fair to Mo, trapped away from civilization, with strangers and a big surprise. Remember Corey's tearful reaction? I do. Now whose being mean?"

"Also remember, Corey got a nice dinner and their rocks off like never before. He was well rewarded."

Bob refocused us with a reality check. "Frances, you said you were out at school. How did Mo miss the memo?"

"All the juniors know my story because we get graded on in-class participation, it was inevitable they'd find out anyway. I don't know what the lower classes know about me and never cared. I didn't mention it to Mo because trans never came up in conversation."

"That doesn't sound like your style."

"Truth be told, Gus, I don't know what's going on. Somehow, I've got new and different feelings for this guy than others before. I don't usually go for younger than me. My shrink said they're unconscious residual-protective feelings related to my mother's murder."

"May I be so intrusive as to wonder, *why is that?*"

"The whole story is I jumped into a fight to help Mo even the odds. My therapist scolded me for risk taking without considering alternative action."

"I won't scold you without more information. Why defend strangers in street fights?"

"I don't know why, at the time it seemed right."

"Frances, I thought Bob and I taught you better."

"You did. But something is different about Mo than with Corey. It's not about sex, we haven't even got that far."

"How come your school never contacted me about you in a fight?"

"Yes Frances, if you were in a fight your school is required by law to tell us. They don't get a pass because they are a specialized school"

"Because it was no big deal and off school grounds."

"Damnit! … I'll have a chat with your principal."

"Have you and Mo talked to see if *your* feelings are mutual?"

"Duh, not yet. I'll talk to them and see what's what at the country house."
"And?"

"Lately, we started eating lunch together, and before you ask, my friends call me a *cradle robber* and shun Mo as too young. His friends treat me as if I'm from outer space and dangerous. We eat lunch, that's all, no way can we have meaningful talks with all the freaks staring at us with evil eyes."

"Tell you what, come out to Mo as trans face to face, and if he doesn't die from a heart attack, we'll consent to spend a weekend in the country deciphering space-alien and untouchable-youth with tea leaves."

"Why would they have a heart attack? There is nothing wrong with me a little surgery can't fix. By the way, just so you know, Mo and I both prefer coffee to tea."

"Duly noted." In response to my comment Frances made a face and stuck out her tongue. I could not resist documenting it with my cell phone's camera. That resulted in more unflattering faces and raised middle fingers for me to record. The best photo was a thumb in each ear, open palms facing the cellphone-camera, fingers waving and tongue wagging side to side.

To restore a semblance of order, or ad to the disorder, Bob asked, "Frances, are you sure Mo hasn't a clue about you?"

"I can't tell … but I don't think so. Bob can you please control your husband. He is in deranged form today, and pestering me with cell phone-photography?"

"I try, Frances, I really do try. But the man is inveterate when over-caffeinated."

"What I'd really like to know is, how Gus is so knowledgeable about straight boys?"

"Now that *is* a long XXX PG-17 story for when you are older."

"I'm older now than when I walked in this restaurant. Tell me please."

"You two stop, we are not discussing my sordid youth this early in the day. What we *are* discovering is Frances' affair of the heart. More info please."

"No, no, no, and so far, it's a boring story. Trust me, you wouldn't be interested."

"Our afternoon is free, and as you know, we are always desperate for amusements beyond the funny faces you make and concerned looks other dinners give us."

"Bob, are you mocking me?"

"What … would I do such a thing? Gus has that franchise."

"Act your age, Bob."

"Yes, Bob, we are supposed to set a fine example for Frances. And I don't know why it doesn't stick."

"At my age, Waldo said I'm allowed a second adolescence. To achieve that end, I surround myself with teenage role models all day, every day at school. Yet, Frances is still a mystery to me."

"I give up, this morning you two get to be the mean girls in this family. But I want the title back before Gus tries to keep it."

"Come on, Frances, you know sooner or later you want to tell us about your pugilistic adventures outside the boxing ring."

"Gus, as usual, I'm in a losing battle with two *adults who behave like naughty small children*. Did Joseph have to put up with your childish behavior?"

"He did. But usually blushed his way out of it. Unlike you who stands up to two against one and goes down for the count."

"I don't."

"Then tell us about violent acting out to impress this Mo character."

"Ugh, first they are not a character. Second, I wasn't trying to impress anyone just even up the odds. You two are impossible."

"Yes, you hint in that direction, repeatedly. So, what happened?"

"Last week the combination lock on my hall locker was giving me trouble AGAIN! Through no fault of my own I was running late for the therapist's afterschool appointment. She is so strict and subtracts late time from my session's forty-five minutes. Lately she's threatening to double it. I rushed to the subway, which I never take because the bus is cleaner but too slow. Anyway, I saw a commotion up ahead by the subway's entrance next to those fenced-in basketball courts.

"When I got to the subway a kid from my school was surrounded by bully thug types calling them names. Just as I turn to go down into the subway the bullies pushed and shoved the student. Something inside me snapped, I've been bullied myself by creeps like that. I know exactly how it feels to be pushed and tripped. Yes, I know, I know, I know, I should have thought before I acted, but instead I ran over dropped my book-pack and started knocking heads. Soon the boy from my school and I were fighting the attackers, back against back. It didn't take long before we were the only ones standing and the crowd watching cheered us.

"I grabbed my bookbag and headed for the subway in a hurry, and the guy I fought with said, 'Where are you going?' I said 1105 York Avenue. They said, 'Hop on my bike, I can get you there faster than the train.' And they did.

"After my appointment, I was only five minutes late by the way, Mo was waiting outside the building. *I said, 'What are you still doing here?'* They replied, 'I want to buy you a slice of pizza or an Italian ice for helping me out.' I told them it wasn't necessary. But they insisted and bought us each an ice cream at that all-natural place over on First Avenue. Mo's vegan."

"Is he any good in a fight?"

"They make up for sloppy technique with gusto. But everything else about them is excellent."

"Sounds like a decent fellow, come out to him and let us know how it goes. Bob and I must go up to the country house this coming weekend to make decisions Mike won't. If you can get off work and Mo is still cute, they are welcome to spend the weekend with us."

****

At a home cooked dinner at our place, for a change, setting the table Frances was glowing as she said, "Guess what? Mo is female to male transsexual. I wasn't expecting that! Instead of what I was dreading it turned out copacetic."

"Sounds like happy news."

"Not completely sure, Mo said I'm too self-absorbed, need to lighten up, and find my center. I don't think I agree with all that new-age gobbledygook?"

"I like him already. What does the name Mo stand for?"

"Monaca. Mo fits the image better."

"What do you say, Bob?"

"I think so far Mo sounds like an interesting person who buys winners ice cream after fights. I like ice cream."

"Mo treats me as if I'm 100% girl, and they like girls."

"Think he's ready to accept all of you?"

"Behave, Gus, they haven't been introduced yet. Though Mo definitely likes the look and feel of my breasts if that's a clue."

"It's a start."

"Mo had top surgery. Their pecs are hard because they do weight training."

"How'd you discover that? No, wait, don't tell. I like mysteries."

"Mo told the family doctor of being afraid of breast cancer; it runs in their family. That's all it took, and snip-snip all done in the doctor's office."

"Will he continue with surgeries?"

"Mo won't consider bottom surgery. They like to get off too much."

"You seem to like this Mo more than a little."

"You're right for a change, Gus."

Bob put on his schoolteacher face and with reluctance said, "Frances, I never expected to ask you this, but are you sure *you* can't give Mo a baby?"

"I already told both you guys … or maybe Joseph did. I shoot mostly clear thin cum. It's clear, slippery, and not sticky like boys' white gooey baby making cream."

"Right, I do remember, it's hard for accidental parents to forget their teens ejaculation stories. Does Mo menstruate?"

"*I don't know,* that is not something I'd ask. We just met. It's not a well-mannered question. You both should know better, that is a private female only subject."

"Thank you for the correction miss manners. Is it possible there's a need for a menstruation chapter in the official transsexual's etiquette guidebook?"

"What guidebook?"

Bob tag teamed in, "The one you should write with Mo in your free time to elucidate cretins like your foster dads."

I tagged in and Bob out. "What happened to our being Goths? I was considering multiple piercings."

Bob tagged me out and him in. "Your extra time between changing diapers."

"Spare time, Bob, really! I never have an extra minute for myself, and I know I can't make a baby."

"*On the contrary,* you have time for an affair of the heart with Mo. Along with *all* your other activities."

"What are you trying to say?"

"It wouldn't be healthy or wise to spread yourself too thin a year away from high school graduation."

I gave Frances a cold reality check and said, "Frances have you considered adding hours to the day to accommodate your too busy life?"

"If only I could. But like we say at the dress shop, alterations guarantee a perfect fit. Don't worry, dads, I take your point. I'll invite Mo to do homework with me and we'll discuss our schedules."

"Back to where this lively conversation started. I'd like to know that Bob and I will not have to deal with you and Mo multiplying the population while still in high school. We don't do diapers. Babies are fragile, and we break things."

"Gus, it is not socially acceptable to have this conversation during a repast. Somebody should have taught you that. Jeez, do I have to do everything around here?"

"Isn't that a gender double standard?"

"What do you mean, Bob?"

"Talking about foster kid's ejaculate viscosity is acceptable but the other is not. It all comes from the same general geography."

"What world do you live in?"

To steer us back on track I said, "A different one than yours."

Bob intervened just in the nick of time before I said something needing an apology later. "Or maybe, Gus, we aren't as desperate for entertainment as you first supposed."

"You're right, Bob. I won't ask Frances why she's so aggressively defensive this morning."

"Good!"

"Is it because you and Mo have gotten beyond exchanging spit, secrets and taking your shirts-off?"

"The United States Constitution says I have a right to privacy. I'm taking the Fifth Amendment."

"Then new question, have you had Mo up to your apartment?"

"I can't believe how well you're defining the word *intrusive*. Gus, do you really want to get all up in my business like some sad old fuddy-duddy?"

"Duh! I'm too young to be anybody's fuddy-duddy or denied grandfather hood."

"Okay, stop, enough is enough … Mo is a fantastic kisser, not all rude, grabby hands like most boys their age."

"I suppose that's reassurance of sorts. Got anything else to put our pregnant minds at ease?"

"Mo is gentle but firm, sweet but takes charge. So far, they are a real keeper. They treat this young lady like I expect to be treated."

"Where do you play touchy feely kissy-face if not in your apartment?"

"His aunt's home when they have to baby sit. I haven't mentioned my apartment yet."

"Why not?"

"I want to do this right and take it slow, sequential and natural for a change. There's no need to rush something this good."

"Wouldn't smooching be more comfortable at your place without a baby to watch? What are you afraid of?"

"I'm not afraid of anything. It's only I'm not ready to explain how someone my age owns an apartment on Fifth Avenue. Mo is different, I don't want to screw it up talking about my crazy life too soon."

"Unbelievable, Frances has a whole apartment in the closet?"

Throwing her hands in the air showing exasperation, Frances said, "Busted! Maybe there *are* parts of my life I'm not ready to broadcast."

"Ugh, like what?"

"You guys are more relentless than usual today."

Indicating she should put her hands down, Bob said, "I believe you've mentioned that."

Right away I said, "May I suggest decaf coffee for you?

As if I hadn't spoken, Bob said, "Why are you still in the closet with Mo? I thought coming out as trans would free communication."

"Bob, you know perfectly well my life is not so simple. I'm rich, own my own home, never have to work, and have you two grownup gay protectors, it's a lot to explain. I'm not ready to tell Mo I'm not an ordinary teenager. Or why I'm not in a group home or surviving hand to mouth panhandling on the street as I was destined to be."

Still attempting to be relevant, I said, "What does your shrink think?"

"All *you* need to know is I like Mo, a lot, and they know it. Respect that! And do me a favor, leave the head shrinking to the head shrinkers. I'll figure out telling who, what, where, and when, on my own."

"Since Mo doesn't know about Bob and me, I hope you don't expect us to dress in drag for the whole weekend. Falsetto gives me a sore throat and it's hard to lip-sink a conversation with you as ventriloquist."

"In my dress shop apprenticeship's professional opinion, you two hairy beasts could *not* pull off drag even if we applied makeup with a cement trowel. Nothing personal, but don't even try!"

"Frances, you really know how to thwart drag queen aspirations. You're in the wrong business."

"Not to worry, I did tell Mo I have two gay foster fathers, neither of which are flaming queens like some boys at our school. They are curious to see how you flounce and swish without flaming."

"Well now, see that, common interests. Bob, we'll need to practice our coordinated high kicks."

"I should warn you they are more politically opinionated than we usually stand for in our family."

"That's all right, I still want to meet the transsexual boy who captured my little girl's heart. When exactly do Bob and I get to say hello and maybe drown the brat? Flounce and swish indeed, maybe while watching his deep breathing water."

"You two better be nice. I'll try to set it up for this Saturday."
"Bob, I suppose we'll have to get our hair and nails done to pass muster."
"Be nice for my sake Gus … okay? It's important to me you don't scare Mo away."

CHAPTER 23. Masturbation for Two

In Frances' estimation, my Mercedes S-class was too ostentatious for a few humble days away from the city with our yet to meet, reportedly cute, house guest. By a two to one vote, it was decided to take Bob's Volvo for the weekend trek to the country house. I did not object strongly to the decision since the accounting department at my workplace was on a tear to curtail mileage on company cars' leases about to expire.

At my job, heated automobile discussions went on ad nauseum before, during, and after meetings. When everything was said and done, at issue was to switch to environment friendly electric or hybrid small vehicles or keep the big fancy German gas guzzlers that impress. It was a fifty-fifty standoff at work, environment versus status quo, no clear winner in sight. I worked at diplomatically being above the fray. After all I'm only one of the guys who sign the big checks.

Since I and my company car had lost the vote at home, it naturally fell on me to get Bob's sedan washed inside and out. It was overdue for a thorough cleaning, so I spang for the exorbitant bucks to have it professionally detailed. However, I saw no reason to share that information and be accused of shirking. After all what's the point of shirking if everybody must know while I'm supposed to set an example for the adolescent family member. In the meantime, while I was out and about galivanting, Bob and Frances telephoned an order for weekend food for me to pick up after the Volvo was scrubbed sparkling clean.

The running around car cleaning and grocery gathering gave me time to ponder our girl-boy apparent falling in love personality change. It brought out a playful, softer self we seldom saw in our usually hyperactive, hard-edged competitive Frances.

My husband and foster child were waiting at the curb in front of 210 Fifth Avenue as I drove up. We loaded Frances' luggage, switched drivers, and headed out. As soon as Bob turned the Volvo onto Third Avenue, Frances phoned Mo and gave him street by street travel updates, complete with changing arrival time estimates based on traffic. We pulled up to his East Harlem tenement building, just as Mo walked out the entrance door holding the other end of a cellphone conversation with Francs in the back seat. Spotting us, he bounced down the stoop-stairs to the car.

In response to the sight of a bounding house guest, Bob hit a dashboard-button and the trunk lid opened. Mo detached himself from and then deposited his hiker's backpack in with our weekend food supplies, Frances' baggage, and closed the trunk.

He entered the car through the back-door Frances pushed open for him. After brief knuckle bumps hello. We were headed northwest to the George Washington Bridge and across the Hudson River to oxygen rich clean country air, good for rejuvenating overworked urban dwellers like me and Bob.

Mo was about Frances' height, less curvy, more male angular physiology. The boy appeared to weigh less and looked younger due to a slight spattering of facial acne. He had close-cropped thick-straight-brown hair above bushy eyebrows with long eyelashes over big dark-chocolate-colored eyes. A slight aquiline nose and full lips suggested indigenous ancestors.

Both of his weight bench-developed muscular arms had colorful tattooed sleeves, wrist to elbow. Mo's tattooed forearms covered in bright colored flowers interlocked thorny stems, encircled grotesque gray-tone human skeleton skulls. The image was a macabre scene of life and death. The tattoos moved when he flexed which he did often. His tight black T-shirt over gym-built shoulders, back, and abs, was so tight it looked painted on to show anatomical details.

A gray hoodie sweatshirt was tied loosely around his waist at belt height atop faded skinny-leg jeans. Mo wore new out of the box looking, high-top blue-green sparkly sneakers over black-ankle-socks. His outfit looked like a fashion magazine photo of a sixteen-year-old urban-punk teenager in the market for acne-cream.

"Nice backpack, Mo, you do a lot of camping?"

"No. I borrowed it from a neighbor. He's an outdoors nut but wasn't using it this weekend."

After a long uncomfortable pause, Bob filled the void. "So, Mo, what are your plans for after high school?"

"Wait, wait, wait, don't be interrogating them, we all want a friendly casual weekend. No pressure please."

"Frances, I was making *polite* conversation, not interrogating Mo. At the moment, my high school classes are writing vocation essays. The subject is on my mind."

"I can take it."

"I don't want you to have to, Mo."

"Frances, I told you they'd think I'm too ghetto for you." That said, Mo took a deep breath, sat up stiff at attention, and puffed out his flat chest ready to receive a firing squad bullet. After a long silent awkward pause, he realized there was no way back from his comment and said, "If I'm too street, just pull the car over and let me out. I can figure out how to get back over that bridge on my own. I'm self-reliant."

"You also a little touchy today, Mo?"

"NO! ... I already told my sweet lady this wasn't a good idea. I only came to please her. Feel free to hate me for not being same as you."

Bob, slowed the car, pulled onto the shoulder of the parkway, stopped, took the car out of gear, and turned in his seat. "We don't know you and you don't know us. To that, we generally avoid hate when possible."

"I just knew this trip would be a disaster."

"Frances is this going as planned?"

"Not really. But if he leaves the car, I'll be getting out with him."

"You *do* know this is rutting season for New Jersey black bears, right?"

"What has that to do with anything, Gus?"

"Frances, as I recall there was a time when you had an aversion to being eaten alive by wild animals. Bears are omnivores, rutting increases their appetites, and this is New Jersey"

"Hey, Frances, why doesn't your friend Mo like me? Do I need to point out I'm the only nonwhite person in *my* car?"

"What's race got to do with it?"

"I don't know, for some reason it keeps being brought up to me. I wonder if I should change my hair style?"

"Frances I've seen Bob do real interrogations with enemy combatants. Like he said, so far, he's just having a polite conversation."

"I don't think Bob is the problem after all."

Getting antsy Bob said, "Does that mean we can proceed?" Frances nodded her head yes. It appeared to me Mo was retaking our measure, and Bob quickly got us speeding along the parkway.

"What offense did Bob and I commit?"

"Maybe none. I'm guessing Mo's hormones are out of whack."

"You guess that because why?"

"Me, sometimes I get all weird-wacko-emotional when I'm feeling out of place or stressed. Like maybe Mo is right now with you two big lugs bullying them."

"Who, us cause stress?" Bob and I exchanged a slapstick disbelieving face.

"Come on, Gus, you two are intimidating on a good day."

"But Bob hardly said two words and I'm mostly behaving."

"Mo, my dads are really good guys, they just don't always know how to show it."

"Oh, yeah, really?"

"They saved my life and supported my foster brother becoming straight in a foreign country."

"What do you want from me, Frances?"

"Just make small talk with those two in the front seat, Mo. They aren't intellectual giants but usually figure out how to be civilized."

"See that, Bob, we're not as smart as you always say." Keeping his eyes straight ahead on the road, Bob threw a sideways right-fist and hit my bicep. "Ouch!"

Mo stayed quiet but it appeared he might be mulling over what Frances said. Finally, he shrugged his gym-built shoulders and a resigned looked wiped across his face. "I apologize, I went heavy with my testosterone injection this morning. I'm bad, I wanted to impress you and did the opposite. Can we start over?"

"Fresh start huh, sure, okay with me. Bob, they want a do over, can you be magnanimous without punching me?"

"What would *you* like to talk about, Mo?" Bob said this balling up another fist with me in mind. I blocked the blow, the car swerved, and we exchanged an unexpected cut the fooling around, it's dangerous, look.

"Let's finish what I think you want to know and get that behind us. I've never been arrested, was never in a gang, I don't steal, I hate violence, I never use drugs not prescribed by a doctor, I don't eat anything that had a mother, and I like Frances beyond her coming to help me in a big fight. What else do you want to know?"

"What you just said and how fast you said it reminds *me* of being a teenager in olden times."

"Yeah, me-too, Gus. It is hard to forget that feeling the first time meeting a boy or girl-friend's parents and feeling unfairly judged under a microscope at a gross age disadvantage."

"Amazing! You guys got exactly how it felt, plus boosted by a hormone shot known for aggression."

"Mo, if we lived in earlier times, I'd be expected to ask your intentions toward our Frances. But she has trained us *not to ask questions of that nature* or suffer serious consequences. So, I won't ask."

"I don't mind, you can ask me anything since I was rude."

"Well, hmm, then?"

"The answer to that question is, I like Frances and we are friends with potential for more. By the way this is a nice car."

"Mo are you into cars?"

"Not really, the Internet says drivers of expensive cars like this one will be the first to go headless in the coming revolution. You already knew that, right?"

Dumbfounded, I looked to Bob for an explanation.

As was his habit, Bob came to my rescue. "This is my car, it stopped being luxurious five years ago when I bought it second-hand. It looks and smells nice because Gus just washed it thoroughly inside and out. Mo, when do you expect the revolution to start?"

"Soon, I guess. I've heard when the big clock shows zero middle class left in America. That's the signal for poor people to kill the rich. Then society gets a new beginning with equality for all."

"What clock, Bob?"

Frances gave me a look in support of her comment *my being less than a mental giant,* and condescendingly said, "The giant billboard size digital clock in the South Bronx facing the Willis Avenue Bridge from Manhattan. How come you don't know the poor people's revolution is coming? With everything else, are you, elitists too?"

Never one to acknowledge my faults or keep my mouth shut, I exposed more ignorance. "No. Somehow my current events feed missed the advertising. Just how does one get headless?"

Mo seemed to relax into his seat, watching us bickering about something I didn't know, and he did. "The poor used scrap-metal to build guillotines in abandoned gasoline-driven auto's junk yards."

"I didn't know that."

"Each borough except Manhattan has at least one abandoned automobile graveyards. They're building guillotines from discarded wrecked hulks. I heard Long Island has too many guillotines and is donating some to New Jersey. They're floating them over on barges."

"Huh, how do you suppose I missed all that?" To compensate for my ignorance, I passed around plastic containers of healthy snacks. Being healthy teenagers, both Frances and Mo lit up at the chance to feed their faces low carb, fruit, nuts, and veggie snacks.

Keeping his eyes on the road as I fed him nuts and dry fruit, Bob said, "Mo, what's the revolution going to look like? Clearly, I'm not as well informed as you."

"In a coordinated assault, nationwide, on a Friday, during evening rush hour, the plan is to park the guillotines alongside heavily congested traffic interchanges. Then pull ritzy motorcars off the road, occupants out, and behead them. Traffic flow will improve with only small cheap cars on the road."

"What happened to the heads and bodies?"

"The heads go on big spikes along the motorways, the bodies get burned in the cars."

"Is that it?"

"No. When vehicular traffic moves smoothly again, the guillotines will travel on sidewalks to luxury apartment buildings. The residents there, coming in or going out are beheaded at their front door. At the end of day those bodies get dumped in the river to feed the fish and birds. Those heads go up on poles as more proof the revolution is on."

"What about resistance, like say law enforcement?"

"Before the authorities realize it, and can do anything, the rich will have disappeared like the middle class they priced out of existence. The authorities will join the revolution or get beheaded, and the poor will establish a fair and just equality for all."

"That's it?"

"No. After the poor tear down the one percent's monuments to their greed, like the banks, bitcoin will be the official money, and everyone will get a deposit once a month whether they want it or not."

"Who is going to build the new post revolution society giving out bitcoins?"

"I'm not *that* into it, I don't know, someone, I suppose."

"Frances, is that how you see Bob and my end?"

"No, no, no, Gus, you always say you and Bob aren't rich, you only live luxuriously."

"What makes you think bloodthirsty mobs could tell the difference?"

"In case they can't, Mo and I with some classmates plan to start an underground railroad for the unjustly accused not rich. Like you two. We will smuggle you to

Costa Rica. It's supposed to be nice there. It's all prearranged ground travel by bus in the middle of the night."

"So, to circle back, Mo, what are your plans for after the revolution?"

"If I can keep my grades up, my dream is to become a middle-school physical education teacher. But the word is they have waitlists except for jocks with high-school-letters, and I'm not a sports star or have any inside connections. Most likely I'll end up a personal trainer. I'm told if you build a lucrative clientele, you'll always have work, and the pay isn't bad. It fits in the gig economy to defeat labor unions and communist healthcare and pensions."

"Side stepping your upside-down politics. Do you have any other interests?"

"The earth is our home, it's on fire. The rich don't *care* that's why they must die. No offense intended."

"Honest, we aren't rich by a long stretch, and who we know that's rich is in the closet about it."

"POINT OF ORDER FRONT SEAT!" Lowering her voice to normal volume Frances said, "I think it only fair that the backseat gets to ask the front seat questions. After all, you don't want to continue to monopolize this journey, now do you?" I took the look on her face, eyes glaring, as a threat.

"Front seat to back seat, message received, go ahead back seat. Or is it 10-4, no, maybe it's over and out? I get lingo confusion between 1900 and year 2050 chatter."

Bob in rare form could not resist a snide quip. "I think now you're supposed to say *goodnight sweet princess* not 10-4."

Frances glared at Bob and said, "Watch it, Dad, this girl has teeth."

"Yes, sweet princess, ask quickly, while we still have our heads attached to answer with."

"Mo should ask since you two are all up in their business. Go ahead, Mo, ask my foster fathers anything you want to know."

"That's okay, Frances, I don't mind their questions. They do have a right to know who sleeps in their home."

"Please, please, please interrogate them like they did you. They won't mind, my dad's may not be bright but have endurance while running."

"Ugh okay … ugh … how about … I don't know … since you already told me Bob is a teacher what kind of work does Gus do? If you want to say"

"I am a partner in a small private enterprise. We salvage failing companies by doing the grunge work they should have done in the first place. I like my job when we are successful, and like most small businesses it's a feast or famine rollercoaster ride."

"Gus, you mentioned grunge work. Is that like some kind of private sanitation?"

"Gus is being modest … hard to believe right? He buys businesses about to go broke, makes them successful and then sells them. That's what he meant by salvage."

"Oh, okay, I see, you are more like a corporate raider than private sanitation Mafioso."

"I like to think of what we do is social work for floundering dreams about to go under. We save companies and their workers' jobs in ways that makes sense for everyone involved. That's what I meant by salvage."

"Um ... actually that sounds like a good thing, saving jobs."

"If that is a compliment, any chance I may ask you a personal question?"

"Like what?"

"Who are you Mo? What are your values beyond beheading the rich?"

"Nobody ever asked me that."

"Bob, and I, told you about us. How about the same from you?"

Give me a minute ... okay ... I saw a T-shirt summer before last that said, *'Work like you don't need the money, love like you've never been hurt, and dance like no one is watching.'* I always dance like no one is watching, and the other two things *will* make sense when I'm older. Now, are you going to make fun of me for finding my mindset on a T-shirt?"

"Mo, we just met. Why would you think I'd make fun of you?"

"Frances says you tease her constantly."

"Frances starts it, our response is self-defense. You, Mo, are our guest. Bob and I don't insult our guests unless it's absolutely necessary."

"Is that a new rule, Gus?"

"No, Bob, just keep the car on the road. For the record, I like Mo's philosophy, wherever it came from."

"Oh okay, so, do you all go to church on Sundays as a family?"

"We don't, Mo, but I'm certain we can find a denomination you'd like to attend. There are a lot of churches out here in rural America."

"That's not what I meant. I was trying to make conversation. As you can see, I'm not good at it."

"You're doing fine. Mo, do you go to church every Sunday?"

"My parents go to a small Pentecostal storefront church three times a week. I get all dressed up and go with my aunt to a big Catholic Church for holidays. You know Christmas and Easter."

"Is religion why you live with your aunt?"

"No. My parents make an exception for me when their church preaches against transsexuals. We're the same blood and they remember all the trouble trying to make me somebody else when I was small

Frances put on her mean girl face, and said, "Mo, are they interrogating you again."

"I don't mind saying why I live with my aunt now that I'm over the hormone flush."

"Before Frances says it is none of my business. I *am* curious why you don't live with your biological family. They sound supportive."

"It's a long story."

"This drive has a way to go."

"My parents' New York City Housing Authority apartment on Webster Avenue in the Bronx is in Savage Skulls' gang territory. When I started junior high school, four years ago, the gang thought I was 100% boy, based on how I dressed, walked, and talked. It happened right after my family gave up trying to make me a girly girl. It was such a relief when I got to wear boy clothes full time. In other words, we solved one problem and got another, the gang tried everything including strong arm threats to recruit me."

"No matter what there's always a hiccup. Right Frances?" To acknowledge my comment Frances only stuck her tongue out at me. It seemed she was trying for her best behavior and almost getting there.

"Mo, don't let my dads interrupt you."

"After several recruitment attempts, the gang finally understood my *no* meant *no*. So, they said they'd kill my little brother and my parents while I watched, then butcher me slowly, if I didn't join. I told my folks. Now my little brother lives in Long Island with my grandmother. I live in Manhattan with my aunt Auria who's a cop and my disabled cousin Tina, and my dad sleeps with a pistol under his pillow. Apartments in public housing are hard to get."

"Would it be out of line asking if the fight Frances joined with you was gang related?"

"I don't mind saying. But you live too far downtown for them to bother you."

"We'd like to know."

"Two days before that fight I went up to the Bronx for my mother's birthday. I didn't notice being followed coming back until I got off the subway in Manhattan. When I figured out what was going on, I ditched the gangbangers, before they could jump me."

"Good for you."

"The day of the fight, I checked to see if they were watching my subway stop. The Skulls had sent down a bigger crew and they saw me just when I spotted them. I tried but couldn't get away and suddenly they were all over my ass. Then Frances jumped in."

"Do Bob and I need to worry about Frances' safety from that gang around your school?"

"No. The Savage Skulls territory doesn't go that far into the Spades turf. Plus, it was humiliating for them to take a beatdown from a girl. Know what I mean?"

"Frances, do you have anything to contribute that might ease our concerns?"

"What you three don't know is, the day after the fight I spoke to our school safety officers' supervisor. I reported being accosted after school, at the subway going to my therapist's appointment. Later that day she pulled me out of class and said she filed an official complaint with the local police precinct's gang task force. Our school is supposed to be in a gang-free zone. She also said she had assigned her officers to monitor those basketball courts for gang activity as a follow up. Don't worry about me. You know I take the bus to school, remember? And for now, Mo doesn't use that subway stop."

Bob slowing down said, "Speaking of such things, this will be our only pit stop. Use the restroom if you need to or not." We all piled out of the car at the rest area. Frances went into the lady's room, and Mo followed Bob and I into the men's facility and took a booth.

****

Natures' calls answered, we got back into the car relieved. "This has been quite an enlightening road trip. Does the backseat have any more questions for us up front? Or is the question-and-answer period over so the oldies but goodies sing along can lighten the mood."

The two teens exchanged an expectant look I could not read. I assumed it meant oldies, but goodies were not high on their list of fun activities. Then drawing in a determined slow breath Frances said, "Mo and I have been talking about the word desire. Anyone not deaf dumb and blind can see you both desire each other."

"Hear that, Bob?"

"Neither of us are who the other imagined wanting, yet here we are attracted."

"Why not just see how it goes?"

"I'll tell you why. Part of me thinks Mo and I together is incomprehensible. Our plumbing is backwards, and yet part of me gets hard at possibilities. I'm deadlocked, I can't keep my hands-off Mo, and my brain says I'm an idiot for wasting time with no potential."

I glanced at Bob for the support I expected to be there and said, "How can we help?" At the same time, I thought, *I'm out of your depth with these two kids.*

"When Joseph said Felicity gets him and vice versa, I was jealous. I never had that and would love someone to understand *me* that way … I think."

"Frances, if you don't know your objective, how can you achieve it?"

"Maybe it's like when you and Bob finish each other's sentences or touch each other for no reason I can see."

"Frances, are you building a riddle?"

"Not exactly, maybe, sort of I guess, Gus."

Bob and I exchanged a look, we had arrived at the same thought at the same instant. "So, Mo do you like grand opera?"

"I don't know opera, grand or tiny."

"I was thinking twentieth century Italian composer Giacomo Puccini's operas. He wrote about love with obstacles, like what Frances was saying."

"Name one opera like our situation and I'll listen to it?"

"*Turandot,* Mo, there is a riddle, decapitations, and implausible love to unlock passion."

Without forethought Bob contributed to the subject. "Puccini died before the opera was finished, so his students completed it using his musical sketches."

Frances triumphantly said, "See, that's exactly what I was talking about, how you two finish each other's thought."

"Is that what the opera is about?" Mo's face had relaxed showing interest. Frances was right, as a teenage boy with girl parts, Mo *was* cute.

"It takes place in ancient China. To court the beautiful, icy cold Turandot, suitors had to solve her riddle."

"Or what, hide their face and run away ashamed they got the wrong answer? What chump losers, Hee, hee, suckers!" Mo appeared completely relaxed as he snarked his words wearing a naughty boy grin.

"No, Mo, nothing that simple. Suitors' heads were chopped off for giving the wrong answer."

"With a guillotine?"

"Nope, big sword. At that time in China everyone wore a queue, a single pigtail on the back of the head. It was to show alliance to the emperor and made decapitation easier. Just pull the queue up and cut the head off. Plus, the queue served as a ready handle for carrying severed heads."

"Shit! Those old Chinese were terrible? Guillotines are more humane."

"In addition, the condemned were tortured before their execution."

"Why?"

"Women in Turandot's family were abused by men. She wanted revenge for the past abuse. In its unstated yet grand way, the opera portrayed the heteronormative binary gender battle for dominance while severed heads piled up."

"Are you two trying to scare Mo away, before we even get started?"

"Frances, you suggested obstacles to love and a riddle, Mo mentioned decapitation. Naturally, Bob and I thought TURANDOT."

To take the heat off Frances, Mo said, "How does that opera horror-story end?"

"Calaf, solved Turandot's riddle and her icy heart melted. Like all good fairy tales, they lived happily ever after."

"Mo and I only need to get beyond some physiological contradictions, then happily ever after could be us."

"Contradictions?"

"Like Mo and I don't fit the other's ideal physical type. Remember, that's what we were talking about before opera got in the way."

"And?"

"We still want to touch each other in ways … well, more than just friendly."

"Frances, I can see your pops don't understand. Maybe they need more specifics."

"Okay, Mo, so when I joined the Gus and Bob household, I noticed they were into each other for absolutely no reason I could see. Sometimes they even communicated without speaking, their eyes talk. I could have written books about what their looks back and forth meant. It is that closeness I want with you, Mo."

Not keeping my opinions to myself, I said, "If it is true love, nurture it, let it grow. If it is something else, wear it out, enjoy yourselves."

Bob talking more to me than Frances, said, "Isn't talking it over in the car, while driving, a step toward making impossible possible?"

"Bob what we want is physical action, not talk, just drive the car will yah please."

"Huh, listen to your words. Could it be you've got shared assets rather than diversity issues, and don't know it?"

"What do you mean?"

"Frances, lately Gus and I harp on what the most with you?"

"Maximize potential."

"If it were possible for you to trade organs with Mo, would that be satisfactory?"

"Except that can't happen because medical technology isn't advanced enough."

Bob saw we'd lost the kids in an attempt not to state the obvious, so he said, "At my school, attraction, desire and intimacy are part of the sex education curriculum in health class. Have you spoken to your health educator?"

Mo gave Frances a quick glance. I suspect for permission before saying, "At our school sex education is about pregnancy prevention, and sexually transmitted diseases. There is next-to-nothing about what gay people do for sex, and *zero* about transsexual sex."

"Did you checkout the library?"

Eager to prove Bob and I wrong, Frances bulldozed her way into the discussion. "The trans books at the public library are outdated, like from the 1940s and 1950s, before my grandfathers were born. Our school library doesn't even have those books. The only thing remotely current at school is 1990s public health prevention pamphlets about AIDS and drug resistant STDs."

"Have you done an online search?"

"Online is the opposite problem, it has too much information, mostly from religious nutjobs there way or no way, kooky-scientists' free-love, weirdo-fanatics' health improvement sects, and cult-religious-politicos predicting doom and gloom for existing. It takes forever to find anything useful online that isn't loaded with truth-decay."

"That sounds like my Ph.D. research, little usable information and too much misinformation masquerading as God given knowledge. But hey, maybe the earth really is flat, and the creationist's warped pseudoscience overrules the true scientific method."

In a feeble attempt to change the subject to something less politically religious, I said, "Nobody said life was going to be easy. By the way, is rain predicted for today, Bob?"

Ignoring my ineffectual attempt at topic change, Mo said, "Bob, do you think Frances and I are wasting our time wanting a romance when we aren't who the other dreamed about?"

"Mo, what you think matters, not Gus or me."

"Frances thinks so and has had a lot of experience with sex."

"Again, what do *you* think, Mo?"

"I don't want to be embarrassed trying something that fails, while I don't have any clothes on."

"Don't rush Mother Nature. Take as much time as *you* need, there's no hurry to get frisky you've got decades ahead for it."

"But how will I know if it's true love?"

"Affairs of the heart are universal; millions of books were written to help mortals understand it. Why not start reading poetry books together?"

"Mo, don't get Bob and Gus started on, 'Wait till you're older.' It's their one size fits all for every occasion. I expect to hear that from them until I'm dead and buried."

"See, Bob, Frances was paying attention after all. We might be getting through with small increments."

"I don't understand, Gus, what's the problem waiting till life experiences and maturity guide her behavior with knowledge."

"Daddies Gus and Bob, back here on planet earth, Mo and I are primed and ready for getting physical, not reading poetry."

"Jeez I'm driving. Don't distract the driver with lude and lascivious accident-causing evocative mental images."

"Yes, if you are going to talk dirty you need to find me ear plugs. I get grossly uncomfortable when you kids talk about exchanging body fluids."

"Anyone can see you guys love each other, and Joseph says he loves Felicity. That's all Mo and I want, not talk or reading!"

To turn the heat down, I said, "Frances, slow down, give yourself a break. You're already familiar with the mechanics of sex, now intellectually find the fuel that powers passion from reading books."

"Are you saying *what I think you're saying?*"

Seeing Frances revving up for an agitated attack, Mo intervened and said, "Gus, would you tell us how you and Bob fell in love? It might help us in our quest."

"Sure, after college while serving in Middle East war zones, we'd seen each other around between missions. In our situation you never knew who you'd see alive or in one piece again, so we connived to meet on the QT, at first to talk. Then trust grew along with feelings, and it got physical. That was during the military's 'Don't Ask Don't Tell.' If you wanted to use us as models, you'd trust your hearts and give your brains a rest when it's time to get sweaty. That's what we did. But hey, we were in our twenties, and bad guys kept trying to kill us and our soldiers. Every time we said goodbye, there was a chance we'd never see each other again."

"Thanks Gus, let's see if I have what you said right? 'Trust your gut, when it feels right do it if it doesn't, don't.'"

Reenergized Bob brightened up. "That sounds like the Cliffs Notes version. Keep it simple, wait till Mother Nature gives a shove."

I jumped back in with closure on my mind. "I know you don't want to hear this, but don't get more physical until you've talked it through. Now, about the weather, is it going to be pleasant all day tomorrow or what?"

"Mo, isn't this what I told you to expect from my foster dads?"

Bob forged ahead ignoring the kids' resistance. "What I know from observing in my world; if you are in love, the physical will find a way, *if you will be patient.*"

"How could you know that?"

"Profoundly disabled people fall in love and produce children. If they can do the deed, able-bodied, you two can figure out what works for you."

"Huh, is there a how to book for handicap sex?"

"Focus on being close, and let nature guide the rest."

"But I don't want to feel silly."

"Frances, you're trying too hard, stop the performance anxiety."

"Huh, of course, … what did I expect … you put it all back on us to wait for an elusive inconclusive future. Thank you very much, Bob. That was not helpful, at all!"

I had enough of her attacking Bob. "Frances, I miss the new era of you being nice, what happened, did it fall out of the car at the rest stop?"

"Oh great! Mo, now Gus is playing shrink!"

"And you are dodging the help you asked for, why?"

"Uh oh hmm sorry, I'm all … what's the word Bob likes to use … discombobulated."

"Frances what's blocking you from throwing caution to the wind?"

"It's complicated."

"What's new?"

"I'll tell you against my better judgment. My fervent wet dream is having a stud fuck my hot wet pussy while I scream in ecstasy. But I don't happen to have a pussy, and doubt Mo can make me scream with theirs."

"One nice thing about dreams and fantasies is they change."

"I don't think so, Gus. I've overheard gay boys at my school say, 'The most tragic thing is two tops or two bottoms in love and no way to consummate.'"

"Bob, Frances seems worried about gay top or bottom pairs having full sex lives. Do you have an opinion to help our wayward child?"

"Sure, I do. In the high school universe, I teach in, when two tops or bottoms find each other in love, they add the word variable to their role-identifier. It's expedient and their love life naturally becomes more interesting from giving and taking new experiences. The kids call it expanding their horizons. We teachers look the other way."

"It's more complicated than that. If I start getting familiar with a real natural vagina, how could I possibly make do with an imitation created from my spare parts."

"Bob, didn't Darwin say something about that?"

"Yes, adaptability, I believe he wrote a whole book about it. Frances, want to borrow my copy?"

With a pout, Frances said, "Does it say anything about neither of our sex fantasies fit the others?"

"Is that all you think about? No wonder you're stuck." Bob said this while accelerating to pass a big slow-moving truck on a steep incline.

"There's more to it than that."

"Elucidate please."

"I can't believe I'm about to tell personal stuff to two adult strangers I just met today."

"Does it have anything to do with your earlier hormone's flushing?"

"How'd you know?"

"Lucky guess."

"Frances and I have what's called animal attraction. If we were heteronormative, she would be pregnant, and I'd be looking for a job to pay for baby supplies. We have animal attraction without role models or an instruction manual."

"Which means you'll both have to write the book. It could be fun."

"The more I realize it's hopeless, the more I want Mo's body in my hands. What I want most is totally doomed, and now with Grandma's wealth I'm used to getting what I want. So, am I crazy or did you gay dads spoil me?"

"Hmm, let's see, you asked for help that's not crazy … spoiled uhm most likely Bob did that. All right, now for something completely different are you open to radical?"

"Like what?"

"Disclaimer, in no way do I encourage either of you to violate this State's age of consent laws. Do you understand and agree?"

"Why for the gods' sake bring the state into it! In this car we're a family driving out of state."

"Gosh, interstate commerce … then it becomes a federal matter. Bob and I don't carry enough liability insurance for that."

"Get on with it, where do I sign? You know, Gus, you are an incurable agist. Age is just a number, get over it!"

"Then tell me why the law of the land imposes incarceration as punishment for statutory rape."

"Hopefully, what you are going to tell us is worth this overblown build up Gus. OKAY, check the agree box, I'll sign whatever to get this over with."

"Suspend all previous sex fantasies for an exercise. Step 1, Undress each other while making out hot and heavy. Then when you are ready take turns pleasuring yourself in front of the other, as if you were alone, and *no one was watching.*"

Bob showed his disapproval. "Yup, this is radical. Our insurance won't cover it."

"Didn't I warn you Mo, Gus, can go one extreme to another."

Mo asked, "And come?"

"Yes, the buildup wouldn't have much point without a climax. Switch back and forth doing and watching before it reaches the point of no return. Give each other a heads up before revealing a cum face."

"Gus, I didn't expect such graphic sex discussed in a car ride out of the city. What was the point?"

"With time you'll learned your partner's hot-erogenous zones and their how-to techniques. Next time, take turns pleasuring those spots on your mate, like they do for themselves. Communicate back and forth what feels good or not, be completely uninhibited giving and receiving."

"Like only one person is watching?"

"Right, I think you got it, Mo. Good sex requires excellent communications."

"WHAT! WAIT A SEOND! No way, jerking off is for kids, and best done alone in the dark when everyone is asleep."

"Who told you that?"

"Joseph, he learned those rules living in group homes."

"Here's a secret, for this experiment don't limit yourselves to group home rules."

"I'd be embarrassed performing solo sex, even for an audience of one. I prefer dark with my eyes closed."

Sometimes Bob cannot help being pedantic. "Visual feedback is an important part of sex. Light some candles, just don't burn down the house."

Catching his drift, I said, "Frances, it is about building trust in stages, with someone you care about who is doing the same with you."

"No way! I'm blushing just imagining doing what you suggested. You're both dirty old men. Do you know that?"

"Frances, it appears you are not interested in the advice you asked for. No problem, you'll remember this conversation when *you are ready for a spectacular shared sexual release* with the love of your life. Whoever that may be."

"Gus, I didn't ask for deviance!"

"Aw, gee whiz."

"Now I'm sorry I brought sex up with you and Bob. I should have known better."

"There is the required proof you are not old enough for grownup sex. You can't even talk about it without getting embarrassed."

"I'm ready for romance, not perversion. I was born ready for love and never got much."

"How about you, Mo?"

"Same as Frances. I wouldn't feel right rubbing myself off in front of a spectator. Do you guys intend to watch too?"

"Absolutely not. Right, Bob?"

"You asked for our help. We gave what we had. Try again in five years, who knows the answer might be different."

"That's it? Gus, that's all *you* got?"

Bob came to my rescue and said, "With time if your love is strong, you will reveal your secret quirks, and accept your mates as gifts. That's the fuel that keeps intimate relationships going for decades."

"Ugh! So, you front seat men say we in back are not hopelessly young if we get kinky weird, and show each other our private self-sex, right?"

"Look at that, Bob, they *were* actually listening rather than just waiting to challenge every last thing. Do I get points for effort or what?"

"Double bonus points for trying. Ah, but alas, minus zero points for succeeding."

"I don't know about points. I'm thinking demerits, many demerits for making us think about aberrant sex acts, right, Mo?"

"Well actually, Frances, if there was a lot of kissing and touching before, I might be willing to risk mortal sin on show and tell self-sex. I like getting off, and I want to see your cum face. But only on condition you don't laugh and make fun of me?"

"Mo, you know I love kissing you, and my foster dads know I never turn down a challenge. But be careful with my two fathers. You just saw how weird they can get without warning."

Bob and I exchanged a look, then paused it for emphasis, "*Teenagers.*" But we had the presence of mind to keep our mouths shut as the kids fell-into a dynamic lip-lock clinch, hands busy groping. I tried to ignore the slurpy guttural sparks with heavy breathing coming from the back seat. That failing, I put my head on Bob's shoulder and rubbed his thigh to distract myself. He rose to the occasion which helped. Fortunately, traffic was light.

When the heavy breathing soundtrack in the back seat reached a peak, I said, "Please stop that and take a break until we get home. You two are a driving hazard steaming up the car's windows."

"Don't you mean wait until we get to that grungy no-tell motel? See, I still know the house rules."

I sat up straight and gave Bob a sideways glance and got back the affirming quick look I was hoping for. "Frances the thing about rules is knowing when to break them."

"WHAT! No no-tell-motel? Afraid we'll bring home bedbugs? I heard there's an epidemic."

"It's known the world around, when individuals spend time exchanging spit, the number sixty-nine shows up on their menu."

"What happened to no explicit sex talk, and no sex in the house ever?"

"That is usually correct, but you both inject different hormone supplements. I'm thinking better safe than sorry if someone has an adverse hormonal reaction to the other."

"I wonder what brought that on?"

"We don't know the result, if you two ingest each other's hormone mix, straight from the source."

"That's considerate, I like you two thinks ahead."

"Right, Bob and I want to be present to call poison control and medical assistance if necessary."

"Uh huh, consequently, no motel tonight. Then bedbugs *are not a concern.*"

"I think she's got it. Let's sing songs from *My Fair Lady.*"

"You two really do care. I'd kiss you, except kissing Mo is more fun."

"We'd need bibs if you kissed us right now."

"Just so you know, Mo, my foster dads are not big giving hugs or kisses, except to each other."

"Hey, what happened to the smooth highway? Why did this road suddenly get so bumpy? It feels like you got a flat."

"You were too busy with your hands in my bra to notice we turned off the highway onto a state route two miles back. This rutted ride is a private road my foster dads keep saying they are going to repaved but never do."

"Are we almost there?"

"See that gray house with red trim … there … through those trees … no, on the left? That's our country house."

"Wow, it's a big old Victorian. Do each of you get your own floor?"

"No. The third floor is a mostly unfinished attic. I store my artwork up there. Would you like to see the art I've made?"

"Sure, cool, … but then where do *we* sleep?"

"We all use bedrooms and bathrooms on the second floor. The first floor is living room, den, dining room, kitchen, and a half-bathroom. We also have free weights, punching bags and other workout gear in the basement."

"Cool!"

Turning back to me Frances said, "So, Gus, your advice is share with each other how we get off alone? Is that it? Any other naughty words of wisdom to put us on the right path?"

"A gentleman and scholar once told me, 'Any problem can be an opportunity, depending on your approach.'"

"Was that wise person a Vietnamese-American high school English teacher?"

"Oh, that's right, you know the love of my life and husband, Bob."

CHAPTER 24. Baggage

"Good morning. Did everyone sleep well?" Then judging my audience more accurately said, "Whoops, my foster child in residence would say that question is intrusive. So, don't answer." Pointing my spatula with less enthusiasm I said, "Coffee, tea, juice on the table, and toast and muffins in the bread warmer. Mo, if you don't see what you want ask."

"Thank you, Gus, it smells fantastic in here. My mouth is watering."

"This morning's breakfast choices are pecan or blueberry or, in Frances' case, unadorned pancakes, with eggs how you like them on the side. Those cute little sausages in the Pyrex are vegetarian. They're made from processed soybeans and lots of sage. These big, delicious, greasy, fennel sausages in the black cast-iron-skillet had faces and mothers in a previous life."

"It all smells like breakfast, yum."

"Finally, here comes sleepy head Bob to complete our quartet." Bob strode over, and I put my spatula down. We exchanged a good morning hug, and his toothpaste flavored kiss met my coffee breath.

After a drowsy sounding, "Good morning," Bob's attention shifted up a notch. Abruptly he looked like a schoolteacher taking attendance and stated the obvious. "Gus, you notice something different with these two?"

And there went my hope for the weekend's weather report while munching breakfast. "Are they taller?"

"Take a closer look."

"Ah yes, Frances has packed on a few extra pounds?"

Frances flipped me the bird, her usual reaction to our father daughter kidding.

"Now I see what you mean, Bob. They are glowing."

"What do you suppose caused the radiance?"

"Can't imagine. I would've noticed a nuclear detonation nearby."

"Huh, could it be they found God? The locals say she keeps a summer home around here." In response to Bob's words and lascivious grin, Frances, and Mo swallowed hard and blushed. "You know, Gus, if we were gracious hosts, we wouldn't inquire how these two slept … or if they did."

"You're right, Bob, we shouldn't be presumptuous. Especially since I already inquired and immediately retracted the question. You know how local law enforcement disapproves redundancy. How do you want your eggs cooked this morning, kids?"

Mo busily munched veggie sausages held on a fork, alternating bites with a toasted, buttered English muffin held in his other hand. At the rate veggie sausages were being consumed, there would be none left for Frances if she didn't hurry and eat. I had to admit the little links looked and smelled appetizing.

"You two going to tell Gus and me how it went, or do we guess?" Bob said this half in jest.

Frances looked dismayed then after a loaded silence said, "Since you dads are so interested in our business, it would be cruel to deny you a small tidbit from last night. Gus, plug your ears in case any sexy bits stumble out."

"How generous! I guess Bob would settle for a tidbit rather than a total news blackout. But wait, do I get to finish the breakfast I just made for us? I find it hard to plug my ears and stuff my face at the same time."

"Okay, Gus, I'll tell the special abridged version, just for you. That way you can keep your greasy finger out of your ears. *We spent the night swearing vows of celibacy.* Happy now?"

"Weird, must have been ghosts, squeaking your bedsprings all night. But there were periodic breaks long enough for ghosts to catch their breath. Okay, celibacy, shall I call the Vatican?"

As usual Bob came to my support. "Gus is right, it had to be the house ghosts getting randy."

"I guess we all agree. Subject closed. What's the weekend weather prediction?"

Bob wasn't ready to let it go and said, "The truth is, I was looking forward *to hearing a detailed report on celibacy.* Now, I'll have to read the Pope's new book."

"Frances, was the physical aspect of celibacy as impossible to achieve as you forecast in the car yesterday?"

"Gus, I guess you will have to finish your breakfast out on the deck or plug your ears and eat later. Mo, you see how my dads tease me?"

Bob forged ahead still half asleep. "An image of you making the impossible possible did fit the squeaky bed springs' soundtrack that kept me awake last night. No, it was those horny ghosts."

"Dear Bob, if you get what you want … will you shut up about it to Gus who has to leave the room?"

"Gus doesn't have to leave if you followed his suggestion."

"We didn't do his *show and tell skit.*"

"Why not?" Feigning distress, I couldn't hold back.

"It sounded too old fuddy-duddy perverted for us, Gus."

"Then may I be so curmudgeonly as to inquire the origin of your morning glow that kept me awake all night?"

"Okay, okay, okay but only because Bob wants to know."

"Good girl."

"Bob, plug Gus' ears when appropriate, I'll give you the high sign, otherwise he can't stay."

"Fine. If you didn't do show and tell, what then?"

"Mo got on top and rode me like a stud. Flat on my back, legs spread wide it was like my wettest wet dream come true. With wet oral action before and after the wild ride. We came together and individually, all night. The only reason I didn't scream with every orgasm was consideration not to wake you old folks."

"That was thoughtful, right, Bob?"

"I've experienced how cranky you two get when your sleep is disturbed. You know, like this morning."

"Phew! I'm so glad you left out the sexy bits for Gus's sake. I completely forgot to finger stuff his ears."

"I concur, my old heart couldn't take an unedited heavy breathing replay of last night. Bob is right! Graphic images would have upset my delicate equipoised sensibilities, for the day."

"Gus, judging from your tone of voice, do I understand you disapprove of Mo's and my sex success? Don't you know you are supposed to be happy for us?"

"Congratulations."

"Where's the high five 'you go girl?'"

"It's built in the CONGRATULATIONS."

"I can tell you don't mean it. What's your problem dad?"

"No problem, I *am* happy for you, compliments, mission accomplished. Now, let's talk about the weekend weather report."

"No, something is up with you, Gus! I can feel it. Are you mad we didn't do what you suggested? Usually you aren't so dictatorial."

"Leave it, Frances, enjoy your success, your breakfast is getting cold and the sausages you like are all gone."

Bob came to my rescue and said, "Frances, change of topic, Mike is coming over at eleven. He, Gus, and I will probably be involved with the layout of homeless trailers most of the day."

"What's the big deal about that?"

"It appears there is a flood problem every spring and we never noticed, out of sight out of mind. Will you rustle up lunch for Mo and yourself?"

"Sure, if there are still veggies from our garden in the freezer."

"There are, especially those big zucchinis. Use as many as you can, they take up a lot of space."

"What's for dinner?"

"We'll cross that bridge after the trailers are high and dry."

"If Gus's breakfast left enough of the eggs we brought from the city, I could make a frittata for lunch and zucchini parmigiana for dinner. We have mozzarella in the freezer from when it was on sale. Gus bought a lot."

"It was half price."

"What dinner are you planning?"

"We brought salad fixing and French bread from the city. I could serve spaghetti on the side and use up jars of Joseph's homemade pasta sauce. We always have dry pasta on hand."

"Will you make enough to invite Mike and Eleanor?"

"Sure, a salad, garlic bread, zucchini parmigiana with pasta, and just to be safe, I'll bake a chocolate cake for dessert. That should be more than enough for six people."

"Yum, I'll phone Mike and see if he can spare us a dozen or two of eggs. Anything else you need?"

"Ask Mike to bring Hans. I'd like him to meet Mo."

"Is that it?"

"Now that Mo and I started our honeymoon, I want to include them in our family."

"Mo what do you think about joining this dysfunctional family? The one you met less than twenty-four hours ago?"

"Sorry, say again, my brain is still preoccupied with last night in bed. I never thought it could be *that* good. Oh, did I cross a line?"

"Frances requested you join our family."

"But I already have a family. If you guys want more foster kids, I'm sure there are agencies with loads looking for homes."

"Frances, you missed a step. First you need to know what Mo wants, before involving Bob and me."

"Gus, you are gloomy today. Jeez, you are supposed to be happy Mo and I were a hit after speaking our fears out loud yesterday. Why aren't you celebrating with us?"

"Frances, sit with your good feelings, enjoy them, and stop bugging me. Today, Saturday, is my day off."

"I won't quit until you tell me why you're so grumpy. Yes, I mean you, Grouchy Gus! I'm not stopping till you tell me."

"Trust me, you don't want to hear what I have on my mind this moment. Leave it and let us get ready for planning a multiunit homeless camp in a flood zone."

"NO, no, no. Tell me, what's your problem foster daddy Gus! You're being a wet blanket. I WANT TO KNOW!"

"Do you want me to leave? I could take a walk or go work out in your basement gym."

Having my back as usual Bob said, "Mo, that's up to you. Despite this current situation, we try for democracy around here."

"Mo, stay, I think *this is* about Gus being mean. You need to know what kind of family I've invited you to join."

I glanced over at Bob he'd already heard my thinking about what Frances was trying to drag out of me. We'd discussed it and arrived at the same conclusion.

"Frances, I don't mind picking up after you and cleaning up your messes. Today, I see a pattern, and it's troubling."

"I don't know *what* you are going on about. Teenagers are supposed to be messy."

"Frances, I for one refuse to be part of yet another of your self-sabotage self-punishments."

"What sabotage? Now what are you talking about? I love Mo, and how they make love to me."

"Then let's leave it at that, shall we? Anyone know the weather for today?"

"No. Why you *are not happy* for me? I love you and know you love me, what's your problem?"

"I suppose you want a list?"

"ABSOLUTELY!"

"Don't say I didn't warn you."

"Tell me!"

"You developed your artwork to the point collectors and agents offered you one person shows in galleries, so you stopped making art. When your classical guitar teacher said you progressed beyond his level of teaching competence and wanted to refer you to his teacher, you quit the guitar. The moment your boxing gym said you were ready for Golden Gloves competition you stopped going."

"I'm a teenager and allowed a changeable mind."

"Since we've known you, bottom surgery was your objective. Then when Corey said he wanted what you wanted, you dumped him."

"You're wrong, that's not self-sabotage. Why would I or anyone go against their own best interest?"

"Ask your shrink? I flummoxed."

"I'm asking you, Gloomy Gus. You're the one who connected all these unrelated dots."

"I see a pattern. It needs to be broken if what you say you want *is* what you want."

"NO, No, no, I don't want to hear any more of this claptrap."

"Yes, you do, the proof is you forced it out of me."

"Why would I sabotage my happiness with Mo? It doesn't make sense!"

"My guess is you have a belly full of self-hate."

"I DON'T!"

"Homosexuals are introduced to self-denigration at such an early age, many are unaware of it, and then never completely shed the unknown affliction over a lifetime. I'd bet big bucks it's the same or worse for transsexuals."

Mo had been looking uncomfortable as the conversation heated-up, and finally had enough. "How can you say it's worse for transsexuals? We have as much right to be here as you do!"

"For most homosexuals, the big conflict is internal expectations. Mo, for your troops it is both internal *and external*. It's twice as hard for your breatharian to pretend and still keep a semblance of authentic self."

"How could my successes trying something new show self-hate when I'm lucky to be alive. Answer me that Glum Gus!"

"Do you feel worthy to be alive, after so many you knew and cared about are not?"

"No. Of course not, how could I without being a totally heartless, cold bitch?"

"An image you are cultivating, parttime."

"I only pretend to get you going."

"A universal excuse in the vernacular is called *fear of failure*. For those of us society won't accept, it's really *fear of the success*. We can't permit ourselves achievement recognition because *it would expose us to shame for existing.*"

"What's that got to do with me?"

"You asked for my help, I sincerely called it how I saw it. That wasn't what you wanted, fine, just move on."

"NO. What help are you offering now, spell it out dad?"

"Break your negative cycle of succeeding up to a point then quitting before it gets too real. Commit to finish what you start. Begin fresh and clean with Mo and follow through no matter how bumpy the road."

The color drained from Frances' face, she'd heard me, and I hit a nerve. Her shoulders and chest bobbled barely perceptively, and tears were ready to spill over bottom eyelids. But she set her jaw ready to fight. Frances could not allow herself to cry in front of Bob, I, and Mo over facts she didn't want to accept, yet felt true. But the girl inside her needed to cry a river at the revelations. The boy inside her would rather have a fist fight.

Mo had been watching and listening to our exchange. He shot up out of his chair and went behind Frances, put his hands on her shoulders and gently massaged. "Come on, baby, let's split this place." Turning to me his face fierce, eyes burning, Mo said, "How could you be so hurtful to my sweet lady?"

Also standing and moving, Bob spoke with authority from behind my chair. In a calm command voice, he said, "We love Frances and want to see you both have a shot at happiness, without the burden of unpacking moldy old baggage."

"It didn't sound like love to me."

"Frances dragged it out of Gus. She insisted to know. Mo, if you care about her, think about what you just heard. As families go, we don't hold back, Frances knows that. Tough love is never pretty but works for us."

Chapter 25. Transition Camp to Evolution, and Non-immaculate Conception

Getting the homeless encampment up and running was not as simple as Mike envisioned. Nevertheless, Bob, Mike, and I met and resolved the stream of big and small obstacles that came with such an on-the-fly project. We overcame each hurdle with a positive attitude, and that soon became the optimistic tone for the camp.

The biggest issue for the powers that be became our refusal to sign a one dollar ninety-nine-year lease for use of our dedicated acre. The powers and lesser stakeholders were anxious to get on with their more lucrative, less socially responsible activities. Consequently, they begrudgingly settled for a one dollar renegotiable one year lease as better than nothing. Sadly, civic planning had not progressed beyond find a place to dump the homeless out of sight, without increasing property taxes. No way could Bob and I, facilitate a no future for the homeless beyond our temporary fix. So, in a way what happened was our fault.

Down at ground level it took creative ingenuity to develop paid internships at actual workplaces for our homeless guests. Next came negotiating community college free tuition for job training leading to better paying jobs. Then financing had to be found for training to work at sheltered workshops for our disabled temporary residents. Rural women and men with big hearts and of good will stepped up to help, when asked.

For those few unable to handle any of our structured training to employment programs, the Red Cross created intensive closely supervised inhouse training using the shelter's own childcare center as a training site. The few labeled untrainable, learned their label was wrong, while gaining a marketable skill as childcare workers with work experience.

Working with other professionals, Joey's high school guidance counselor took the lead fitting distinct pieces of *train to work* together to create a successful program for all who wanted employment. It was her idea to add inhouse training for those rejected by more formally structured preparations.

Finally, over budget and behind schedule, big yellow school buses, and multicolored Red Cross and church passenger vans ferried homeless families and single women with children to the Mike and Elanor Morgan Transition Camp. Establishing the facility had been Mike's idea. He and Eleanor were proud, Bob, and I proposed their name for it. We owned the land and were entitled to naming rights.

Our highly motivated homeless families and individuals came from all sorts of makeshift temporary shelters or living in their cars. The big attraction was a promise of work leading to permanent affordable housing. Our County Mental Health Department (CMHD) received a state grant to screen out untreated, or nonmedication compliant mentally ill, and or those too addicted to function in the Morgan transition job training program. Alternative housing with treatment was made available for those screened-out. The Red Cross handled the camp's intake process after the CMHD screening approved new guests.

It did not take long before our back acre of federal emergency management unadorned white trailers, with part time paid and volunteer staff, was full and a waiting list started. The promise of work leading to housing brough in many people who had given up hope of ever having their own home again. Their ability to wait to get into the program was proof to us they were motivated to succeed, and the wait also screened out those with resources or other options, from the truly needy.

During the initial three months it took the county's homeless to get housed with us, Frances and Mo were a big help on weekends. In addition to shopping, preparing our meals, and laundry, when asked, our kids took on all sorts of assignments that fell through the cracks, or paid staff refused due to time restraints. As the back-acre project came to fusion, Frances' attitude about housing the homeless on it changed from negative to positive. She even had constructive operational suggestions based on her early childhood experience living in women's shelters.

To spend more weekend time with Mo and our back-acre children, with regret Frances gave up her part-time dress shop job. Bob and I had different opinions about her quitting a job she liked and became good at. She promised it was not from fear of success but rather deepening her relationship with Mo and their work helping homeless children. Frances had developed a genuine kinship with the camp's kids. She spent her own money buying them coats, gloves, and shoes. We worried because she had little real-world work experience, unlike Joey who had labored to survive from a young age. Like good parents, Bob, and I, kept our opinions to ourselves.

The first weekend we did not go to the country house to trouble-shoot the Morgan project's latest snafu, Frances showed Mo her apartment for the first time. It was a Saturday, supposedly for them to catch up on school homework. The apartment showing did not go well. Mo left in a huff before any schoolwork was done.

Mo had previously agreed to join us for Sunday brunch the following day. When he stomped into the restaurant late, his body language loudly broadcast, *Beware, dangerous anger about to detonate.*

"Hey, Mo, what's up?"

"I just came here to tell you three I'm breaking up with Frances! And I hope I never see any of you people again!" Mo spit out his words and turned to trudge out of the eatery.

Speaking to his back, I said, "Don't we get a reason?"

Half turning back toward me, he said, "You had to know Frances has a fancy-smancy apartment across the street from where you live. I was the dupe, the chump-sucker you kept conned in the dark."

"What's wrong with her apartment?"

"She isn't who she pretends to be."

"Like how do you mean?"

Mo reluctantly turned completely around to face me. He was hooked but not landed. "It's not the apartment, it's the secret of having it. How am I supposed to love her when she keeps secrets as big as an apartment? I thought I knew Frances. I don't, she's duplicitous! Yes, I too know some big words."

"At first, I didn't want to scare you off by being more out of the ordinary than usual. Then over the months together, the time was never right to tell you with my working and then our weekends in the country with the homeless kids."

"Excuses, excuses."

"I didn't want to upset you. If these two hadn't kept bugging me, I would have waited much longer to tell you. It's their fault you're distressed right now."

"Thanks for sharing, a little late and a dollar short."

"Mo, please sit down and let's talk about why you want to break up over a stupid apartment."

"How can I ever trust you, Frances? You are not an honest person! If I knew you were such a raging capitalist, I'd never have kissed you the first time."

"Mo, please sit down and let me explain. You are here now, don't make it a wasted trip. You really love breakfast, and breakfast here is the best."

Frowning deeply, Mo stiffly slid into the booth next to Frances and threw me a challenging look in the process.

"Bob has held me back from giving you two relationship advice. But if you are breaking up, I'll tell you what I think, anyway. Mo your anger is not about that apartment, it is about ego. I noticed you guys building up to a clash of egos for a month."

"Don't hold back, Gus, go ahead, blame us the victims."

"In my travels, it takes two egos to want a divorce or to make a relationship work when it's not."

Bob jumped in, cutting me off. "Except, Mo, if this is about you think you can have power and control over Frances. For your physical safety I'd strongly advise against trying that."

"She's not so tough. I can handle myself. Bob, are *you* threatening me?"

"No. Is this really the pissing contest you want to have right now?"

"Not really!"

"My unsolicited suggestion is you two go for a walk and talk over misunderstandings. Gus and I usually find there's enough fault to go around after we talk."

"That'd be a waste of time! What's the point? I already know she has a secret apartment."

"Make two lists, one, reasons to stay together, and the other reasons to split. The longest list wins."

"Huh, that sounds like an action plan. I'd need energy to do that. Maybe I should have breakfast first. It smells scrumptious in here, and I haven't eaten since yesterday's lunch. I was *that* upset, Frances." Frances daintily passed Mo, her mostly untouched gargantuan vegetarian breakfast plate. Then they both nibbled from the same dish.

Despite being young, Frances and Mo had gotten to a place well beyond infatuation. They were at serious relationship building before the overdue apartment showing fiasco. While Bob, and I, chowed down on a hardy breakfast, Frances and Mo's defensive postures melted away. Mo's injured party righteous aggression dissipated looking at Frances watching him. At the end of the meal the two young lovers left the restaurant hand in hand looking adoringly at each other, leaving Bob and I to flip a coin to see who would pay the bill.

****

One year passed with nothing earth shaking or even all *that* out of the ordinary occurring with our family. Joey reported school in England was going better than he expected and wished us all the best with the homeless on weekends. The same could not be said for the authorities under whose authorization Eleanor and Mike's camp flourished. It often felt like the camp was a calm smooth-functioning island in a sea of bureaucratic typhoons, one coming right after another. For the most part we ignored the storms and worked to keep the camp's mission on tract and our weekday lives separate.

However, Bob noticed something Mike, Eleanor, and others missed. The education and psychological quality of the newer camp residents was trending lower than our original homeless guests. It seemed as we graduated workers to their own permanent homes, they were replaced by harder trainees, with poor work habits, who could only see the end goal, not how to get there. Prognosis for their success was not good.

****

Bob, Frances, Mo, and I left for the country house earlier than usual to prepare the house for a small first anniversary party to celebrate the Morgan Camp. Our small get together was for a select group who were instrumental creating and maintaining the enterprise. The next day Saturday afternoon, at the elementary school auditorium, the homeless kids were putting on a Charles Dickens-ish play, acting out their personal stories. Frances and Mo had been instrumental helping the children write and perform their tales.

Saturday night, Bob and I were giving out certificates to current and past successful camp residents. It would be followed by a community donated, modest potluck buffet dinner for camp residents, alumni, and staff, held in the high school cafeteria. Sunday afternoon the Morgan Transition Camp choir and soloist were giving a secular concert at the village Synagogue. Sunday night at a fancy dress up dinner at the Ski Lodge Resort Casino, village and county elected officials planned to give speeches to honored guests and dignitaries. They would describe the Eleanor and Mike camp as a model, and its demise and metamorphosis to a new bigger location, the future. Bob and I were invited as special guests to receive a round of applause for our contribution creating the model whose lease was expiring and not renewed. It wasn't because they didn't have another dollar.

Heady with our success getting the homeless employed and then permanently housed and the subsequent affordable housing building boon creating construction jobs that required many camp residents as worker trainees, the village council and county political leaders scrambled to reap credit then parlay it into self-aggrandizement.

The Algonquin Resort Hotel Health Spa, and Golf Links, a bloated white elephant for over 150 years was sitting on 400-acres of pristine isolated real estate technically in the village zip code. It finally gave up its ghost after decades of swimming in red ink. No buyer could be found for the lien-heavy property desperately in need of extensive expensive repairs and billion-dollar modernization.

Old, stodgy county officials talked demolition of the 200-room hotel and turning the golf course, swimming pool, and boardwalk restaurant area into a public-private park retail mall with huge parking lot. However, no money could be found for demolition or even seed money for a stripped down 400-acre park sans mall and mammoth parking. The old turgid bureaucrats were constantly met with a question they could not answer. What cash-strapped rural village could afford a new park during an unfunded homeless crisis?

Rabble-rousing, young-blood village politicians, whippersnappers less than sixty years old, were unified in wanting to save the old Algonquin structure as an historical artifact. They evolved a plan to turn the original old Hotel into a kind of social service mega mart. It would provide one stop shopping for all public services away from the gaze of the tax paying public. To please the old-timers, it would indeed have a larger parking lot than at present.

The overzealous young-bloods' good intentions lumped, halfway houses for released convicts, deinstitutionalized mental patients, posttreatment sex offenders under State supervision, unwed teenage mothers, battered women with and without children, court mandated instead of jail residential drug and alcohol treatment, all in the west wing of the hotel. The east wing would house public health department and its sexually transmitted disease clinic, parole, sanitation, and of course residential homeless services, including those newly developed by Morgan transition camp. All programs would be housed under the one leaky old roof. The plan was all clients would mingle in common areas, go for a swim, play golf, and to learn life skills from each other.

Rather than prepare each space independently and move in programs when rooms were ready, the county and village managers voted to have all programs move in on the same day with a parade led by the high school marching band. The rational for an all at once move on the first of the month was to collect rent to pay for necessary building repairs to make spaces habitable. The future intention of the planners was the mega-mart would be self-sustaining from rent and parking fees once repairs brought it up to code.

Sadly, most programs like the Mike and Eleanor Transition Camp paid no rent, and few of their clients owned cars or had discretional funds for parking fees if they did. What was about to happened was a classic example of good intentions gone bad from inadequate research leading to insufficient planning and resources. For example, no one would have anticipated the huge hit to earmarked tax revenues when landlords of public service offices, private charities, and small nearby businesses were suddenly faced with a glut of empty real-estate nobody wanted or needed to rent. The mass exodus to the Algonquin would made the village central business district a ghost town overnight and ripe for something new, street crime of every ilk.

Part of my problem was the Algonquin project came out of nowhere like a flash of lightning, was voted on at a late-night session and became a reality before counter proposals or even informed public comment could be heard. The hard-to-reach, isolated, obsolete country club spa was destined to destroy necessary social programs by inaccessibility. Small nonprofit community service programs barely surviving from fundraiser-to-fundraiser could not afford to procure and maintain passenger vans to transport their clients back and forth to required court or medical appointments.

Nevertheless, eager young politicians proclaimed in the rural media that Algonquin day clients and hotel residents would be happy to swim and frolic together in the country clubs bathing facilities, relax with free yoga classes, and even golf together.

Someone had resurrected and reprinted a 1920 Algonquin advertising poster showing people wearing antiquated bathing attire in the spa-resorts swimming pool while old white duffers golfed in the background. The poster reprint seemed to appear everywhere and gave the public a false impression of what was about to happen to local public services programs.

Eleanor was convinced it was all about the Republicans' intention to scuddle the successful Mike and Eleanor Morgan Transition Camp because it worked well and only cost a meager amount to operate. She fervently believed most politicos from both parties were against social service benefits not intended for the pockets of their wealthy constituents. Mike blamed the Democrats with tall tales to tell against labor unions. He had a different cast of characters and motivations than his wife to blame. They typified the opposite points of view of the few county residents interested in what the politicos were up to in their name. Most citizens didn't want to be bothered unless it affected their personal property tax.

Bob and I tried to stay out of the fray of political finagling that would unintentionally punish the poor, addicted, and otherwise disabled. Then realizing what they'd done, call it compassionate fiscal conservatism. We were happy to get away from the mean-spirited heartless lying politicians in stretch limousines and have our lives back from frontline homeless boot camp issues every weekend. At the same time, we acknowledged with sympathy, to Mike and Eleanor seeing their brainchild dismantled and moved to the Algonquin had to be difficult, after its success.

****

Our simple pre-party Friday night meal was at seven P.M. It left plenty of time for party preparations before friends and other good guys dropped by at nine P.M. for drinks and mostly finger-food. The party was our small kickoff for Mike and Eleanor Morgan Homeless Camp's weekend of high and low one-year anniversary celebrations and last gasp final.

For Bob and me, the dinner table was morose. Celebration seemed the opposite of ego-braggadocio about to undo a year of hard work to break the cycle of homelessness for those we sheltered. It felt personal, it wasn't. It was thoughtless, and inconsiderate at the expense of those without voice to protest being made further invisible.

Frances and Mo were absorbed ticking off potential problems in the children's play. No one at our table had appetite for anything except Frances' two-layer, crumbled-cookies-on-top icebox cake. She had not made it since Joey went to England. It had been a favorite at our house, sweet, cold, multitextured tasty, the comfort food from generations ago.

Beginning to clear away the dessert things, Mo said, "Are we expecting party guests *this* early?"

"No way! We aren't setup."

"Right, Mo hasn't started to stuff the celery ribs with blue cheese. Frances isn't ready to julienne veggies for the spicy peanut butter dipping sauce, and Bob has yet to put chips in bowls. I may have to lend him a hand."

"Who's going to drag out that totally unnecessary six-foot-long, over-stuffed deli-meat death sandwich?" Frances said this pointing a finger at me.

"Since that tacky humongous nitrate filled thing was Gus' idea, he should lay it out in mortuary fashion surrounded with white lilies. Is it too late to call the florist?"

"All right, Mo, I'll supervise sandwich placement, but will need a few extra hands for help. Six feet is a lot of meat-filled-sandwich."

Hands on hips, exasperation showing on Frances' face, she said, "We don't need supervision. Gus, what we *do* need is you to put that ungodly thing outdoors for the carnivorous animals."

"Everybody stay calm, we'll be set up before the guests arrive."

"They're here, and by the way a punch would have been so much better than an open bar. But as usual you two daddies never listen to me. I don't know why you keep a girl like me around, other than to prove I'm always right."

"Frances, we value your input, just don't always take it."

"What should I say to whoever just drove up?" Mo said this watching the three of us interacting family style as usual.

Looking at his watch, Bob said, "This always happens, someone gets the time wrong. I wish they'd go away and come back later."

"Do something about that or I will." Frances said this heading to the kitchen to start preparing finger food.

"Fine, I'll tell them to come back when we are ready. It'll be faster than trying to put them to work and slow down preparations."

Bob and I were talking as we walked to the front door anticipating hearing about an imagined immanent drop everything crisis that required immediate attention or the sky would fall in on the homeless encampment.

Mo, who had followed us, glanced through the front-door side-glass panel and said, "It's a rental car license plate on an economy vehicle. I never saw it around here before."

"Nobody rents cars out in these parts.",

"That's true, Gus, most of your unscheduled visitors drive ratty old pickup trucks, or those big shot long-limousines. Oh look, do you guys know the attractive young woman getting out of the car? She's a looker."

"No. Wait could the driver be …"

"It sure looks like and moves like him …"

"… except he's taller, heavier … grownup."

Bob and I threw open the front door and stepped out onto the porch. Mo stood at my side.

At the sound of the door being unlocked, Frances rushed from the kitchen, then followed us outside drying hands on her apron and muttering, "I'll give them a piece of my mind."

When she saw who it was, she screamed as the new arrivals ascended the porch-steps and approached. "JOSEPH! Why didn't you tell us you were coming? Give me a hug!" Where upon she grabbed him in a tight bear hug and kissed his neck like a thirsty vampire searching for an artery. He returned her greeting with slightly less enthusiasm.

Mo and Felicity looked uncomfortable at the prolonged intense greeting.

I said, "Joey if we knew you were coming, we'd have met you at the airport."

"Come in, come inside." Bob made the invitation physical, swinging an outstretched right arm. Then he and I relieved them of suitcases.

'This is Felicity Heimerman. Felicity, these are my foster dads Bob and Gus.

Squeezing the life out of me a second ago was Frances, and you I don't know."

"Hello, nice to make your acquaintance. I've heard so much about all of you. Do I get a hug?"

Stiffly with little enthusiasm, Frances and Felicity exchanged a brief brittle formality hug and noncontact cheek air-buzz.

"*Hi, I'm Mo.*"

"Oh, sorry, sorry, sorry, this is Mo, my significant other. Can I get you two something to drink, coffee, tea, maybe a soda?"

Bob and I led our kids and their significant others into the living room. Joey and Felicity snuggled into the love seat, Frances and Mo curled up on the sofa, and Bob and I took our usual easy chair rocker-recliners.

Viewing our expanded family with pride, I said, "Joey you're early for the party. Did Mike invite you, and forgot to tell us …"

"… have you eaten, are you two hungry?" Bob looked ready to go make them a sandwich.

"We're okay, right, Felicity?"

"Yes, I'm fine. We stopped on the way for a snack. We don't have juicy-sloppy-joes in England."

"Don't fuss you guys, I'm family and she is too by association. What party, Gus?"

"Friends and neighbors are coming over at nine for drinks and snacks. Joey, you know most of them from when you lived here."

"Like whom?"

"Your high school guidance counselor, Mike and Eleanor, the Thompsons, like that."

"Joseph, tonight must be divine intervention, I made your favorite dessert, and there's plenty left over for the party guests."

"Oh, Frances, what *is* his favorite dessert?"

"Don't you know?"

"*No, I don't.* And we supposedly know everything about each other. Obviously, I'm in deficit."

"*Icebox cake.*"

"He never mentioned it. Why is that do you suppose?"

"No idea."

"May I ask how this confection is prepared?"

"It couldn't be easier Felicity …"

"I'd like the recipe if it is not too much trouble to write down."

"Sure, no problem."

"On rare occasions I give Joe little treats. *When he's been good.*"

"It couldn't be simper, no baking and everything comes right out of a box."

Mo saw a situation heating-up and jumped in to draw Felicity's fire away from Frances. "Except the fruit cocktail comes from a can. Drain it well before you mix it in the vanilla pudding and don't forget to refrigerate for at least four hours before serving."

"Thank you, Mo, could *you* please write out the recipe? Oh, never mind, Joe probably knows it. It's his favorite. *Only I wasn't privileged to know that for some reason.*"

It appeared Frances took a second to think then rethink, while Mo spoke with Felicity. Frances seemed to consider her icy reception to Felicity, and arrived at a conclusion about jealous culpability, then contrite said, "Felicity, put a graham cracker crust in a 9"X13" Pyrex. Then place a layer of vanilla pudding mixed with a large can of *drained* fruit cocktail in the crust, and then cover with a layer of chocolate pudding. To guild the lily I top it with vanilla wafer cookie crumbs, and a generous dollop of whip cream on the side of each dish. Silly me chattering away, let me go get you some."

"*Please, don't bother.*"

"No bother, I have to serve it up for the party guests anyway." With that said, Frances got up and rushed to the kitchen.

Felicity's face suggested she was upset about something more than icebox cake. Being new to us, she was ignored with apprehension like an unexploded ordnance in our midst nobody wanted to detonate.

"Joey, if Mike didn't invite you to the swan song weekend for our 'House the Homeless' misadventure, to what do we owe the honor of your visit?"

"Gus, Mike and Eleanor are quite upset their dream is being programed to fail after its success. I'm not surprised they forgot to mention your party. Mike is usually not talkative, but he bent my ear on the phone for an hour on how unfair things have gotten here. He thinks you and Bob should have fought much harder for keeping the camp."

Bob responded to what Joey directed to me. "We know their feelings and gave the camp quite enough time and money. They know it was local politicos who scuttled what was working and were only listening to themselves."

"Mike should have told us you were coming. Tonight, is a small get-together to say goodbye to those who helped, don't be disappointed you came such a long way for not much."

"Gus, we didn't know about your party. Felicity and I have something important to talk over with you and Bob."

"Then don't keep us waiting, what is it?"

"Just when you two thought I was out of your hair, I'm back."

"Speak, number one foster child."

"Is it possible for us to talk in private?"

"Joey, you know my aversion to making Cliff Notes. Frances and Mo are members of this family and I'd rather they hear directly from the source rather than my or Bob's recollections forgetting key details."

"I do remember that proclivity, Gus. Only the thing is, this subject may be embarrassing for Felicity."

"Don't worry about me, honey. I won't let you embarrass me … when I can embarrass myself. Your family is exactly as you described them, except Mo who seems a nice enough chap."

Just then Frances returned from the kitchen and handed a dessert plate, fork, and cloth-napkin to each visitor from England. She stood back to watch as they tasted her easy, fast, treat, and then said to Bob and me, "What did I miss?"

When no one spoke, Frances looked around gaging the room's tension and said, "Is everybody okay in here."

Mo whispered from behind his hand into Frances' ear. "Felicity is upset about something, but we don't know what."

"Your dessert is quite lovely. I fancy it and can see why it is Joe's favorite. We have something similar in the U.K. called trifle, Joe also favors it."

Joey jumped into the conversation to head off a possible skirmish. He said to no one in particular, "Felicity's hormones have been playing hell with her moods lately."

At the word hormones, Frances and Mo exchanged looks I could not imagine trying to unpack.

Mission accomplished, Joey put his arm around Felicity and tenderly said, "We're both tired from the long flight, let's talk it over with Gus, Bob, and family tomorrow."

"No. Joe I'd rather know whether this trip was a waste, tonight. If it was, we can go straight back first thing tomorrow."

"If that's what you want, and they don't mind, why don't *you* tell them?"

"I'll start and you finish, how's that?"

"Go for it, sweetheart."

"Joe and I are undergraduate physics majors, at the top of our class. I'm not bragging, it is why we did something we shouldn't and almost got kicked out of school."

Bob sternly said, "Like what?"

"We took and aced a microbiology elective last semester. Most days we had time to kill during the boring class full of nincompoop nonscience majors looking for an easy impressive grade. While wasting time in the microbiology laboratory we performed some goofy experiments to amuse ourselves instead of getting caught sleeping or texting. We were trying to look busy but didn't know much about what we were playing around with and got unexpected results. No matter which way we tried, we couldn't explain what happened, or why, and then the trouble started."

"For those of us unenlightened, what are *you* talking about? Frances, please sit down, we can collect their dessert dishes later."

"Sorry, Gus. There are microorganisms that if put in a petri dish with noncompatible microbes either fight or commit suicide. Those results are 100% provable every time. Joe and I put three different killer germs in the same petri dish expecting to watch winners, losers, or at least interesting three-way slams. Instead, all three fell in love, mated, and created a new supper germ unlike the three parents.

Then when we introduced its relatives, big newbie destroyed genetic relations with a mad vengeance. When we introduced unrelated germs to our three-parent hybrid it devoured them but with less fervor."

Half to himself, Mo said, "I could see a colorful animation of this story with lots of bright Day Glo-smarmy-colors and silly loud chomping music. Oh, I'm sorry, continue with your story, please."

"One of the less boring microbiology professors proctored an in-class exam and nosing around found Joe and my unauthorized experiment, hidden. He was gutted and accused us of every infraction imaginable, including endangering public health. Our scholastic futures looked finished. At a meeting he called with our microbe teacher and the head of the department, we were threatened with expulsion from the university. But Joe had the presence of mind to document our unapproved experiments and strange results. At the meeting, the profs went from being vindictive angry to fascinated by what we discovered. Joe why don't you tell them what happened next."

"Let me apologize if Felicity and I are boring you."

"So far, we are not bored. I for one am fascinated. How about you, Bob? … See Joey, he is not bored either. Please go on with threatened expulsion after you went through so much to go to England."

"Gus, remember I know when you're being ironic."

"Duly noted my prodigal son."

"As you remember it was bad luck then good luck that got me to Oxford. So more good luck came when our microbiology professor presented our paper, with his name attached, naturally, to a scientific journal. It was published and Oxford took the credit. For our part, the university offered Felicity and me graduate classes while still undergraduates and created a special fast track program for us to get our bachelor's in physics and a master's in microbiology simultaneously. But there is a catch. We must also finish an accelerated program designed to attain simultaneous MDs and PhDs. It's a lot of work but we are up to the challenge."

"Wow!"

"Holy mackerel!"

"Joey you never mentioned wanting to be a medical doctor."

"Apparently, there is a critical shortage of research Medical Doctor Pharmacologists. According to our faculty committee advisor, Felicity and I have a talent for microbiology, but must earn multiple degrees to capitalize on it. The university wants to help us fill an international gap."

"Damn, Joseph, how am I supposed to compete with *you*?"

"Frances, you and I were never in competition. Just be your genuine self, the one we all love so much. You're worth much more than a bunch of paper to hang on a wall."

Grumbling, half to himself, Mo said, "Before I met Bob and Gus, I was used to being the smartest guy in the room. Now I know how Hans felt being pushed down the pecking order in this family." Sulking, Mo's face showed his perceived loss of status.

"Felicity, sweetheart, why don't you tell them the rest?"

Taking Joey's hand in hers' Felicity said, "I'd rather you did, honey. They know you and won't be quite so appalled."

"As Gus likes to say, *long story short*. We were so excited from our good luck from goofing around in microbiology lab, not getting kicked out of the university, and offered free special fast track intensive handling. I forgot to use a condom and now Felicity is pregnant."

"Don't all look disappointed; I'm not embarrassed to say I prefer to feel Joe inside me without a condom. I hate rubbers are the European, Asian, and most of the Americas preferred method of birth control."

"Why?"

"I don't like having that latex barrier between us, separating us when we make love."

"And now you're pregnant."

"Reproducing our own replicas was always my plan, only it was to happen later, after we finished our education."

Tired of sitting passively, Bob, couldn't let her last comment go unchallenged. "Degrees don't finish an education. We live in a time where continuing education is required. It's called professional development ..."

Frances suddenly looked animated, wiggling around on the sofa she couldn't wait for Bob to finish speaking. "Pardon me for interrupting, Bob. Joseph, what happened? Did you wake up one morning and get hit by a bolt of heterosexualism?"

"No, not exactly, it happened like our foster dads said it would."

"How?"

"Felicity and I, strangers, were assigned to be lab partners in Zoology. We became friends and then study partners in common classes. Step by step like Gus and Bob said."

"And?"

"Before our friendship became intimate, I explained my sexual identity indeterminacy, and I might discover at age sixty or ninety I'm gay and want to make up for lost time. She said, "Let's just deal with the present moment and let the future come as it will."

"Um uh, oh, so what's your plan now, Felicity?"

"Good question, my parents are observant and would never let me to use the morning after pill. Even if I could get it from the National Health Service without their knowing, and I can't."

Looking around the room I could see confusion on Frances' face. Before she could add more ambiguity, Mo said, "I think I understand, it took forever for my strict Pentecostal parents to accept me as transsexual. What will you do in the meantime?"

As if waiting for that cue, Joey sat up straight and said, "Bob and Gus, do you guys remember when Mike asked you to take me in as a favor to him?"

"It's a little hard to forget with you looking all grownup sitting right here."

"I'm asking you guys for the same favor you gave Mike. Felicity and I *want* this baby but can't handle it and finish our degrees at the same time. Would you two raise our baby for its first five years? We have been guaranteed to write our own ticket to a prosperous interesting work-life, in five years. As Frances says, 'Please, please, please.'"

"No! Absolutely not, Gus and I know nothing about babies and given our usual workload don't have time nor inclination to learn. For your baby's sake give it up for adoption."

"Joey, did you ask Felicity's parents for the same favor?"

Felicity stirred in Joey's arms and answered for him. "They are Orthodox Jews my father's mother my grandmother is a Holocaust Survivor. My family would have to cast me out and sat Shiva if they knew I was pregnant out of wedlock, by a goy."

"That sounds harsh."

"Don't misunderstand, I love them dearly, and know they made sacrifices for my education. We just believe differently. Joe and I are closer in that department."

"Okay, fine, Joey, what Bob and I do know is the first five years of a baby's life are the most formative. If you want to give your child a fair shot at a decent life, do what Bob suggests."

Entreating Felicity, Bob said, "Go for adoption, your parents won't need to know, your baby gets parents with time and interest, and you can study worry free."

"Bob, our problem with adoption is we can't control who gets our child and how they'll raise it."

Wishing we weren't having this discussion and suddenly feeling left out it, I said, "Back here on earth, Joey, what's your other option? As I recall, you didn't appreciate being handed around as a small tyke. Why put your own through that? Let the professionals find a suitable home with people willing to meet your baby's needs with love. I AM RIGHT and you know it?"

"Gus, another option we've discussed is one or both of us drop out of school. That would be a major sacrifice of our education and future to put on a baby."

"Is it a girl or a boy?"

"Frances, it's a zygote less than six weeks, we don't know yet."

"Have you chosen names?"

"If it's a girl, she'll be Matilda, after Matilda MacKinsey. If it's a boy, he will be Benjamin named for Felicity's late uncle Ben Heimerman."

I couldn't help myself from asking with so much of their private lives already on display. "Joey, are you planning to convert to raise your children in the Jewish faith?"

"I'm not sure, I never had strong feelings about religion, other than singing hymns. We've decided to let our kids decided when they are old enough to make informed consent. I'll see what they want. I might follow the kids' choice for their sake."

"Doesn't that surgery cause problems for most adults?"

A small ironic smile played on Felicity's lips as she said, "Joe warned me about his gay dads. I'm only in your home minutes and you want to know about my son's briss."

"Guilty."

"There is such a thing as a Shalom Briss. They cut off the tip of a carrot instead of the penis, God likes carrots too. You can all relax I wouldn't let Joe be incapacitated in the bedroom. I love him too much."

Frances and Mo wore blank faces up to that comment. The idea of Felicity protecting Joey seemed to energize Frances physically to stand up. "Felicity, would you consider letting me raise your child? I may not look the part but I'm rich and will learn infant care between now and you deliver. One thing I discovered from the Morgan homeless camp is my maternal instincts are alive and active."

"How old are you, Frances?"

"I'll be eighteen soon and get my driver's license. I'm already an emancipated minor with my own fully paid for apartment. I'm ready, willing, and able to parent your child ..."

Joey jumped into the conversation curtly cutting off his foster sister. "Frances, raising a baby is a big commitment and a lot of responsibility. What about your bottom surgery?"

"Joseph, Mo doesn't believe more surgery is a good idea, I love Mo, what he thinks matters to me. If for some reason that changes, your child would be seven the earliest, I could do the change legally. Most likely if I *did* alter my thinking, I'd wait till middle age, by then your baby would be an adult."

Not having expected Frances' offer, and her standing presenting it like a lawyer in court. To buy time to consider it, Joey deflected. "What do you think, Felicity?"

"I think Frances is in love with you, Joe. She as much said so when we arrived. The real proof is she made your favorite dessert and *I did not even know what it was.*"

"Felicity, you are making a big deal out of nothing."

"Joe, you told me it was never serious between you two. Now Frances wants to raise our child! Really, you call that no big deal?"

There were six of us in the room and I for one was not interested to watch Joey and Felicity have a spat, so said, "Felicity, could there be a different reason Joey never mentioned ice box cake?"

"Like what?"

"It's personal but not about Frances or you."

"Precisely what are you lollygagging about, Gus? Oh, sorry if that came out rude. I didn't mean to be rude."

"When Frances joined our family, weekend weather permitting, she and Joey took motorcycle day trips to get to know each other. Bob and I encouraged them. After one such outing, they returned with a dusty battered 1930s Depression era cookbook. Joey paid five cents at a yard sale for the scruffy dogeared book. The kids were determined to recreate each recipe using modern-day ingredients. Though nutritious the food was unappetizing without lots of condiments, with one exception, we all liked the ice box cake. Joey, admitted remembering the dessert as something his grandmother made for him before she died."

"What does that have to do with anything?"

"Maybe going to England was a chance for Joey to reinvent himself. My guess is he didn't want you to know about his formative years being shuffled around in poverty."

"Or maybe he hasn't been honest with me about feelings toward Frances and her for him. Did you see how they greeted each other? It looked like they were in heat."

"Appeared pretty normal to me. Sometimes, Frances can be a bit rambunctious."

"By English standards, my people are not well off, I am not ashamed of that. Why would Joe not tell me about his favorite anything unless the reason was reprehensible. Otherwise, none of this makes sense?"

"What Bob and I know is Frances and Mo love each other deeply. Joey told us, you Felicity are his one and only. He says you get each other, which is rare these days of GPS hookups in a hurry."

"Then why not tell me about a favorite? I could have made it for him. I think Joe has feelings for Frances which complicates all this talk we're having."

"She is my foster sister, *of course I have feelings,* and you and I *will* discuss this alone later."

"But Joe, Frances is awfully young to be a mother?"

Frances had been standing behind seated Mo, her hands rubbing his shoulders while she listened. Her face showed a range of emotions, finally settling on goal attainment rather than ready to attack in retaliation, her usual domestic look. As Joey was about to answer Felicity, Frances cut him off and said, "Soon I'll be eighteen, four years older than my mother and father when I was born. I'm still here, doing fine despite my parent's age."

"But Frances, young people are supposed to revel in carefree fun, get thoroughly partied-out before settling down to raise a family."

Frances stood tall, made direct eye contact, held it and said, "Felicity, you are not that much older than me and you're contemplating relinquishing your carefree freedom and independence for five more years of difficult schoolwork. Raising your child, I won't have your inflexible school distractions. Mo would you help me raise their child?"

Mo perked up, took then kissed her hand, and beamed. "Absolutely, you know I love children. You've seen me co-parent my disabled niece and we look after some of the homeless kids like they're ours. Children are the future of the world, they are precious."

Ignoring Mo, Felicity said, "Frances, your offer is generous indeed. I'm just not sure what rules we'd need to have beyond I am Joe's first and only mate no matter what your or his feelings to the contrary."

"Bob and Gus taught me to live by rules. This is mine, if I raise your baby you don't get, her or him back unless that's what they want, and are old enough to know what's in their best interest."

"WHAT ARE YOU SAYING, *we don't get our baby back?*"

"You can visit, even go on vacation together. But this child gets what Joseph and I never had, constancy of a home, loving attention, and money enough to live up to potential."

Felicity's face sternly digested Frances' words, then after a brief self-deliberation, gained vigor and said, "Sorry, Frances, I want my baby born and to live in England, that's where we reside. But thank you so much for the kind offer."

"With an American father and an English mother, the child should be intitled to dual citizenship."

"For the next five years Joe and I will live in England. We'd like our son or daughter to learn sophisticated English culture and live close enough to visit."

"Did you expect Gus and Bob to move to England?"

"No. But they are much older."

"Well, I *can* agree to move overseas if Mo is willing. Mo you willing to live in Great Britain for a while?"

"Sure, why not. As long as we are together."

"Then it's settled, we will move to the U.K. until you finish school. However, after you graduate, we are not following you around the world to live for the sake of your work opportunities. Remember, this child gets constancy of a secure home, over everything."

"Would you agree to that in writing?"

"Yes. I have a great lawyer who does first rate work. If you allow me and Mo to raise your baby, we'd consider parenting a collaboration. Joseph and I have experience as brother and sister working out problems."

I got an urge to nudge them to a conclusion before they went off on another tangent. "Frances what will you do with your apartment if you move to England?"

"If you and Bob aren't interested in managing an Airbnb, Allison Ajax might do it for a percentage of the fee. I'd trust who she screened, or I could just warehouse it. Money is not the point, I already have much more than I could ever spend. Gus, we are talking about a baby's future, not real estate, get with the flow dad."

Joey had clearly been gnawing on the unexpected offer of child rearing by his foster sister. "Gus, Bob, Mo, what do you think of Frances' proposal?"

"We live across the street from Frances' New York City apartment and intend to keep this country house into our dotage. Speaking for both of us, our foster kids their spouses and children are always welcome in our homes. In addition, as you know, I have connections from work in England that could help Frances and Mo get setup there."

"Frances … Felicity and I would like to sleep on your magnanimous offer, if that's okay?"

"I expected you would Joseph. Just out of curiosity which way are *you* leaning tonight?"

"Right this instant my forgetting to wear a condom in the heat of passion and the result is a troubling abstraction I'm nevertheless responsible for. On the other hand, finishing our education is concrete solid for our future. That's how I feel right now. Once the baby is born and has a face and personality all bets are off. I need a deep think on this. We hoped Gus and Bob would make it easy. But I get it, they are still parenting me."

"Joseph, you know me better than anyone ever has. It would be a privilege to raise your child, giving her or him everything we missed. Remember, you know me and now met Mo, we are not anonymous strangers with bizarre beliefs and strange practices."

"*Don't* push it, Frances. Let me work it out in my head in bed tonight."

"Okay, okay, okay, but from one foster brat to another, you'd be a fool to give up your education for forgetting a condom and an unborn baby who may not even like you."

Felicity had been cold toward Frances until she offered her unborn infant a home. Practicality helped her warmup but with serious reservations. "Frances why would you want to give away freedom, and resources for our child? Are you still in love with Joe? Is that what this is really about?"

"I'm in love with Mo and it's mutual. Joseph is my brother and I call *that* brotherly love. I'm willing and able to give your baby loving kindness because I want it to have what I missed. Your infant will be a member of the caring family you see in this room. We may not be a village, but together we can be indominable."

"Impressive sales pitch."

"My foster dads taught me by example it is better to give than receive. Joseph knows me well he can give you a letter of reference if required."

"If my question was inappropriate, I apologize. Lately I do and say the silliest things, my academic self may be growing maternal instincts at its detriment."

Making another direct eye contact connection, Frances spoke from the heart. "Okay, I can see you want more reasons why. What might help with your decision, Felicity, is I have good reason to expect a short life. Whether I have bottom surgery or not, I can't reproduce healthy offspring due to opposite gender hormones taken from an early age. I have considered long and hard where my fortune goes after I'm gone. For political reasons Mo will just accept a tiny portion, and that only to please me."

"Sounds like a heavy burden for a young person to carry."

"It has been my dream to give a little child all the love and care Joseph and I never received until Gus and Bob took us in as teenagers. When my time is up, leaving someone I reared with compassion, decent values, and the means to live respectably and responsibly ends a cycle."

"What cycle?"

"I learned from my maternal grandmother, her mother my great grandmother was cold, cruel, and hated children. As a result, my grandmother did not want to give birth to my mother but waited too long for an abortion. My mother hated her mother, for cause. If I'd been born a heteronormative female, like I should have been, most likely I would have passed the family curse on to another generation."

"How does that relate to my baby?"

"My being transsexual from birth forced my mother, like it or not, to protect me from a hostile world of hate. I learned at my mother's knee how to stand up to injustice and fight. I can do right by your baby at a time when worldwide more children than not are hungry. And I can provide for the rest of your child's life and their offspring in the process."

"You make a strong case, *except*, it looks to me like you are in love with my Joe."

"Everyone in this room who knows Joseph loves him. Mo and I are the only ones present willing to devote ourselves and my immense wealth to your unborn progeny *full time* and do it properly."

"I fancy that."

"Felicity, Mo and I may be considered freaks by some, but we know how to fight to the death for what's right. With Gus and Bob having our backs we are invincible."

"As you've mentioned."

"How are you leaning tonight?"

"We came to America looking for help from Gus and Bob. It was Joe's idea, I was skeptical."

"Of course, you never met any of us. We are an awesome family."

"Frances, if I'm correct you are offering our baby Joe's whole family to parent it. Really, how could I refuse?"

Mixed emotions showing on his face, Joey said, "Am I reading you right? Felicity, it is not like you to flipflop, especially about something important."

"Joe, I'm not vacillating. Frances made an excellent case for our child's care until we have the wherewithal to fully take over as parents."

Looking unsettled Joey glanced at the faces in the room. Clearly, he was looking for an answer. "I don't get it! A few minutes ago, you and Frances were practically at each other's throats over ice box cake."

"That is correct, Joe, and right now I think she is what is best for the baby, us, our education, and this family's role in our future. I'd call that a win. If it doesn't work out, we'll have more children."

"What changed?"

"I saw sincerity and steely resolve in Frances' eyes. I learned to read those links to the soul from you, Joe. After you sleep on it, I hope you agree with me."

The doorbell started ringing and didn't stop until all invited guests, and a few others arrived. Joey helped me march the six-foot Cuban sandwich out of the kitchen and onto the living room buffet where it was devoured before Bob, Frances, and Mo, could get their healthy munchies ready for the party guests to eat. Meanwhile Joey, then Bob helped me keep the bar stocked and drinks topped up.

At elven ten, everyone was feeling all right, conversations were buzzing, people looked buzzed from the booze. Then suddenly cells phones started going off in unison causing one hell of cacophonic racket. Some chimed, beeped, rang, or played tunes, all at once. Conversation stopped and most male guests left in a rush.

I sought out Eleanor Morgan and asked, "What just happened?"

"Fire. Gus, you invited a bunch of volunteer firemen to your party."

"That's the only kind we have. Where's the fire?"

"The Algonquin, it's an all-response code, sounds bad."

About the Author

Peter Melillo was born in New Haven, Connecticut, moved to Tucson, Arizona, at age seven, then moved to New York City at age twenty-five. In 2013, JM Snyder Books published a collection of twelve of his gay war short stories: *For Man and Country*. In total, JM Snyder Books published sixteen short stories by Peter Melillo online as e-books. In 2018 Querelle Independent published *Fairy Swatter*, six short stories with murder as a side issue, as well as *Improbable: Male Love Stories*. Peter can be reached at peteramelillo@gmail.com.